Titles by Laura Griffin

"Pitch-perfect plotting, taut suspense, compelling characters. A master of romantic suspense, Laura Griffin keeps getting better. I love the Tracers series!"

—Allison Brennan, *New York Times* bestselling author

SNAPPED

"*Snapped* rocks!"

—*RT Book Reviews* (Top Pick)

"Electric chemistry between two believable and interesting characters coupled with the investigative details make this page-turner especially compelling."

—*BookPage* (Top Pick for Romance)

"Laura Griffin mesmerizes. . . . A captivatingly passionate romance where danger is around every turn."

—*Single Titles*

"If you want a knock-your-socks-off romance, here it is."

—*The Reading Frenzy*

"You won't be able to put this book down."

—*Fresh Fiction*

"This gripping, vivid tale has a great pace that delivers plenty of suspense."

—*Fallen Angel Reviews*

"A gripping, white-knuckle read."

—Brenda Novak, *New York Times* bestselling author

UNFORGIVABLE

"Features the perfect mix of suspense and romance that make Catherine Coulter, Iris Johansen, and Tami Hoag popular with both women and men."

—*Booklist*

"The science is fascinating, the sex is sizzling, and the story is top-notch, making this clever, breakneck tale hard to put down."

—*Publishers Weekly*

"Interweaves frightening murders with a compelling romance."

—*Single Titles*

LAURA GRIFFIN

Untraceable

POCKET BOOKS

NEW YORK LONDON TORONTO SYDNEY NEW DELHI

Pocket Books
A Division of Simon & Schuster, Inc.
1230 Avenue of the Americas
New York, NY 10020

This book is a work of fiction. Names, characters, places, and incidents either are products of the author's imagination or are used fictitiously. Any resemblance to actual events or locales or persons, living or dead, is entirely coincidental.

This Pocket Books paperback edition May 2013

POCKET and colophon are registered trademarks of Simon & Schuster, Inc.

For information about special discounts for bulk purchases, please contact Simon & Schuster Special Sales at 1-866-506-1949 or business@simonandschuster.com.

The Simon & Schuster Speakers Bureau can bring authors to your live event. For more information or to book an event, contact the Simon & Schuster Speakers Bureau at 1-866-248-3049 or visit our website at www.simonspeakers.com.

Interior design by Julie Schroeder
Cover design and hand lettering by Jae Song
Landscape by mail4cindi/stock.xchng
Photo of rain by Marcelo

Manufactured in the United States of America

10 9 8 7 6 5 4 3 2 1

ISBN 978-1-4767-2973-2
ISBN 978-1-4391-6318-4 (ebook)

For Doug

CHAPTER ONE

Melanie bumped along the pitted road, almost certain she wasn't lost. She peered through the darkness and drizzle, searching for nonexistent landmarks. Had she missed it again? No way. First left after the low-water bridge—

She spotted the yellow porch light and sighed. Finally. Sex and Mexican food. She'd been craving both all day—in that order—since Joe had called to tell her he was off tonight.

The Blazer pitched down, then up again, its worn shocks responding to every rut as she neared the house. She pulled in behind Joe's Honda and noticed the house's darkened windows. Maybe the game had ended. With a giddy rush, she gathered up the carryout bag and pushed open the door. The smell of warm tortilla chips mingled with the cool dampness of the spring night. She glanced at the house again—

And froze.

The back of her neck tingled. She heard a voice from her past, a faint echo at first, then a whisper. She gazed at the house through the raindrops as the whisper grew louder.

Go, go, go!

And she did, numbly dropping the takeout food and yanking the door shut. Turning the key and shoving the Blazer into gear. Shooting backward down the driveway, then retracing her course, only the gentle bumps were bone-jarring now as she sped toward the highway with a hammering heart.

He was there.

How did she know? She just knew. Something about the house told her, something she could figure out later. She tried to keep the Blazer centered on the road as she rummaged for her phone. Her trembling fingers dialed Joe.

Voice mail.

Tears burned her eyes. She reached the paved highway and slammed on the brakes just as a sports car zipped past.

Think, damn it. What would Alex do? The tires shrieked as Melanie pulled onto the highway and groped for a plan. She had one. She *had* a plan.

What was it?

She took a deep breath. Her emergency kit was in the back. She could leave this instant, no stops. She could go to her safe spot.

But what about Joe? She slowed again. She had to go back.

A pair of headlights winked into her rearview mirror. The objective part of her brain registered the height, the shape, the spacing. The rest panicked.

She floored the gas pedal. Her pulse skittered as the

car behind her sped up, too. The speedometer inched past sixty, but still the lights behind her refused to fade. Her hands clenched the steering wheel. Her heart pumped furiously. He couldn't have found her. Not now.

Why hadn't she listened to Alex?

A curve in the road. She jerked the wheel, then struggled for control. She felt the spin coming, felt her stomach drop out as the tires glided across the asphalt. Brakes squealed—or maybe it was her scream—and a wall of bushes rushed at her. Metal crunched. Her nose hit the wheel.

Then nothing. Just the rasp of her breathing and the *tip-tap* of rain over her head. No air bag. She clutched her abdomen and tried to take stock. Blood, warm and coppery, seeped into her mouth.

He's coming.

The thought spurred her body into action. She pushed at the door, heavy because of the angle. She was in a ditch. She threw her shoulder against the door and muscled it open. Branches snapped at her cheeks as she heaved herself out of the car.

The only light nearby was a head lamp, now buried in leaves. Rain pelted her face. She blinked at the surrounding gloom and tried to orient herself.

She heard a low rumble—like thunder, but not. It was a pickup, diesel engine, somewhere behind her. She listened, paralyzed with terror, as the rumble ceased and a door slammed shut. He was *here*. The nightmare she'd imagined so many times, in vivid detail, was happening.

She clawed wildly at the vines and branches. Panting now, she crashed like an animal through the woods. No car. No phone. No emergency kit.

A distant whir growing nearer. Tires on pavement. She scrambled toward the sound. She broke through the foliage just as the car whizzed by.

"Help!" she screamed, waving her arms at the shrinking taillights.

Her mistake hit her. She ducked back into the bushes, but it was too late. He was right behind her, closer now, so close she could hear his grunts and breaths.

Move! she willed her rubbery legs. She choked back a sob as he came closer, closer. Then *smack!* she was on the ground, her legs pinned. No air, no breath. She scratched and elbowed and kicked, her heel hitting something soft. A moan. She jerked herself free and lunged for the road. Another car—she heard it, saw its lights beckoning her to safety. Just a few more feet . . . She reached for the light, the pavement. She clawed at the gravel.

"Help! Stop!"

A hand clamped around her ankle and dragged her back.

Two days later

Alex Lovell downed her last sip of tepid coffee, slung her camera around her neck, and checked her watch. Late again.

Fortunately, the subject of today's surveillance liked to sleep in. Less fortunately, he lived in his girlfriend's apartment near campus, which meant parking was going to be a bitch. As a backup plan, Alex grabbed the orange traffic cone that lived in the corner of her office and helped her get away with damn near anything.

Outside, an early morning downpour had snarled traffic. Alex cast a glance over her shoulder as she hurriedly locked the office. Cars inched along Lavaca Street, and she tried to decide which route to UT would be fastest.

A shadow fell over her.

"Scuse me, ma'am?"

She surveyed the man's reflection in the glass door before answering. Boots, jeans, western-style jacket. His six-foot frame was augmented by a cowboy hat. Was this guy for real?

"Think I might be lost," he drawled.

She turned around. "Cattle Raisers Association's two blocks over."

He smiled slightly, and the lines bracketing his mouth deepened. "I'm looking for Lovell Solutions."

She nodded at the words etched on the glass door beside her. "Looks like you found it."

"Are you Alexandra Lovell?"

"Yes," she said, certain this wasn't news.

"I have something to discuss with you. Only take a minute," he added, as she glanced at her watch.

"What's your name?"

"Bill Scoffield."

"What do you do?"

"I'm a lawyer."

She eyed him skeptically. Tufts of white hair peeked up from his shirt collar, and a slight paunch hung over his belt buckle. She put him at fifty-five. Her gaze dropped to his boots, shiny black ostrich. She'd been in Texas long enough to recognize expensive footwear.

She thought about this month's receivables. "Five minutes," she said, glancing at her watch again.

She dropped the cone on the sidewalk and unlocked

the door. "And I'll hang on to that SIG while we talk, if you don't mind."

You would have thought she'd asked him to surrender his dick. His gray eyes narrowed as he fished the pistol out from the holster beneath his jacket. He passed it to her, butt first.

She led the way into her air-conditioned reception room. It lacked a receptionist. Alex glanced at the door to her messy office, which thankfully was closed. As the visitor removed his hat, she walked behind her assistant's recently vacated desk.

"Little paranoid?" He glanced pointedly at the security camera mounted up near the ceiling.

She shrugged. "You can never be too careful." The last man she'd let in here armed had put her in the hospital.

Alex nodded at a vinyl chair. "Have a seat." She placed the pistol on top of the file cabinet behind her and settled into a swivel chair. "What can I do for you, Mr. Scoffield?"

He deposited his hat, brim up, on the mini-fridge beside him. "I'm here on behalf of a James Bess. I have it on good authority that his estranged daughter hired you a few months back."

"I don't know any Bess."

"Melanie Bess? Married name Coghan?"

"Never heard of her."

"Well, that's too bad. See, Melanie's come into some money, and it's my job to get it to her." He watched her, as if to see whether "money" was Alex's magic word. Sometimes it was. But at the moment she was more interested in determining this guy's agenda.

She tilted her chair back. "Where'd you say you were from again?"

"Midland," he said. "Drove in this morning."

"Long trip. You probably should've called first."

They stared at each other for a moment. He pulled a photograph out of his jacket pocket and slid it across the desk. "You recognize Melanie?"

The picture showed a smiling teenage girl posing for the camera in a cheerleading uniform. Curly hair, laughing brown eyes, dimple. She looked a lot like Alex had in high school, only blond and popular and with big breasts.

"She's pretty," Alex said. "I'd definitely remember her."

"Listen, Miss Lovell." He leaned forward and rested his elbow on the desk between them. "I really need to find Melanie. Her daddy just passed away. She's got a lot of money coming to her, and I bet she could use it. Last I checked, she wasn't exactly flush, if you know what I mean."

"Have you tried the Internet?" Alex tipped her head to the side. "The online White Pages can be an amazing resource these days, if you're trying to find someone."

He frowned at her across the desk. She watched neutrally as he stood and tucked the photo back into his pocket, then rested his hands on his hips and gazed down at her. "How good are you at finding people?"

"If you can afford it, I can find them."

"How much to track down Melanie Bess?"

She shrugged. "I'm pretty booked up right now. It would take me at least a few days to get to it."

"The money'd be good." He produced a business card and passed it to her.

She stood and slipped the card into the back pocket of her jeans. "I'll think about it."

He collected his hat, and she followed him to the door. When they were out on the sidewalk, she returned the pistol, and he wedged it back into his holster.

"You think about my offer, now." He tipped his hat and strolled away.

In the side mirror of her car, Alex watched him head east, toward Congress Avenue, and turn the corner. She took out her phone and keyed a three-word message. She flagged it "urgent" and pressed Send.

Alex drove a five-year-old Saturn that got great gas mileage and almost never went into the shop. A surveillance vehicle it was not.

Despite a battery-powered fan, Alex spent her morning sweltering in the Saturn's front seat and waiting for a subject who never showed. By lunchtime, she was ready to call it quits. But the guy's insurance company was her top-paying client, and they were giving her good money to tail him with her camera wherever he went.

So Alex stayed. And sweated. Between PowerBars and a sprint to the corner gas station for a much-needed break, she made dozens of calls searching for any trace of Melanie Bess.

By evening, she'd found one.

Alex was on the move again now, still unable to believe it. The low-profile life she'd gone to great lengths to set up for Melanie was no more. Melanie had quit her job, canceled her utilities, and moved out of the Orlando apartment she'd rented under a corporate name just six months ago. And then Melanie committed the cardinal sin for women on the run.

She came back.

The news burned in Alex's chest as she navigated the ruts of the gravel road. All that effort, and her client had come right back to the place she'd tried so hard to leave behind.

Alex passed a weathered wooden sign for Shady Shores RV Park. She crossed the low-water bridge and hung a left at a gnarled oak. Another quarter mile of scrub brush, and there it was: 15 Moccasin Road, the house number stenciled right on the mailbox.

Alex gazed with apprehension at the modest wooden cabin. It was so *small*. And *dark*. The dread that had been nipping away at her for hours took another bite.

Alex scanned the nearby cabins and trailers. Some had been boarded up, others simply abandoned. Most lakefront property in Austin was expensive, but this scrap of land looked to be the exception. She glanced at the rusty spires rising over the tree line. The nearby power plant probably wasn't doing much for property values.

Alex parked in front of the house and unfolded herself from the car. She shook out her stiff legs and studied the overgrown yard. No cars, no sounds. The place seemed deserted. Maybe it was, and Melanie was merely using it as a dummy address.

And maybe Alex was giving her too much credit.

Six months. Six *months* and she'd come right back to Austin. What was she thinking? All that time, all that wasted effort . . . Alex nursed her anger. It was easier than dealing with the steadily creeping fear.

A breeze stirred the cypress limbs overhanging the house. Goose bumps sprang up on her arms, and she rubbed them away as she trekked across the weedy lawn to the front stoop. The screen squeaked as she pulled it open. No bell, so she rapped on the wooden door.

Alex let the screen slam shut and walked around back, where she found a sagging wooden porch. She mounted the back steps and tried the doorknob. Unlocked.

"Hello?"

She listened intently, but heard only the faint buzz of motorboats in the distance. With a growing sense of foreboding, she stepped over the threshold.

The kitchen was tiny, with a 1950s fridge, a gas stove, and a Formica table in the center. Alex walked through the room. She picked up a Budweiser can from the table and shook it. Half empty. Warm. In the living room, a tired tweed sofa took up the wall beside the front door, opposite a surprisingly new flat-screen TV. Magazines littered the coffee table: *People, Cosmopolitan, TV Guide*. Alex put down the beer can and shuffled through them all. The issues were current, but no mailing labels.

She peeked her head into the bedroom. A queen-size bed with a plaid green bedspread dominated the space, hardly leaving room to walk. On the nightstand sat an empty water bottle. Alex stepped into the cramped bathroom and pulled back the shower curtain. Pert shampoo on the side of the tub and a pink razor. Nothing on the sink.

She returned to the kitchen and spied a bit of white plastic on the floor. An earbud. Just one. She picked it up. It looked like it belonged to an iPod.

A blinking red light on the kitchen counter caught her eye. Two messages on the answering machine. Alex tapped Play. A long beep, and then a woman's voice—not Melanie's—filled the room.

Hey, it's me. Gimme a call. Another long beep, and then a dial tone.

Alex went to the back door and peered out. Almost dusk. The bushes and trees formed a shadowy purple backdrop, allowing only fleeting glimpses of the lake beyond. She caught a flutter of movement by the water and stepped out onto the porch. Nothing. Just her eyes playing tricks on her in the twilight.

She pulled the door shut behind her with a thud and tugged her phone from her pocket. She dialed Melanie, yet again, as she made her way down the steps. For the fifth time today, she waited through the computer-generated greeting.

"It's me," she said. "I really need to hear from you. I—"

Alex halted and stared at the shoe print on the step. Not mud. Was it . . . blood? She squatted down and illuminated the print with the light from her phone.

Blood. Dried. Old. But definitely blood. Her gaze traveled up the steps, to the door. More droplets, a smear.

She stood up suddenly and felt dizzy as her gaze followed the trail from the door out to the yard. Feet heavy with dread, Alex followed the narrow dirt path through the grass. She batted her way through the mesquite bushes until she stood on the spongy shore of the lake. She gazed out at the water, at the distant twinkle of houses on the opposite side. Guilt, thick and bitter, clogged her throat.

Alex jumped, startled, as her phone beeped. The call had ended.

She should call the police. Or 911. But she couldn't do it. She had to think of another way.

The photo flashed into her mind—a teenage Melanie with curls and dimples. Alex gripped her phone and cursed.

Something snapped, like a twig, and she glanced over her shoulder. Behind the windows, an orange flicker.

Fire.

The earsplitting blast knocked her off her feet.

CHAPTER TWO

Heads turned when Nathan Devereaux entered the Smokin' Pig. Ignoring the looks, he went straight to the bar and pulled out his wallet.

Janelle whistled. "What happened to you?"

"Long story."

She lifted an eyebrow.

"Trust me," he said, mustering a smile for her, "it'd bore you to tears. My order ready?"

She pursed her lips and studied him. Then she poured two fingers of Dewar's, slid the glass across the counter, and sauntered into the kitchen.

Nathan's attention drifted to the basketball game playing on a TV above the bar as he waited for the Scotch to kick in. But when Janelle came back, he felt just as lousy as he had when he'd walked in.

She put an aromatic bag of barbecued ribs on the bar beside him. "Witch hazel," she said. "On a warm washcloth, right on that eye. If that doesn't work, try alfalfa tablets."

"Alfalfa tablets."

"Or arnica cream."

She was speaking Greek, but he nodded anyway and slid her a twenty. "Thanks," he said. "Keep the change."

And then he was back in his car, finally headed home after a never-ending shitstorm of a day. It had started at 7:40 A.M. when he'd watched the ME's crew pull a waterlogged body out of Lake Austin. It had ended thirty-five minutes ago when he'd finished booking a pair of sixteen-year-olds for murder.

Nathan eased into his garage—more carefully than usual because his vision was still wacked—and entered his house through the back door. He dropped the food on the counter but realized he couldn't eat yet. He was too pissed. The Scotch hadn't helped, and he knew the only real cure was waiting for him outside. He stashed his dinner in the fridge and went into the bedroom to change.

Two hundred reps later, he lay on his weight bench, soaked and winded, but in a better mood. He could have clocked the kid. He'd had the chance. He'd had the provocation. But his partner had jumped in and, with one look, stopped Nathan from taking a career-threatening swing at a cranked-up gangbanger not half his age. Instead of returning the right hook, Nathan had settled for slapping some cuffs on him and hauling him downtown.

Now Nathan's gut clenched right along with his biceps. The scene on that street corner had been a bloodbath. Three victims—all still in high school. One of the kids' mothers had seen it, and her shrieks still rang in his ears.

What a waste. Nathan sucked in a breath and pushed the bar up. One more time. And again. And again. What a goddamn waste.

"Pretty impressive."

His elbows buckled, and he dropped the bar onto the bench frame. A woman stood in the doorway of the garage. He sat up and wiped sweat from his eyes.

Nope, he wasn't seeing things. Alex Lovell stood right in his garage against a backdrop of pouring rain. Her dark hair was plastered to her head.

She walked over and plunked a hand on her hip. "On second thought, you look like hell."

He hadn't been this close to Alex in months. He noted the fresh scrape on her chin, the dirty arms, the grass-stained jeans.

He glanced up into those whiskey brown eyes. "You seen a mirror lately?"

"No." She crossed her arms. "But it can't be worse than you. You been beating confessions out of people again?"

Her sarcasm hit a little too close to home. He grabbed a towel from the floor and mopped up his face.

"How'd you find me?" he asked.

She tipped her head to the side, obviously insulted by the question.

He'd forgotten how short she was. The bench put him at eye level with her breasts. He hadn't really noticed them before, but in that wet shirt—

"Quit ogling. I have to talk you." Her gaze wandered the room for the first time, skimming over his black '66 Mustang. It was the other half of his garage that captured her attention. Not a car person, apparently.

He stood and draped the towel around his neck, recovering some of his cool. Alex Lovell was at his house. His pulse thrummed, but that was probably from the weights.

She met his gaze briefly, then stepped away. "What's with all the shelves?"

"Ask my ex-wife."

She turned her back on him and paced the length of the wall. Some men had power drills and a tool bench in their garage. For years, Nathan had had Santas. And wreaths. And boxes and boxes of designer glass ornaments.

Alex surveyed the empty plywood shelves. "Your ex a big reader?"

"She's a Christmas fiend. She needed half the garage just for her stuff. Took it with her when she left, though."

"You sound heartbroken."

"Come inside. I'll get you a beer." *And clean up that face, too.* The more he looked at her, the more he got a sour feeling in the pit of his stomach. Alex was up to her neck in something, and if she needed to talk to him about it, that couldn't be good.

He held the door for her and continued to ogle as she stepped inside. He should have called her months ago. He should have done a lot of things.

She stood in the middle of his kitchen and glanced around.

"Smells like hamburgers."

"Barbecue," he corrected. "You hungry?"

"No." She pulled out a chair and sank into it with a sigh. She rubbed her grimy arms and shivered.

Nathan dragged open a drawer and tossed her a dish towel.

"Thanks."

She blotted her face, then her neck. And that's when

he saw it. The tiny, crescent-shaped scar above her top lip. That scar would be seven months old now.

"I need your help."

He tore his gaze away from her mouth and looked at her eyes. "With what?"

She stared down at her mud-caked Nikes. "This is harder than I thought." She glanced up at him. "Could I have a drink first? A Coke or something?"

He pulled open his fridge and retrieved two Bud longnecks, even though she'd told him once that she hated beer. He twisted off the tops and handed her one.

"Thanks." She took a long sip and rested the bottle on the table with another shudder.

Nathan's stomach tensed. The Alex he knew from before didn't scare easily. And it was fear, not cold, that had her shivering in his kitchen. She took another swig, and his gaze slid over her slender neck, her mud-spattered T-shirt. It stopped at the hole in her jeans.

"You're bleeding." He whipped the towel off his shoulder and dampened it under the faucet. Then he crouched down in front of her.

"It's nothing."

But he was already tugging up her jeans to reveal an ankle holster, which held a SIG P228. The pistol shouldn't have surprised him, but it did. Her pale calf was streaked with blood, and she flinched as he pushed the denim up farther to uncover a deep gash in her knee.

"What'd you do?" He dabbed at the blood.

"I tripped. Earlier. It's nothing—*ouch*!"

He pulled a giant splinter of wood from the wound

and glared up at her. Blood gushed from the cut, and he pressed the towel against it.

"Hold that." He replaced his hand with hers and went to get some first-aid stuff. His supply was limited, but he rummaged through the bathroom cabinet until he came up with some gauze and hydrogen peroxide.

He knelt in front of her again. "Sit tight."

"Damn, that *hurts*!" She clutched his shoulder as the cut bubbled and foamed. He poured more antiseptic and grabbed her foot as it shot out to kick him in the stomach.

"Easy, now."

Her grip tightened, and she let out a string of curses. The bleeding slowed. She drank and looked away. By the time she'd emptied the beer, he had her knee wrapped in gauze and taped securely.

He sat back on his heels and looked up at her. "You were saying? You need my help?"

"I'm not sure I want it now." She scooted her chair back. "You're a sadist!"

He watched her steadily, relieved to see the fire back in her eyes.

"Spit it out, Alex."

She jerked the leg of her pants down. Then she looked at him and took a deep breath.

"I need to report a murder."

He crouched there, staring up at her, but she couldn't read his expression. Probably because of all that nasty purple swelling around his eye. He rubbed the bridge of his nose and winced.

"Alex . . ."

He stood up and leaned back against the counter. Then he plowed his hands through his scruffy dark hair and gazed down at her until she wanted to squirm.

"You need to call a lawyer," he finally said.

A lawyer? What . . . ? "*I* didn't kill anyone!" she sputtered.

But she could tell he didn't believe her.

"I think someone killed a woman I know." The words made her queasy. "She was a client."

"You *think* someone killed her."

"No, I know. At least, I think—"

"Where is she?"

"Huh?"

"Your client. Where's the body?"

"I don't know. That's the thing. I was looking for her—"

"If you don't know where she is, how do you know she's dead?"

"Because I can't find her. Anywhere. She won't answer my calls or my text messages."

He uncrossed his arms and seemed to relax again. "So maybe she left town."

"She did. But then she came *back*." Alex shot a glance at the ceiling, straining for the last bit of patience she needed for this conversation.

"She *did* leave town," she explained. "Months ago. I helped her disappear. You know, drop off the radar."

She watched his reaction. Some of her techniques weren't exactly legal, which he probably knew because he was frowning at her.

"You do this a lot?"

"What?"

"Make people disappear."

She shrugged. "It's kind of a niche business. Sometimes people want to start over. For a lot of reasons. I
show them how. I'm pretty good at it, actually."

Not good enough. Not this time. Alex gazed down at her
slimy shoes. God, she was a mess. Maybe she shouldn't
have come here.

"So if you showed her how to disappear, how do you
know she's really gone?"

Alex got up and walked to the sink. She pumped soap
into her hand and lathered up her arms, then nudged
him aside and pulled open a drawer.

"I met Melanie back in October." She dried off with
a fresh towel and finger-combed her hair. "She came to
see me after a fight with her husband. He'd beaten her
to a pulp."

"You should have called the police."

"I wanted to, but she refused." Alex tossed the towel
on the counter. "I started making arrangements for her.
It took a few days. She gave me a little money, and I told
her we'd settle up later, after she got a job. I told her to
try waitressing."

"Why?"

"You get paid in tips, mostly. If you can find someone to pay your wages off the books, it works out. She
got moved, got on her feet. We were in touch for a little
while at first, but then I stopped hearing from her. I did
some searching today and found out she'd blown her
own cover."

"How?"

Alex huffed out a breath. "Every way possible. She

ditched the waitressing job and went to work at some clinic, doing almost exactly what she'd been doing here."

"Makes it easier to track her down," Nathan commented.

"Exactly. And then I found out she'd been flying to Austin. Long weekends here and there, over the last two months. And *then* I found out she moved right back here. Right back to her asshole husband."

"She move in with him?"

"No." Alex scoffed. "But she may as well have. It took me ten minutes to find her, once I knew she was back in town. Her husband probably found her quicker than that. I went looking for her—"

"Don't tell me you confronted this guy."

"I didn't," she said. "But I checked out the house—"

"You broke in."

"And then it caught fire."

"It caught *fire*? What the hell did you do?"

"Nothing! Someone burned it! On purpose. It had to be. I think it's a crime scene. I saw traces of blood on the back porch."

"What did the fire investigators say?"

She glanced down.

"Alex? You gave a statement, right? Don't tell me you just peeled out of there."

She closed her eyes, ashamed of what she'd done. She'd taken off like a teenager afraid of getting caught. She'd messed up, but it was too late to go back and change it.

She opened her eyes and looked at Nathan, wanting to make him understand, but also wanting to protect his opinion of her. After last fall, she knew he thought of her as smart, maybe even brave. Tonight she'd been neither of those things.

"I was scared," she said simply. "Something about the place felt creepy. Like someone was lurking around. And when I saw the fire, I panicked. I couldn't think of what to do, so I came here."

His expression softened. Maybe he'd just realized that she'd known where he lived, that she'd had an interest in him long before tonight's catastrophe.

Well, so be it. She'd never been good at coy.

"I need to go back to that house," she told him. "I think Melanie might have died there, and I need you to come see. I want your take on it."

He sighed heavily, as though he sensed this was going to be much more complicated than she'd led him to believe.

He was right. And he didn't even know the half of it.

"You'd better stop," Alex said, glancing through the windshield. A foot of water streamed over the bridge, according to the metal depth marker, but Nathan didn't slow.

She glanced at him across the front seat. "Look, the last thing I need is your flooded-out car on my conscience."

But he looked totally unconcerned as he sailed right over the bridge, spraying water on both sides. Then he pulled over to let a boxy red fire engine rumble by. Its sirens were silent, and it was the second rig they'd passed since they'd left the highway.

Alex didn't need to navigate farther. A crowd of people milled around in the center of the road. They turned and squinted at Nathan's headlights, but didn't step aside. Nathan pulled onto a relatively high patch of grass across from Shady Shores RV Park.

"You wait here."

"But—"

"We can poke around later. I need to see who's here."

He got out and slammed the door before she could object. Alex crossed her arms and heaved a sigh as he disappeared past the reach of the headlights. More waiting. Just what she needed.

Patience had never been her strong suit, and she found it ironic that such a big chunk of her professional life was spent waiting around for things to happen.

Her personal life was the opposite, and she liked it that way. When she saw something she wanted, she steeled herself for possible rejection and then just went for it. None of this moping around and wishing some guy would call.

So why hadn't she called Nathan? She'd run into him here and there since they'd met last fall. They had some mutual friends, and their paths tended to cross. But they'd kept it light, professional. Maybe it was the shock of everything that had happened today, but Alex wasn't feeling very professional toward him right now.

She caught a glimpse of him, talking to a firefighter beside a red Suburban. He was probably using his cop status to get all kinds of info not available to lowly citizens like herself. Law enforcement was a fraternity, and Alex was well aware that she'd never gain access to the club. She operated on the fringes, but she liked it that way. More flexibility. More room to bend the rules.

Alex squirmed in her damp jeans. Nathan's car was

like a sauna. She decided to do some investigating of her own and popped open his glove box: proof of insurance, Maglite, bullets, lighter. Hmm . . . Closet smoker? Doubtful. Probably more of a Boy Scout, always prepared.

Her phone vibrated in her pocket, and she jerked it out, hoping it was Melanie. But she didn't recognize the number.

"This is Alex." She waited a few beats. "Hello?"

The call ended, and she stared down at the screen, her heart racing now. Was it her? Was she reaching out, finally, after a dozen urgent messages?

Alex clicked over to the Web browser and keyed the phone number into a search engine. No matches. She redialed the number and sat through about twenty rings before hanging up.

The crowd had dispersed now, and Alex didn't see Nathan. She watched the red Suburban containing the last firefighter roll away. Then she grabbed the flashlight out of the glove box and trekked across the road, sweeping the ray of light back and forth over the soggy grass until she found a strip of yellow crime scene tape. Beyond the barrier, the house had been reduced to a pile of charred debris. Steam curled up from the cinders and danced in front of the flashlight beam.

"Hey."

She gasped and whirled around. "Dammit, you scared me!"

"I told you to stay in the car."

"What did you find out?" she asked.

He took the light out of her hand and turned it off. Right. Better not to broadcast their activities.

"I talked to the captain."

"And?"

In the darkness, her senses were sharpened. The air smelled like summer camp. Nathan smelled like damp leather from the jacket he wore to conceal his gun.

"They got here pretty quick," he said in that low, southern-tinged voice. "No casualties."

"Okay. And they're sure about that?"

"They brought in a couple of canines. No bodies under the bed, if that's what you were thinking."

That was exactly what she'd been thinking. She felt relieved. But then she recalled the bloody shoe print, facing out, as if someone were leaving.

"One of the dogs picked up an accelerant. Also, there was a propane tank somewhere in the kitchen. It exploded in the fire, pretty early on, based on witness accounts. Couple people at the RV park heard the boom before they even noticed the fire." He paused. "They reported a white Saturn racing down the road soon after that."

The last part was loaded with disapproval.

"I think there was a gas stove," Alex said, redirecting the conversation. "I didn't smell anything funny inside the house, though. No gas, nothing . . . decaying. I was standing right behind the house when the explosion happened."

Nathan didn't say anything to this news, but Alex sensed he wasn't thrilled by it.

"Could a stove just blow up like that?" she asked.

"I doubt it," he said tightly. "Not unless it'd been tampered with."

Alex swallowed hard and glanced around in the

dimness. It seemed like they were alone, but she couldn't tell for sure.

If the neighbors had seen her here, had someone else? And had anyone gotten her license plate?

"Show me where you saw the blood," Nathan said.

She took back the flashlight and led him around to the back of the property. She aimed the light beam beyond the crime scene tape.

"There was a porch," she said, but it was gone now, reduced to a pile of burned wood. A blackened beam lay in the middle of it all, its surface all cracked and scaly, like alligator skin. "So much for the shoe print."

"You remember anything about it?" he asked. "Did it look like a man's or a woman's size?"

"I don't know. It was only the front part." She walked toward the lake. "What if we got some Luminol out here? Maybe someone trailed blood away from the house."

"That'd be a huge long shot with all this rain," he said. "Not to mention the fire hoses."

Alex's temper flared. "Well, we have to do something! This is a homicide scene. Don't you want to look for evidence?"

He stepped closer, until he was a big shadow beside her.

"You're worried about your client. I get that. But for all you know, she's hanging out at some bar right now, living it up with her friends."

"She doesn't *have* any friends. That's one of her problems."

He sighed, and Alex tried to tamp down her annoyance. "Look, something's wrong," she insisted. "I was here. I saw blood. And then someone, for some reason, burned this house down. I'm no homicide detective, but that tells me we might be standing on top of a murder scene."

"You want to know the first rule of murder investigation? It's real simple. Have a body."

"I told you, she's—"

"Yeah, I know, she's missing. If you really think something happened to this girl, you need to go down to the police station and fill out a missing-person report. Get it on record, along with your suspicions about her husband."

"I can't do that," Alex said quietly.

"Why the hell not?"

"Because her husband's a cop."

CHAPTER THREE

Nathan stared at her, hoping he'd heard wrong but knowing he hadn't. "You want to say that again?"

She turned her back on him and trudged over to the car, the flashlight a glowing pendulum beside her. Nathan followed. Whatever she had to tell him, she didn't want to say it out in the open. He slid into the driver's seat and waited for her to explain, but she just sat there picking at the rip in her jeans.

"Who is he?" Nathan demanded.

"Craig Coghan."

Craig Coghan. Nathan almost laughed, it was so absurd. "You think Craig *Coghan* murdered his wife?"

"I know he did."

"Alex . . . I know the guy."

"What, you think you couldn't know a man who beats his wife? Wake up, Nathan."

"I'm not saying that, I just . . . Shit, he's a friend of mine, okay? He's a good cop. I find it pretty hard to believe he'd—"

"He's a terrible cop," she said. "And a terrible husband, too. And don't talk to me like I don't know what

I saw. My client was a mess. I have photos of it. And I checked out her story."

"And?"

"And she's credible, so just forget about explaining this away. Melanie was scared enough—despite her husband's threats—to move halfway across the country to get away from him. Craig Coghan is dangerous. And I don't care who he's friends with."

Nathan's mind reeled. Coghan. Nathan *knew* the man. They'd played in a basketball league together a couple years ago. Nathan had been out for beers with him countless times.

"This is why I need your help."

He turned to face Alex, who sat in the dimness on the other side of the Mustang, her back pressed against the door. He could feel the tension radiating off of her.

"I can't just show up at APD and start asking questions," she said firmly. "I want to gather evidence first. Discreetly, without tipping anyone off. And when I've got something solid, I want to take it somewhere else. Maybe the FBI. Or the D.A. Someone outside the police department."

Nathan shook his head. She was in for an uphill battle. And it wasn't just because the guy was a cop. They didn't have a *body*. Coghan worked narcotics, but any cop worth his salt would know plenty of ways to hide a corpse. And get rid of evidence. And craft an alibi.

"When did you last hear from Melanie?" he asked.

"It's been months. But the airlines have a record of her flying here from Florida five weeks ago. And she didn't fly back. So that's the window I'm looking at."

A depressingly big window.

Nathan tore his gaze away from Alex's shadowy silhouette and stared through the windshield at the gloom.

"Will you help me?" she pleaded. "Quietly? Without tipping anyone off?"

"That's going to be tough," he said. Try impossible. How could he work a homicide without anyone in the department knowing? She was talking about an investigation that was the purview of Internal Affairs. Nathan hated IA rats. And he wasn't about to become one.

"It's important," Alex pressed. "Melanie came to me for help. I feel responsible for her now, and I won't screw this up. Not again. So if you can't do this discreetly, I'd rather you not do anything at all."

The tone of her voice pulled at him.

"Will you do it?"

"Yes," he said, knowing he'd just made a promise that was going to be nearly impossible to keep.

Alex's eyelids grew heavy as Nathan wended through Austin back to his house in Northwest Hills. She rested her head against the window and gazed out at the glowing porch lights moving past. Melanie had lived in a neighborhood much like this, but on the other side of town. She'd had a job and a marriage and a seasonal wreath on the door. Anyone looking at her life from the outside probably figured she was happy.

"Tired?" Nathan asked.

"I guess." She closed her eyes and sighed. She wished she could just go to sleep and wake up tomorrow knowing Melanie was safe in Florida, where she should have been, and this day had all been a dream.

"The adrenaline's wearing off," Nathan said. "You're about to crash."

Alex opened her eyes and sat up straighter. She couldn't crash. Not yet, anyway. She still had work to do tonight. She had a timeline to build—Melanie's timeline—and she needed her brain alert and functioning. Maybe she'd go home and make a pot of coffee.

Alex looked across the car at Nathan. He hadn't seemed to mind being dragged away from home to go check out a hypothetical crime scene.

"You probably work pretty crazy hours, huh?" she asked.

"I'm used to it. Hardly think about it anymore."

He had a good profile. Strong, masculine lines. And from this angle, she couldn't see his bad eye. She liked the way his hair brushed the top of his jacket. It made her want to run her fingers through it.

"What?" he asked, glancing at her.

"Nothing."

She looked into the side mirror. Three cars back, she saw the same pair of headlights that had been behind them ten minutes ago. The lights were low, square, and set wide apart. An American-made sedan, if she had to guess.

"So how'd you find her?"

"Huh?"

"Melanie Coghan," he said. "You said it took you ten minutes, once you knew she was in town. How'd you do it?"

The sedan behind them hung a left, and Alex turned her attention to Nathan. "I had her phone number, so it was easy," she told him.

"I thought you said she wasn't answering."

"She wasn't." Alex smoothed her T-shirt. She really was a mess. She hoped she didn't smell bad, too, after slogging around in the mud tonight. Nathan smelled like leather and freshly showered man, and it was getting to her. She'd been having a hard time keeping her distance since he'd cleaned up back at his house.

"Okay, I give up," he said. "What am I missing?"

"I called Domino's. Actually, I called Domino's, Pizza Hut, and Papa John's, but Domino's was the one that had her."

"So she ordered a pizza . . . ?"

Alex shifted in her seat to face him. "They track customers by phone number in the computer. It was a simple pretext. I gave them Melanie's number, placed an order, and they confirmed an address on Moccasin Road. Then I canceled the order and went looking for Melanie."

Nathan turned onto his street, where Alex's car sat in front of his house. She was almost too tired to drive home. She needed to rally.

"That's good," Nathan said. "I wouldn't have thought of that."

She shrugged. "People give out information all the time. You just have to know who to ask." Nathan parked in the driveway, and Alex shoved open her door. "Thing is, with Melanie, it shouldn't have been so easy." She got out and slammed the door. "*That's* what pisses me off."

Nathan came around to her side of the car. He glanced

over her shoulder, at the Saturn parked in front of his house, and then met her gaze.

"So you told her to keep a low profile when you sent her off to Florida," he said. "And you're upset because she didn't follow your advice."

"Bingo." Alex sighed. She tucked her hands in her back pockets and looked at her feet. "I guess I didn't drill it home hard enough. She *never* should have come back here. And then after she did, she got sloppy, blew off everything I taught her."

"Her fault, not yours. You need to let it go."

She glanced up at him. It was too dark to see his expression well, but his warm southern voice surrounded her. He was from Louisiana, and his voice in the dark made her think of the bayou.

He was staring down at her now, and a shiver moved through her. He lifted his hand to her chin, and she held her breath as he brushed his thumb over the scar above her lip.

"I've been meaning to ask you," he said, "how you've been doing all this time."

Since last fall, he meant. All this time since a professional hit man had busted into her office and tried to beat information out of her. She'd called Nathan afterward and kind of lost it.

She looked away. "I've been okay," she said.

His hand dropped away. "I should have called you."

"No big deal." Why did she have this knot in her stomach? She stepped away from him and fished her car keys out of her pocket. "Well . . . thanks for your help tonight."

He stood there, watching her.

"I'll touch base tomorrow," she said, "see what you found out."

She took another step back, then turned and started toward her car. His street was quiet. No cars, no pedestrians, not even a barking dog.

"Be careful," he said after her.

She glanced over her shoulder and waved. "I will."

Sophie Barrett didn't always believe in horoscopes, but some days she had to admit they were pretty damn accurate.

Good fortune will befall you when you least expect it. Sophie drove down Lavaca Street and confirmed that, no, her baby blues were not deceiving her. There was an empty parking space *right* in front of her destination. Meaning that although it was rush hour, and downtown, and congested, she *wouldn't* have to hike it three blocks from the nearest parking garage in the drizzle. Her hair and her silver sling backs stood a chance of making it to the interview unscathed.

Sophie rolled past the space, then reversed into it with perfect ease. She'd always been a good driver, and she handled her SUV like it was a coupe.

Lovell Solutions. She read the lettering etched on the glass and glanced at the rearview mirror. Her lipstick was flawless. No need to risk sitting here primping within plain sight of that glass door. Alex Lovell was probably inside, and Sophie was determined not to let him think she was a bubblehead. Being blond had its advantages, but there were disadvantages, too. Sophie adjusted her push-up bra, smoothed her satin blouse, and slid out. After quickly dropping a few quarters into the meter, she hurried to the entrance.

This must *work out,* Sophie told herself, and put her hand on the door. It buzzed, startling her, and she pulled it open.

The office was cool after the humidity outside. Her eyes adjusted to the dimness, and she took in everything at once: the mismatched chairs, the worn sofa, the black metal desk. A woman stood behind it, staring at her.

"May I help you?" she asked.

"I'm here to see Alex Lovell."

"About?"

"I have an important matter to discuss with him."

The woman came around the desk and stood in front of Sophie. She had curly dark hair that fell to her shoulders, brown eyes, and no makeup. Good cheekbones, though. Nice lips, too, although she didn't look like the collagen type.

Sophie let her gaze flick down to the woman's faded jeans. Not much of a dress code here, but then she'd heard that about Austin.

"Is he in?" Sophie asked.

The receptionist tipped her head to the side and gazed up at her. "Do I know you from someplace?"

Sophie smiled. "It's possible. Have you been to the Velvet Note?"

The woman tucked her hands into her back pockets. "You're the singer. I remember you now."

This was going better than she'd hope. Maybe this woman would put in a good word for her.

"I'm Sophie Barrett," she said, extending her hand.

"Alex Lovell." She gave Sophie's hand a firm shake. "What did you want to talk about?"

"Uh . . ." She glanced around, flustered. Was this a joke? Mitch had said he wanted to *kill* Alex Lovell. He'd said he wanted to strangle him with his bare hands.

He had said "him," hadn't he?

"You're Alex Lovell?"

"I am."

"I'm sorry, I—"

"Did you need something?" The woman glanced at her watch. "Because I'm on my way out, actually. I've got to be somewhere, and I'm already running late."

Panic surged through her. "I need a job," she blurted.

"Excuse me?"

"I lost my job because of Alex Lovell. *You*. And I need a place to work now."

And that had come out all wrong. Sophie closed her eyes and clasped her hands together. Desperation was not attractive.

When she opened her eyes again, Alex had her arms folded over her chest and was watching her with a chilly expression.

Sophie took a deep breath. "Let me start over."

"Please do."

"Mitch Kohl used to be my boss. After you came to . . . visit him last month, he was arrested. Put in *jail*." Sophie paused for emphasis.

"That's generally what happens when people get arrested. You want to explain how that means I owe you a job?"

"I worked at Mitch's club. It's closed down now because he can't make the rent."

"Mitch Kohl's a lying deadbeat who owes twenty-two months' back child support. He's got three kids living in Austin. Did you know that?"

Sophie stepped back, away from the harsh tone. "I wasn't aware—"

"The Velvet Note's in Dallas, anyway. What are you doing down here?"

"I'm here for the music," Sophie said, before she could censor herself. But maybe honesty was her best strategy. This woman wasn't going to be swayed by cleavage and guilt. "I'm trying to get my singing career started. Austin's got a big music scene."

"And you figured you'd sweet-talk me into letting you work for me."

"I guess so."

"Doing what?"

"Well." Sophie straightened her shoulders. "I have a minor in photography."

Alex's eyebrows arched.

"I figure you take a lot of pictures? Of, you know, people cheating on their wives? Stuff like that?"

"Actually, most of my clients are insurance companies," she said. "And I take my own pictures. What else you got?"

Sophie darted her gaze around the office. She noticed the piles of papers, the overflowing trash can, the software manuals stacked on the floor beside an empty Dell computer box.

"I'm good with computers," she lied. "And I'm *super* organized. I love to file."

Alex laughed at this, and Sophie realized she'd gone too far.

Still, she seemed to be considering it.

"You must really want a job," Alex said.

"I do."

"How old are you?"

She thought about tacking on a few years. But this woman was a PI. "Twenty-three," she answered.

Alex looked her over again, and her gaze lingered on Sophie's French manicure. "Look, Sophia—"

"Sophie."

"I actually *do* need an assistant. But I run a lean operation here. The wages are low, the hours suck. And I know PI work might sound glamorous, but it's really pretty boring. I doubt you'd be up for it."

Alex's candor only made her want the job more. She could almost *feel* it within her grasp, when just minutes ago, she'd thought she'd blown it.

"It sounds perfect," Sophie told her. "I want to live in Austin and pay my bills. You need an assistant. I'm not looking for a career or anything—just a day job."

"That your Tahoe?"

"Huh?"

Alex peered around her. "On the street there. Is it yours?"

"Yes."

"You mind using it for work?"

She had it! "Not at all."

"Good. I'll need the keys." Alex held out her hand. "And your license, too. I need to run a background check."

"I don't—"

"Look, I've got to be somewhere ten minutes ago. I'm not about to leave you here with eight thousand dollars' worth of office equipment unless I have some collateral. You want the job or not?"

"I want it."

"Good. Then you can lend me your car. I'll call you from the road, fill you in on everything else while I drive. Answer the phone and be ready to take notes."

Sophie felt like she was stepping off the edge of a stage into thin air. A total stranger was going to hire her for a job she couldn't do and drive away in her car. It was crazy.

She dropped her keys into Alex's hand.

It wasn't as if business could get any worse, Alex mused, as she headed across town in Sophie Barrett's Tahoe. Why not hire an underqualified, overdressed office assistant?

Alex was ninety-nine percent sure she was going to regret this decision, but the thought of spending yet another day melting in the Saturn had pushed her over the edge.

The Tahoe had possibilities. The Tahoe had black-tinted windows, a spacious backseat, and plenty of room to spread out a computer during endless surveillance gigs. And best of all, it was registered to someone besides Alex, so that if anyone—say, Craig Coghan—should happen to see it around, he wouldn't link it back to Lovell Solutions.

Alex turned into the parking lot of Coghan's gym and maneuvered the hulking SUV between two cars. She spotted the white Dodge pickup on the opposite side of the lot.

Right on schedule. Looked like the guy's routine

hadn't changed since Alex had run surveillance on him back in the fall. If he remained true to form, he'd spend another twenty minutes here at the gym before reporting in for work at APD. Like most cops Alex knew, Coghan's schedule tended to start out predictable, then get increasingly chaotic as the day wore on, meaning that if Alex hadn't caught up to him by lunchtime, it was a good bet she wouldn't find him until he returned home for the night.

Alex tucked her hair into a baseball cap, entered the gym, and rode the elevator up to the second floor, where the workout room overlooked downtown traffic. She darted her gaze around. Glass, mirrors, and Spandex as far as the eye could see.

"Can I help you?"

She turned her attention to the guy sitting at the reception counter behind a stack of towels. "Hi, there." She smiled. "I wanted to inquire about a membership here."

"Sure." He pulled a brochure out of a drawer and slid it across the counter while Alex stared at his enormous pecs. The kid was practically bursting at the seams.

"Your first consultation is free," he said.

"Thanks."

She spotted Melanie's husband at the far side of the room, leaning on a treadmill and talking to a brunette in yoga pants. Coghan was every bit as muscular as Alex remembered him, possibly even more so. Had he been spending a lot of time at the gym since his wife left? Alex tugged the bill of her cap lower and watched him, trying to determine whether he was coming or going.

"Is that a yes?"

She snapped her gaze back to Steroid Boy. "Excuse me?"

"Would you like to schedule a free consultation?"

Coghan picked up a water bottle from the floor and started walking toward Alex. Then he turned into the men's locker room.

"I'll think about it." Alex slid the brochure into her pocket and ducked back into the elevator.

She needed three minutes. Five, at the most.

She tried to look nonchalant as she approached Coghan's pickup. The truck bed was empty except for a crushed beer can. She glanced inside the cab. No alarm, which was a pleasant surprise. Alex slipped a Slim Jim from her purse. With well-practiced movements, she slid the tool between the window and the weather stripping, caught the lock rod, and popped the lock.

It was your typical man's truck cab—empty fast-food cups in the console, McDonald's wrappers on the floor, a phone charger plugged into the lighter. She checked the glove box and the console. Nothing incriminating.

Alex sighed. What had she expected? Some empty gas cans, maybe? Bloody handprints on the dash? The guy was a cop, and she gave him just a bit more credit.

Alex reached under the passenger seat and felt around for a smooth metal surface. After finding one, she pulled the GPS from her purse and attached the magnetic mount box to its new hiding spot. The device was motion-sensitive and would come to life whenever the truck started moving, which would preserve its battery life. She glanced up at the row of windows facing the street. Time to clear out. She slid from the cab, relocked the door, and returned to her car.

Now she'd track him. She wanted to see his every move. Arrogance was Craig Coghan's Achilles' heel, according to Melanie, which meant he thought he could get away with anything. Including murder.

CHAPTER FOUR

Nathan was up to his knees in garbage when his phone buzzed for the second time in ten minutes.

"It's yours, Dev," his partner called from a neighboring Dumpster.

Another buzz.

"Goddamn it," Nathan muttered, snapping off a Latex glove. He dug the phone out of his pocket and checked the screen. Alex. He'd missed two calls.

"What's wrong?" he demanded, and was answered by silence. "Alex?"

"Nothing's wrong, it's just . . . you sound upset. Did I interrupt something?"

"No."

"Having a bad day?"

Nathan gazed down at the putrid remnants of food and grease leaking from the trash bags. "Everything's peachy. Why?"

"I just got a lead. On that thing we talked about last night." Alex obviously thought she needed to be guarded on the phone with him. "I thought we'd get together later, maybe compare notes."

Compare notes. That assumed Nathan had something to compare. He didn't. His whole morning had been derailed by a convenience store holdup. After hours of legwork he'd turned up the terrific lead that some homeless guy had seen someone who *might* fit their shooter's description tossing something that *could* have been a handgun into this Dumpster.

"I'm in the middle of something," Nathan said, nudging aside an empty milk carton with his shoe.

"Well, how about dinner? We could meet somewhere and exchange information. I know a good Chinese place—"

"No," he cut in. He was standing on top of enough rotting Chinese food to feed an army of roaches. "Anything but Chinese. And it'll have to be late. I've got about ten things to do before I can knock off, so—"

"How about the Smokin' Pig at nine o'clock?"

She'd read his mind. Or maybe she just remembered it was the place he'd taken her the night they'd first met. He'd bought her a beer. Then she'd sat there and cracked one of his cases wide open. Nathan had been impressed. More than impressed—he'd been intrigued. And he'd been meaning to call her ever since to ask her out on a date.

But he hadn't done it, and now she'd beaten him to the punch.

Although, this meeting tonight didn't seem like much of a date. Her voice was all business, and she wanted to "compare notes." Didn't that sound exciting?

"Nathan? You there?"

He glanced at the rank, unidentifiable ooze clinging to his pant leg. "Make it nine thirty," he said. "I've got to run home first and shower." And it wouldn't hurt to toss his clothes in an incinerator.

"Nine thirty, then. Don't be late," she said, and clicked off.

Nathan stuffed the phone back into his pocket as Will Hodges poked his head over the side of the rusty Dumpster.

"Hot date?" his partner asked.

"Nah, just work."

Hodges lifted an eyebrow. The kid could smell a lie from a mile off. It was uncanny. And one of the reasons he made a good homicide detective, despite his age.

"You know, Courtney's got this friend—"

"Forget it," Nathan said.

"So it isn't just work."

Nathan glanced at Hodges, who, sure enough, was smirking at him.

"It's nothing," Nathan said. "Just Alex Lovell. I'm helping her out on something."

But Hodges still didn't look convinced.

Screw it. Maybe the kid could help him.

"Hey, you ever heard anything about Craig Coghan?" he asked, tugging the glove back on so he could keep digging.

"Narcotics guy?"

"Yeah."

"Don't really know him," Hodges said. "Good reputation, though. What's he need with a PI?"

"His wife hired her." Nathan crouched down to lift up a black plastic bag. About a hundred glass bottles cascaded out, and the smell of stale beer blended with the ripe mix of rainwater and garbage.

"Thought he was divorced," Hodges said, his voice echoing from inside the metal box.

"More like separated, I think. You haven't heard any dirt on him?"

"I haven't heard much, except that he got promoted last fall to head up the narco squad. Hey, I found something."

"What?" Nathan stood up and craned his neck to see into the neighboring Dumpster.

His partner knelt amid the garbage bags, beaming. He held up a nickel-plated pistol with a wilted lettuce leaf stuck to the barrel.

"Money," Hodges said proudly.

"Yep." And it was. They had their murder weapon. Nathan yanked off his gloves and shook loose the egg shell attached to his shoe. All they needed now was a shooter and a confession, and they'd have this case wrapped up with a big red bow.

Nathan wasn't holding his breath.

For the second evening in a row, Alex pulled up to Nathan's house and parked beneath the giant pecan tree that shaded his front yard.

Pecan trees, landscaping. The place was so domestic, it was hard to believe a jaded homicide detective lived here. Alex had never owned a house. She didn't cook or entertain, didn't like gardening. She spent most of her time working and thought of her one-bedroom apartment as a convenient place to sleep and stash her things.

Alex tossed her baseball cap on the Saturn's passenger

seat and finger-combed her hair. She considered lipstick, then ditched the idea. This was business. Period. She got out of the car and slammed the door.

The house looked dark, but Nathan's Mustang was in the driveway. She walked up the sidewalk and a floodlight blinked on, startling her. She looked for movement behind the windows flanking the front door but didn't see any. Alex rang the bell and waited. And waited. And rang again. A light switched on in the hallway. The door swung open, and Nathan was standing there, a blue bath towel slung low around his waist.

"You didn't get my message?" He stepped back to let her in, and she tried not to gape at his nicely sculpted chest as she entered the house.

"I did get it," she said. "That's why I'm here. This can't wait until tomorrow."

He closed the door and strode past her into a darkened hallway. "You'll have to talk fast, then. I'm on my way up to Round Rock for a suspect interview."

He'd said as much in his phone message half an hour ago when he'd canceled their dinner plans. Alex had been disappointed, and not just because she had something important to show him. She'd spent her entire day conducting surveillance, and she'd been looking forward to some conversation.

The man she'd wanted to converse with led her back to the master suite. Like the rest of the home's interior, it had "bachelor pad" written all over it. Alex hesitated a moment before stepping into his bedroom. It felt steamy and smelled like Irish Spring from his shower. A black floor lamp stood in the corner, providing the only light.

Not much furniture to speak of—just a bureau and a king-size bed with a simple black spread.

Nathan stood at his closet with his back to her. "My day got trashed. Literally." He grabbed some clothes and walked into the bathroom. "Sorry about dinner, but there's nothing I can do." He swung the bathroom door closed, but left a slight opening so she could hear him. "It's taken us weeks to locate this kid, and we need a confession out of him."

Alex was well aware of Nathan's reputation. He'd been nicknamed the Priest—not because of any kind of devout lifestyle, but because of his legendary ability to get a confession. Nathan had the gift of gab and a knack for getting people to talk to him. Alex wasn't sure how he did it, but she'd fallen for his techniques a time or two herself.

"So what'd you need to tell me?" he asked over the buzz of an electric razor.

Alex looked around uncertainly. No chair, so she perched on the corner of his bed, resisting the urge to glance at the sliver of reflection in the bathroom mirror.

She had so many things to tell him, she didn't quite know where to begin. So she started at the top.

"I checked out that attorney." She heard a towel hitting the floor and pants being pulled on.

"What attorney?"

"His name's William Scoffield. He came to see me yesterday morning about Melanie. That's what prompted me to try and contact her."

He jerked the door open now and stood there, buttoning his cuffs. White shirt, charcoal slacks. His work uniform, or so it seemed.

"What did the attorney want with her?" he asked.

"You really should get that eye looked at. It's even worse today."

He dragged open a bureau drawer and fished out some socks. "The attorney?"

"Some sort of probate issue," she said. "Told me he was handling Melanie's father's estate. That she just inherited property in west Texas."

"You think he's legit?"

"Seemed to be." Alex remembered the way he'd handled his cowboy hat, removing it indoors and placing it brim up on the table. "I checked him out. He's registered with the state bar. And Martindale-Hubbell lists him as a partner with a firm out in Midland."

Nathan reached for the shoes sitting beside his closet. He sat down on the bed beside her, and the mattress sank. "What about the inheritance?" he asked.

"State has a record of a Midland County man by the name of James Bess passing away several weeks ago. Melanie never told me much about her family, except that she wasn't on good terms with them. It seems to fit."

He propped his foot on his knee and tied his shoe. "So that's your big lead? A lawyer who is who he says he is?" He stood up and reached for the belt coiled on the dresser, right beside his Glock.

"That wasn't all I did today."

"What else did you do?" He quickly put on his belt and threaded it through his holster.

"I followed Coghan."

His hands stilled on the buckle. He stood there, watching her, and the scowl on his face would have been scary, even without the bruise.

"What?" she asked.

"It ever occur to you that a cop *might* just notice you tailing him around all day?"

"I did it from a safe distance." She omitted the part about breaking into the man's truck to plant a GPS she could track with her cell phone.

Shaking his head, he finished buckling and adjusted his gun. "And what'd you find out?"

"He made some weird pit stops."

"How do you mean, 'weird'?"

"Well, he's a narcotics cop, right? Head of some task force?"

"Yeah." He rested his hands on his hips.

"So . . . I'd expect him to spend his time at the police station," she said. "Or maybe in the really crime-infested neighborhoods, doing drug raids and stuff."

"Yeah?"

"He spent half his day over in Captain's Point. In his personal vehicle."

Nathan muttered something she couldn't hear as he walked out of the bedroom.

She followed him. "Don't you think that's a little upscale? I mean, Captain's Point isn't exactly a hive of nefarious activity."

Nathan went into the kitchen and jerked open the fridge. He grabbed two cans of Red Bull and handed one to Alex. This was dinner, apparently.

He leaned back against the counter and popped open his can. "I'm not really following how Coghan spending the day in Captain's Point means he murdered his wife."

"It doesn't. I just think it was odd. Don't you?"

"I think your theory's odd." He took a long swig, then

set the can down on the counter. "Not only that, I think you're underestimating who you're dealing with. You don't think Coghan's eventually going to notice you tailing him around town? He probably already knows his wife hired you just before she left. You're aware of that, right?"

"So?"

"So the guy's probably pissed off." He glanced at his watch and grabbed his car keys off the counter. "I have to go now." He stepped closer and gazed down at her. "We can talk about this again tomorrow, but leave Coghan alone, okay?"

"I haven't told you the best part yet." Alex pulled a clear plastic bag from her back pocket and handed it to him.

His dark brows knitted together. "What's this?"

"An earphone," she said. "Like, for an iPod. I found it at the house last night, on the floor. Then everything went sideways, and I forgot about it until I was getting dressed this morning. It was in my pocket."

Nathan held the bag up and studied the white plastic earbud.

"You see that brown stuff on there?" Alex pointed at the bottom part, just above where it looked like the wire had been cut. "I think it's blood."

Nathan shot her a glare and handed back the bag. "Just what are you planning to do with this?"

"We can have it tested, try and find out who the blood belongs to."

Nathan shook his head and looked away.

"What?"

"This isn't some TV show, Alex. I can't just order up a DNA test whenever I feel like it."

"But this is important evidence." She held up the bag again. "Look at that and tell me you don't think that's blood on there."

He shrugged. "Sure, maybe, but it doesn't mean anything."

"It means we have evidence," Alex protested. "If it's Melanie's blood, it proves something violent happened to her just before that fire. Or maybe the blood might belong to her killer."

"Alex." He gazed down at her again, and she bristled at the condescending tone of his voice. "Do you have any idea how backlogged our crime lab is? DNA tests are time-consuming as hell, not to mention expensive. Typically we don't even do them unless we've got a suspect charged and on his way to trial."

Alex's stomach twisted with disappointment. She wasn't sure if it was what he was saying or how he was saying it that bothered her more.

"You're telling me you won't do this," she said. "You won't even consider what this evidence could mean—"

"It's not evidence!" he snapped. "Alex, you broke into some house, you picked up someone's personal property, you *removed* it from a supposed crime scene—"

"It *is* a crime scene. You said it was arson—"

"Now you want me to send it to the lab and ask for a DNA test? And then what? It doesn't matter whose blood it is, if it even is blood. There's no chain of custody. The evidentiary value of it is zip."

She stepped back, stung by the harshness of his words. He wasn't even willing to consider the fact that she'd found something important. He was too caught up in all the standard procedures.

She gazed down at the bag in her hand, at the brown smudge on the cord. Anyone could see it was blood. What if Melanie never turned up and this was the only evidence out there that something bad had happened to her?

"Fine." She shoved the bag back into her pocket. "If you won't investigate this case, then I will."

She handed back the can of Red Bull. "Thanks for dinner," she said, and strode for the door.

CHAPTER FIVE

The sky was still dark and likely to stay that way for another half hour when Alex pulled into the almost-empty parking lot. Nathan watched her swerve around a pothole before sliding into a space beside his Mustang. She got out of her car and slammed the door.

"Morning, sunshine," he said.

She eyed him grumpily over the roof of her Saturn. "Is this place even open yet?"

"It will be when we're done."

"Done what?"

He walked over to where she stood, hands on hips, scowling at him in the drizzle. He glanced at her feet and saw that she'd followed the directions he'd given her over the phone twenty minutes ago.

"You wore your Nikes," he observed.

"You can't be serious about that."

"Why not?"

"It's *raining*. And who in the world exercises at this hour?"

"It's barely sprinkling." He smiled. "Don't be a wuss."

"I'm absolutely a wuss. I need coffee." She glanced

longingly over her shoulder at the café. A light had come on and someone was taking down chairs, but the sign still said CLOSED.

"Thirty minutes." He draped an arm over her shoulder and steered her toward the lakefront trail. "Then we'll have breakfast and talk over your case."

She thrust her chin out.

"I'll go easy on you," he added. "Four miles, max."

She snorted and shook off his arm. But then she pulled her ankle back behind her and started stretching her quadriceps. "You'll be lucky to get a mile out of me. I haven't jogged in ages."

They waited for a break in traffic, then crossed Lake Austin Boulevard. When they reached the sidewalk, he broke into a trot. She joined him soon enough, and he shortened his stride so she could keep up. She was a small woman. Petite, some would even say. But Nathan never thought of her that way, probably because of the force of her personality.

"How do you stay in shape?" he asked, as they veered off the paved sidewalk to the gravel path that hugged the shoreline.

"What makes you think I'm in shape?"

"You look it. And you have the gear, too, so you must do something."

"I have all kinds of gear," she said. "You never know when you're going to need to tail someone to the gym."

But Nathan wasn't buying it. She was barely breathing hard, and they were moving at a good clip. He increased his stride and led her onto the concrete pedestrian bridge. Cyclists blew past them. Early morning traffic *whoosh*ed back and forth on the car bridge just above. On the other side, they veered left onto the trail that paralleled the lake's south side. Traffic was sparse today. Looked like the cool, damp weather was keeping everyone snug in their beds at home. He glanced at Alex.

"How'd your interview go?" she asked, and he caught an edge in her voice. Or maybe he'd imagined it.

"Good."

"You get your confession?"

He hadn't imagined it.

"Yeah." He looked over again, but her face was unreadable. He guessed she was still pissy about their canceled dinner plans. Maybe he should feel smug about that.

Or maybe he should have his head examined. Alex Lovell wasn't the type to sit around pining for a man to go to dinner with her.

Hell, for all he knew, she already had a boyfriend. He should probably just ask her.

"How's business?" he asked instead.

"Busy," she said. "Lots of insurance work lately with the economy down like this. No one wants to pay anybody."

"Including you?"

She sniffed. "I get my bills paid."

He'd bet she did. She was tough.

Except when it came to Melanie Coghan.

"How about you?" She shot ahead of him to squeeze past an overhanging tree limb. When he reached her side again, he noticed she'd picked up the pace.

"Busy."

"I keep reading about gang shootings in the paper."

"Some of that," he said. "We're getting a lot of turf wars, drug deals gone bad. Plus the regular ration of crap."

"City's expanding," she said.

But that wasn't all there was to it. Even given the swelling population, crime was on the rise, gangs were making inroads, the murder rate had spiked. APD was hiring new recruits as fast as they could get them, but that didn't seem to help. There weren't enough old guys like himself. Not that thirty-eight was old, necessarily, but they needed more experience out there. Anyone with more than five minutes on the job was stretched thin.

Sure, there were good days—the collars, the confessions. The feeling of deep satisfaction when someone actually went to trial and got put away. But there was the bullshit, too—the never-ending paperwork, the plea bargains, the perps who went to jail, then got spit right back out onto the same streets to pull the same shit Nathan had nailed them for the first time. With every new arrest, Nathan was feeling like he was winning the battle but losing the war.

By the time they reached the second pedestrian bridge, his T-shirt was soaked through, and not with rain. Alex was in the lead now. He'd told her four miles, and she seemed to be holding him to it. The fact that she knew the trail told him she wasn't as much of a stranger to exercise as she let on.

Another fifteen minutes, and they were back in the parking lot. Nathan untied his car key from his shorts and unlocked the Mustang. He tossed Alex a white towel from the duffel he kept in the backseat. Then he stripped off his wet T-shirt and pulled on a dry one. He caught Alex checking out his chest as she blotted her face, but she quickly looked away.

"They're half full already," she said.

"Best pancakes in town."

"Really?" She sounded surprised. "It looks like a dive."

"It is."

Alex tossed back his towel. He locked his car and led her into the restaurant, where the hostess he knew gave them a booth in the back corner, which was his preferred spot.

Alex slid in across from him, and he felt a warm shot of lust. Her brown eyes were bright and alert now, and her cheeks were pink with all that freshly oxygenated blood. Just like the other night, he could see the shape of her breasts through her damp T-shirt.

"Y'all ready to order?"

He snapped his attention to the waitress.

"Pecan pancakes, link sausage, orange juice, and coffee," Alex said.

"Whole wheat or buttermilk?"

Alex made a face. "Buttermilk. Definitely."

"I'll have the same," Nathan said.

When the waitress left, he looked at Alex. "I've got some questions for you before I can really dig in on this thing."

She leaned back in the booth. "Shoot."

"I need to know the exact day Melanie left town and the exact day you last heard from her, if you can remember."

"October fifth, January third."

"You sure?"

"Positive. I just reconstructed the timeline from phone records."

"Okay, and where'd you move her?"

"I told you," she said. "Florida."

"Whereabouts, exactly?"

"Orlando."

He watched her, looking for the telltale signs that she was lying. Nathan was good at gaining people's trust. And he knew that, for whatever reason, he hadn't fully gained Alex's.

"What?" she asked.

"You're being straight with me?"

"Why wouldn't I?"

"I don't know. Why wouldn't you?"

She crossed her arms.

"I spent about an hour on your case yesterday. Airline has a record of Coghan heading up to Portland the weekend of November fifth."

"So?"

"And an apartment locator in Salem ran a credit check on Melanie on October eighteenth. A cable company in Salem did the same for her a week later. I'm guessing if I took the trouble to look, I'd find some ATM debits in Oregon right about that time, too."

"You would," Alex said.

"But she was in Florida."

She arched her eyebrows and looked at him impatiently.

"Just making sure." He leaned back and watched her. She was good. Thorough. She'd been just as good and just as thorough on the last case he'd seen her work, the case of Courtney Glass, who now happened to be married to Nathan's partner. Courtney had gone to Alex last fall when she was flat broke, neck deep in trouble, and looking to disappear. Alex had helped her. Both Hodges and Nathan had searched high and low for Courtney but had turned up nothing but dead ends. If Courtney hadn't slipped up, she might have stayed lost forever.

The coffee came, followed by two plates heaped with steaming pancakes. Nathan welcomed the distraction. He didn't much like remembering Courtney's case. He particularly didn't like how it ended with Nathan inadvertently leading a hired gun straight to Alex's door. The fucker had been looking for Courtney, and thought Alex would give up her client's whereabouts after a good beating.

"Coghan's trip up to Portland," Alex said now as she poured syrup over her pancakes. "We can assume he was looking for Melanie?"

The scar above her lip moved as she talked, and Nathan watched it, feeling the familiar anger. He pictured her in her office, all cut up and bruised, and his gut tightened.

"Nathan?"

"I never assume anything. I'll have to check it out."

"I also planted some bogus ATM transactions in northern California, just after she left."

"How'd you do that?"

"Friends in the area," she said. "I sent a couple of them Melanie's ATM card. Told them to make a withdrawal, FedEx the card back, then go have a drink on

Melanie for their trouble. I wanted to make it look like she was moving around the region, looking for a place to settle."

She gulped down some orange juice, and he watched her, wondering where she'd picked up her trade. This niche business of hers was like a civilian-run witness-protection program. And despite the complexities involved, she seemed to have a handle on everything.

"Did Coghan have any travel to California?" she asked. "Maybe he rented a car or dropped one off?"

"I didn't see anything. But like I said, haven't spent a lot of time yet."

"Let me know what you find out."

"What is it with you and these basket-case women, anyway?"

"What do you mean?" she asked.

"I mean, if business is good, why take all these crap cases? They're dangerous. And they don't pay."

She shrugged. "Not everything's about profit."

"I thought you were a businesswoman."

"I am. My insurance cases pay me nicely."

He studied her face, trying to see past the attitude. Finally, he shook his head. "I don't get you."

She leaned closer, and he caught the gleam in her eyes. He'd struck a chord.

"Let me ask you something," she said. "When you get called to the scene of some murdered woman, who's the first person you look for?"

"Husband or boyfriend."

She nodded. "And if the victim was in an abusive relationship, odds are even higher that's who killed her.

Some women try and get out, but that's when they're in the most danger. These guys don't exactly take rejection well."

"So you step into the middle. You have any idea how reckless that is?"

"Not reckless," she said. "Carefully calculated. My clients follow my advice, they get free."

"So what happened with Melanie?"

She looked away. "I'm not sure. I thought she understood the danger of coming back here. I can't figure out why she did."

"Where do these women hear about you?"

She forked up a bite of pancakes. Chewed thoughtfully. Washed it down with a sip of juice. "Here and there."

"Meaning?"

"Courtney was a referral. A friend of a friend. Some of them I get through a shelter, I think. I'm pretty sure someone at one of the places in town has my number."

Perfect. Someone was sending Alex these people. Parking trouble right on her doorstep, over and over again.

"Melanie get you through a shelter?"

"She never went to one," Alex said. "She was too scared."

Nathan didn't comment. He wasn't sure fear was what had kept Melanie away from any shelters. He still had his doubts about Coghan's wife. Alex had been way too eager to accept her story at face value. Nathan knew some of his reservations stemmed from his relationship with Coghan, but another part was experience. He'd learned that most things were much more complicated than they seemed. And people—particularly desperate ones—lied like rugs.

"These are great." Alex nodded at his plate. "Aren't you gonna eat?"

He frowned down at his breakfast. Stabbed a link of sausage.

"How'd you get into what *you* do?" she asked. "You've got a lot of crap cases yourself. Can't be the pay."

She seemed to like throwing his words back at him.

"I wanted to be a cop since I was a kid."

"Why?"

He watched her for a moment. She looked genuinely interested, not like someone making small talk.

"My family ran a bar in the French Quarter," he said. "My dad was always getting called out of bed to go meet the cops, hear about how some punk had busted into our place, looking for money or booze. When I got old enough, he started letting me come along."

"So cops were your heroes."

He shrugged. He'd never really thought of it that way, but Alex would. She was an idealist.

"How'd you get into PI work?" He scooped up a bite of pancakes and watched her.

"I always liked computers," she said, as if that explained it. "I tried working for other people, but I do better on my own."

"Problems with authority?"

"I like to call my own shots."

More interesting than what she'd said was all the stuff she'd left out. Nathan had looked into her background— not that he'd ever tell her that. She'd grown up in Urbana, Illinois, the daughter of two university professors. She'd gone through her freshman year of college there, receiving what had to have been a nice break on tuition at U of I, where her parents worked. But then she'd dropped out. Three years later, she'd founded Lovell Solutions in her hometown. Then she'd taken the show on the road, apparently, moving herself and her company to Chicago, San Francisco, and most recently, Austin.

She was just twenty-nine. She'd been here two years, and it looked like she planned to stay. Unless she got itchy feet again.

"What?" Alex said now, and dabbed her mouth with her napkin. He'd been staring.

"Nothing." He glanced down at his plate, which he'd somehow managed to clear, despite all the distractions. Alex had cleared hers, too.

She downed a sip of coffee and checked her watch. "I hate to eat and run, but I've got an appointment over in West Campus. Is there anything else you need to know?"

"The date of your last payment from Melanie."

"October fourth. The day after she hired me."

"That was it?"

"Yep."

Shit, she'd let the woman walk all over her.

"That about covers it, then," he said. "I'll do some more digging today, see what I can find out."

"Whatever you do, be discreet. I don't want this getting back to Coghan." She tried to pass him some money, but he waved it off.

"My treat," he said.

"No, mine." She slid out of the booth and tucked the bills under her coffee mug. "You're spending time on this case for me. I feel like I owe you."

"You don't owe me anything yet. I haven't done jack."

She smiled down at him. "Yeah, but you will."

Sophie twisted the last screw into the shelving unit with the little metal tool and stepped back to admire her work. Not bad. And this one had taken only half as long as the one she'd built yesterday. The main challenge had been deciphering the instructions that had come in the bag with all the different-size screws.

Someone knocked on the glass, and she whirled around.

A visitor. Her first visitor, and she was on her knees surrounded by files. She jumped to her feet and smoothed her skirt down as she walked over to the door. Alex hadn't shown her how to buzz someone in from her desk. Sophie added that to her mental list of questions as she pulled open the door.

A tall man loomed on the sidewalk. He looked at least six-two, but it was hard to tell because of the cowboy hat.

"May I help you?" she asked crisply.

"I'm here to see Alexandra Lovell." He stepped forward, and Sophie caught a whiff of tobacco.

"Ms. Lovell isn't in right now." She leaned back against the door and ushered him inside. "Would you like to leave her a message?"

He hesitated a moment, then stepped into the office and removed his hat to reveal a shock of white hair. His gaze roamed over the mess and then paused on the open door to Alex's office.

"May I get your name?"

"Scoffield. Bill Scoffield."

His voice had an east Texas drawl to it. Sophie was

an expert on voices. She could place almost anything and sometimes made a game out of it.

"You know when she'll be back?" he asked.

"Anytime now, I expect," Sophie said, although she had no idea when Alex was coming back. She was doing some sort of surveillance, and it was taking much longer than she'd originally said. Sophie stepped over a stack of files and opened the drawer she'd organized this morning. She found a pink message pad and jotted down the man's name.

"Anything you'd like me to tell her, Mr. Scoffield?" She glanced up, and he stood right by Alex's door, peering into the office. Sophie stepped into his line of sight and pulled the door shut. "A message, maybe?"

"Just tell her I dropped by." He gazed at her a moment, then he settled the hat back on his head and walked out.

Sophie watched him go, feeling uneasy. She didn't like his interest in Alex's office. She didn't like something else about him, either, but she couldn't quite place it.

She got down on her knees and resumed her shelving. Another knock, and she turned around, expecting the cowboy again.

But it was someone else.

No walk-ins for two days, and now they were flooded. Sophie hurried to the door and pulled it open.

"May I help you?" she asked, trying not to flinch when she saw his face.

"I'm looking for Alex." He sauntered into the office and turned around. "She in?"

The man had a friendly voice. Southern. Louisiana or Arkansas would be Sophie's guess.

"I'm sorry, she's out right now."

He ambled around the room, taking in everything, it seemed, despite the injury to his left eye. "You expect her back soon?"

"I don't really know."

"And who are you?" he asked, pausing beside the desk she'd just organized.

"I'm Sophie. Alex's assistant."

He nodded, then glanced down and thumbed through the Rolodex.

Annoyance overcame her intimidation, and she rushed over. "And you are?" She picked up the Rolodex and slid it into a drawer.

"A friend of Alex's."

Friend, as in boyfriend? Doubtful. He looked too scruffy, even for Alex Lovell. The navy blazer and gray slacks were probably meant to make him seem civilized, but they didn't quite do the job. Maybe he was a loan shark. Or some angry husband whose wife's PI had caught fooling around, and now he was out for revenge on Alex—

"Place is looking good." He stepped over to Alex's office door and stood there listening, as if wanting to confirm that no one was behind it.

Sophie crossed her arms. "May I take a message for you?"

But the man was more interested in checking out the reception room. His gaze drifted over the results of Sophie's last two days of work: the two bookcases, which she'd unpacked and assembled from the dusty Ikea boxes leaning against the wall; the newly organized file cabinet, which now doubled as a table for the coffeepot.

"Looks like you've been busy."

"Yes, well . . ."

He smiled, which went a long way toward calming her nerves. He had a nice smile. "Relax," he told her.

"Excuse me?"

"You seem kinda jumpy."

"I'm not, really. I just—"

"I bet she's a tough boss, huh?" He stepped closer. "She's good, though. At what she does. You're lucky she hired you. She's a pretty quick judge of character, so you must have made a good impression."

Sophie felt herself smile, even though something told her she should stay on her guard.

"Listen," he said smoothly, "I really need to find Alex, and she's not answering her cell. Where is she, exactly?"

"I'm not sure." Sophie perched on the desk and took a sip of coffee, then casually placed the cup on top of the note she'd made earlier. "But I'll be happy to get her a message."

He plunked his hands on his hips, revealing a gold shield clipped to his belt. "You know where she is, but you don't want to say. Is that right?"

"I'm not at liberty to disclose—"

"Honey, I'm a cop. And I need to talk to Alex. You can tell me."

She gazed up at him, warmed by a sudden wave of trust. "She's doing surveillance all day," she told him. "That's all I can tell you. But I'll be happy to get her a message for you, if you like."

"Thanks." He smiled again, a flash of perfect white teeth. "Just tell her I stopped by."

And then he was across the office, pulling open the

door. He glanced over his shoulder at her. "Good luck with the new job."

Sophie smiled as the door whisked shut. He was cute. Sexy, even, if you overlooked the dings.

A thought struck her.

"Wait!" she rushed to catch him. "You never told me your name!"

She pulled the door open and poked her head out, but he was already gone.

CHAPTER SIX

A lex had never ruptured a disk in her back before. But she was pretty sure that if she *had,* she wouldn't be eager to heft a kayak eight feet in the air.

"Lying liars who lie," she murmured, zooming in on her subject. This was well worth the thirty-plus hours she'd sat roasting in a car, waiting for this guy to emerge from his girlfriend's apartment. Standing on the running board of his Nissan XTerra, the subject centered the kayak on the luggage rack. He pulled a bungee cord from his pocket and tossed it down to his pretty female helper. Together, they started securing the boat.

Alex zoomed in closer, making sure she got a shot of his smiling face as he reached over the roof to hook the cord. What a faker. He hopped down and went back inside the apartment. Five minutes later, he returned with a huge cooler. Alex got a shot of his carefree grin as he loaded the ice chest into the cargo space. When the XTerra pulled away, Alex followed.

A little sunset kayaking? The SUV turned south, toward Town Lake, and her suspicions were confirmed.

Alex hung back discreetly, excitement fluttering in

her belly. She had him, finally, after days and days of nothing. This was just the footage she needed to wrap up this project and get paid. Then, at last, she could give Melanie her undivided attention.

The subject pulled into a lot near a lakefront boat ramp and slid into a handicapped parking space. Alex double-parked on the opposite end of the lot and fumbled for her camcorder. This was too good to be true.

The passenger door jerked open. Alex dropped the camera in her lap as Nathan ducked his head in.

"Hey! Don't sneak up on me like that."

He smiled. "Making a movie?"

She muted the sound on the camera. "Get in," she said. "And don't slam the door."

He obediently slid in and eased the door shut. "This a company car?"

"It is now." She lifted the camera and zoomed out for a wide shot of the couple unfastening the boat. The woman wore cutoffs and a T-shirt with Greek letters emblazoned across the front.

Alex glanced at Nathan. "How'd you find me?"

"Tailed you over here from West Campus."

"Bullshit."

"'Fraid not."

Alex bit her lip. She would have noticed a tail. She *should* have, but maybe she'd been distracted. She needed to be more careful.

She returned her attention to the subject of her surveillance. A few more seconds of him, and then she zoomed in on the license plate to underscore his identity for the insurance company that was paying his claim. Some collegiate-looking people wandered over from a nearby picnic table and exchanged greetings. Soon they were unloading the cooler, stowing it beneath the picnic table, and putting a pair of boats into the water.

Alex grabbed her tote bag from the backseat. She pulled out a khaki baseball cap—her quickie disguise of choice—and tugged it down over her unruly hair. "You coming or not?" she asked.

"I don't know. What are you doing?"

"My job." She rummaged through the tote for her black Astros cap. "Here, wear this." She handed it to him. "That eye's a little too conspicuous."

Alex found an empty park bench facing the water. She placed her bag beside her and arranged the camcorder within it so that the lens peeked through the custom-made hole in the bag's side.

Nathan sat down next to her.

"So what'd you want to tell me?" she asked.

He gazed out at the shimmering water where Alex's subject was kayaking with his friends, practically guaranteeing a big paycheck in Alex's future. But she couldn't have cared less at the moment. Nathan had something to say, and she could tell from his suddenly grim expression that she wasn't going to like it.

"I checked out Coghan today," Nathan said. "It was real interesting."

Her shoulders relaxed a little. They hadn't found a body, thank God. "And what did you come up with?"

He stretched an arm out over the back of the bench. "Well, for starters, he just received a commendation from the chief of police. He got promoted last fall to head up the anti–drug task force—no small achievement—and he's got a pristine record." He paused, as if wanting this to sink in. "I checked with Human Resources, too. Not a single complaint about him in fifteen years of service."

Alex's mouth dropped open. "You checked with *Human Resources*?" Of all the places to check ...

"I also checked police reports. Coghan's got nothing linked to him about domestic abuse. No calls from Melanie or the neighbors, nothing. Not even a noise complaint."

"You don't believe me." Alex's breath caught. "After everything I told you, you still don't believe me."

"Melanie Coghan never reported any kind of abuse. Not once." He rested his elbows on his knees and gazed at the lake. "But that's not to say APD hasn't heard of her. Your client's got an interesting reputation, did you know that?"

She couldn't believe she was hearing this. He didn't *believe* her.

"Rumor is, Melanie Coghan's a nutcase," Nathan said. "She actually showed up at the station once, shitfaced drunk, and got into it with her husband, right there in the parking lot. She cursed him out. Told him she was leaving him. I talked to a patrol officer who says he saw the whole thing."

"What are you trying to say?" Alex asked.

"I'm saying, all that doesn't jell with your helpless, battered wife running away from her husband."

"I can't believe you." Alex snatched up her tote bag and stalked back toward the parking lot.

Nathan followed. "What can't you believe? That I checked into some facts before tossing around accusations?"

"I asked you to do this *quietly*." She shook her head.

"Human Resources is the gossip mill of any office. Don't you know that? You're going to tip him off! He's probably out right now, getting rid of evidence!"

"Alex." Nathan took her by the arm. "Listen to yourself. You're not making sense."

"*I'm* not making sense?"

"No." He gazed down at her. She actually caught a flicker of concern in his expression, but she didn't care. She was too mad.

"I understand that you're worried about your client," he said. "But you've got to get some perspective here. All you have is one woman's story. And no evidence. And you're accusing a veteran police officer of murder."

She looked down at her feet and swallowed the lump of frustration in her throat. He didn't believe her. And worse, he'd betrayed her trust.

"Let me ask you this." His gentle tone made her chest hurt.

"What?"

"Does Melanie owe you money?"

"A little." A lot, actually. Alex had paid the security deposit on her Orlando apartment out of her personal bank account. Ditto her utility deposits.

"You think it's possible she's avoiding you because she doesn't want to pay?"

Alex looked away. It was possible. But she didn't believe it.

In her heart of hearts, she believed Melanie was dead. And in her heart of hearts, she believed Craig Coghan was responsible. Melanie had come to Alex for help. She hadn't had anyone else to turn to, so she'd turned to Alex.

"Alex? Isn't it possible you've got this wrong? That you've made a mistake?"

She gazed up at him and felt the bitterness expand in her chest. He'd opted to trust his colleague over her because the guy was a cop. She'd always heard about the Blue Wall, but she'd never seen it up close like this.

She stepped back, away from him. "The mistake I made was thinking you'd help me."

Captain's Point was a luxury subdivision carved out of a hillside overlooking Lake Travis. During the dot-com heyday, hordes of thirtysomethings had built huge custom houses and thrown lavish parties there. Times had settled down, though, and now many of the houses were owned by retired couples or banks that had foreclosed after some Dellionaire couldn't make his payment.

Alex wended her way through the neighborhood, too distracted to be dazzled by the pseudo-Tuscan architecture or sweeping sunset views. Nathan was wrong. That's all there was to it. Alex didn't care how many commendations Coghan had under his belt, the man was a wife beater, and probably a murderer, too. And just because Nathan couldn't find a record of something didn't mean it hadn't happened.

Of all the things he'd discovered during the course of his nano-second-long investigation, one thing stood out. It was the parking lot scene, when Melanie allegedly showed up at Coghan's workplace, drunk and verbally abusive. It didn't sit well with Alex. For one thing, Melanie had told Alex once that she didn't drink. And for another, the meek, mousy woman who'd walked into Lovell Solutions all those months ago had seemed completely incapable of staging a scene like that. Alex couldn't imagine Melanie threatening her husband at all, much less in public and in front of his coworkers. Was it possible Coghan had planted a witness to some imaginary fight?

Or was it possible there was another side to Melanie, a side Alex knew nothing about? In addition to the trembling, terrified victim who'd gone through a box of Kleenex in Alex's office, maybe Melanie also happened to be a loudmouth drunk who didn't mind humiliating her husband at his workplace.

But if she truly was afraid of him, why spark his temper in such a dramatic way?

It didn't make sense. And it put the first nugget of doubt in Alex's mind. Maybe she didn't know Melanie quite as well as she thought she did.

Melanie's return to Austin had been stupid. And her actions once she'd come back had been sloppy. But Alex's background investigation had been sloppy, too.

Of course, none of that accounted for why Coghan was spending his workdays in Captain's Point, stopping in at various houses. Alex passed the first of three homes that had been on Coghan's agenda. She turned a corner and drove past the other two. Yesterday, each of the three houses had had cars in the driveway. Now, as dusk fell over the hillside, those driveways were empty.

Alex parked her Saturn down the street at a utility easement. After her run-in with Nathan, she'd dropped by the office to give Sophie back her Tahoe. Alex had been curt to the point of rudeness, and her new assistant was probably wondering what had put her in such a bitchy mood. But Alex hadn't explained. Instead, she'd sent Sophie home, closed up shop for the night, and come here.

Expensive gas lamps flickered along Treasure Trail as Alex hiked up the hill to the first house on her list. Luckily, there weren't a lot of nosy neighbors out and about. But Alex liked to be prepared for contingencies, so she'd tucked a clipboard under her arm. On it was a petition for improving water quality, which gave her a reason to be wandering around the neighborhood gleaning information from people.

A breeze cooled her bare arms as she neared the house. The two-story entrance was lit by an outdoor chandelier. No interior lights on, though. No cars, no dogs barking, no flutter of movement behind the closed curtains. It looked like no one was home, but she made her way up the cobblestone sidewalk and rang the bell anyway. After several minutes of waiting, she walked around to the wooden gate leading to the backyard.

She hesitated a moment, listening for the slightest growl or rustle of plants that would mean she wasn't alone. Then she stepped into the yard and quietly closed the gate behind her. In the dimness, she could barely make out the shape of a spacious swimming pool surrounded by rocks. The water looked murky. Dark shapes hovered at the bottom, and it took her a moment to realize they were leaves. And branches. From the looks of it, the pool hadn't been cleaned in months.

Alex stepped closer to the house, beneath a covered patio where the visibility was even worse. She pulled a penlight from her bag and shone it around.

An empty terra-cotta planter stood beside the column closest to Alex. The plant in it was shriveled and dead. Other than that, the patio was empty—no chairs or chaise lounges or stainless-steel barbecue pits.

And then she got it. *Duh.* This was a vacant house. She aimed her light inside the windows to confirm it. Not a stick of furniture anywhere, not even a rug—just bare tile floors.

What the hell? Alex checked the other two houses on her list and found them vacant, too. She drove out of Captain's Point more puzzled than ever. What had Coghan been doing here?

Alex pondered the question all the way across town until her grumbling stomach broke her concentration. She hadn't eaten all day, so she pulled into a Dairy Queen and ordered a Hunger Buster with cheese, a chocolate milk shake, and fries. While she waited at the window, she took out her phone and logged onto Google.

The first two addresses netted nothing, but she got a hit with the third. It came up as part of the online directory for the Austin Camera Club. The club's president, evidently, had lived there in the not-so-distant past.

"Ma'am? Your order?"

Alex glanced up at the impatient teenager trying to hand her her dinner.

"Thanks." She took the sack from him and pulled away. A warm, oniony smell filled her car, and she dug french fries from the bag as she made her way home.

What was Coghan up to? And did it have anything to do with Melanie? Even if the man was in the market for a house, Alex hadn't seen any FOR SALE signs. Plus, Captain's Point was well above a police officer's pay grade.

Alex pulled into the driveway of her garage apartment and glanced at the main house. The glow of the television in the living room told Alex that Thelma was home tonight instead of out playing bunco with her girlfriends. She climbed the metal stairs leading to her door, stepping over the gray tabby curled up on her welcome mat. Sugarpotamus stood up, arched, and stretched as Alex unlocked the door. He sniffed the bottom of the takeout bag and mewed plaintively. Thelma fed him table scraps all the time. No wonder the poor thing weighed eighteen pounds.

"Not for you," she told him. "You're on a diet."

Alex pushed open the door, and the cat darted inside. She stepped in behind him.

And saw the man-size cowboy boots parked right beside her sofa.

CHAPTER SEVEN

"How'd you get in here?" she yelped.

Troy Stockton watched her from his sprawled-out position on her couch. The side of his mouth curled into a smile. "I never forget a hide-a-key."

"My alarm was on!"

"I never forget an alarm code, either."

Alex glanced at the keypad beside her door and saw that he had indeed entered her code. She slammed the door and dumped her purse and takeout bag on the table.

She didn't care for the fact that he'd let himself in here. She cared even less for the fact that he was stretched out on her sofa, all relaxed and gorgeous, while she stood there all tired and disheveled. She'd envisioned her next meeting with him countless times, and every vision was the same: Alex would be somewhere—preferably at a bar surrounded by men—looking sexy, but uninterested. Troy would be there, too, looking tortured and desperate to win her back.

"I told you to *call* me. Not show up here." She strode into her kitchen, catching her reflection in the microwave as she went. Yikes. It was worse than she'd thought.

Troy sauntered into the room with the athletic gait she remembered so well. She never should have called him. But she'd only wanted him on the phone, not in her apartment.

He propped his shoulder against the wall and crossed his arms. "Three voice mails," he said. "All urgent. You didn't think that'd get my attention?"

She turned her back on him and busied herself at the sink, filling a bowl with water. The fact that she still had the power to get his attention made her feel funny. Good, yes, but also a little uncomfortable.

"I needed to talk to you about something." She shooed Thelma's cat back outside and put the bowl down for him beside the welcome mat. "It's about a case."

Troy smiled slightly and heaved a big sigh. "I figured that when you mentioned the Delphi Center."

His disappointment was feigned. He must know he had a lot of groveling to do if he wanted back in her life. She planned to make him do it, too, because she'd missed him. But as a friend only. She wasn't about to get burned twice.

"So let's hear it," he said. "You said you needed a favor."

"I do." Alex got two plates down from a cabinet and carried them to the table. She took out her burger and fries. "Bring me a knife, would you?"

He retrieved one from the drawer beside her oven, but she refused to be impressed that he'd remembered her kitchen even though he'd been in it only a few times.

She cut the burger in half and divided the food. Troy sank into a chair, and she winced as it creaked under his weight. She told herself not to feel self-conscious about her consignment-store furniture and her cheap Target dishes. Troy had more money than God, but he wasn't a snob about it. It was one of the things she'd always liked about him.

"Here," she said, and slid a plate in front of him. "You'll be more likely to say yes on a full stomach."

He chomped into the burger as she sat down at the table and poked a straw into her shake.

"I've got this client," she started. "I helped her disappear about six months ago."

Troy's expression hardened. He knew all about her work with runaway wives and girlfriends. Alex was pretty sure his mother had been in a similar predicament once upon a time, but Troy didn't talk about his childhood much, and Alex had never asked.

"Here's the problem," Alex told him. "She came back to Austin, and I think her husband found her. Now she really *has* disappeared."

Troy ate silently as she explained the events of the past three days. When she'd finished, she took the clear plastic bag from her purse and placed it in front of him.

She went to the refrigerator for some water. A six-pack of Dos Equis sat on the top shelf. He'd remembered her aversion to beer, evidently, and brought his own. She grabbed one of the bottles for him, annoyed that her grudge was weakening. And he hadn't even begun to grovel.

"You want this blood analyzed, is that right?" he asked.

She popped off the cap and handed him the beer. "You guessed it."

Troy raked a hand through his longish brown hair.

He'd always reminded her of Brad Pitt, and it wasn't just because of the name.

"You still have that contact at the Delphi Center?" she asked. "The forensic scientist?"

"Mia Voss," he said. "She's a tracer. Works in their DNA lab."

"You guys still in touch?"

"Just talked to her a week ago. She's helping me out with some research."

Alex slurped up milk shake. "New book?"

"Same one," he said, then frowned at his empty plate. "It's really dragging this time. I keep running into walls."

She felt a twinge of sympathy. Troy was a bestselling true-crime writer, and he constantly dealt with police departments as he researched homicide cases for his books. Sometimes he had to go outside regular chan-nels to get information, which meant he had a mind-boggling list of contacts in all areas of law enforcement. One of those contacts had referred him to Alex several years ago. Troy had needed to track down someone in the federal witness protection program for an interview, and he'd hired Alex to do it.

It was, without a doubt, the toughest assignment she'd ever been given. And she'd succeeded.

As had Troy's book, which had been picked up by Hollywood and made into a movie.

Less successful was the affair they'd started last December. Troy had a wandering eye, and Alex had a zero-tolerance policy.

"So do you think Mia could run this for me?" Alex nodded at the earbud.

"For a fee," he said. "The Delphi Center's a private

lab, so it won't be cheap. Especially not if you want it soon. When do you need it?"

"Immediately."

"That might take some persuasion."

"That's your department," Alex said, getting up from the table. "I was hoping you could call your friend and put in a good word for me."

He came up behind her as she rinsed the plates.

"I'll do you one better," he said when she turned around. "I'll take you there myself. They're about an hour south of here, near San Marcos. We can go tomorrow."

She folded her arms over her chest and watched him. Troy lived on the lower Texas coast, which meant he'd come a long way to do her this favor. And he probably expected her to let him spend the night. Which she'd be happy to do.

"You have a hotel room somewhere?" she asked.

He hooked his thumbs through his belt loops. "Thought I'd stay here."

It was that warm, seductive look that had haunted her for weeks after the party they'd attended on New Year's Eve. She'd also been haunted by the image of him in a lip-lock with another woman at 12:01. And 12:02. And 12:03.

Alex smiled, savoring the moment, if not the memory.

"You're more than welcome to stay here," she told him. "You can have the couch."

Mia Voss peered through the eyepiece and sighed, then made a notation on her report: *Odocoileus virgianus*. Her detective was going to be disappointed.

"Great news."

She looked up from the microscope to see Darrell standing in her doorway. He had a Starbucks bag in his hand and a grin on his face.

"You brought scones?" she asked.

"Muffins." He pulled out a chocolate cupcake and started peeling away the paper. "But I'm willing to share. Want some?"

"I'm good, thanks." Mia ignored the shower of black crumbs as she slid the file aside and gave Darrell her full attention. "Okay, let's have it. I could use some great news this morning."

"Remember that case that came in last week? The one from Dallas?"

"The blue jeans," she said. How could she forget? The jeans had been saturated with so much dried blood, they could have practically stood on their own. The crime scene must have been horrendous.

"That's the one," Darrell said. "We got a forensic hit."

"You're kidding."

"The perp's profile matched one from a murder scene up in Oklahoma City. Crime's five years old." He popped another chunk of cake into his mouth. "I just talked to the cold case squad up there, and they're reopening the file. Dallas PD's got some fresh leads for them."

Mia snapped off her latex gloves and tossed them in the biohazard bin. Now she was smiling, too.

Hits were a reason to celebrate. In Mia's line of work, the only thing better than a forensic hit—which linked crime scenes together and generated new leads for the police—was an offender hit, as in, not only was this

DNA profile already in the database, but they knew *whose* it was. Offender hits were the reason Mia got up in the morning.

She tucked her hands into her lab coat and watched Darrell polish off his breakfast. As a computer tech at the Delphi Center, Darrell's job included entering DNA profiles into the national database on behalf of the lab. Letting the scientists who worked those cases know that their efforts had made a difference went above and beyond his job description.

"Thanks for telling me," Mia said. "You didn't have to do that."

"No problemo. Hey, catch you later, okay?" He lobbed his trash into a wastebasket and sidestepped the visitor approaching her door.

Mia's smile widened. "Well, if it isn't my favorite Texas Ranger. What brings you here?"

"Hadn't seen your pretty face in a while."

She walked over and gazed up at those gray eyes she remembered well. "Still full of bull," she said.

"You got a minute?"

"For you, I've got hours. What's up?"

John Holt stepped into her cramped, windowless laboratory and glanced around. "Nice digs."

"It's not much to look at, but everything's top of the line."

"I believe it." His gaze landed on an electron microscope that probably cost more than he made in a year. "Looks pretty high tech. And the building's nice, too. Never been here before. Thought I was walking into the Parthenon, all slicked up."

She dragged a stool from the corner of the room and nodded at it. "Have a seat."

"Don't mind if I do." He sat down and crossed his feet at the ankles, displaying a familiar pair of cowboy boots. Mia hadn't seen Holt since she'd worked at the state crime lab in Austin. Two years had gone by, but it looked as though he hadn't changed a bit.

"Just dropped off a tissue sample with your evidence clerk," he said.

"Something wrong with the facilities in Austin?"

The twinkle in his eyes faded. "This is a special case."

"Okay." She stepped closer. "How can I help?"

"Sample's from a floater recovered in Travis County. Body's a mess, no prints. We're having a hell of a time getting an ID. I need a DNA profile so I can see if he's in the system somewhere."

"Okay." So far, everything sounded standard. "When do you need it?"

"Yesterday."

Standard again. "I'll do my best," she said. "What's this about?"

"That, I can't say. Only that it's highly sensitive. After you generate the profile, send it straight back to me."

"Our database tech can enter it—"

"Not this time." His gaze locked with hers.

Mia folded her arms over her chest, trying not to get defensive. "Background checks on the tracers are very thorough. I trust every one of my colleagues, so—"

"I'm sure you do." Holt stood up and rested his hands on his hips. His silver star gleamed at her, reminding her of the early days of her career when she'd paid her dues at the state crime lab. "I'd tell you more about it if I could, but you're gonna have to take my word for it. It's a sensitive case. You're the only person I trust."

She nodded. "All right, then. I'll start on it today."

"Thanks." He squeezed her arm affectionately. "I sure appreciate it."

When he was gone, she stared at her empty doorway until the telephone yanked her back to the present.

She picked up the receiver. "DNA."

"You have visitors down in the lobby, Mia."

She checked her watch. It would be Troy and his detective friend. Another face from the past. Mia glanced at her reflection in the glass cabinet. She tucked a wayward curl back into her ponytail and sighed. It had been years since she'd had a good hair day and almost as long since she'd had a good date.

Troy Stockton. Here we go.

"I'll be right down," she said.

Nathan pulled into work and knew it was going to be a shit day. All the clues were there: no coffee filters, a sopping wet newspaper, a sharp pain behind his eyeballs every time he looked at the sun.

Maybe Alex was right and he should get his eye checked out. Or maybe his headache had more to do with her than the punk who'd sucker punched him a few days before.

The station house was buzzing with activity as Nathan walked in. Only Friday morning, and the weekend rush had already started. Nathan hiked up the stairs to his department, trying to recall the last time he'd had two consecutive days for recreation.

"Yo, Dev."

He turned to see Hodges coming toward him, a manila folder in his hand. More reports Nathan hadn't had time to read.

"We got a problem," Hodges said.

Nathan ducked into the break room, where the coffeepot was empty, of course.

"What's the problem?" he asked, fishing his wallet from his pocket and turning to the vending machine.

"Floater from Lake Austin," Hodges said. "Strangling victim."

A Coke thunked down, and Nathan retrieved it from the machine. "What about him?"

"I followed up on that phone number we found on the matchbook in his pocket," Hodges said. "Took me a while to track it down."

Nathan popped the top and chugged, eyeing his partner's face over the top of the can. Hodges looked much too intense for the average day at the office, even in homicide.

"What?" Nathan asked.

"It's a corporate account, belongs to A.L. Enterprises."

"Yeah. And?"

"And that's a shell company," Hodges said. "Owned by Alexandra Lovell."

Alex hadn't expected one of the world's foremost DNA experts to be cute. But that was the first word that popped into her head as she watched Mia Voss walk across the lobby.

Alex told herself to reserve judgment, at least until the woman opened her mouth. When Mia reached them,

Troy pulled her into a hug while she regarded Alex with curious blue eyes.

"You must be Alex," she said, and Alex could tell by her tone she'd been expecting a man.

They exchanged a polite handshake. "Thank you for seeing us on short notice," Alex said.

"Troy tells me you're down from Austin. So . . . you're with APD?"

"Not exactly," Troy said. "Hey, you mind giving us the tour before we head up to the lab? Alex has never been here."

"Sure." Mia glanced at the visitor's badge clipped to Alex's shirt. "Looks like you're all checked in."

She led them across the spacious lobby toward a pair of Doric columns. Alex wasn't sure what to make of the place. Or the guide, for that matter. Besides the predictable lab coat, Mia wore faded jeans and ankle boots, and her strawberry blond hair was pulled back in a black scrunchie. Alex suddenly wondered whether this pretty young doctor was one of Troy's many ex-girlfriends.

Alex cut a glance at him as they walked. Instead of signing in as Alex had and having his driver's license swiped for a criminal background check, he'd simply pressed his palm against a screen at the front desk. The receptionist had waved him right in. How had he gotten that sort of clearance? She'd asked, but he'd shrugged off the question, which had only piqued her curiosity.

They passed through the columns and into a long corridor, and the architecture fast-forwarded into the twenty-first century.

"We call this wing Plants and Ants," Mia said over her shoulder. "Our botanists and entomologists work here."

Alex glanced back and forth at the glass doors as they passed. Behind each one, she saw stainless steel counters and sinks, lots of cumbersome-looking equipment, a few scientists in goggles peering into microscopes.

"Is it my imagination," she whispered to Troy, "or are we going down?"

"We are," Mia said from several steps ahead. "I'm taking you past our Bones Unit. They work in the base-ment."

The temperature cooled as they descended. Alex had thought the complex looked large from the front steps, but she'd had no idea it extended so far underground.

Mia came to a double glass door. She rested her palm on the screen to the right, and the panels parted. A wall of cold air hit them.

"This is where we do cadaver research," Mia said. "All the workrooms are closed off, but the entire section stays at about fifty degrees."

Alex rubbed her bare arms and wished for a lab coat like Mia's. As they moved through the corridor, she gazed through a long window at a group of people with clipboards and eye shields huddled around a table.

"That's Osteology." Mia stopped and nodded at the glass. "Looks like a class going on right now."

Alex craned her neck, but she couldn't get much of a view. "What are they looking at?"

"A skeleton," Mia said. "They brought it in from the body farm this morning."

Alex sent her a questioning look.

"We've got about a hundred acres southwest of the building where we research decomposition. How human remains react under different conditions—car trunks, ponds, open fields."

Mia resumed the brisk pace. "Used to be, the country's primary body farm was in Tennessee. But we get different kinds of weather and wildlife out here, so ours is more helpful for law enforcement agencies in the Southwest."

Mia led them around a corner and stopped at an elevator. When the doors dinged open, she stepped inside and flattened her palm to the screen before pressing the button for the sixth floor, which was labeled DNA/COMP. Alex read the other choices: IDENT, TRACE, PHOTO, QD.

"What's 'QD'?" Alex asked.

"Questioned Documents. I'd take you by there, but they're hosting VIPs today. Some group from Britain, I believe."

"Delphi's getting attention from all over the world." Troy smiled slyly. "Almost like Quantico."

Mia shot him a look. "Better than Quantico."

The doors dinged open, and Alex kept her skepticism to herself as they stepped into a sunlit hallway. She squinted up at the glass ceiling. "Guess you get to work in the solarium?"

"Actually, no." Mia led them down the hall as Alex gazed down through the floor-to-ceiling windows at the courtyard six stories below. They passed another interior window, and Alex stopped short. "Holy hell," she muttered.

"Knew you'd like this part," Troy said.

Alex gaped at the enormous room filled with sleek

new machines: computers, servers, 3D laser scanners. A trio of latex-gloved men stood around a table at the end of one of the rows. One of them slowly waved a scanner over a skull, and the image appeared on a nearby screen.

"That's Digital Imaging and Cyber Crimes." Mia looked at Alex. "I take it you like computers?"

"Yeah." Alex itched to go explore, but she had a feeling her visitor's badge wouldn't get her inside.

Troy leaned in close. "Jealous?" he asked, and his breath was warm against Alex's ear.

He was talking about the computers.

"Not really," she said. "I just upgraded, so I'm not in the market."

Mia passed another row of windows, and Alex saw more scientists with eye shields working at tables. Then Mia stopped at a door and did her palm routine again. The panel slid open.

"This," she said, stepping inside, "is where I work."

They followed her into a windowless room, and the door slid shut with a *whoosh*. The space was dim, the only light coming from a desk lamp sitting on the counter beside an open file folder.

Alex glanced around. The center of the space was occupied by a rectangular, slate-topped table. Three microscopes were arranged in a neat row on top. On the far wall were shelves filled with glassware: beakers, test tubes, lots of other stuff Alex couldn't identify. A red biohazard bin sat tucked in a corner.

"Is this all yours?" she asked Mia.

"Not really. Most of our DNA tracers work in the bigger lab next door. I like this room because it's dark, and I work with lots of alternative light sources, chemicals that fluoresce, stuff like that." Mia gestured to a stool. "Have a seat. Show me what you brought."

Feeling a bit self-conscious now, Alex pulled out the plastic sandwich bag containing her "evidence." It seemed out of place here, amid all the cutting-edge equipment. She passed it to Mia.

"Hmm." She held up the bag. "Next time, use paper."

"Paper?"

"To transport evidence," Mia said. "Plastic containers can accelerate the deterioration of biological specimens. So what is it you want to know about this?"

"Well." Now Alex felt even more self-conscious. "First off, I'm not sure whether it's blood."

"Let's find out." Mia reached for a box on the counter behind her and snapped on a pair of surgical gloves. She pulled down a metal arm suspended from the ceiling and switched on a light. The glare was intense, and Alex was reminded of visiting the dentist's office.

"I'll just do a quick TMB test," she said, taking some supplies from a drawer. She tore a piece of paper from a wide roll, arranged it on the table, and emptied the plastic bag on top of it. Then she dampened a cotton swab with some sort of liquid and bent over the earbud.

"What's that?" Alex asked.

"Distilled water." She dabbed gently until the tip of the cotton swab was pink. Then she dampened a paper strip with the water and held the swab against it. "This is a Hemastix strip." She glanced up. "We're looking for it to change color. Sort of like a home pregnancy test."

Troy eased closer. Alex pulled up a stool and sat down to wait. Soon the paper turned greenish-blue.

"It's blood," Mia announced. "Next question, is it human blood? I would guess yes, since it's on an earbud, but you never know. Just this morning I tested blood droplets on a pair of boots that belong to a murder suspect. *Odocoileus virgianus,* unfortunately. White-tailed deer." She sighed. "My homicide detective isn't going to be very happy. Anyway, I'll run what's called a precipitin test to be sure."

Alex glanced at the cotton swab. "Aren't you worried about using up the sample?"

"It's okay. We've got methods now to replicate DNA so that we can get a usable sample from a very small amount. I can get one off a single hair follicle, if I need to."

"I'm pretty sure it's human blood, given the circumstances," Alex said. "The question is, whose?"

"You want a DNA profile," Mia stated.

"I guess." Alex glanced at Troy. He hadn't told her that when he set up the appointment?

"And I assume you also want us to run it through the database for you."

"Depends." Troy claimed the stool beside Alex, and she felt reassured by his closeness. "Alex believes the blood belongs to a murder victim."

Mia's brows arched. "A victim? Would they be in the missing-persons index?"

"What's that?" Alex asked.

"The national DNA database has three main parts," Troy said. "One is for profiles lifted from crime scenes—that's the forensic index. Then there're profiles from offenders. The third part is missing persons. Profiles from un-IDed remains."

"It also includes donated profiles," Mia added, "from families who are looking for someone, hoping they'll turn up someday."

"I see." Alex felt the weight of her ignorance. "Sorry, but this isn't really my area. Tracing people in cyberspace, I know all about. Tracing people through genetic codes, I'm way out of my league." Alex looked at Troy. "I doubt Melanie's in the database, though. I mean, I'm the only one who even believes she's missing. And she doesn't have a criminal record."

Mia tipped her head to the side, clearly confused. "I'm sorry. I'm not sure I understand your objective here. Your department thinks someone was murdered? And they sent you here to—"

"I'm not a police officer," Alex cut in. "I'm a private investigator. One of my clients disappeared, and I think there was foul play involved."

Mia gave Troy a look, but Alex couldn't decipher it. Had he misled her about why they were here today? Or maybe she was annoyed to be wasting her time with a civilian.

"Alex is trying to convince police that her client is dead," Troy said. "She wants a murder investigation. But the only evidence she has is this"—Troy nodded at the earbud—"and a burned-down house, where her client was staying. Alex thinks the killer set fire to the place to conceal the crime."

Mia leaned back against the counter and folded her arms. "So there isn't even a case yet, really. Just your belief that something bad happened to this woman."

"That about sums it up," Alex said.

Mia watched her for a moment, drumming her fingertips against her sleeve. "All right." She shrugged. "Works for me."

Alex stared at her. She was going to help. Alex hadn't really believed it until just this moment, and she didn't know what to say.

"What?" Mia glanced at Troy. "That's why you came here, right? To make your case?"

"I'm just surprised," Alex said. "Getting the tests run . . . this detective I know made it sound like such a big deal."

"I get that a lot," Mia said. "Old dogs, new tricks, and all that. Most cops still look at DNA as something used to prosecute a case, not investigate. It's one of the biggest problems we're up against." Her voice took on an edge as she talked. "With the technology available now, that's so shortsighted. We can use DNA to put a weapon in someone's hand. To put a perp at a crime scene where he claims he's never been. We can pile up evidence and pressure someone into a confession, save the taxpayers a big trial. But that's not happening right now because the system is broken. We've got this amazing technology, but we're really only using it to prosecute cases that have already been solved."

The room fell silent, and Mia's words hung in the air. Alex realized this woman was on a mission.

"Sorry." Mia rolled her eyes. "Bottom line, yes, I'll help you. I assume you brought me another sample? Something I can compare to this blood, see if I get a match?"

Alex pulled another plastic bag from her purse, this one containing the envelope Melanie had given her last

October when she'd put a down payment on Alex's services.

It was the only payment Alex had managed to collect from her.

"I watched Melanie lick this envelope." Alex handed Mia the bag. "Will that work for you?"

She smiled. "Like a charm."

CHAPTER EIGHT

Troy turned onto Alex's street, and she glanced out the passenger window for the hundredth time today. No tail. But still, she felt uneasy for some reason.

"What's wrong?"

She shrugged. "Nothing, really. I just like to keep tabs."

His brow furrowed. "You worried about something?"

"Force of habit."

He pulled into the driveway behind her Saturn.

"Thanks for the ride." Alex scooped the box of leftovers off the floorboard. They'd spent the afternoon walking around San Marcos and then stopped for drinks at a restaurant on the river. Drinks had become dinner. Now it was dangerously close to nighttime, and they still hadn't dealt with the tension hovering between them.

Alex shoved open the door and got out. Troy walked her up the stairs, like she'd known he would, and stood patiently behind her as she fished her keys from her purse.

"You driving back tonight or tomorrow?" she asked,

unlocking the door. She turned to face him and immediately knew the intention behind his warm, steady look.

"That's up to you."

Her stomach fluttered. He wanted to come inside and pick up right where they'd left off before New Year's.

And she wanted to say yes.

"Thanks for your help today," she said instead.

He gazed down at her.

"This case is important to me. And it means a lot that you gave up so much of your time to help me with it."

"But you're still mad," he stated.

"I'm not mad." And she wasn't. Not anymore. The anger had lasted only a few hours. The hurt, though—that had stuck with her for months.

Troy rested his hand on her shoulder. He didn't look upset. Just resigned.

"I know you're going to think this is bullshit," he said, "but I *am* sorry."

She watched him, waiting for more. But he simply looked at her.

"Thank you," she said finally. Where was the rest of it? The sweet talk? The seduction? This man was really good at the seduction part, and there was a strong chance he'd be able to sway her if he put some effort into it. Part of her wanted him to.

Another part of her was thinking of Nathan. She kept remembering him crouched in front of her the other night in his sweat-soaked T-shirt, cleaning up her knee and ignoring her while she cursed at him.

And then for some reason she felt guilty for standing here on the verge of inviting Troy inside. Where had that come from?

Troy dropped a kiss on her forehead. "Night, Alex. Lock up tight." Then he went down the stairs and slid back into his car.

Alex stood on her doorstep and watched as he backed out of the driveway. She stayed there, thinking, until the sound of his engine faded completely into the night.

The Ferrari 360 Modena turned the corner, and Nathan watched Alex watch it go. When she finally stepped back inside, he sat in the Mustang for a few more minutes, collecting his thoughts.

Or, more accurately, grinding his teeth over the realization that Alex had spent the day with some rich hotshot while he'd been busting his ass trying to find her.

He got out of his car and slammed the door. A dog barked nearby as he crossed the tree-lined street to the Hyde Park mini-mansion where Alex rented a garage apartment. Nathan had thoroughly scoped out the place earlier in the day, though why a woman who kept a brand-new Mercedes and a pristine-looking 1960 Ford Sunliner stashed in her garage should need to take a boarder was a mystery. Nathan walked around the side of the garage and glanced through a dusty window. The Sunliner alone was worth at least a few years of what Alex probably paid in rent. But maybe the rich old bird liked the company.

Nathan hiked up the stairs noisily and wasn't surprised when the curtain behind the glass pane shifted and Alex peeked out at him. Then the door swung open.

She fisted a hand on her hip as he looked her over. Sometime in the past three minutes, she'd changed into—God help him—blue satin pajama pants and a tight-fitting tank top.

He dragged his gaze back to her face. "Hi."

Sighing, she ushered him inside and closed the door. "Excuse me while I fire my assistant." She turned and pulled a cell phone from the purse sitting on the breakfast table.

Nathan caught her wrist. "She didn't give me your address."

"Then how'd you find me?"

He lifted an eyebrow. It hadn't been easy. Alex had a vast array of privacy shields, and every bit of information he'd had on her linked back to her business address.

"I'm not kidding," she said. "I need to know."

"I used your pizza trick."

She crossed her arms. "I never order pizza."

"No, but you like Hunan Cafe."

She rolled her eyes and walked into the kitchen. She jerked the fridge open and grabbed a Coke from the top shelf. A half-empty carton of Dos Equis sat on the shelf, too.

Nathan's irritation returned. "Where have you been all day?"

A look of amused disbelief came over her face. "Out."

"You didn't answer your phone."

"I was busy," she said. "You want a drink?"

"No."

She popped open the Coke and took a sip.

Nathan forced himself to let it go. How she spent her time was none of his business. Neither was her personal life. Or the fact that she kept her fridge stocked with beer she didn't drink.

He turned his attention to the apartment. A flat-screen television sat on an empty bookcase opposite a striped blue sofa. The coffee table consisted of a scuffed black camp trunk. Cardboard boxes lined the far wall beneath a pair of windows, reminding him of her office the first time he'd seen it. The place looked as though she'd just moved in, but the Chinese restaurant had orders for her dating back two years.

"Don't you ever unpack anything?" he asked.

"Not if I can help it. I like mobility." She scraped back a wooden dining chair and sat down. A sliver of black lace peeked over the waistband of her pants, and Nathan's imagination kicked into gear.

"So what's going on?" she asked.

"Did Melanie Coghan have a boyfriend that you know of?"

Alex's face paled. "You mean she's . . . dead?"

"No." He frowned. "At least, we don't know that."

"You said 'did,' as in past tense."

"Okay, *does* she have a boyfriend? I need to know if she's seeing someone. Someone here in Austin."

Alex shook her head slowly. "She didn't say anything. Not to me, anyway."

"You think it's possible?"

Alex watched him, wide-eyed. Gone was the snippy attitude. She was worried about Melanie.

"You mentioned she'd been taking trips to Austin," he reminded her. "You think she was meeting somebody?"

"I don't know. Maybe. It would explain a few things. It would be incredibly stupid, though. What better way to piss off her husband than to come back here and have an affair, right under his nose?"

"I can't think of one."

Alex shook her head and muttered a curse.

"It's not your fault," he told her. "Whatever she was doing, she ignored your advice."

Alex gazed up at him, her eyes wary. "What's this about, anyway? What aren't you telling me?"

"We recovered a floater from Lake Austin on Tuesday."

Her eyes widened. "Was it—"

"Adult male. About five-ten, one-sixty. Dark hair. He sound familiar at all?"

"No."

"We're still working on an ID." He stepped closer. "In the meantime, I need to know why your phone number was in his pocket."

"*My* phone number? Why would some dead guy have my phone number on him?"

Nathan pulled a notebook from his jacket, flipped it open, and rattled off the number.

"That's not my number," she said.

"It was scrawled on a book of matches. It's to a cellular account registered to A.L. Enterprises."

A lightbulb seemed to go on. "It's Melanie's safe phone."

"What's that?"

"It's just a regular cell phone. But it's part of her emergency kit. Or it's supposed to be."

"Why is it in your name?"

"I give all my clients a safe phone. Or at least this kind of client. They're supposed to use it only in an emergency. It's part of this kit I tell them to put together in case their cover gets blown. They keep some cash, a phone, a simple disguise, like maybe a hat and wig. I also suggest they keep a prepaid gas card, any prescriptions—whatever they need to take off at a moment's notice."

"But why is this registered to you? Why not a prepaid cell phone?"

"Mostly, they use prepaid phones. This is just for emergencies. And I have the number, so I can track them, if I need to. The phone companies have gotten wise to pretexts from PIs, so it's gotten harder and harder to gain access to other people's phone records. This phone is in my name, so it makes things easier."

"And I'm assuming you tried this with Melanie?"

"The very first day," she said. "The last call bounced off a cell tower in Florida months ago. I've left messages on it and Melanie's prepaid phone, but the mailboxes are full now. I don't think she's retrieved anything. I figure she took the battery out. Or maybe Coghan got rid of it somehow. Even the GPS wasn't working."

"Interesting. And how would you know that, exactly?"

She cleared her throat. "I sort of have this friend in emergency dispatch. I explained the situation and convinced her to ping Melanie's phone. . . ." Her voice trailed off as Nathan stared at her.

"What?" she asked defensively.

"Nothing. It's just, shit, here I am thinking you need a warrant, or at least a badge for that."

"Hey, if you don't want to know the answer, don't ask the question."

He shook his head, exasperated.

"There's something more, isn't there?" she asked. "Something's bothering you."

Everything about this case bothered him. Alex being mixed up in it was top of his list.

"We haven't IDed this floater yet," he told her, "but we think he may have had a gang affiliation."

"Why do you say that?"

"I can't disclose the details."

"Nathan, I need to know what's happening."

He watched her for a moment, debating whether to trust her. "This is confidential," he said finally.

"Okay."

"Whoever strangled this guy cut off some skin before dumping him in Lake Austin."

She cringed. "Why?"

"Tattoo removal. We see it sometimes with gang murders. You kill off a rival, take away his symbols. It's kind of like the ultimate 'fuck you' to the rival gang."

"But if you can't see what was there, how do you know it was a tattoo?"

"We don't. It's just a possibility. Course with this link to Melanie, and to *you*," he added pointedly, "we realize it might not be that simple. We'll know more when we get an ID. Unfortunately, the whole department's slammed right now. We're in triage. My lieutenant just ordered me to lay off this John Doe homicide and tackle stuff that's more solvable."

"But I thought gang killings usually involved guns. Didn't you say he was strangled?"

"Maybe someone didn't want any noise. Or any slugs recovered. Hell, I don't know. Maybe this has nothing to do with gangs, and someone's simply trying to make it harder for us to identify this guy. His fingertips were in bad shape, so even if he's in the system, it's going to be tough to get an ID."

Alex shook her head and looked down at her bare feet. He could tell she was worried, which was good. Worry might make her careful. But it was the guilt on her face that really bothered him. He slid his hand up her arm and rested it on her shoulder. She glanced up.

"Stop doing that," he said.

"What?"

"Thinking this is your fault. Melanie was a grown woman. She made her own bad decisions."

"You think she's dead."

"Maybe," he said. And at her worried expression, he couldn't help giving her a sliver of hope. "Or maybe she's just avoiding you. Could be she's involved in something shady, something that drew her back to town."

"Like what?"

"I don't know. Right now, anything's possible. Sounds to me like she never told you the full story about why she left."

Alex shook her head and glanced away. She looked so pretty sitting there, and sad, too.

It was time to go before he did something stupid.

He dropped his hand from her shoulder. "You need to be careful," he said sternly.

"Me?"

"Whatever this is, it involves you now. And until we get a handle on it, you need to watch your back."

CHAPTER NINE

Alex drove through Nathan's neighborhood and was struck again by how domestic everything looked. People were out walking dogs, pushing strollers, and collecting Sunday papers off the sidewalks. Why did he live here? He couldn't have very much in common with these people anymore. Alex pulled up to the curb and wondered if the white Saturn that kept appearing in front of his house had generated any gossip yet.

Nathan answered the door in jeans and a rumpled white T-shirt. She smiled at his bed head.

"Sleeping in?"

He stepped back to let her inside. "What time is it?" he asked, and his voice was husky.

"Almost nine."

He went straight for the kitchen, and she trailed behind him through the living room. "Looks like you pulled an all-nighter."

"Got in at six," he said, rubbing the back of his neck. He went to a cabinet and pulled down a yellow tin of coffee. He put a new filter in the coffeepot, then dumped in half a dozen heaping scoops. He added water and switched on the power.

Alex glanced at his bare feet. The cuffs of his jeans were stained with something.

"Double homicide."

She snapped her gaze up to his. He'd noticed her noticing the blood. He must have come straight home from work and fallen into bed.

"Guess I'm going to have a tough time talking you into a run this morning," she said.

He leaned back against the counter and looked her over. His attention lingered on her bare legs.

"I could probably be persuaded." He held her gaze for a long moment, and her cheeks warmed. The pot gurgled and hissed beside him.

She turned around and opened a cabinet. Dishes. She opened another one. Cups. She pulled two down and poured coffee, even though the pot had barely started brewing. She passed him a half-full mug and took a sip from the one in her hand.

"Whoa." She made a face. "It's strong."

"It's the chicory," he said. "Plus you didn't let it finish." He downed his in one gulp, then plunked the cup on the counter. "Gimme a minute, and we can go."

He disappeared into the back of the house, and she stood in his kitchen, sipping coffee and questioning her decision to show up here unannounced on a Sunday morning. It felt a little too . . . something. Intimate, maybe? She put her mug in the sink and went to the front door to wait.

Nathan appeared a minute later in shorts and running shoes.

"How far?"

"Four-point-six miles," she answered, leading him down the sidewalk.

"You clocked it already?"

"MapQuested it. We're going to Mount Bonnell. If we take Mesa from here—"

"I know where Mount Bonnell is."

She heard the amusement in his voice and glanced at him over her shoulder. "What?"

"You're funny," he said.

"Let's go."

She set a brisk pace, determined to redeem herself from the last time, when she'd had to hide the fact that she'd been sucking wind the whole way.

He switched places, so he was running on the outside and she was closest to the sidewalk. His protective streak again.

She cast a sidelong glance at him, admiring his straight posture and the way his T-shirt stretched taut over his chest. He caught her looking.

"I don't remember you being in this kind of shape," she said.

"When?"

"When we worked together last fall."

"It's Hodges."

"What?"

"Will Hodges, my partner. Guy's a fitness nut. Figured I needed to kick it up a notch or he'd make me look bad."

"I've met him before," Alex said. "How old is he, anyway? He looks pretty young."

"Twenty-nine."

"You've got a decade on him."

"Not quite," he said, and she sensed she'd touched a nerve.

"You've got almost a decade on me, too." She smiled and picked up speed, and of course he responded to the bait. Men were so predictable.

Because of their ridiculously fast pace, they reached the trailhead in almost no time. He led the way up the uneven stone steps. For a while they hiked in silence, passing a few other people out soaking up the morning. It was a popular trail, and it ended at the highest elevation point in the city.

Alex spotted a large boulder on an outcropping of rock just off the path. "Let's sit down."

She rested against the rock and glanced around. The sun cast sharp shadows over the hillside, and a chilly breeze stirred the trees. Alex closed her eyes and took a deep breath of the sweet, piney air. "I love this smell."

"Mountain cedar," he said. "Lot of people can't stand it. Gives them allergies."

"I like it."

"Spoken like a native Texan."

"I'm not from Texas."

He propped his shoe on the rock and looked down at her. A sheen of sweat covered his skin, but he wasn't winded. Alex took another deep breath. Hot guy. Another scent she liked.

"So what do your parents think of you chasing down deadbeats and insurance cheats?"

She looked away. "I don't know. Why?"

"Seems like they'd want you home in Urbana."

She glanced over at him. She'd never told him much

about her background, and she wondered if that slip had been intentional.

"They probably wouldn't mind." She shrugged. "I didn't ask them, really. I just left."

"Why? I hear Urbana's a nice town."

"It is."

"But?"

"It's too, I don't know . . . settled, I guess."

"Chicago too settled, too?"

"Not really."

"San Francisco?"

She narrowed her gaze at him. "What's your point?"

"You move around a lot. Come on." He jerked his head toward the trail, and she fell into step behind him.

For a while, they hiked without talking. The trail grew narrower, and the trees and scrub brush thinned out as they neared the top.

"So let's hear it," he said.

"Hear what?"

"What you need today." He glanced back over his shoulder. "Don't tell me you came to see me because you love jogging."

"Maybe I like your company."

"Maybe you need a favor."

"Have you always been this cynical?"

"Yep."

"Okay, you're right," she said. "I need a favor."

He didn't break his stride as they moved up the increasingly steep hillside.

"I went back and canvassed the neighborhood over on Moccasin Road."

"And?"

"And I talked to some people who noticed a Honda sedan and a Chevy Blazer at that cabin in the weeks before the fire." Alex struggled to keep up with him as she talked. "One woman said she saw the Blazer in a ditch just off the road around ten on the night of the eighteenth. There was a red tow truck there. A pickup, too. Maybe it was Coghan's."

"She get a tag number?"

"No."

"On *any* of the vehicles?"

"No."

"What color was the truck?"

"She couldn't remember for sure. Something light."

"Lot of pickups in Texas," he stated, and for some reason his tone of voice ticked her off.

"I'm aware of that. But wouldn't there be an accident report or something? Maybe someone called the police?"

"I can look into it."

"Thank you," she said, and he didn't respond. He was probably annoyed that she kept peppering him with requests. But at this point, she didn't really care. Nathan was her best contact at APD, and she needed help.

He took her elbow and pulled her close to the trees. A couple squeezed past them on the narrow trail, and Nathan nodded hello. When they were gone, he gazed down at her with those clear blue eyes, and her stomach did that little flutter.

"I'm doing you a lot of favors," he murmured.

"And?"

"And it's only fair to warn you. I'm keeping score."

CHAPTER TEN

Nathan ignored the neon fast-food signs lining the feeder road. He'd skipped lunch and dinner. It was nearing midnight now, and he could have used a hamburger something fierce; but more than he needed food, he needed to talk to Alex. And she wasn't going to like what he had to say. He dialed her number with one hand while using the other to swerve into the fast lane.

"Hello?"

"Hey, it's me."

She said something, but it was drowned out by the wail of a guitar. "What?"

"It's Nathan."

More noise, and then "Have to talk louder."

"Nathan Devereaux." Jesus, where was she? "I ran down that *lead* for you."

She said something, but he didn't catch it.

"Where the hell are you?"

The noise stopped abruptly. "The Roadhouse," she said, clear as a bell. She must have gone outside.

"Eli's Roadhouse? Off the interstate?"

"You know another Roadhouse in town?"

Her sarcasm grated on his nerves. Not to mention the vision of her standing outside some noisy biker bar talking on her damn iPhone.

"Did you say you ran down that lead for me?"

"Yes." He tried to keep the annoyance out of his voice. "I need to talk—"

"Want to have breakfast tomorrow? You can fill me in."

He exited the freeway and pulled up to a stoplight. It was a quiet Monday night. Not too many cars out. Sounded like all the action was going on at Eli's.

"Nathan? How about eight A.M. at that pancake place?"

He heard a whoop of laughter followed by the snort of someone's Harley.

"Are you outside? You know, that's a crappy neighborhood. The parking lot backs right up to a strip club and—"

"I'm going back in," she said. "So I'll see you for breakfast then? Eight o'clock?"

He imagined her rolling out of bed and coming to meet him. After sleeping with some biker she picked up.

Shit, he was being a jerk. She wouldn't do that. She wouldn't pick up some stranger at a bar.

But what did he know? And what was she doing at Eli's Roadhouse? The place was a rat hole. Nathan had practically grown up in bars, and he knew exactly the kind of people who frequented ones like Eli's.

"Are we on, or not?"

"We're on," he said.

"Good. See you tomorrow."

Then the music was back, and she clicked off.

* * *

Troy watched Alex zip the phone into her purse and elbow her way back through the crowd. Whatever that was, she didn't look happy about it. She hitched herself back onto the stool beside him, dropped her purse on the floor, and picked up her drink.

"You okay?" he asked over the noise.

"Yeah." She took a gulp of rum and Coke.

"You don't look happy."

The band ended their set with a loud flourish, and the crowd clapped and whistled.

"It was my detective friend," she said.

"Something come up?"

"Nothing urgent."

"So what's the problem?"

She rolled her eyes. "He's on my case about safety. Thinks this place is a dump."

"Hey, I wanted to meet at El Rancho. This place *is* a dump."

"Yeah, but it's got atmosphere." Alex pushed her empty glass across the bar and traded nods with the bartender.

Typically, Alex wasn't much of a drinker. But something was bugging her tonight, and Troy was determined to figure out what it was.

"Guess your detective friend doesn't know about your SIG," he said. "Maybe your concealed carry permit's a little out of date?"

"You were saying?" she asked, changing the subject. "About the Delphi Center?"

The band filed off the stage to take a break, and Stevie Ray Vaughan's "Caught in the Crossfire" started up on the jukebox. Troy took a swig of beer and then picked up where he'd left off.

"Mia called me last night," he said. "She wants to talk to you."

"She has the results already?"

"She has something."

"Is it Melanie?"

"She wouldn't give me details over the phone," he told her. "She said come by in person, she'll explain everything then."

Alex eyed him suspiciously. "She didn't tell you what she had?"

"Nope." Troy had asked, of course, but she'd been unusually tight-lipped.

The bartender brought over a second Crown and Coke, and Alex stirred it thoughtfully with the slender red straw.

Troy watched her, kicking himself again for fucking things up so badly. Alex was hot. Not in an obvious, pole-dancer kind of way, but in a subtle way he found way more attractive. Their few weeks together last Christmas had forever changed his view of short, small-breasted women.

She glanced up at him, and the suspicion was back.

"What?"

"Pretty fast turnaround," she observed. "I thought DNA tests took forever."

"It's a private lab. And you said it was urgent."

"I'm guessing she charged me a rush fee, too, then."

"It wasn't bad."

"You paid her already? She said she was going to invoice me!"

"I took care of it," he said.

"But—"

"It's no big deal." He clinked his beer bottle against her glass. "You can get the drinks."

Her spine stiffened, and she got that look on her face. It meant she was pissed at him. And she had no idea how much that turned him on.

What was it with this girl?

He gazed at her for a few moments, trying to figure it out.

It was the brains, he decided. Smart women did it for him. It was the same way with Mia. There was something there, some kind of vibe they gave off. They drew him in like a magnet, then fucked with his head. Alex was a master at it. She was doing it right now. He'd spent the better part of a week—and a crapload of money—doing her a favor, and still, he could tell he was no closer to getting back in her bed than he had been when he'd gotten her first phone message.

Troy swilled his beer and plunked the bottle on the counter. Truth was, he didn't mind helping her, even without the sex. He respected what she did for a living. He respected *her,* and there were far too few women in his life he could say that about.

"There's something else," he told her.

She glanced up, and her face fell. "It's Melanie, isn't it? They identified—"

"It's not about Melanie."

"What then?"

"It's about the Delphi Center," he said. "I'm here to recruit you."

Her eyebrows shot up. "Me?"

"That's right."

"For what?"

"Their Cyber Crimes Unit. It's a growing field, and they're looking for people. Mia asked me what kind of skills you have. I told her, and they want you."

The look on her face was pure astonishment. "What on earth would I do there?"

"Anything," he said. "Everything. The possibilities are endless. They run down identity theft, child porn, credit card fraud, you name it. You're great with computers. You'd be a natural at it."

"But . . ." Her voice trailed off as the bartender stopped by to check on them. "But I don't even have a degree. The people over there are doctors and PhDs and—"

"Your skills are in high demand right now. Who gives a damn about a degree? You know the Internet better than anyone. They could use you."

She stirred her drink and shook her head. "I've already got a job. One that I like, too. I've built a business."

"So do some freelance for them. Couple of projects here and there, see if you like it. I can tell you right now, you'll like the pay."

"I don't know."

"Think of everything you'd learn." Then he pulled out the big guns. "Think of the equipment and software you'd get to use. They demo stuff that hasn't even hit the market yet."

Her eyes locked with his, and he knew he had her.

"Why are you telling me this?"

He shrugged. "I thought you'd be interested."

"No, I mean, why *you*?" Her gaze narrowed. "You're connected to Delphi Center, aren't you? And not just through Mia."

Troy glanced away. He'd known this would come up. "I'm on their board," he said.

"How'd you get on their *board*? You must have—" She broke off abruptly and stared at him, wide-eyed. "Oh my God, you're one of them, aren't you? You're one of those anonymous benefactors who freaking funded the place."

He just looked at her.

"Oh my God." She closed her eyes and shook her head. "I knew it was weird. How you just breezed right in and—"

"Look, there are a lot of people involved," he said. "It's not just me. They're doing groundbreaking work over there. It's attracted attention. Anyway, talk to Mia. She'll fill you in."

She watched him for a long moment. "Fine, I'll talk to her. But this isn't going anywhere. A lot of what I do is in the gray, legally. I'm not exactly a model citizen."

"You never know."

Actually, he did. Delphi knew all about Alex's background, and they wanted her anyway. They wanted her because of it. The sort of experts they needed for cyber crimes weren't sitting around writing software manuals.

But Troy let it go.

For a while, they drank and traded small talk. When Alex's second rum and Coke was gone, she rested her chin on her fist and gazed down into the glass.

Her mind was on Melanie again; he could tell.

"How's your case coming?"

"The same." Her voice was glum.

"Hey, perk up. Maybe your detective will come up with something."

"He's not *my* detective."

But the tone of her voice sent up a red flag. He was onto something.

"You seeing each other?" he asked.

"No."

Again, too emphatic.

Troy smiled. He never would have pictured Alex Lovell with a homicide cop, but there was something poetic about it. Not that it would ever work out. Cops were notoriously bad at relationships. Plus they were cynical, and Alex was a closet idealist.

She glanced up at him. "So are you coming with me?"

"Where?" Troy glanced over her shoulder at the bar entrance.

"The Delphi Center."

A guy stood at the door, staring at Alex. His gaze shifted to Troy.

"I could, but I don't need to," he said. "You're on the list now."

"The list?"

The man was shorter than Troy—probably five-ten— but powerfully built under that cheap blazer. His gaze scanned the bar briefly, then homed in on Alex again.

"Yeah, you're all cleared." Troy took a last swig of beer. "You don't need an escort anymore. Just call Mia."

Alex looked surprised by this news. She looked even more surprised when the homicide detective appeared at her side.

"Hi." The man ignored Alex's gaping stare and

extended a hand to Troy. "Nathan Devereaux," he said coolly.

They shook hands. "Troy Stockton."

"*What* are you doing here?" Alex asked him.

"I need to talk to you." The man's voice was flat, his eyes hard. His gaze veered to the Dos Equis bottle sitting at Troy's elbow.

"I thought we were meeting tomorrow," she said.

"Now's better."

Alex looked pissed again, but this time it was directed at the plainclothes detective. Lucky bastard.

Troy tugged his wallet from his pocket and tossed a couple twenties on the bar.

Alex frowned. "Where are you going?"

"Home," Troy said.

"But—"

He kissed her mouth to shut her up. And to annoy the cop.

"Take care." He looked down into her startled eyes. "I'll call you next time I'm in town."

Alex watched, shocked, as Troy left the bar.

"You had something you wanted to tell me?"

She spun around to face Nathan, who'd made himself comfortable on Troy's vacated stool. He flagged the bartender and asked for a Scotch.

"I can't believe you just barged in here! I was with someone."

"Looked like he was leaving."

Alex couldn't believe this. What if she'd been on a date?

Or maybe that was the point.

The bartender slid Nathan's drink across the counter and cleared away the beer bottle. Nathan turned on his stool and tossed back the Scotch as he looked out over the crowd. She watched him, simmering. Then his attention settled back on her. For a long moment, they just stared at each other, his blue eyes burning into hers in a way that made her heart pound.

She didn't know what to say, so she grasped for an easy topic. "My test results are in," she said. "From the Delphi Center."

Nathan's gaze flicked to the door. "That where you ran off to the other day?"

"Troy has an in there. A DNA expert."

"Yeah? What did he say?"

"*She* said I can come by tomorrow and she'll walk me through her findings."

His gaze swept the room again, then returned to her. "I looked for that accident report," he said. "Didn't find anything. I also called around town. None of the towing services has a record of it."

"But the witness said she saw a tow truck."

Nathan didn't respond.

"You think Coghan might have, I don't know, paid someone to keep it out of the records?"

"Could be." He shook his glass, rattling the ice cubes. "You're not even sure Coghan was there, though, are you?"

"The woman saw a pickup—"

"She couldn't even remember the color," Nathan cut in.

"Well, it was raining out. And she told me she'd just taken a big dose of cold medicine."

"Sounds like a great witness," he quipped. "I also checked up on Coghan for that night. Our dispatch records have him at a drug bust over on East Fifth about the time your witness said she saw the truck at the accident scene."

Coghan had an alibi. Alex should have expected him to, but for some reason the news came as a disappointment.

"Maybe he got the dispatcher to lie for him," she said. "Maybe it's part of his cover-up."

Nathan lifted an eyebrow, and Alex's temper sparked. She'd had enough of his skepticism.

"How much more proof do you need that something is terribly wrong here?" She slapped her hand on the bar. "Melanie's *missing*. Doesn't a dead body in the lake near her home mean anything to you? And what about the car wreck?"

"Okay." He cocked his head to the side. "What's your theory?"

Alex deflated. "I don't know, exactly. There was some kind of struggle at the house, I think. That's why I saw blood. Maybe Coghan kidnapped Melanie. Maybe she had a boyfriend who went after them in the Blazer, and then Coghan killed him, too. Then dumped them in the lake."

"And his alibi?"

"I don't know, okay?" She slid off the stool. Troy had left enough money on the bar to cover her drinks, so she grabbed her purse from the floor and headed for the exit.

She heard the scuff of Nathan's shoes on the pavement behind her as she crossed the crowded lot to her car. She dug her keys from her purse and clicked open the locks.

She reached for the door handle, but he reached around and leaned a palm on the door.

"Wait," he said.

"What for?" She whirled around. "You don't believe me. No matter how much evidence I throw at you, it's all some big misunderstanding. No way could a buddy of yours, another *cop,* be capable of killing his wife."

"That's not what I think."

"But you're not willing to go out on a limb," she accused. "Not if it means implicating someone with a badge."

"That's not true, either."

He gazed down at her calmly. His hand was still flattened against her car as she glared up at him. For a moment, time seemed suspended as he eased closer, close enough to feel how angry she was. Close enough to feel her heart pounding furiously in her chest.

And then his hand was in her hair. Her breath caught. And every muscle tensed as he leaned down and kissed her.

CHAPTER ELEVEN

Shock ricocheted through her body. His mouth was warm, firm, and then she felt the scrape of his stubble against her skin as he slanted his head to the side and kissed her. He tasted sharp, like alcohol, and the hot maleness of it made her dizzy.

Vaguely she heard the grumble of trucks and motorcycles. Vaguely she felt the vibrations beneath her feet, the cool metal of the car as he eased her back against it. Then it was the hard wall of his chest she felt, as his hand held her head steady and his tongue tangled with hers. Her mind was still reeling, but her hands slid up, over his shoulders, and her fingers curled into his hair. He tasted good. Desire pooled inside her as his lips moved over hers and she rocked her hips against him.

"Come home with me," he said against her mouth.

She kissed him. She didn't want to stop, didn't want to talk. She just wanted those long, deep kisses making her light-headed. He gripped her hips, pulling her up on tiptoes, and she could feel the hard heat of him through her jeans.

"Alex." His voice was lower, more urgent now. "Come home with me."

She leaned back and looked up at him, tried to catch her breath. Those blue eyes flared again as he stared down at her. She wanted to go home with him. Something told her that she shouldn't, that she should be wary. But she wanted to go anyway.

"I—"

A loud growl cut her off. She turned to watch a pair of bikes roar past.

Then the warmth of his body disappeared, and he stepped back from her, scowling. Her heels sank back to the ground as he jerked a phone from his pocket.

"Devereaux," he snapped.

He shot her a heated look. She turned to reach for her door handle, but he caught her arm.

Wait, he mouthed.

She waited, patiently, tucking her hands into her pockets so he wouldn't see that they were trembling. One kiss, and he had her trembling. What would happen if she spent the night with him? He talked quietly into the phone, but continued to pin her with that hot, penetrating look.

She glanced away. Slowly, reality came back as she stared out over the Roadhouse parking lot. It was crowded with pickups and motorcycles and SUVs. The smell of exhaust mixed with garbage from a nearby Dumpster, and the combination snapped her out of her lustful daze.

Which was a good thing, because she could tell by Nathan's half of the phone conversation that he had to go in.

Finally, he clicked off and stuffed the phone in his pocket.

"Work?" she asked.

He nodded.

She turned and pulled open her door. He didn't move to stop her this time. She slid behind the wheel and glanced up at him, but his face was difficult to read. Would he come over later? The thought made her nerves flutter. But he wouldn't. Probably not. They didn't know each other well enough for him to come knocking on her door in the middle of the night expecting sex.

Sex. With Nathan Devereaux. She fumbled with her keys.

He leaned a forearm on her car and dipped his head down. "Sorry about the timing," he said.

"Not a problem."

"I could call you later . . . ," his warm southern voice trailed off, and the suggestion was delivered with a meaningful look.

She gazed up at him, and she knew. This was a bad idea. For many reasons, starting with the fact that he was on his way to a death scene. And more important, she was still angry at him. He didn't believe her. He didn't respect her judgment in the most important case of her career.

"Don't call," she said.

He looked surprised. Then cautious. "Okay. You still want breakfast tomorrow?"

She glanced at her watch. "It already is tomorrow." She fixed a smile on her face. "You're going to be out late. Let's forget the breakfast. Just give me a call if you have something new for me."

"Something new?" He frowned.

"About the case."

The twenty-four-hour convenience store closest to the crime scene sold coffee that smelled halfway decent but tasted like sludge. Nathan had downed way more than his share of it over the years, but it was 4:50 in the morning, and he couldn't stomach the thought. He snagged a Red Bull from the refrigerator case. As the door slid shut, he glanced up into the convex mirror and spotted Britney.

She wore a red jacket with a fake fur collar that matched her blond ponytail. Nathan watched in the mirror as she bought a pack of Camels. He went to the register and when he stepped out of the store a minute later, she was already halfway down the block, sucking on a smoke.

Nathan put in a brief call to Hodges before circling his Taurus around to intercept her at an alley several blocks north. He rolled down the window, and she stopped short.

"How's it going, Britney?"

Her expression went from alarmed to guarded, and she kept walking.

Nathan pushed open the door and got out. "Don't do this the hard way," he called after her.

Her tall black boots stopped just shy of the sidewalk. She turned.

"I got nothing to say to you." Her gaze darted around, but the street was nearly deserted.

"Guess I'll do all the talking then."

"I'm not going to the fucking station."

"Have I ever asked you to? Let's go for a drive." He pulled the back door open for her and waited. After another uneasy glance around, she walked behind the car and slid in.

Nathan backed out of the alley. He watched her in the rearview mirror as he navigated side streets all the way to Interstate 35, which ran like a dividing line through the city.

"How you been?"

Instead of answering, she bent over and snuffed out her cigarette on his floorboard. Then she jerked the pack out of her pocket and lit a new one.

Nathan crossed under the freeway and turned south. She flashed him a hateful look until he passed the turn-off to APD headquarters. Then he cut through some middle-class neighborhoods and pulled into an all-night fast-food restaurant.

"You hungry?" he asked.

"No."

"I am." There was no line at the drive-through, and Nathan picked up a sack of food before heading a few blocks south to a park.

He opened Britney's door for her. She took a last drag of her cigarette and crushed it under her boot as she got out. The night was damp and chilly. She hugged her coat around herself in a gesture that struck him as oddly childlike. Nathan led her to a picnic table, then sat down and pulled out a pair of warm, foil-wrapped tacos.

"Eat." He placed one at the spot across from him, and Deanna Perry, aka Britney, twenty-two, originally of San Antonio, reluctantly sat down.

"I'm sorry about Tammy," he said.

"You didn't kill her."

Nathan popped open his Red Bull and glanced at her. The lights from the nearby parking lot allowed him to read her expressions as they talked. "Any idea who did?"

She looked away.

He unwrapped his taco and took a bite. Britney, so named probably because of her long blond extensions, tapped another cigarette out of her pack and lit up.

"You guys both work for Little J, don't you?"

She glanced at him and shrugged.

"He and Tammy getting along lately?"

She squinted at him as she took a drag. Twenty-two, and already she had the beginnings of crow's-feet. But fading looks were the least of her problems if she stayed in her current profession.

"J doesn't get along with anybody," she said. "He's an asshole."

She turned to blow her smoke away, and Nathan's gaze slid down to the pink scars that dotted the back of her neck. The woman whose body he'd watched get loaded into a meat wagon earlier tonight had had similar scars. Nathan figured Little J liked to brand his girls with his cigarette during oral sex.

"He the kind of asshole who'd shoot a woman at close range, then put her in a trash can?"

She tossed her smoke away and swung her legs over the bench as she turned to face him. "Probably." She glanced at his half-finished taco and started unwrapping the one in front of her. "But not Tammy. She was worth too much."

Nathan noticed the tremor in her hands as she lifted the taco to her mouth and took a bite. She chewed slowly, staring down at the table, and he wondered if she was thinking about her ever-waning life expectancy.

"You girls knew each other how long?"

She shrugged.

"She was from San Antonio, right? You knew her from home?"

Another shrug, which Nathan took for a yes. She peeled off a strip of tortilla and nibbled on it. Nathan watched her, waiting.

"She wanted to be a singer," Britney muttered. "That's why she came here. Told me how great it was." She picked the sausage out of the taco and ate it. "We shared an apartment for a while."

"Where was she living lately?"

"Wherever."

A pair of headlights swept over her face as a car pulled into the lot behind them. A guy got out with a pair of black Labs, and Britney looked around warily.

"I need to get back," she said.

"I'll take you back." Or at least, as close as she'd let him. He'd interviewed her before, and she always wanted him to drop her off somewhere no one would notice her getting out of an unmarked police vehicle.

Nathan watched her shred the tortilla. Finally, she lifted her gaze to his.

"I need your help," he said.

She looked away again.

"A name? A car? A reason? Even if it's just a rumor you heard."

"I haven't heard shit."

"She was your friend, Britney. And now she's dead."

"Yeah, that's because she's stupid, all right?"

"How was she stupid?"

She wiped her nose with her cuff, and Nathan could tell she was near the breaking point.

"How was she stupid?"

Maybe Britney knew her friend had been an informant for APD. Most likely she did, but Nathan sensed she wasn't talking about that. If it was just about that, Britney herself wouldn't be sitting here having this conversation.

"Britney?"

She stood up and stepped over the bench. "You're the big detective." She turned her back on him. "I don't want shit to do with this. You figure it out."

Nathan woke up and winced at the glare. He squeezed his eyes shut again, but the obnoxious dinging continued.

Fuck it. He got out of bed, yanked on some jeans, and stalked across the house. Hodges was a dead man.

But it wasn't his partner standing on his doorstep.

"Hi." Alex shoved a paper cup into his hands and breezed past him. "How was your night?"

"Long."

"When did you get in?"

"Two hours ago."

She turned to face him. "I took a guess you'd be off this morning because you were out all night. Am I right?"

Nathan set the coffee down on the hall table. He took in her freshly showered hair, her snug-fitting jeans and T-shirt. He walked across the foyer and leaned a hand against the door frame behind her. "You smell like coconuts."

She rolled her eyes. "I'm serious."

"So am I." He gazed down at that lush pink mouth he remembered from last night. He wanted to pull her into bed with him and finish what they'd started. "What'd you have in mind?"

"A field trip."

He picked up a lock of hair and curled it around his finger. She held his gaze, and he liked the way she pretended not to notice his chest.

She cleared her throat. "I have to go get my lab results. I thought you might come along. If you're off, that is."

"I'm off."

"Would you like to come?"

He lifted an eyebrow.

She ducked under his arm and picked up the coffee cup. "Here." She thrust it at him. "It's a venti. I figured you'd be tired. You want to join me or not?"

Nathan watched her a moment. She didn't seem pissed off anymore, which was good. Still, there was a big gap between not pissed off and ready to get naked. He had his work cut out for him.

"I could rally," he said. "I have to be in court by two, though."

"That'll work."

"And I have to shower."

"I'll wait in the car."

Alex pulled off the interstate and checked her mirrors.

"What do you keep looking for?"

"Nothing," she said.

He gazed at her over the top of his aviator sunglasses. How did he always know when she was lying?

"Someone's been following me."

His glanced at the side mirror.

"Not right now."

"When?"

"Last night," she said. "A few times before."

"He followed you home from Eli's?"

"No way. I ditched him."

Nathan shook his head, clearly unhappy at her little revelation. "You get a plate?"

"No," she admitted. "It's usually an American-made sedan. A Taurus, I think. Once it was an Explorer."

"Sounds like a police tail. You think it's Coghan?"

"Not last night."

"How can you be sure?"

"He was at the Smokin' Pig. Or at least his truck was."

Another look over the tops of his shades. She could almost feel the tension filling up the car.

"What?" she asked.

"You put a snitch on Coghan's truck?"

Actually, she'd put the device *in* his truck, but she didn't feel the need to mention that.

"Are you *trying* to incite this guy?"

"I'm trying to protect myself. This way, I can track his moves from a safe distance using my cell phone."

He shook his head again. "I told you before, you're underestimating him, Alex. He's not stupid. And if he's not on to you now, he soon will be. And then you've got more to worry about than Melanie's whereabouts."

Alex sighed, annoyed by the paternal tone. And the fact that he was probably right.

The turnoff came into view, and she was glad for the distraction. She pulled up to the cast-iron gates, gave her name, and had a moment of panic as the guard flipped the pages on his clipboard. He checked her vehicle tags, then her driver's license. Finally, he gave her a nod, and the gate slid open.

Alex followed the curving road through the sloping limestone hills. They had about a mile and a half to go, if she remembered correctly.

"You familiar with the story behind Delphi Center?" She was searching for more neutral ground.

"The Jones family," he said. "Some oil heiress funded the place."

Alex's gaze flicked to the mesquite bushes and prickly pear cacti dotting the landscape. A group of buzzards circled in the distance, and she remembered what Mia had said about a body farm.

"She lost a kid, wasn't it?"

"Her daughter," Alex said, following the curve around a twisted oak tree with an enormous green canopy. "Vanessa Hayley Jones. Student at UT. She was spending the summer at her mom's house in Houston. Got up one morning, went out for a run, and never came home. Two weeks later, her body was discovered in Buffalo Bayou."

"Strangled, right?"

"And raped." Alex's gaze followed the buzzards. "The mother's a widow. Loaded. She brings all kinds of hell down on HPD until they get an arrest. They collar this guy Wayne Korbin. Turns out, he's a convicted sex offender."

"I remember the trial," Nathan said. "It was a media circus. They didn't get the death penalty."

"Life, no parole," Alex said. "There were a couple holdouts on the jury. Anyway, about five years later, a technician at the state crime lab was running a decade-old rape kit. He got a cold hit."

"Lemme guess. Korbin."

"Six months later, there's another hit. Korbin again. To date, they've linked six separate rape kits to this scumbag. If even one of those kits had been tested earlier, he could have been locked up before he killed Vanessa."

Nathan didn't comment. She supposed he'd left his outrage behind years ago. Or maybe it had morphed into that cool determination with which he approached his murder cases.

"Anyway, by the time they got to like the third case, Vanessa's mom was over the edge," Alex said. "She took the entire Hayley family oil fortune and gave it away. Ninety-two million dollars. That's the endowment behind the Delphi Center. Most of it, anyway. They've processed an incredible number of rape kits since they opened. Part of their mission is to help clear the backlog."

She pulled around a bend, and the complex came into view.

"Whoa," Nathan said. "Looks like the Parthenon. On top of a golf course."

Alex steered up the curved driveway, impressed yet again by the gleaming white structure atop a lush carpet of Bermuda grass. The manicured lawn looked all the more out of place because it was surrounded by the untamed flora of the Texas Hill Country.

Alex pulled into the visitors' lot and found a space. They got out, and Nathan glanced up.

"Awesome, isn't it?" she asked.

"Beats the hell out of our crime lab. We're rigged together with duct tape and chewing gum."

Alex gazed up and couldn't believe someone wanted her to work here. She couldn't imagine it. She turned to Nathan. "You ready?"

"Lead the way."

They ascended the wide marble steps. Nathan pulled open the glass door for her, and they were assaulted by a blast of cool air. He peeled off his shades.

"Fair warning, this place is frigid," she told him, as they walked past the security guard and presented their IDs at the reception desk. The attendant checked his computer, made a call on his phone, and then handed them a pair of visitor badges. Alex had notified Mia on the way down here that Nathan was coming.

"Oh, and another thing? Mia's pretty young," she said, "so don't be surprised when you see her."

"How young?" Nathan asked, clipping his badge to the pocket of his blue Oxford shirt, which matched his eyes.

"I don't know. Early thirties? Pretty young for all the degrees she's got."

She heard the distant ding of an elevator, and turned to see Mia striding across the lobby.

"You weren't kidding," Nathan murmured. As she approached them, Alex saw Nathan taking in the pony-tail, the freckles. If not for the lab coat with the Delphi logo, the woman could have passed for a grad student.

"Alex. Detective Devereaux." Mia smiled. "Right this way, please."

Alex had expected to head for the elevators, but instead Mia led them through a pair of exterior glass doors. They ended up on the lawn again, only this side of the complex faced a rocky gorge.

"It's so nice to get a break from the rain," Mia said cheerfully. "Thought we could talk outdoors."

Alex's bullshit meter clicked on, but she didn't comment as Mia led them over a flagstone path to a picnic table beside a pecan tree. They sat down—Mia on one side, she and Nathan on the other.

Mia turned to Nathan. "So you're a homicide detective? Is this your case?"

"It isn't officially a case yet, so no," he said.

"Well, I hope these results will be helpful to you. Whatever comes of this."

What did that mean? Alex wasn't sure, but she braced herself for bad news.

"Okay, let's start at the top." Mia took a spiral pad from the pocket of her coat. "The sample you brought me is Type A-positive blood. That's tied with O-positive for the most common, found in thirty-three percent of the population. The subject is also a secretor."

"What's that?" Alex asked, before she could stop herself. She didn't care, really. She just wanted to know if the blood was Melanie's.

"They secrete antigens, proteins, and enzymes, indicating their blood type, into other bodily fluids," Mia said. "Most people fall into this category. Only about twenty percent of the human race would be classified as nonsecretors."

Mia flipped a page, and Alex shifted impatiently.

"Also," Mia continued, "your subject is male."

"Male?" Alex leaned closer. "Are you sure?"

"Yes."

Not Melanie. Her shoulders sagged with relief, and she looked at Nathan. "Could it be Coghan's? Maybe there was some kind of struggle?"

"Who's Coghan?" Mia asked Nathan.

"The missing woman's husband."

"Craig Coghan," Alex said. "Could the blood be his?"

"Not unless he's dead," Mia said.

Nathan and Alex stared at her.

"Your blood sample matches a profile recently entered into the missing-persons index. Some unidentified remains."

"How recently?" Nathan asked.

"Yesterday morning."

"Are you sure?" Alex asked.

"Absolutely. I ran both profiles myself."

"You ran both." Nathan frowned. "Who submitted the other sample?"

"I'm afraid I can't tell you that."

"Why not?"

"I'm afraid I can't say."

Nathan glanced at Alex, then back at Mia. "Did this other sample come down from Austin? Maybe a floater pulled out of the lake?"

"I'm not at liberty to disclose the details."

Nathan scowled. "Isn't that the point of this place? Cooperation among law enforcement agencies? Everyone helping one another?"

She smiled weakly. "I understand your frustration. But this is an unusual case. Please understand my position."

Nathan sat back, looking seriously annoyed. He was thinking this DNA profile belonged to that murder victim he believed was Melanie's boyfriend. That case was *his,* supposedly, yet he knew nothing about someone sending a sample to the Delphi Center for testing.

"There's more," Mia said. "I recovered some perspiration from the earbud. Same donor as the blood."

"So the blood came from whoever was wearing the earphones." Alex looked at Nathan. "Presumably the victim, not the attacker, right? Who would wear earphones to attack someone?"

Nathan didn't comment.

"Also, we recovered a latent fingerprint from the earbud," Mia continued. "A partial, actually. We ran it through AFIS, but no hits."

"Maybe it's mine," Alex suggested.

"It's not," Mia said. "We have your prints on file. Anyway, a single partial print is a long shot, but I wanted to check for you. So that's about it for the earbud. You can pick it up from our evidence clerk on your way out."

Mia tucked the notepad back into her pocket. "Just one more thing. I took the liberty of sending your envelope to one of my colleagues. Were you aware there was a trace substance inside it? A fine white powder?"

"Coke?" Nathan asked.

"I don't know," Mia said. "I asked one of our chemical tracers to take a look at it when he gets a chance. I'll let you know."

"This substance was *inside* the envelope?" Alex asked.

"Yes."

Nathan looked at Alex. "Maybe it's baking soda," he said sarcastically.

Yeah, right.

Mia checked her watch and stood up. "I wish I had

more time today." She turned to Alex. "Have you had a chance to think about our offer?"

Nathan stood up then, too, and Alex felt his gaze on her face as she floundered for a response. She'd convinced herself Troy's words were just that—*words*.

Alex got to her feet. "Troy was a little vague. I wasn't sure he was serious."

"He was," Mia said. "He speaks highly of you, and we'd be very interested to have you in for an interview with our Cyber Crimes Unit." She pulled a card from the pocket of her lab coat. "My cell number's on the back. Call me and I'll tell you more about it."

Alex avoided Nathan's gaze as she accepted the card. "Thank you."

"We've got some talented people here, Alex. I think you'd fit right in."

CHAPTER TWELVE

Nathan spent the first half of the return trip conducting a cryptic telephone conversation with Hodges. When the call ended, he gazed out the window, his expression conveniently shielded by sunglasses.

He was cutting her out of the loop again. Alex waited calmly, but by the time they reached the Austin city limits, her patience was gone.

"So what do you think?" she finally asked.

Nathan turned to look at her, but his eyes were hidden behind mirrored lenses. "Probably pays better than PI work. I think you should go for it."

"I meant the *case*. What'd you think of Mia's findings?"

He glanced away.

She gripped the steering wheel, trying to tamp down her frustration. After all they'd been through, he still didn't consider her part of his inner circle.

Maybe she *should* take a job at the Delphi Center. At least it would give her some legitimacy with cops.

"Your friend's back," Nathan said.

She glanced over and saw that he was looking at the side mirror. Alex checked the rearview.

"Three cars behind us," he said. "Changed lanes two minutes after you did."

Nathan was right. The boxy black sedan looked familiar. And whoever was at the wheel was subtle enough that Alex hadn't even noticed the tail this time.

"Pull into a gas station," he said. "We can fuel up, then switch drivers. When he picks us up again, I'll see if I can get a tag."

"Uh, thanks, but no."

He arched a brow skeptically. "You think you can handle him?"

Instead of answering, she took the next exit off the interstate. The sedan stayed with them, but managed to hang back about five car lengths.

"Don't run the yellow," he advised as she approached the first stoplight. "He'll know he's been made."

Alex shot him a withering look. "Would you like me to tell you how to write a traffic ticket?"

She cruised through a few intersections until she'd reached a residential area. This part of town was somewhat hilly, which would help with her strategy. She spotted the turnoff she wanted and pulled into a middle-class neighborhood. She turned down a semi-busy street and glanced at the mirror. He wasn't visible, but that didn't mean he wasn't there. She got to the crest of a hill and quickly darted her gaze around in search of a FOR SALE sign. No luck.

The sedan appeared behind her, about a hundred yards back.

Another hill. This time she spotted what she needed. In the yard, a sign. In the driveway, no cars. She floored the gas pedal, then whipped up into the driveway and cut the engine.

"Get down," she said, pulling Nathan's arm and ducking her head down.

They were hunched over the console, their faces just inches apart. Her gaze dropped to that mouth that had sent shock waves through her body last night. She wanted him to kiss her again. She glanced up and saw that he was watching her. He looked as though he could read her mind.

A delivery truck roared past. Then the quiet *whoosh* of a car.

"Think that was him?" she asked.

"It sounded right."

Slowly, they both straightened and peered out the back window. Alex started the car and backed down the driveway. The street was empty now. She sped through the next several intersections, looking up and down side streets for any sign of the sedan.

"Pretty good," Nathan said.

"'Good' would have been catching up to him and getting a license plate." She glanced down another empty cul-de-sac and cursed.

"Ah, don't be so hard on yourself. You caught him off guard. Anyway, I've got to be in court in half an hour."

"You want me to drop you off?"

"Just take me to the station," he said. "I can pick up a car."

By the time they pulled into the lot behind APD, Alex's frustration with him had returned. Where was the trust? The cooperation?

"Just pull over here," he said, pointing to a narrow street beside the employee lot.

Alex pulled over and blew out a sigh. She shoved the car into Park.

"I appreciate the ride." He turned and grabbed his blazer off the backseat. Then he lifted the paper evidence bag out of the cup holder. Thanks to Mia, the bag containing the earbud now had an official evidence label on it, complete with a bar code and a list of signatures. "Mind if I hang on to this?" he asked.

She looked at him for a moment, confused. "What happened to 'zero evidentiary value'?"

"Let me worry about that." He pulled a pen from the pocket of his jacket and scrawled his name on the evidence label, just beneath hers. "I'll get you a receipt for this, okay?"

"Okay."

He tucked the bag and the pen safely into his pocket. He looked her in the eye. "Be careful."

With a sigh, she put the car in gear. "I will."

"And Alex?"

"What?"

He leaned across the console and kissed her—hard.

And then he left.

Nathan's phone rang the instant he walked out of the police station.

Alex. They'd been playing phone tag for two days now, and he had a strong suspicion she was dodging him.

"Hi," he said.

"Guess what. I was right about that truck."

Nathan unlocked his car and slid in. This was work related, as he should have guessed.

"Turns out there *was* a wrecker called out to Moccasin Road a few weeks ago to pull a Blazer out of a ditch," she said. "Lone Star Towing. The towing company's records show—"

"How'd you hack into their records?"

"I didn't. I made friends with the clerk in their office," she said. "Their driver took the car all the way up to Greene's Automotive up on Highway 183."

"That's a hike from Moccasin Road."

"I know. It was a cash transaction, and the driver claims he doesn't remember much else. But the Blazer could be a secondary crime scene. I'm thinking, if you can find out what happened to it—"

"I got it, Alex."

Pause. "I'm just trying to help."

"I know. What are you doing right now?"

Silence as she analyzed the question.

"I'd really like to see you tonight," he said. Was that clear enough? A second ticked by. And another.

"Tonight doesn't work," she said, and he thought he heard regret in her voice. "Maybe tomorrow."

"Sure, I'll call you."

They clicked off, and he tossed his phone onto his dashboard. It rang almost immediately. He saw Nicole's number on the screen, and his evening took another nosedive.

"Yeah?"

"Well, well," his ex-wife greeted him. "Don't *you* sound happy?"

"I'm not."

"Meet me for a drink," she said. "It'll cheer you up."

Not likely.

"I'm tied up right now."

"Well, untie yourself. This is important."

He very much doubted it, but twenty minutes later, he parked his Mustang and walked into the Randolph Hotel. Stuffy as ever. He crossed the spacious lobby and entered Lariat Lounge. As soon as his eyes adjusted to the dim lighting, he spied Nicole at the bar.

He could tell she'd come from the office. Her hair was back in her typical loose bun, and she'd draped a jacket over the back of the bar stool. She wore a fitted black skirt and a white silk blouse, the price of which would probably give him a heart attack. Thankfully, her shopping habits were no longer his problem.

He walked over. "Hi," he said, and kissed her cheek. She smelled like Obsession, which set off a little warning in his head. He'd always liked that perfume on her, and she damn well knew it.

"I ordered you a Dewar's," she said.

He glanced at her Tanqueray and tonic and nodded. "Thanks."

"Thank *you*. I know how busy your evenings get."

One of her little darts. Nathan's crappy hours had been one of the primary problems in their marriage. The other had been money.

His drink came, and he took a sip, eyeing his ex-wife over the glass. "You look good," he said, because it was true.

She smiled. "You look good, too."

He waited for her to get to the point. When she tucked

a strand of blond hair behind her ear, he knew she was ready to begin.

"I keep hearing your name come up."

"Let me guess," he said. "Adamcek wants to recruit me over there to work for him?"

Nicole gave him a peevish look. She was an assistant district attorney, and Nathan's feelings for her boss—the Travis County D.A.—were no secret.

"I'm hearing it from our investigators," she said. "And some cops."

"Such as?"

"Cernak, McElroy, Webb—"

"Webb's a blowhard."

"That's not the point. Sounds like you're asking a lot of questions about Craig Coghan."

Nathan shifted his attention to the stage across the bar where a brunette woman in a slinky black dress was adjusting the microphone.

"Are you?"

"Am I what?"

"Asking questions about Coghan?"

"I ask questions about a lot of people," he said. "It's my job."

She picked up her glass and took a sip. He could tell she was annoyed.

She shook her head. "I don't understand you."

"What don't you understand?"

"For a man with your intelligence, you're extremely oblivious to politics."

"I think the guy's dirty," he said.

"You're way out in left field with that."

"I mean it."

"I can tell. But you think you might want to leave this to IA? Coghan has some serious connections in this town, and you're not doing yourself any favors."

He shrugged.

She put her hand on his arm and leaned closer. "You ever wonder why you've been doing the same crap job for the same crap pay going on twelve years now?"

"I'm good at it?"

She shook her head, exasperated. "Always sarcasm. I'm trying to do you a favor, Nathan."

"Well, don't."

She sighed and looked away.

He felt a twinge of guilt. Maybe she was honestly trying to help him. She'd never understood his priorities. They'd both grown up working class, but Nathan didn't fantasize about climbing any social ladders. Nicole did. He didn't blame her, really. He just didn't share her willingness to make nice with people he thought were assholes.

And if his questions were pissing off people in the D.A.'s office who thought Coghan hung the moon, Nathan didn't much care. The D.A. was a weakling, and Nathan was fed up with watching the dirtbags he arrested plead down to minor offenses.

He sipped his drink and tried to take the edge off his mood. It didn't work. What was Alex doing tonight? Three nights in a row, she'd been busy. Was she out with Troy Stockton again? Nathan had disliked the guy on sight, and he liked him even less since he'd checked him out.

He glanced at Nicole, who was silently smoothing her cocktail napkin. He could tell she was hurt by his don't-give-a-shit attitude. He decided to change the subject.

"How's Mandy?" he asked.

She glanced at him, surprised. "Fine."

"She graduates in May, doesn't she?"

"That's right." Again, he'd surprised her. Nathan always had had a soft spot for Nicole's youngest sister.

"Tell her I said hi, would you?"

"I will." She smiled slightly. "Mandy always liked you."

"She's a good kid."

She put her hand on his arm again. "*I* always liked you, too."

"Yeah, up until you didn't."

She tipped her head to the side and looked at him for a long moment. "You dating anyone now?"

"No."

"Well, you should be. You're too much of a workaholic. It isn't healthy."

She shifted closer, and he smelled her perfume again. It reminded him of coming home from parties with her.

He finished off his drink. "I need to go, Nikki."

She dropped her hand to his thigh and gave him a look he knew well. "No, you don't."

"Yeah, I do."

"No." She leaned closer and smiled. "You really don't."

CHAPTER THIRTEEN

Mia watched through the glass as Alex Lovell completed her second round of tests.

"How's she doing?" she asked Ben.

"She's good," he said, and she caught the admiration in his voice. "I can't believe she doesn't do this for a living."

"She does."

Ben propped his shoulder against the window as Alex's fingers flew over the keyboard. "No, but I mean she's not a badge. She's got no formal training, not even a degree. She's all instinct."

Mia lifted an eyebrow in Ben's direction. Evidently, the tracers' star cyber cop had a crush on their newest recruit.

His attention remained fixed on Alex as Mia looked him over: spiky dark hair—a little overboard on the hair product, wire-rimmed glasses, a fondness for geeky logo tees. He had a decent build, but Mia doubted that a set of nice pecs and a genius IQ were going to give Detective Blue Eyes anything to worry about.

"Would you look at that?" Ben clucked. "She did it again."

Mia followed his attention back to the computers, where Alex was pointing at the screen, explaining something to Ben's supervisor.

"What, exactly, are you guys having her do?"

He sighed absently, and Mia recognized the sound: *I'll do my best to explain it, but this is way beyond you.* Mia heard that sound a lot at the Delphi Center. Everyone here was an expert in something or other, and it wasn't always easy translating technical jargon into plain English.

"Okay, you're familiar with online classifieds, right?" Ben looked at her hopefully.

"I guess so."

"I'm talking Craigslist, Kijiji, Zac's Page. There are hundreds."

"Okay."

"So all those sites are major venues for underground communications. Chat about illegal activities. Right now, Alex is in the Personals section of Zac's Page, where we've seen a recent spike in pedophile traffic."

He turned to gaze through the glass. Alex's hands were in motion on the keyboard again as the head of Delphi's Cyber Crimes Unit watched over her shoulder.

"Okay, so she's identifying the suspicious ads?"

"That's part of it," Ben said. "And that's hard enough. A lot of these guys are clever. They're really good at disguising what they're after, speaking in code."

Mia watched Alex point to a line of text, then key something in.

"We've got guys on here looking to swap KP collections—"

"KP?"

"Kiddie porn. We've got guys looking for prepubescent girls. We've got mothers on here pimping out their children—"

"That's sick."

"That's just the tip of the iceberg. You wouldn't believe some of the twisted shit we see on a day-to-day basis," he said, and Mia gave him a look because, hey, she saw some pretty twisted shit herself.

"Okay, right," he said. "You probably would believe it. Anyway, first you have to spot the illicit ads, then translate them, and then figure out the real identities behind the screen names. Everyone hides behind anonymizers and remailers."

She gave him a blank look.

"An anonymizer supposedly lets someone surf the Net anonymously. A remailer program is designed to strip away header info and replace it with info that's untraceable. There are loopholes, though, and Alex seems to know them all. It's amazing. No prep. No formal training. She shows a lot of potential."

"So I take it you're going to offer her a job?"

"We did, but she didn't want it." He shook his head. "She's pretty noncommittal. It's weird. She wasn't interested in a salary."

Mia glanced at him, startled. She'd never met anyone truly immune to money. "You couldn't get her on board?"

"Oh, she's on board," he said firmly. "She agreed to do some contract work for us."

"So what'd you offer her?"

"That's the cool part." His voice bordered on reverence now. "The woman loves computers. Instead of money, she wants access to our toys."

Sophie nervously scrolled through the playlist on her iPod as she waited for Alex's call. She landed on Neko Case, sang the opening bars of "Hold On, Hold On," then started the song over and sang it again.

Last night's gig had wreaked havoc on her vocal cords. All that smoke. She should have turned down the job, but she was trying to get her feet on the ground in this town, and she wasn't in a position to decline anything, not even an early night gig in Lakeway, where the absence of a smoking ban attracted bar patrons.

Her phone vibrated. She plucked out her earbuds and answered the call.

"Okay, I've got him," Alex said. "He's in a black Chevy Caprice. We're heading toward you, should be there in about five minutes. You all set?"

Sophie glanced at the shopping bags in her front seat. "Yeah."

They clicked off, and Sophie gathered her props. She hustled across the parking lot to the mall entrance and waited just inside the glass doors. It took longer than five minutes—probably due to rush-hour traffic—but finally, she spotted Alex's Saturn.

Sophie's stomach flip-flopped. Her first surveillance job. She tugged down the brim of the White Sox cap Alex had given her and straightened her sunglasses. She set down her shopping bags for a moment and rubbed her palms dry on her sweatpants. It was stage fright, nothing more. She could do this.

A black sedan turned into the lot, just north of where Alex had entered. The driver slowed, probably looking for Alex's Saturn, which was making a leisurely pass down a row of cars. Alex pulled into a space. She got out of the car and crossed the parking lot with a purposeful stride.

Alex entered the mall just beside the door where Sophie stood watching. They didn't make eye contact. Sophie kept her focus on the sedan as it eased past the entrance and turned down a row at the far edge of the lot. It was the perfect lookout point, slightly elevated so that someone could look out over the parking lot and see any activity. Not too many cars around, either—a Porsche Carrera that some protective owner had parked away from the crowd and, several spaces down, a gray Mercury Cougar. It was the ideal location.

Which was why Alex had known their guy would choose it. As predicted, he passed the Porsche and turned into a tree-shaded space about four spots in from the Mercury.

Sophie's car was the Mercury, which she'd rented this morning at the airport. She picked up her shopping bags and headed for it now.

Her palms got clammy again as she neared the Chevy. A man sat in the front, a vague shadow she could hardly see because of the tinted windows.

Sophie glanced away and kept walking. She hummed softly to calm her nerves. Numbers had never been her thing. She wasn't good at recalling them, but Alex had taught her some mnemonic devices.

She cut a glance at the license plate. 3–2–9-J-G-T.

Three twenty-nine, jolly good time. It didn't make sense, but it rhymed and she could remember it. She repeated the phrase over and over in her head as she unlocked the car and dumped her bags in the backseat. Then she slid behind the wheel and pulled the phone into her lap. She called Alex on speakerphone so she wouldn't have to lift the phone to her ear.

"You get it?" Alex asked eagerly.

Sophie rattled off the tag.

"And what does the driver look like?"

"Hard to tell," Sophie reported.

"What's he doing?"

"Talking on his phone, I think. Doesn't look like he's going inside."

"Okay, call me if that changes. I've gotta go."

Sophie hung up and smiled. *Mission accomplished.*

She backed out of the space, careful not to glance at the sedan. As she neared the parking lot exit, she looked in the rearview mirror.

The Chevy's door opened. A bulky man in a baseball cap hefted himself out of the car, tucked something under his jacket, and shut the door. He headed for the entrance.

Alex strolled past Williams-Sonoma and inhaled the tantalizing scent of fresh banana bread. She resisted the urge to step inside for a sample as she waited for Ben's voice in her ear. She'd used the Web browser on her phone to run a search on the license plate. When it came back "unavailable," she'd called Ben. The tracers had access to databases not available to mere mortals like herself.

"You still there?"

"I'm here," he said. "Otto's thinking."

"Otto" was the pet name for the computer housing the latest-and-greatest vehicle-search program.

Alex paused beside the window and let her gaze roam over an outrageously priced set of cookware.

"Hmm . . . That's funny," Ben said.

"What?"

"It's coming up as 'blocked.' "

Alex's phone beeped, but she ignored it. "What does that mean?" she asked him.

"Could be a government car. Or maybe an undercover police vehicle. Usually, I'd be able to see that, though. Maybe it's just a program glitch."

Alex gazed absently past the pans at the cooking demonstration going on inside the store. Her mind conjured up possibilities.

"This is weird," he said. "Let me look into this for you and call you back."

Her phone beeped again. "Okay, thanks." She clicked off with Ben and switched to the other call. "Hello?"

Alex watched her own reflection in the glass. A large figure loomed behind her.

Time slowed down.

The man reached inside his jacket. Sophie's voice echoed in her ear, like she was screaming across a canyon: *He's coming!*

Alex's brain raced forward, but her feet seemed mired in quicksand. The man closed in. Adrenaline overcame her shock, finally, and she lunged away from him.

A giant hand clamped around her upper arm. "Don't

scream," he growled in her ear. Something hard jammed into her ribs.

She sucked in a breath. Panic zinged through her. She lurched the other way, but the grip tightened.

"Don't make a scene."

She glanced around frantically. People were everywhere—shoppers, mall walkers, kids in strollers. But no one was looking at *her*.

And she realized her mistake. She'd assumed she'd be safe here, in this sea of people. She hadn't made herself safe; she'd put *them* in danger.

They stumbled past a water fountain, and he jerked open a door marked EMPLOYEES ONLY. A scream tore from her throat and was silenced almost instantly by a meaty hand over her face.

Now she couldn't breathe.

A new wave of panic seized her, and she kicked and clawed at him. He was behind her now, with his hand over her mouth and nose, as he wrestled her down the corridor toward another gray door.

Alex shook her head violently, struggling for air. The edges of her vision started to spot. He was going to kill her. Somewhere in the panicked fog, she thought of her SIG. Zipped inside her purse. Sandwiched against her hip. She reached for it with her free hand, then realized she was still holding her phone.

"Alex? *Alex?*" Sophie's soft, tinny voice called out as the man hauled her through another door into a stockroom.

She dropped the phone and fumbled for the purse. Her lungs burned. Her vision tunneled. The world dimmed.

She bit his finger, hard.

"*Shit!*"

He hurled her away from him. She smacked into something hard and dropped to the floor.

"Fucking bitch!"

She sucked in air. Her head swam. She spied her purse on the ground and grabbed for it just as the man lunged toward her and the door they'd just come through flung open.

"*Police! Freeze!*"

For a split second, she stared in shock at the man in the doorway, his feet wide apart, his gun raised. A cloud of Sheetrock exploded beside his head.

Alex rolled sideways, away from the blast. Another shot rang out. She scrambled to her feet, raced down the aisle, and dove behind a wall of shelves.

Footsteps thundered close by. She glanced around desperately. The room was dim. Musty. Miles and miles of shelves and boxes and crates, two stories high.

"*Police! Freeze!*" the voice bellowed again.

Where was her weapon?

In her purse. On the other side of the wall. She flattened herself on her stomach and commando crawled toward the end of the row. She paused to listen. Footsteps, two sets. A slide and shuffle as somebody raced down a row, then changed directions. Then a shrill female yelp and a door slamming open.

Alex stumbled to her feet. Keeping her head down, she darted around the wall of shelves and spotted her purse on the floor. She snatched it up, jerked open the zipper, and yanked out her SIG.

She was armed.

She was alive.

Another slamming door. Then a round of high-pitched chatter as people—department store workers, she guessed—reacted to the commotion.

Alex slung her purse over her shoulder and winced at the unexpected pain. She glanced around. Her gaze landed on her now-silent phone, covered in a snowy layer of plaster, on the floor near the door. She snatched it up and tucked it into her bag. She was eye to eye with the bullet hole in the wall now, and a fresh wave of fear gripped her.

A door crashed open behind her. Footsteps thudded down the row, and she whirled around, weapon raised.

The white-haired policeman. He stood motionless at the end of the aisle. Only his gaze moved—from her face, to her weapon, then back to her face again. At his side, he held a familiar pistol.

"Don't shoot," he said calmly.

Slowly, Alex lowered her gun. Slowly, the man moved toward her. Fear and anger and confusion swirled through her head as he stopped in front of her.

"Your name's not Bill Scoffield," she said.

"No, it isn't."

CHAPTER FOURTEEN

The voice was the same, though. *East Texas, maybe Nacogdoches,* Sophie had said. But Scoffield was supposed to be from Midland.

"Where is he? That man?" Alex nodded toward the far side of the stockroom, where the chatter was reaching a fever pitch.

"Lit out across that parking lot."

"But . . . shouldn't you guys go after him?"

"What 'guys'?" He tucked his weapon into a holster beneath his jacket, and for the first time she noticed the star pinned to his lapel.

"It's just me," he said. "And anyway, he's long gone. You can put that away." He nodded at her SIG.

"I need to see some ID first."

He rested his hands on his hips and sighed. Then he tugged a leather folio from the inside pocket of his jacket and flipped it open.

Alex eyed the photograph, then the name beneath it: *John Holt. Texas Ranger.* She glanced at his badge again. The *cinco peso,* it was called. And the lawmen who wore them were legendary throughout Texas.

"Okay?" He flipped the case shut and tucked it back into his pocket.

She slipped her gun into her purse beside her dusty phone.

The door beside them burst open and a pair of wide-eyed security guards rushed in, walkie-talkies drawn.

"Police," Holt said quickly. He whipped out his creds again and flashed them at the guards.

"We got a report of gunshots," the larger one said, and his gaze dropped to the bits of plaster and dust on the floor.

Holt turned to Alex. "Lemme take care of this. And then we need to talk."

Alex opened her mouth to protest, but her phone chimed. Holt turned away to calm the security guards while Alex checked the screen.

Sophie, of course.

"What *happened*?" she squeaked. "Are you all right?"

"I'm fine."

"I was about to call 911! Are you sure—"

"Positive. I've gotta go now, though, okay? Call you later." Alex clicked off as the guards strode past her, talking into their radios. Their footsteps faded to the other side of the stockroom.

"Where are they going?" Alex asked.

"Parking lot," Holt said. "They need to check everything I told them so they can put it in their reports."

"And what did you tell them?"

He watched her for a long moment. "We need to talk," he repeated.

"All right. Talk."

"Not here. Come with me."

Alex followed him through the bowels of the shopping mall as he made a few phone calls. Pipes creaked and hummed around them. They passed a whistling janitor, a security guard. After a few more twists and turns, they came to another gray door, this one with MALL SECURITY stenciled on it in black. Holt opened the door. A large African American man in uniform approached them. He and Holt exchanged words. Then the ranger opened yet another gray door and nodded for Alex to step inside.

The small, putty-colored room had cinder-block walls and a low ceiling. A fluorescent strip of lighting gave everything a sickly hue. Alex entered the room, propped her good shoulder against the wall, and crossed her arms. "Talk," she said.

Holt pulled the door shut behind him. He glanced around, then dragged a metal folding chair over and sank into it. For a moment, he just looked at her. Then he stretched out his long legs and crossed his arms.

"You're hard to keep up with."

She didn't respond.

"You don't return phone calls, either."

"I didn't want your job," she said simply.

"You could have told me."

She shrugged and looked away. She was still shaking, and she squeezed her arms closer to her body, hoping he wouldn't see it.

She met his gaze again. "You've been following me."

"I've been following someone *else* who's been following you."

"Same thing."

"Not really."

"That guy back there," she said, "the one who shot at you. Do you know who he is?"

"We're working on that. My guess is, he works with Coghan. Are you sure you don't recognize him from anyplace?"

"I'm sure." Alex bit her lip and tried to conjure up details that might help with the guy's identity. Just remembering him made bile rise up in the back of her throat.

"He had a black sun tattooed on his hand," she said. "And olive skin. I think he's Hispanic."

Holt nodded.

"He was strong, too. For his height, I mean."

"I'll make a note of that." Holt cocked his head to the side and frowned at her. "You want an ice pack? That cheek's starting to swell."

"No," she said. "Who's 'we'?"

"What?"

"You said, '*we're*' working on his identity."

"That would be me," he said. "And some colleagues."

Colleagues. Talk about evasive. Alex tried for patience, but her stomach was twisted in knots and she could feel the shakes coming on.

"I thought you were alone," she said.

"On this assignment, I am." He smiled slightly. "I drew the short straw today."

"What is this, some kind of police corruption scandal?"

He watched her calmly. It must be the training. Flying bullets and foot chases didn't seem to faze him. But Alex still felt woozy. She hugged her arms closer.

"I'm going to tell you more than I should," he said now, "because I think you can help us."

She stared at him and waited.

"I'm looking for Melanie Coghan," he said. "That wasn't a lie."

"Why don't you ask her husband what happened to her?"

"We're not real eager to tip him off that he's under investigation."

"Who's investigating him?" she persisted. "Besides the Texas Rangers?"

"That's not something you need to worry about. Let's just call it a task force and leave it at that."

"So this is a corruption thing? Or are you simply investigating him for murder?"

His steady gaze was her answer. Alex rolled her eyes and looked away. Of course not. Why put together a task force over the menial matter of a woman's death? This was probably about money. Probably Coghan was on the take from the drug dealers his narco squad was supposed to be busting.

Alex pushed off from the wall. "I can't help you. I don't know where Melanie is. My best guess is, you should try dragging Lake Austin."

"We did."

She blinked at him. They'd dragged the lake? Even Nathan didn't know about that.

Unless, as she'd begun to suspect, he was holding out on her.

A little knife twisted in her chest.

"Why don't we back up a bit here, all right?" Holt said. "I want to know why that man tried to kidnap you. You have any ideas?"

"He wasn't terribly chatty."

"Did he ask you any questions?"

"No."

"What do you think he wanted?"

"It seemed pretty clear he wanted me dead." She suppressed a shudder.

He watched her a long moment. "Where did Melanie go after you helped her leave town?"

"You really don't know?"

He shook his head.

"I helped her get settled in the Southeast," she said vaguely. "That was back in the fall. I haven't heard from her lately, though."

"Does she know you're looking for her?"

"If she's alive, she does. She know *you're* looking for her?"

"Yes. But we haven't seen or heard from her in six months."

Alex shook her head. This case just kept getting more and more complicated. He hadn't seen Melanie since Alex helped her leave town, supposedly because her husband was beating her. Alex could have kicked herself. Melanie had misled her about almost everything since the day she'd walked into Lovell Solutions.

"I think I'm getting the picture here," she said, and watched Holt's reaction carefully. "I'm guessing you approached Melanie back in the fall. Maybe you wanted her testimony?"

"She can't testify against her husband in court. Not about this, anyway."

Alex pursed her lips. She *could* testify about domestic

abuse. Spousal privilege didn't apply to that. But this task force wasn't interested in Melanie's home life, evidently. "So, what'd you want from her?"

"We wanted her to wear a wire around Coghan and some of his associates. We thought she might be able to get us some good intelligence about their operation."

"And risk her life doing it."

He paused. "Her life was already at risk."

Unbelievable.

"You scared her off," Alex stated. "Hence, she came to *me* so she could disappear."

Holt nodded.

"Well, I think she has disappeared," Alex said. "I suggest you and your task force find another inside source. Oh, and maybe open a murder investigation while you're at it. I believe Coghan killed her, along with her boyfriend."

"Joe Turner," he said. "The one we found in Lake Austin."

"I didn't realize he'd been identified."

"Melanie ever tell you about him?"

"No."

"You seem hostile, Alex."

"I don't appreciate being lied to and manipulated, *Bill*."

The side of his mouth twitched up. "Ah, come on now. Don't tell me you've never had to lie to get a job done."

Alex's phone chimed again, and she fished it out of her purse. Nathan.

"Hi," she said.

"Hi there."

Just the sound of his voice made the tremors start again. Alex turned away from Holt. "I can't talk right now."

"What's wrong?"

"Everything's peachy," she said, borrowing one of his phrases as she tried to keep her voice even. "Listen, can we talk later? I'm in the middle of something."

"Call me."

She shoved the phone into her purse and checked her watch. Almost seven. She could feel her composure slipping, and she needed to get home. She was getting that acidy feeling in her stomach, and the walls of this little room were starting to close in.

"I need to go."

Holt didn't say anything, and she moved for the door.

He stood up and reached around for the knob, effectively blocking her. "I need you to stay in touch."

She glared up at him. "Why don't you and your task force stay in touch with me? You can start by giving me a call when you find out the name of the asshole who just attacked me."

"We're working on it."

"Like you're working on finding out who killed Melanie?"

He didn't say anything as she gazed up at him. Finally, he turned the knob and pulled open the door.

"Stay in touch, Alex," he told her.

"You bet."

Alex parked illegally in an alley two blocks from her building. She ignored the gestures and horn blasts as she darted across Lavaca Street and jogged to her office. She would spend five minutes, ten tops. She'd send Sophie home, collect her laptop, and then close up shop. Then she'd go home and fall to pieces in private.

She rapped impatiently on the glass. Sophie buzzed her in.

Her assistant took one look at her and jumped to her feet. "Oh my *God*!" She came out from behind the desk. "What happened?"

"Long story." She tossed her purse on the sofa and went straight for her file cabinet. She yanked open the top drawer.

"Alex, what—"

"What happened to my files?" she demanded.

Sophie stepped back, visibly rattled by her tone. And probably her appearance, too, by the appalled look on her face.

"What'd you do to these files?"

"I, uh . . . alphabetized them."

"Where's Scoffield?" Alex pawed through the folders. What was this crap?

"He's under 'B' for Bess. The Melanie Bess case. You said—"

"Don't screw with my stuff." She spotted the neat little tab within the Bess file: SCOFFIELD, WILLIAM. Alex muttered a curse and jerked the folder from the drawer. She couldn't believe she'd fallen for it. She should have hunted down a photograph. Sure, there was an attorney named William Scoffield practicing law in Midland. Just like there was some guy Bess who'd died recently in Midland County. But neither of those people had anything to do with Melanie Coghan. Bess was a common name. Holt had probably searched the death records, then built his story from there.

"Alex, I think you need some ice." Sophie's worried gaze shifted to her cheek.

Alex took a deep breath. She reminded herself that her assistant was only trying to assist her. "I'll get some at home."

"But, Alex—"

"I just need to grab my laptop." She shoved the file under her arm and strode toward her office. "You can head out now," she said over her shoulder.

"But—"

"Don't worry about the rented car. We'll return it in the morning."

"But you have a client—"

Alex pushed open her office door.

"—waiting for you."

She stopped cold.

The file slipped to the floor. Her jaw dropped open. She stared at the pale, black-haired woman slumped over her desk, snoring.

Melanie.

CHAPTER FIFTEEN

"I've been *trying* to tell you, you have a client waiting."

Alex dragged her gaze away from her desk and looked down at Sophie, who was crouched on the floor now, scooping up papers. She stood up, brushed the hair out of her eyes, and thrust the folder at Alex.

"Here," she said.

"When did she get here?"

"An hour ago. She insisted on waiting in there with the door shut. I think she was worried about somebody walking in."

Alex took the file and gazed down at it dumbly. Melanie was alive.

"I couldn't leave until you got here," Sophie said. "But I'm late for a gig now. So if you don't mind . . ."

"Go. Please. Sorry to make you late."

"I'll see you tomorrow."

"Tomorrow," Alex repeated, staring at Melanie. *Melanie*. Right there in her office.

She heard the door open and whirled around. "Sophie, wait!"

Her assistant paused in the doorway.

"Don't tell anyone about her, not a soul."

Sophie looked insulted. "Give me some credit," she said, and walked out.

Alex turned back to Melanie. Her spiky black hair stuck up from her head. Her cheek rested on her folded arms, and she looked completely and totally *out*. If it hadn't been for the snoring, Alex would have thought she was dead.

She *had* thought that. For weeks now.

She pulled her office door shut behind her and locked it.

Melanie was alive.

A lump lodged in Alex's throat as she adjusted to this new reality. She stepped over to her desk and stared down at Melanie.

As if sensing her presence, Melanie stirred. The snoring stopped. Her eyes fluttered open. She sat up abruptly and shot back in Alex's rolling desk chair.

"Long time no see," Alex said.

Her hands gripped the chair arms. "Oh my God, you *scared* me!" she gasped. "I didn't know you were here."

"I work here." Alex tossed the file onto the desk and sank into a plastic chair. She gazed at her client. Melanie's complexion was sallow, and she had dark circles beneath her bloodshot eyes.

"Not looking so good, Melanie."

This observation seemed to shock her. She stared across the desk, incredulous. Then she let out a bark of laughter.

"I'm serious," Alex said. "You look like crap."

She sat motionless for a moment. And then she crumpled. She buried her face in her hands and let out a muffled sob.

Alex crossed her arms and watched the floodgates open. Behind her hands, Melanie cried and sniffled. The scene was much like the one back in October, only then it had been Melanie in the plastic chair and Alex behind the desk.

"I've been so terrified, Alex." She glanced up tearfully. "You wouldn't believe everything that's happened!"

"Try me."

"My whole life's been crazy, every minute." She tugged at the sleeve of her baggy gray sweatshirt and dabbed her nose with it. "I've been so *scared*."

"Guess you forgot my advice about black," Alex said.

"Huh?"

"You blondes. You always want to go black. Or red. I told you, it's too noticeable. You want to blend in, stick with brown."

Melanie's brow furrowed.

Not only did her hair look awful, she'd put on weight. And her skin hadn't seen the sun in months, from the looks of it. Alex wondered how long ago she'd ditched her identity in sunny Florida. The utilities had been disconnected for weeks, but she could have left long before that.

Alex stood up and walked around the desk to her computer. She felt Melanie's baffled gaze on her as she booted it up.

"Don't you . . . don't you want to hear what's going on?"

Alex clicked open her accounting software. "Sure, fill me in."

"Well . . . I came back to town a couple months back. I guess you knew that."

"Figured that out, yeah."

"I was staying at this place on the lake."

"Got that part, too." Alex clicked into the screen she wanted. "You owe me twenty-eight hundred dollars. Just FYI."

"What?"

Alex propped a hip on her desk. "That would be eight hundred dollars' worth of my time. At the bargain-basement rate I gave you. Plus deposits on your utilities in Orlando. Plus the security deposit on your apartment. Any chance I can expect to see that money sometime soon?"

Melanie sat back in the swivel chair. "No."

"Didn't think so."

Alex clicked out of her accounting program and turned to face Melanie, arms folded. "Why didn't you return my calls?"

"I didn't—"

"We had a system, remember? I send an urgent message, you answer. You send an urgent message, I answer. That was nonnegotiable."

"I lost my phone."

"You could have found a pay phone. An Internet café. Something. Do you have any idea how worried I've been? Do you have any idea how much time I've spent looking for you?"

Melanie stared up at her, wide-eyed.

Alex clamped her mouth shut and swallowed all the

bitchy things she wanted to say. Melanie really looked bad. Whatever she'd been doing lately, it hadn't been good for her health.

Alex eyed her suspiciously. "Are you on drugs?"

"*Me?*" Melanie splayed a hand against her chest, and her nails were bitten down to the quick. "I don't touch drugs. I don't even *drink*."

"You look terrible."

Melanie's gaze fell to her lap. "I know." She squeezed her hands together until her knuckles whitened. A tear dripped onto her thigh, making a dark gray dot on her sweatpants.

Alex closed her eyes and tipped her head back. She would *not* be pulled in again. She had to turn off the sympathy for this girl. She took a deep breath.

"You lied to me back in October."

"I know." Melanie's voice was small, almost a whisper.

"Why did you do that? I was trying to help you."

"I didn't think you would. Not if you knew what was really going on."

"What's really going on, Melanie?"

Her shoulders tensed. She hunched over. She sniffled.

"I can't help you if I don't know the truth, Mel. We tried that already. It didn't work."

She nodded, her head bowed.

"You need to tell me everything. Starting at the beginning."

Melanie looked up, her eyes brimming with tears. "He's dead, isn't he?"

"Who's dead?"

"Craig killed him. I know it."

"Who?"

"Joe." She choked out a sob. "He killed Joe."

Alex watched Melanie gaze at her lap as she struggled with her emotions. When she looked up again, she had a question in her watery eyes.

"Joe Turner?" Alex asked.

Melanie nodded.

"Joe Turner is dead. I don't know who killed him."

Alex expected another flood of tears, but instead, Melanie closed her eyes and nodded. She took a deep breath and met Alex's gaze. Maybe she'd known it all along. Maybe the confirmation came as a relief.

"What's going on, Melanie?"

"I'll tell you," she said somberly. "And then I need your help."

Help. As in money.

"What happened to your Honda?" Alex asked.

"What Honda?"

"The one your neighbors saw at the lake house while you were living there."

She glanced down. "That was Joe's. I don't know what happened to it."

"And the Blazer?"

Melanie looked up and wiped her nose again with her shirt sleeve. "That's mine. *Was.* I don't know where it is now. I guess Craig did something with it."

"How'd you afford the car?" she asked.

"Joe got it for me. He wanted me to have freedom to come and go. He didn't want me to feel trapped all the time, like I did with Craig."

Alex shook her head with frustration. She leaned

forward across the desk. "Did you listen to *anything* I told you? Coming back here was the last thing you should have done. What were you thinking?"

Melanie looked down and shook her head slightly. Alex wondered if she'd caught the underlying meaning: *By coming here, you probably got your boyfriend killed.*

Melanie glanced up suddenly. "Have you ever been in love?"

Alex sat back. "No."

"I didn't think so." She gave her an apologetic look. "No offense, but you can't understand."

"What can't I understand?"

"What it's like. What I'm feeling. I needed to be with him." She sighed. "You'll understand someday."

Alex rolled her eyes. What a bunch of bullshit. She wanted to toss Joe's death in Melanie's face and ask her if their little honeymoon by the lake had been worth it.

"Joe and I . . . we had plans. We were going to start a new life together. He'd been saving money for us."

"How?"

Melanie glanced up. "He's a real estate agent. Was. He'd been putting money away so we could start over somewhere. As far away from Craig as we could get."

Alex watched her, trying to gauge whether she was telling the truth. She'd expected to learn that Joe Turner was mixed up in Coghan's operation somehow. She hadn't expected him to be a real estate agent. But maybe that was a front.

"Tell me about Craig," Alex said. "What's he doing to attract the attention of so many investigators?"

Melanie snorted. "What's he *not* doing? He's into

drugs. Prostitutes. You name it. Everything he's supposed to be policing." She shook her head. "I shouldn't say any more than that, though. It's dangerous for you to know too much."

Alex let her drop the subject temporarily. She wanted to keep her talking.

"And how did your Blazer end up in a ditch?"

Melanie took a deep breath, and Alex got the impression she was finally going to learn what happened at the cabin.

"I went for carryout," she said quietly. "Joe said he'd be watching the basketball game when I came home. But the TV wasn't on." She looked over Alex's shoulder, as if envisioning the events. "I guess that's what tipped me off. Everything was too dark. I knew something was wrong." Her gaze fastened on Alex's. "I remembered what you said. About trusting my instincts. So I just took off. But the roads were wet. I lost control of the car and crashed and next thing I knew, I was racing through the woods, and Craig was behind me."

"Behind you?"

"He tackled me. I kicked him, threw gravel in his face. I got free and ran out into the road." She laughed without humor. "Almost got hit by a car, too. That's what saved my life. This woman stopped to help."

Alex looked at Melanie, imagining her in the dark and the rain, running for her life from the man who'd just murdered her boyfriend.

"You're lucky," Alex told her.

She snorted.

"I'm serious. You could easily be dead right now."

"I know." Melanie sighed tiredly and looked away.

"My grandma always said I was like a cat with nine lives. I figure marrying Craig used up about eight."

Nathan stared into the fire and thought of Alex. Where was she? She'd sounded strange on the phone earlier. He'd called twice since then, but she hadn't picked up, and he couldn't shake the feeling that something bad had happened. Something was wrong.

He poked the pile of coals with his barbecue tongs. Then he lifted the metal grate from the deck and dropped it back in place over the fire.

Then again, maybe nothing was wrong. Maybe Stockton was in town again, and he'd called her, just like he'd said he would. Maybe they were out tonight in his Ferrari. Or back at her place, and she was too busy to pick up the phone.

Nathan's temper smoldered as he watched the flames. He cast an annoyed glance over his fence, debating whether to go next door and raise some hell about the noise. He hated country music. And he didn't much appreciate the endless loop of Rascal Flatts on a Thursday night.

He pulled the phone from the pocket of his jeans and checked the screen again. Nothing. He tipped back his beer. Empty. He dropped the bottle into the carton sitting on the deck beside the bag of coals. Three down, three to go. He picked up a cool one and twisted off the top, just as the gate creaked open. He turned around.

"Hi."

His heart gave a kick.

"I rang the bell, but no one answered, so . . ." Alex's voice faded as she walked toward him across the dark patch of grass. "What's cooking?"

"Nothing yet."

She sounded chipper, which was unusual. She had on jeans and a T-shirt. He couldn't see the details in the dimness, but the outfit didn't look to him like something she'd wear on a date.

She climbed the three wooden stairs to his deck. "Sorry to just show up, but it sounded important."

"Important?"

"Your messages." She glanced around at his yard, and he was glad it was too dark for her to see how overgrown it was. She sank into a patio chair and leaned back, sighing. "God, I'm so beat."

"Long day?"

"Very long." She stretched out her legs and tipped her head back to gaze up at the sky. "Pretty night."

He walked over to stand in front of her, and she snagged the beer from his hand. She took a sip and grimaced at the taste. "You have anything besides beer?"

"I've got some wine inside, if you want."

"Sounds great."

She heaved herself from the chair, and he led her to the back door. He pushed it open and ushered her in. The utility room was crammed with about three weeks' worth of laundry, and he shoved a heaping basket aside with his foot.

"Sorry," he said, slipping around her.

"No problem. You should see my place."

"You like red?" The wine was on the counter beside

the fridge, and he pulled open a drawer and rummaged for the corkscrew.

"Red's great."

He glanced over at her and froze. "Holy shit, Alex." He rushed over. "What happened?"

"It's nothing. I—"

"Nothing?" He lifted her chin and examined the bruise on her cheek. The skin there was purple and swollen.

"I bumped into a wall."

He stared down at her, and she glanced away.

I bumped into a wall.

He dropped his hand. He leaned back against the counter and watched her. "A wall," he stated calmly, but white-hot anger was pulsing through his veins.

"It's no big deal," she said, rolling her eyes. "It doesn't even hurt."

"Did Stockton do that?" Nathan would kill the guy. He'd fucking take his head off.

"What?"

"Troy Stockton. Did he do that to your face?"

"No."

"Who did, then?"

She crossed her arms over her chest and glanced around, obviously uncomfortable now in the harsh light of his kitchen.

And then he got it.

This was about her job. She'd gotten hurt working on some case. Probably Melanie's.

"I shouldn't have come over." She shook her head and looked away, looked at everything except him. "I knew you'd freak out."

"Tell me what happened." He gripped the edge of the counter and did what he considered an amazing job of *not* freaking out while he stared at that swollen purple welt.

She sighed. "Look, Nathan, I've had a long day. Let me clean up first, okay? Then I'll tell you everything."

And when she finally made eye contact, he knew she was lying to him. She would *not* tell him everything. She would keep her guard up, like she always did.

But he nodded toward the hallway and played along. "Be my guest," he said.

He watched her disappear and heard the water go on in the bathroom sink.

He loosened his grip on the counter. He unclenched his teeth. He took a deep breath and tried to rein in his emotions.

Anger. Frustration. Protectiveness. He wasn't sure which he felt the strongest, but he needed to get a lid on all three before he said or did something he'd regret later.

Such as tell her to drop Melanie's case. Or, even better, tell her to quit her job. She didn't take orders well, particularly not from him.

He retrieved the corkscrew and slammed the drawer shut. With sharp, jerky movements, he uncorked the wine he'd bought earlier this week, thinking it might help him sweet talk Alex into bed. Instead, he'd nearly ended up in bed with Nicole.

He poured a glass and left it waiting on the counter, then made an ice pack and took it to the guest bathroom. A strip of light spilled out into the hallway. Through the narrow opening in the doorway, he saw her standing in front of the sink in a black sports bra and jeans. Her startled gaze met his in the mirror.

"Hi," she said, and dipped her T-shirt under the faucet.

He eased the door open and placed the ice pack on the counter. "Want some Neosporin for that?" He nodded at the raw, red abrasion on her shoulder. Carpet burn? Pavement? Just conjuring up the possibilities made his stomach turn.

"Guess you've been shopping since my last visit." She glanced at him in the mirror and smiled slightly. "If I keep showing up like this, you're going to have to get some real drugs."

He leaned against the counter now, facing her, and watched her dab at her shoulder with her damp T-shirt. She had a bruise there, too—a nice big one.

"You need to ice it." He picked up the ice pack and braced a hand behind her shoulder before gently pressing the pack against the swollen joint. She sucked in a breath and closed her eyes.

"You want me to take you in, get it checked out?"

"No." She looked up and gave him another weak smile. "It's just cold."

He held her gaze, and something sparked between them. And he was acutely aware of the water running, and her crumpled T-shirt on the edge of the sink, and the swell of her breast just inches from his hand. He couldn't believe he'd let his mind go there right now, but there wasn't a damn thing he could do to stop it. He'd been attracted to her from the instant he'd met her, and she was standing so close he could feel her breath on his neck. His gaze slid down to the black spandex that was rising and falling now, more rapidly than it had been minute ago.

"Why did you say that?" she asked, slipping her hand under his and taking over the ice pack. "About Troy?"

"I don't know." He shoved his hands into his pockets. "I thought maybe you were involved with him."

"I'm involved with him, so that means he beats me up?"

"*Are* you involved with him?"

"Not like you mean."

But Nathan remembered the unmistakable vibe he'd picked up at Eli's. "But you *were* involved."

"Were," she said. "Past tense. But it doesn't matter anyway, because he'd never hurt me."

"He has a record of assault."

Surprise flashed into her eyes. She lowered the ice pack and gazed up at him, and he couldn't tell whether she was surprised that Stockton had a rap sheet, or that he'd taken the trouble to find out about it.

That's right, honey, I'm jealous. And I want you in the worst way. As if she didn't know that already. As if she hadn't figured it out when he'd pinned her against her car the other night and begged her to come home with him.

She trained her gaze on the mirror now and rearranged the ice on her shoulder. "Troy's been in a few bar fights. That doesn't mean he beats women."

She was stalling.

"What happened today, Alex?"

"It's a long story," she said, and before he could protest, she cut him off with a look. "And I'll tell you, okay?

But I don't want to analyze the entire thing right now. I'm not up for it."

He crossed his arms over his chest. "All right."

"Basically, I set up a surveillance op with Sophie. To find out who's been following me."

Nathan struggled to keep his mouth shut as he waited for the rest of it. She rearranged the ice pack again, and he could tell she was using the time to edit the hell out of her story.

"We lured this guy to the mall," she said. "Sophie approached him in the parking lot and got his tag, and I ran a trace on it."

"And?"

"And it all went down as planned until he found me inside the mall and grabbed me. He pulled me into a hallway, and we had kind of a tussle." She flicked a glance at him. "It sounds worse than it was, okay? Just calm down."

"You left out the wall part."

"I bit him, and he pushed me into a wall. Then I got away. End of story."

Yeah, right. Nathan gritted his teeth. "Who the hell was this guy?"

"No idea. His tag came up 'unavailable.' Maybe you'll have more luck running it down."

"Did you even call security?"

"Yes. They wrote up a report. Now I'm done talking about it. Moving on. What did you call me about?"

He simmered for a moment, not at all ready to move on. But he let it go. For now.

"I was calling about Melanie," he said. "I heard a

rumor at work today, and I thought you'd want to hear it."

Her spine stiffened, but she kept her attention focused on the mirror. "What was the rumor?"

"A buddy of mine with the sheriff's office told me they had a crew out the other day, dragging the lake, right where we found our John Doe. They're searching for a second victim, same spot."

Nathan watched—shocked—as Alex's eyes filled with tears. But she blinked them back and pretended to be focused on the ice pack in her hand.

He wasn't sure why her reaction surprised him. Yes, Alex was tough, but Melanie wasn't just a client. Alex really cared about her, evidently.

She cleared her throat. "Who's 'they'?"

"A couple sheriff's deputies, a canine unit, a few feds."

"But it's not the sheriff's jurisdiction, right?"

"Shouldn't be," he said, and she obviously caught the implications. APD had been cut out of the investigation. Again.

"And what did they find?"

"Nothing," he said, but he knew that didn't make the news any easier. "So . . . I'm starting to think you were right about Melanie. Sounds like you're not the only one who thinks she's dead. And if the feds are involved, and if APD's been cut out, then there's something big going on here. Something far-reaching."

She nodded stoically. "I knew that."

"I know, I just . . . I'm sorry to have to tell you."

She glanced down and shook her head, as if she didn't trust herself to talk. Or even to look at him.

He wanted to pull her into his arms and comfort her. But she'd picked her shirt up now, and she was holding it to her chest in a way that told him she wanted space.

"Thanks for telling me," she said. "If you don't mind, I really want to clean up."

"Sure," he said, and then slipped through the door and eased it shut behind him.

He walked back to the kitchen feeling like an insensitive jerk. She'd acted so convinced of Melanie's murder, he hadn't realized she was still holding on to some kind of hope. And he'd just crushed it to pieces.

On the countertop was the big T-bone he'd thawed for dinner. He'd split it with her. He went outside and spent a few minutes reviving the fire. Afterward, he leaned his forearms on the wooden railing of his deck and stared out at the backyard, cursing his neighbors' taste in music as he tried to come up with ways to persuade Alex to drop the case.

You're completely out of your league here—which didn't seem to matter to her. *This goes way beyond your client, and you need to let someone else handle it*—which would be equally unconvincing. And yet another approach: *If you don't drop this case soon, you'll get hurt for real, and we'll be fishing you out of Lake Austin, and I think that would kill me.*

The back door opened, and he turned around.

Alex stood there, silhouetted against the light of his utility room. In a T-shirt. With a glass of wine in her hand.

She pulled the door shut behind her and walked toward him, and his heart turned over in his chest as he realized her hair was wet. And the plain white shirt she had on had come from a drawer in his bedroom. She reached beside him and set her glass on the railing, and he caught the scent of his shampoo in her hair.

His heart turned over again.

"Hi," she whispered, and smiled up at him.

"Hi."

CHAPTER SIXTEEN

This was the hard part. She'd made a play for what she wanted. And now she held her breath, waiting for his reaction, figuring it could go either way.

He wanted her. Or at least he had at the bar. But he was in a dark mood tonight, and she was fairly certain that while she'd been steaming away her aches and pains in his shower, he'd been gearing up for a lecture on the dangers of her job.

Which was *not* something she wanted to listen to at the moment.

She eased closer, brushing her thighs against his and settling her hands at his waist. Little shivers of anticipation danced over her skin.

"What are you thinking?" she whispered.

"You're wearing my shirt."

She pressed her weight into him, and his hands curved around her butt. She felt the exact moment when he realized she had on nothing at all beneath the thin, soft cotton.

"What are you thinking now?" she whispered, and his grip tightened.

He dipped his head down and kissed her. It was hungry, demanding. Possessive, even, in a way she hadn't expected. And she was hungry, too. She'd been lusting after this man for months, and every nerve in her body was alive with the prospect of spending the next few hours naked with him. She couldn't wait. She couldn't wait another minute to discover what it was like to be with Nathan Devereaux.

Especially when he kissed her like this, like he was impatient and needy and every bit as eager as she was. His hands slipped under the shirt and pulled her close, and one of his thick, strong thighs eased between hers. The denim against her skin was like an electric shock, and she gave a little moan.

And then his hands found her waist, and the cool night air touched her skin as his thumbs stroked over her rib cage. She nestled closer, and he made a low sound of approval as his mouth moved along her jaw to the space beneath her ear.

A whoop of laughter made her jerk back and whip her head around to find the source of the noise. His neighbors. She heard a loud splash, followed by another.

She looked up at Nathan in the dark. "Pool party?"

He muttered a curse, and she slid her hands up into his hair and brought his head down for another kiss. She loved his hair, his mouth. She loved the way he kissed. She loved his hands on her skin, his big, warm palms pulling her against him.

Another splash next door.

"We need to get you inside," he said into her ear.

But she liked it out here, and she had the urge to just slip the shirt over her head and see what he'd do.

His hands slid out from under the shirt and moved up to clasp her wrists. "Come on."

And then he pulled her behind him across the deck. She glanced at the Weber and noticed the glowing mound of briquettes.

"What about the coals?" she asked him.

"Fuck the coals."

He tugged her over the threshold, into the laundry room, and kicked the door shut. He led her through the kitchen, then the darkened living room toward the hallway that led to the bedroom.

That he'd shared with someone else, years ago.

She didn't mind, really. But this first time . . . She wanted it to be just theirs. It was silly and sentimental, but she couldn't help it. She pulled him to a stop just beside the fireplace.

"What?" he asked, his voice husky.

"Here."

He glanced around. "On the floor?"

And she smiled at his tone—surprised, but not unwilling.

"The chair," she said, and steered him into a big leather armchair that creaked under his weight when he sank down. The chair was wide and masculine, and she could picture him sitting in it, drinking beer and watching baseball. It turned her on much, much more than some bed he'd shared with another woman.

He gazed up at her, and even in the dim light from the kitchen she could see the heat in his eyes. "Always calling the shots."

"Yep," she said, watching the heat flare again as she knelt in front of him. He wore leather work boots, and she pulled off one. Then the other. Then she pulled off his socks and tossed them away. He reached out and cupped her face in his hand. She kissed his palm, and his eyes darkened some more.

Then she stood up and settled onto his lap. She wrapped her arms around his neck and kissed his jaw, right below his ear where he was scratchy with stubble. He smelled like the grill and, very faintly, like aftershave. She nuzzled closer.

His hands were on her hips again, and he adjusted them until she was nestled right on top of the rock-hard bulge in his jeans.

"You've been in my shower," he said, trailing kisses down her throat.

"Hmm . . . How did you know?"

His hands slid around and up, to cup her breasts. "I'm a detective." He brushed his thumbs over her nipples, and she arched into him. His mouth trailed lower. She sighed happily as she felt the warmth of his mouth on her breast through the thin fabric. He sucked her, hard, and she squirmed in his lap as the warm ache spread everywhere.

He felt *so* good. Everything about him. But he was wearing entirely too many clothes and she wanted to feel his skin under her hands, so she tugged his T-shirt free from his jeans and pulled it up. He lifted his arms to help her, and by the time his shirt hit the floor, she was already bent over, kissing and nipping at his collarbone.

"I love your chest," she said.

His hands found her breasts again. "I love yours, too."

And she smiled because he sounded so earnest, even though she didn't have the kind of breasts men lusted over.

At least not usually. This man was doing a pretty good job. And she wasn't even naked yet.

He seemed to notice that, too, and he caught the hem of her shirt. She lifted her arms over her head and yelped when pain shot through her shoulder.

He froze. "What?"

"Nothing." She lowered her arms and rolled her shoulder. "Just a little sore."

He looked at her for a long moment, and she knew he was going to try to put on the brakes.

"Are you up for this?"

"Yes," she said, and eased her elbow through the armhole.

He flattened his hands on the chair arms and watched her, as if he were afraid to touch her now, and she could feel the passionate mood slipping away. She got the shirt over her head and tossed it away.

"See? I'm fine."

He looked into her eyes, still wary, and she shifted on his lap to remind him where they were. His gaze dropped to her body. Slowly, his hands moved to circle her waist, and she suddenly felt totally exposed. Which she was. His hands glided up her body to curve around her face and comb into her hair.

Gently, he pulled her face to his and kissed her mouth, her chin, her throat. And then the mood was back, only different now, because he was going slower, taking his time. His warm palms settled on her thighs and kneaded them softly as he kissed the side of her neck and she shivered. She tipped her head back and closed her eyes, letting the moment wrap around her, letting everything disappear, all the stress and fear and anxiety of the past few weeks. It all went away except him and his hands and his mouth on her body and the way he knew just how to make her quiver.

"You're beautiful," he said, and she opened her eyes and saw that he was watching her while he touched her.

She felt self-conscious now, so she turned the attention on him, kissing him deeply. She reached for his belt, and he stretched his legs out and leaned back to give her better access. Her fingers trembled as she worked at the buckle. She glanced at his face, to see if he'd noticed, but she couldn't tell. Finally, she got the belt undone and then the snap. She took her time pulling down the zipper. Then he wrapped a strong arm around her waist and kept her from falling backward as he leaned against the chair arm and dug something out of his back pocket.

She sat up on her knees and busied herself kissing his jaw, his neck, his shoulders. His wallet thudded to the ground, and she caught the glint of a foil packet in his hand.

She kissed him. And kissed him. And kissed him again, all the while waiting for the bittersweet pain she knew was coming as he lifted her hips and lowered her onto him.

Her breath caught. She wrapped her arms around his neck.

"Alex?" His voice was tight.

"I'm okay," she said, and kissed him to shut him up. He seemed to believe her because he moved beneath her, rocking into her, as she moved against him, trying to get as close as she possibly could.

And then it was all good, only good, only pleasure, as

they moved together in a blissful rhythm, his hands stroking up her back, then down again. They were together, completely, and with that wonderful friction, she felt the knot of loneliness deep inside her start to come loose. His solid arms wrapped around her, and the urgency was back, along with the impatient, insatiable hunger of that first kiss in the parking lot at Eli's, when he'd seemed to want to swallow her whole. And she closed her eyes and felt the hardness of his mouth against hers, the rasp of his beard, the broad wall of his chest against her breasts as she moved against him and against him and against him. And then his hands were gripping her, moving her, pulling her closer and closer and he called her name again, like a plea, as she shattered and broke apart.

His muscles went rigid, and she held on to the moment as long as she could before she slumped against him and buried her face against his neck.

A minute drifted by. Then another. She rested her head on his shoulder and her palm on his damp chest. She felt his heartbeat under her fingers and loved knowing she'd made it pound like that. His hands stroked up her back and tangled into her hair. He pulled her head back gently and blinked at her with a heavy-lidded gaze.

"Wow," he said.

She smiled.

"I mean it. Where you been keeping all that?"

She kissed his chin, then settled her head on his shoulder again. His arms wrapped around her, and for a while they just sat there, listening to the faint sound of country music next door. Alex closed her eyes and sighed.

He hadn't been holding out on her. He'd told her about dragging the lake. And the knowledge that she could trust him banished the very last of her reservations. She'd completely let her guard down, but now it was time to rebuild it, at least a little. He'd have questions. He didn't miss a thing. And certain details he'd let go earlier, while she was licking her wounds in his bathroom, were going to come back again. He kissed the top of her head, and she felt a rush of regret for all the lying she planned to do.

He didn't say anything as she disentangled herself from him and slid out of his lap. Her knees ached as she stood up and turned around, searching for her shirt. She pulled it over her head and felt his strong arms wrap around her from behind.

"How's the shoulder?" he asked.

"Fine."

"Good. Let's go." And then he caught her hand in his and pulled her toward the bedroom.

"You can't be serious."

"As a heart attack."

"But . . ." she tried to think of a reasonable protest as he towed her down the hallway. "Don't you need a break?"

He halted in the doorway, and before she knew it, he'd scooped her off her feet. She squealed in surprise.

"You're gonna pay for that," he said, and dropped her right onto her bare butt on the bed. Then he sank down next to her, and she rolled into him, laughing.

"I doubt it," she said.

He made a low growl and pinned her beneath him, planting his hands on either side of her head to hold his weight up so he wouldn't crush her, and her heart melted a little because she knew he was still being careful of her shoulder.

"You picking a fight?"

"Yeah." She smiled up at him and hooked her leg around his.

"Good," he said gruffly, and dropped a quick kiss on her lips. And then the lightness of the moment faded as he gazed down at her. She gave in to the urge to reach up and slide her fingers into his hair as she studied his face in the dimness. He was a good man. She didn't want to ruin whatever this was by lying to him. But it was his goodness that was going to stand in her way.

He kissed her again, harder this time, deeper, and that ache of desire started to build again. She wrapped herself around him and pushed tomorrow out of her mind as he made good on his promise to make her pay.

"Remind me never to shower with you again."

Alex turned and glowered at him from beneath a head full of suds. "I was here first!"

"Yeah, well, you've been in here forever. You think you might want to be a little more generous with the hot water?"

She turned around and tipped her head back, giving him a truly amazing view as she rinsed her hair.

"Ladies first," she said, and opened one eye to look at him. "Hey, don't stare at me like that."

"Like what?"

She turned her back on him, feigning modesty. "Like I'm an exhibit in a zoo or something."

He lathered his hands with soap and stroked them over her shoulders, then down her back and over her hips. He couldn't get enough of all those soft, subtle curves. "It's my shower. I'm allowed to stare as much as I want."

She scooped her hair into a ponytail and squeezed the water out. Then she swept the curtain aside, but he caught her around the waist.

"Not so fast."

"It's all yours," she said over her shoulder. "I'm finished."

"Yeah, well, I'm not." He pulled her against him and kissed her neck.

"I thought you said we were running late." She turned in his arms and stroked her hands up into his hair again. She seemed to like his hair for some reason, and he took advantage of her distraction by shifting her back against the tile wall and kissing her neck some more.

"That's if we stop for breakfast," he said, and skimmed a hand over her stomach to rest at the top of her thigh, just to taunt her. "I'm happy to skip the diner, spend some time here."

She let him slide his hands over her hot, slick skin, and after a few minutes, he wasn't the only one willing to sacrifice food and caffeine. She closed her eyes and made one of those little noises that drove him crazy.

"Come on," he whispered in her ear, and she clutched her arms around him. He kissed her mouth, her throat.

She jerked back suddenly. "Did you hear that?"

"No." He kissed her again, but she pulled away.

"Stop, I'm serious. I heard a voice."

A voice.

Nathan reached over and twisted off the water. He strained to listen, but didn't hear anything.

Still, his gut was filling with dread. "Where'd you park?" he asked her.

She blinked up at him. "Down the street. Why?"

Shit.

He swept the curtain aside and jerked a towel off the rack.

"What?" she asked. "Your neighbor was having a party, so—"

"Stay here," he said, and shoved a towel into her hands.

Her brow furrowed, and he realized he'd scared her.

"It's probably nothing," he said. "Just wait in the bedroom, okay?"

Nathan grabbed a towel for himself and slung it around his neck before snatching his jeans up off the floor beside the bed. He jerked the bedroom door shut behind him, just as heels clicked across the marble foyer.

He rounded the corner and nearly bumped into Nicole.

"Morning." She rose up on tiptoes to kiss him, then backed up to look at his wet chest. "You're running late today."

"You should have called."

She rolled her eyes. "Stop bitching. I brought you breakfast."

He took her elbow and steered her back toward the kitchen. "You should have called, Nikki."

He got her all the way to the kitchen before she shook his arm off and gaped up at him. "Oh my God. Are you *with* someone?"

"Yes."

He saw her jaw tighten. Her gaze darted to the living

room behind him, and he hoped like hell Alex wasn't standing there in the hallway watching this conversation. He walked into the laundry room and tossed his towel on the washer, then grabbed a dirty T-shirt from the basket on the floor and yanked it over his head.

"I apologize," Nicole said when he turned around. Her voice was cool, but her eyes were fiery. "You're right, I should have called."

She wore a tailored black suit and heels, which meant she probably planned to be in court later. He noticed the cardboard coffee cups on the table, and felt a pang of guilt. Goddamn it, he never should have kissed her good night at the hotel. This was his fault for putting his tongue in her mouth and thinking she wouldn't take it as some big signal that their on-again, off-again sexual relationship was back on.

"Nicole—"

"Forget it." She picked up her stylish black handbag and strode out the back door, yanking it shut behind her.

Nathan turned around to see Alex walking into the living room. She wore jeans, sneakers, and the T-shirt she'd shown up in yesterday. Damp curls fell around her shoulders.

She didn't look at him as she pulled a key from her back pocket and they pretended not to hear Nicole's BMW backing out of the driveway.

"Want to take your car?" he asked.

She gave him a blank look, and he knew breakfast was off.

"That was my ex-wife. Nicole."

She held up a hand. "Not my business. I've got to get going, so—"

"Don't do that."

"Do what?"

"Act like you don't care."

She crossed her arms. "Why should I care? Your ex-wife stopped by your house. So what?"

"Okay." He searched her face for some kind of emotional reaction. He didn't find one. Maybe she really *didn't* care. Maybe she was the first woman he'd ever known who didn't have a jealous bone in her body.

But then her gaze settled on the coffee cups, and her eyes sparked.

"I've got to go." She turned and headed for the front door, and he followed her.

"I'll call you later."

"I've got a busy day," she said over her shoulder.

"I'll call you tomorrow, then."

She flipped the bolt and walked out. "Tomorrow's busy, too."

"Tomorrow's Saturday." He followed her down the sidewalk. Where the hell had she parked? The street must have been packed last night.

But she was done making excuses. She walked right up to the Monte Carlo red Ford Sunliner parked across the street. It was long and shiny and, with its distinctive body style, a hundred times cooler than his Mustang. She shoved a key into the door.

"Where's your Saturn?" he asked, stunned.

"In the shop." She jerked open the door with a squeak and slid behind the wheel. Original upholstery, too.

"Isn't this your landlady's?"

"It's mine."

In the back of his brain, he heard the faint crack of a whip. He could fall hard for this girl.

If she ever spoke to him again.

He leaned an arm on the window while she shot him an annoyed look.

"Look, I'm sorry, all right? She doesn't usually drop by like that."

"Not my business."

"Yeah, it kind of is your business. We were in the middle of making love."

She glared up at him, and he could tell she didn't like his terminology. Jesus. She was determined to belittle it as much as possible.

"I *will* call you," he said, getting pissed now.

"Fine." She pulled at the door, but he braced his hand against it.

"This is the last time I'm going to say it, Alex. I apologize."

"Drop it," she said. "Now do you mind? I need to get to work."

CHAPTER SEVENTEEN

Alex was late, and she was counting on a trayful of grande lattes to smooth things over. She could have been here sooner, but she'd needed some time to collect herself before she could walk into her office and pull off some semblance of normal.

But nothing was normal. Even a change of clothes and a second shower with her own, non-Nathan-scented shampoo had done nothing to ease the knot in her stomach.

Alex took a deep breath and shook it off. It didn't matter. She hated relationships. And if she made room for one in her life right now, she'd have to deal with the void when it went away.

Alex strode up to the door of her business and tapped her knuckles on the glass. Sophie emerged from behind Alex's closed office door, and her face brightened when she spotted the cardboard tray.

"Oh my God, you read my mind."

Alex stepped into the office and handed Sophie a cup. From behind the closed door, she heard the murmur of female voices.

"Courtney's here already?"

"She's been here almost an hour," Sophie said. "And she's incredible. I'm going to have to hire her before my next round of head shots."

Alex crossed the reception room. "Draw those miniblinds, would you?" she asked over her shoulder. *You never know who might come knocking.*

She should have been prepared for the scene inside her office, but she wasn't. And Sophie was right. Courtney *was* incredible.

"Wow," Alex said. Behind her desk, in the big leather swivel chair, was a completely transformed Melanie Bess.

Courtney shot Alex a look. "You're late."

"I stopped by Starbucks." She set the tray of drinks on the desk.

"You're forgiven."

Which wasn't exactly surprising. Besides being a personal friend, the tall, auburn-haired stylist was one of Alex's former clients. She belonged to a subset Nathan had labeled "basket-case women," although she no longer fit that description, thanks in part to Alex. Courtney had turned her life around and recently managed to land a job at Austin's hippest salon.

Alex fixed her gaze on Courtney's latest masterpiece. "*How* did you do that?"

Melanie cast a sheepish look in Alex's direction. "You like it?"

"Yes." She stepped around the desk for a better view. Gone was the pasty skin, the dark circles. And yet— thanks to Courtney's skill—she didn't have that base-face look that Alex despised. Also gone was the choppy black hair, replaced with a light brown pixie cut that seemed completely natural. And unnoticeable, which was the entire point. Melanie needed to blend in with the crowd, not stand out. And—unbeknownst to Courtney, Sophie, and Melanie herself—she was having a new passport photo taken this morning.

"We made a mess of your bathroom," Courtney said, applying coral lip liner to Melanie's mouth. "But nothing a little Lysol won't take care of."

"I'll do it," Sophie said.

"What did you do to her eyes?" Alex leaned in for a closer look.

"White eye pencil," Courtney said. "On the inner rims. That combined with the eyelash curler really wakes her up. Makes her look younger. My older clients love it."

Alex filed it away. She hardly ever wore makeup. But her mother had told her that might change, right along with her metabolism, when she hit thirty.

"Did you notice the eyebrows?" Sophie propped a hip on the desk and sipped her coffee.

"Yeah, something's different."

"I altered the shape," Courtney explained. "Gives her face a different look. Subtle, but effective."

Alex nodded her approval.

Courtney finished off the face with some light brown blush, accentuating Melanie's cheekbones and further reinforcing the new look. She snapped the compact shut and stepped back to admire her efforts. "Not bad."

"It works," Alex agreed.

Melanie smiled nervously as Courtney rummaged through her shiny silver makeup case.

"I almost forgot." Courtney pulled out a circular container of flesh-toned makeup. "Your scars. Here, bend your head down." Courtney stepped around the chair and dabbed makeup over the circular pink burn marks on the back of Melanie's neck. Coghan had put those marks there, according to Melanie. Some sadistic thing he liked to do during sex.

When Courtney was finished, she dropped the concealer into a Ziploc bag that was already filled with makeup.

"This is for you," she said, handing it to Melanie. "Just remember everything I showed you."

"Thanks." Melanie glanced worriedly at the bag in her hands. "Um . . . how much do I owe you for all this?"

"It's on me." Courtney latched shut her makeup case and looked at her watch. She turned to Alex. "I've got to run."

"Are you sure?" Melanie cast a tentative look at Alex, and Alex knew she was thinking about her outstanding bill with Lovell Solutions.

"It's okay," Courtney said, grabbing her kit, her coffee, and her keys. "I owe Alex a few favors."

"Speaking of favors." Alex cleared her throat. "It would be really helpful if you wouldn't mention to Will—"

"I was never here," Courtney said. And Alex breathed a sigh of relief because, in addition to being a former client, Courtney also happened to be married to Nathan's partner.

Courtney turned to Melanie. "You watch out for yourself, all right? And if you want to make this work, take my advice and do whatever Alex tells you."

Alex smiled slightly, remembering how Courtney had had very little luck following that advice herself.

"I will," Melanie promised.

And Alex hoped to hell that, this time, she meant it.

As strange as it was, sometimes Nathan just couldn't look at a dead body on an empty stomach.

"Fuckin' bad way to go," Webb said, and turned to spit on the pavement.

Nathan glanced up at him from where he was crouched near the corpse. "Hey, you wanna take that shit over there? Away from the crime scene?"

Webb fixed him with another hard stare and swished his chaw around.

Nathan stood up and stepped over a puddle of what looked like urine. He crouched down again and took a closer look at the vic's face. Mid-twenties. Hispanic. And with a bloody wound around his neck that reminded Nathan of the victim they'd pulled out of Lake Austin just a few weeks ago. Baling wire, the ME had concluded. But it was all conjecture because, as with this guy, the killer had taken the murder weapon with him when he'd split the scene.

A line of ants marched from the gaping neck wound all the way up the victim's throat and into his nose and mouth. Nathan's stomach twisted. He wished he'd managed to get more than a few sips of coffee into his system before heading over here.

He'd been called out not long after Alex had left, and he'd spent the entire drive over reviewing last night in his head. It occurred to him now—probably because she wasn't around to distract him with sex—that she'd been acting funny when she'd first shown up. She'd been in a great mood. Tired, but cheerful. Then she'd gotten emotional when he told her the rumor he'd heard about Melanie. And then—strangest of all—she'd seemed happy again. Happy enough to want to spend the night with him.

Her behavior was puzzling, now that he thought about it. And Nathan had never been one to leave a puzzle alone. Something weird was going on, something he felt certain had to do with Melanie's case. He needed to figure out what it was.

A gust of air whipped through the alley, stirring up the putrid smell of death and piss and garbage. Nathan glanced around the vicinity, looking for something he might have missed when he'd first walked up.

"What did the club owner say?" he asked Webb, who had arrived right after the patrol officer.

"Not much. Just that there was a stiff in the alley when he was leaving the place about six twenty this morning. Cocktail waitress inside claims she served the guy a Miller Lite at one thirty, then he skipped his check."

"You tracked down the waitress already?"

"Wasn't hard. She was working overtime in the club, if you know what I mean." Webb leaned against the brick wall on the opposite side of the alley they were standing in. Nathan didn't bother telling him to quit touching shit within the crime scene perimeter. Webb was two years from retirement and made no effort to hide his contempt for all the rules and regulations that had come along with the flashy new forensics available now. Nathan would have taken Will Hodges over Webb any day of the week, but the kid was out sick today, puking his guts up with some stomach bug.

"She's a hooker?" Nathan asked, skimming his gaze

over the victim's skin for any body art. The victim had a black sun tattooed on his right hand, but that was the only thing visible at the moment. Nathan didn't plan to touch anything, even the guy's wallet, until the ME showed up.

"Just a guess." Webb waggled his eyebrows. "She looked dressed to party. Said they had some after-hours thing going on inside the bar last night. A 'private event,' she called it."

Nathan stood up and glanced around. About two feet from the body was a half-empty bottle of Miller.

"What's the plumbing situation inside?" Nathan asked.

"The what?"

"Maybe the john's broken?"

"Hell if I know." Webb turned and spit again. "Ask Angel." He grinned. "That's her name. Angel. You believe that?"

"She a dancer here?"

"Nah, supposedly she's just a waitress. But my guess is they're all working. Probably she knows a lot more about this guy than she's saying. Claims she doesn't even know his name." Webb stepped closer now and frowned down at the victim. "So how do you think it went down?"

"Looks to me like he came out here to take a leak, set his beer there by the Dumpster. Could be the restroom was full, maybe a couple in there or something."

"Wouldn't doubt it."

"Guy comes up from behind, wraps the wire around his neck. Creates that blood spatter there on the wall."

"He'd have to be pretty strong," Webb observed,

squinting at the corpse. "This kid's got to be five-ten, one-ninety. Looks like he works out, too."

"Yeah."

"Tell you what, this reminds me of that one off Highway 71. What was that strip joint they used to have out there?" Webb rubbed his jaw. "Shit, what was it called?"

"I don't know."

"Damn, what was that place? They had three-dollar steaks. This was back five years ago. But still."

Nathan glanced over his shoulder as the crime scene unit rolled to a stop at the end of the alley. "I was in Houston then," he reminded Webb.

"Ah, that's right. Anyways, it was like this. Guy gets it right behind a titty bar. Wire around the neck. Same thing."

"What happened?" Nathan asked, suddenly feeling a renewed sense of appreciation for some of the dead weight in his department.

"I don't remember."

Or maybe not. "You remember a name? A suspect? Anything?"

"Naughty's. That was the place."

"You guys make an arrest?"

"Don't think so," Webb said. "I remember this, though. When we bagged the vic, he still had that wire wrapped around his neck. Messy as shit job. If it's the same guy as now, he's cleaned up his act."

"What happened to the wire?"

"Who knows? Probably still sitting in the evidence room."

* * *

The Honorable Judge Gordon Mueller liked punctual lawyers, polite defendants, and short closing arguments. He didn't tolerate tracksuits in his courtroom, and he had a standing 10:30 A.M. appointment with a pack of Winston Selects.

It was 10:31. Like clockwork, the doors to Mueller's courtroom pushed open, and a stream of people filed out for a fifteen-minute break from the State of Texas versus Luis J. Perez.

The prosecution's star witness slipped through the doors and headed for the men's room. Nathan followed.

"Hey, Craig."

Coghan turned around, and his surprise quickly turned to suspicion.

"Got a minute?" Nathan asked amiably, and nodded at the nearby side door. Without waiting for a response, Nathan walked through the door, just beyond the knot of reporters and bureaucrats milling beside a giant ashtray. He stopped at an empty bench and propped his shoe on it.

"Hey, what's up, Devereaux?" Coghan frowned at his watch as Nathan bent to tie his shoelace. "I'm supposed to be in court."

"This won't take long." Nathan straightened and gave the man a once-over. Shit, he hadn't been this close to Coghan in a while. He'd been bulking up. "How's married life?"

Coghan scowled.

"Yeah, that's what I heard."

"What the fuck does that mean?"

"Looks like we have a mutual friend." Nathan rested

his hands on his hips. "Alex Lovell? She runs a PI shop here in town."

Coghan's expression hardened.

"She showed up at my house last night, big old bruise on her face." Nathan stepped closer. "You wouldn't know anything about that, would you?"

Coghan's shoulders tensed as Nathan got right up in his grill.

"Like I said, Alex is a friend of mine," Nathan said quietly. "You go near her again, I'll fucking kill you."

"Hey, go fuck yourself, Devereaux."

Nathan shoved Coghan in the chest with both hands. He tripped backward a few feet, then lunged forward and landed a hammer-sharp blow to Nathan's jaw. Gasps and yelps went up from the smokers.

Nathan staggered back, stunned by the pain. Then he launched himself at Coghan's gut, and they crashed to the ground. Nathan jabbed him in the nose once, twice, three times. With the third hit came the satisfying crunch of bone, and Nathan jumped to his feet. Coghan sat up and made a grab with both arms, but Nathan evaded him.

Coghan scrambled to his feet just as a few guys in jeans and ties closed in. Reporters, judging by the press passes hanging from their necks. One hoisted a news camera onto his shoulder.

Coghan surged forward, then noticed the audience. He squinted at Nathan with hatred in his eyes. "You're going to regret that."

"Watch out, Coghan." Nathan swished the blood in his mouth and spit on the pavement. "You don't want to be grabbing any headlines."

Nathan turned his back on him and walked away.

* * *

"What do you mean she's not there?" Alex demanded. "I just talked to her an hour ago."

Sophie darted a glance at the phone number she'd written on her notepad. She'd dialed correctly.

"Well, maybe she's *there,*" she told Alex. "But she's not answering."

Alex jerked her cell phone from her back pocket and started dialing, glancing over at the message pad to check what Sophie had written down. She waited and waited, but evidently Melanie wasn't picking up for Alex, either.

"God*damn* it!" Alex said, disconnecting the call. "I swear to God—"

"You think she took off?" Sophie asked, earning a death scowl.

Alex tried the number once again, while Sophie refrained from pointing out that it probably *wasn't* such a good idea to lend Melanie her car.

But Alex must have known that already, or she would have lent her the rental car, which was parked right outside Lovell Solutions.

"She wouldn't just take off," Alex muttered, almost to herself. "She *couldn't*."

"Why couldn't she?"

Alex glanced up, and seemed to realize what she'd said.

Sophie watched her expectantly. She'd figured out quickly that if she wanted to learn this business, she had to ask questions. Sometimes Alex blew her off. But sometimes she let her in on things, like she had with regard to Melanie.

Obviously, though, there were some things she'd left out.

"Why couldn't she just leave?" Sophie asked again. "I mean, she's done it before. You showed her how."

"This time's different," Alex said. "I have stuff she needs. She was supposed to *meet* me in La Grange to get it before she went anywhere."

La Grange, Sophie understood. Alex knew a motel owner in the nearby town who had agreed to put up Melanie—for free—without filling out any paperwork on her. From what Sophie had gathered, the motel owner was a business acquaintance of Alex's. What Sophie *hadn't* gathered was what the "stuff" was that Melanie needed from Alex. Besides the obvious: cash.

But Sophie was beginning to get some ideas.

She crossed her arms. "I thought you told me fake identities didn't work."

Alex glanced up from her phone. She'd been scrolling through e-mail messages, probably looking for something from Melanie.

"They don't," Alex said. "Usually."

Sophie frowned. Alex had told her she didn't buy fake IDs for her clients who wanted to disappear. She'd explained that you never knew what you were buying. You could be buying the identity of someone with major credit problems. Or a criminal history. Or worse, an outstanding arrest warrant. The best way to disappear, Alex had told her, was to erase all possible tracks—digitally speaking, of course. Then to leave false tracks—again, using computers. And finally, to create a new life for yourself well under the radar. Which, Alex had told her, was precisely what she'd helped Melanie do the first time.

This time appeared to be different.

"Are you helping her leave the country?" Sophie asked.

Alex halted, mid–text message, to give her a warning look. "Stop asking questions," she said. "The less you know about this case, the better."

Sophie watched her boss, getting worried now.

Alex had said fake passports were worst of all. Customs and Border Protection had become quite adept at sniffing out forgeries. And who wanted to leave the country with the knowledge that they might not have a way back in?

Melanie must be in some serious trouble. With some seriously dangerous people.

Sophie glanced at the clock, then stood up to gather her purse and the rental car keys. The plan was to return the car by two, to avoid getting charged for another day.

"We need to leave," Sophie told Alex, and she finally put her phone away.

Alex followed her out of the office and paused to set the alarm. Sophie took one look at the car rolling to a stop behind the Mercury and knew they were never going to make the two o'clock deadline.

Nathan Devereaux shoved open the door of some awful-looking gray sedan. Even Sophie could tell it was an unmarked police vehicle; it might as well have had a sign on the door.

And the detective looked worse than his car. The shiner was gone, but now he had a swollen violet bruise on his chin.

He nodded at Sophie.

"Hi," Sophie greeted him. "You get in a fight?"

His gaze settled on Alex. "Bumped into a wall. Where you ladies headed?"

"We have an errand."

Sophie glanced over, startled by Alex's curt tone. She'd never seen these two together, but she'd thought they were friendly. Evidently not.

Nathan leaned back against the side of the Taurus and crossed his ankles, clearly signaling his intention to hang around a while until Alex gave him the time of day.

"I'm on my way to the Delphi Center," he said. "Thought you might want to come."

Alex folded her arms over her chest and watched him a moment. She bent her head slightly and looked at something inside his car. Sophie followed her gaze and saw two brown paper bags sitting on the passenger seat.

"What's in the bags?" Alex asked.

"Not much."

"You want me to come with you, but you won't tell me what you have?"

"I'll fill you in on the way there."

"Sorry, can't do it. I've got a full afternoon."

"All right." Nathan crossed his arms, mirroring Alex. "Let's try this another way. Where's your Saturn?"

Sophie's gaze snapped to Alex, but her boss's expression gave nothing away.

"I told you," she said. "In the shop."

"Uh-huh."

"Look, just tell me what's going on. What'd you get?"

"Ride down with me, I'll tell you all about it."

Alex rolled her eyes. "You're being childish."

"*I'm* being childish." He shook his head. "You're the one playing games here. I thought this was a joint effort."

She scoffed at him.

"Come with me to the lab. We'll get on the same page with this thing. I could use your input."

"My input?" This ticked Alex off for some reason. "Since when do you want my input? You just want to babysit me. Forget it. I've got things to do." Alex stepped toward Sophie and the Mercury, but Nathan blocked her path.

"That girl's bad news, Alex."

"I need to go." She stepped around him and held out her hand to Sophie. "Keys."

Sophie gave her the car keys. She would be driving her Tahoe, and Alex would drive the rental car. Sophie dug through her purse, pretending not to notice the way Nathan had taken Alex's arm and turned her around to face him.

"Please listen to me." His voice was low and urgent now. Sophie would have had an impossible time refusing him. "You need to let this go. She's on her own now."

"I can't do that."

"Alex, I mean it. You're gonna get hurt."

"If the guards give you any trouble, just drop Mia's name. Or Troy Stockton's. He's on their board. I'll put in a call to him—"

"I don't want you to put in a *call*," he said. "I want you to forget whatever shit you're up to and let Melanie take care of herself for a change."

Alex slid into the Mercury and slammed the door.

Sophie climbed into the Tahoe. She'd barely pulled into traffic when her cell phone sang out.

"Did you tell him about Melanie?" Alex demanded.

"No. Maybe he figured it out for himself. He *is* a detective."

Alex cursed.

"Do you really know Troy Stockton?" Sophie couldn't resist asking.

"Huh?"

"Troy Stockton? The author?"

"Oh. Yeah. He's a friend of mine."

"He looks like Brad Pitt."

"Tell me about it," Alex said, as Sophie navigated the Friday lunch traffic. "Oh, crap."

"What?"

"I just got an e-mail from Melanie," Alex said. "She's giving me a number where I can reach her tonight. . . . *Dammit!*"

"What?"

"It's a five-oh-four area code. Where is that?"

"I don't know."

"Five-oh-four. Is that Dallas?" she asked hopefully.

"No."

"Dammit, I knew this was going to happen. She's gone and changed the plan. What is she *thinking*?"

"I don't know."

"If I ever see her again, I swear I'm going to kill her myself."

CHAPTER EIGHTEEN

Nathan didn't know all that many lab rats, but the ones he did know were nothing like Mia Voss. He kept glancing at the name embroidered on her lab coat to remind himself she was an actual doctor.

"So you're trying to build a forensic triad?" she asked, eyeing the paper bags Nathan had lined up on the table beside her microscopes.

"Not exactly." A forensic triad would be evidence that linked a victim to a crime scene to a suspect. "This case is a little more complicated than that, unfortunately."

She tucked her hands into her coat pockets and watched him expectantly.

"The blood on the handkerchief, that's my suspect," he said. "I need you to come up with a profile."

"When was the sample collected?"

"This morning. My DNA's probably mixed in, too, by the way."

Her eyebrows arched.

"Guess you'd say I collected the sample surreptitiously."

"In that case, you can give me a buccal swab for exclusionary purposes." She stepped closer to read the label on the second bag. She donned a pair of eye shields and pulled some latex gloves from the box on the counter. "This one's a wire? I'm not a ligature expert. We've got someone who is, though."

"I'm mostly interested in the DNA," Nathan said, as she unsealed the bag and carefully lifted out a thick length of wire. It was bent and twisted at the ends, and the middle was coated with dried blood. "I'm assuming the blood belongs to the victim," he said. "What I want to know is, can you get anything else off this thing? Maybe some skin cells, or even traces of blood, from when the killer pulled the wire around the victim's neck."

She examined it critically. "It probably depends on whether he wore gloves. If he didn't, I can most likely get something. Ligature strangulation requires some force. How old is this evidence?"

"Five years."

She sighed. "Well, that's good and bad. The good part, five years ago, we didn't have such a problem with the CSI effect. Criminals didn't used to be so knowledge-able about gloves and condoms and leaving behind trace evidence." She carefully tucked the wire back into the bag. "The bad news is, things deteriorate over time. I'll do the best I can."

Nathan nodded respectfully. Mia knew her stuff. He'd bet she did well in front of a jury, too. She was the antithesis of the nerdy, long-winded scientists he'd seen bore jurors to tears during murder trials. The girl-next-door look probably made her seem trustworthy.

"And what's in the little sack?" she asked.

"Scones."

"Scones?" Her face brightened.

"Chocolate almond. From the coffee shop downstairs. Just wanted to thank you for squeezing me in like this on a Friday afternoon."

"I love chocolate almond scones."

"That's what I hear."

Ten minutes later, Nathan eased his dinged Taurus through the Delphi Center's electronic gate. His phone went off, and he dug it out of his pocket. APD. This would be his lieutenant calling to ream him out.

"Hey, Dev," the caller said, and Nathan recognized the voice of Garza over in Auto Theft. "I got a hit on that Blazer. The one you put on our hot list."

"You're kidding." Nathan had been sure the vehicle was a dead end when he'd gone up to Greene's Automotive and found out the Blazer had been "stolen" the day after it arrived for repairs.

"A sheriff's deputy spotted it up in Killeen," Garza continued. "It's at a salvage yard up there. I've got the info here, if you want to take a look."

"Thanks," he said. "Just give it to Hodges, would you? I'm still in San Marcos."

"He's out sick today."

"Shit, I forgot."

"Yeah, everybody's out. First Hodges. Now Webb and Coghan."

"Coghan's sick?"

"Nah, Webb and Hodges are sick. Coghan had some family emergency. Took off about an hour ago."

The back of Nathan's neck prickled. "Where'd he go?"

"I don't know, man." Garza chuckled. "Maybe he went to go get his nose fixed. Heard you belted him pretty good over at the courthouse. What was that about, anyway?"

"Nothing. Hey, just leave that info on my desk, okay?"

Nathan dialed Alex, but she didn't pick up. He tried her work number and got Sophie.

"She's not here," the woman said cheerfully.

"When do you expect her in?"

"I don't know. Maybe Monday? I think she's gone for the weekend."

"Gone where?"

She paused for an instant, but it was enough.

"Where is she, Sophie? I need to get ahold of her."

"I don't know," she said, and he pictured her lying through her pretty white teeth. "She just said she'd be gone for a few days—"

"Is she with Melanie?"

"Melanie who?"

Nathan's phone beeped. APD again, damn it. He took the call.

"What's this shit I'm hearing about over at the courthouse, Devereaux?" This time, it was Lieutenant Cernak. "You and Coghan trying to get us on the news? You have any idea how many reporters—"

"Coghan threw the first punch." And yeah, Nathan knew exactly how many reporters had seen it. Three. He just hoped one of them would get curious enough to start sniffing around Coghan.

"I'm warning you, Devereaux, you're on thin ice. I don't need this shit right now—"

"I'm taking a personal day."

"A *what*?"

"A personal day. Or two. I'll be back in on Monday."

"You're supposed to be on all weekend! Hodges is out. Webb's out. I'm fresh out of sympathy passes, so get your ass in here before I suspend it."

The lieutenant hung up, and Nathan cursed. Where was Alex? And what was she doing? He had to find out because he had a strong suspicion Coghan already knew.

He called Sophie again.

"I *told* you," she insisted. "I have no idea where—"

"Cut the crap, Sophie. This is an investigation. Alex is in the middle of it. Now, either you tell me where she is, or I'll have you charged with obstruction of justice."

"You can't do that!"

"Wanna try me?"

A strained silence.

"I can have a search warrant for that office in about five minutes." Another lie.

"I don't *know*, okay?" She sounded shaken now, and he knew the Bad Cop bit had worked. "All I have is a phone number."

"That's it?"

"Not even the number, really. Just the area code. It's five-oh-four."

Nathan frowned. "What's she doing in New Orleans?"

"I have *no* idea," Sophie said. "You're going to have to ask her."

Alex stared through the amazingly wide windshield and wondered when, not if, this boat was going to crap out on her. She hated the Sunliner. She rarely drove it, in fact, but she'd been desperate for a ride to Louisiana, and she needed one that didn't have a GPS on it.

She glanced at the speedometer, which more or less

worked, and estimated her travel time. Four more hours, including a brief stop for gas. Assuming the gas gauge worked. Her dad's parting words when he'd given her the keys to this thing had been, "She drives great. Just keep her topped off."

Alex didn't understand car enthusiasts. She had no idea why people collected these gas-guzzling road hogs. But hey, free car, right? When she'd received the gift on her nineteenth birthday, she'd been broke, jobless, and in no position to complain.

The Sunliner had been with her in Urbana, Chicago, and San Francisco. And even after she'd moved to Austin and been forced to acquire a car with air-conditioning, she'd hung on to the damn thing. Why? She did not know. It took up way too much space and served no clear purpose, but she'd never quite managed to get rid of it.

Alex rolled the window down and got a nice breeze going. She smelled wet dirt and pinesap, which made sense as she was driving through the Piney Woods of east Texas just after a rainstorm. She knew very little about this part of the state and even less about her destination. She thought of everything she knew about Louisiana. Swamps. Alligators. Mardi Gras.

Nathan Devereaux.

She'd kept busy this morning, but for the last several hours she'd had plenty of time to think about last night. She'd replayed every heart-pounding second from the moment she'd stepped onto his deck and his eyes had gone dark with want. She'd relived his mouth on her breast, his hands around her waist, the sharp feel of him pushing into her.

She'd replayed the calmer moments, too—the ones when they'd lain together in the darkness, getting their breath back. She'd loved that part the most. She'd felt like they were sharing their own private cocoon, set apart from the rest of the world.

And then reality waltzed in.

Alex had been too flustered to do more than eavesdrop in the hallway while Nathan talked to his ex. She'd crammed her feet into sneakers and hadn't had the presence of mind to peek her head around the corner and get a look at the woman. She regretted it now. Alex really wished she'd seen her. She had a deep-rooted desire to know what sort of woman Nathan had once decided to spend his life with.

Alex glanced at the phone sitting silently on the seat beside her. She'd switched off the ringtone just west of Houston. She knew why he was calling. She also knew how persuasive he could be, how smooth he was with people. But Alex had no intention of divulging her plans to him, and the best way to avoid even a chance of that happening was to stay off the phone. No interrogation, no confession. And no meddlesome detectives swooping in at the last minute to botch up the plan. At least she hoped not.

The plan was to meet Melanie at her safe spot and help her leave the country before Coghan or anyone working for him got wind of her whereabouts.

Alex cruised down the interstate, through the dense tunnel of trees. Darkness was falling all around her.

WELCOME TO LOUISIANA.

The sign flew past, and Alex wondered again what had prompted Melanie to choose a safe spot in New

Orleans. She could have gone anywhere. All she really needed was a storage unit—preferably a twenty-four-hour-access place—where she could keep important papers and supplies: her birth certificate, her passport, a roll of cash, a list of important phone numbers. Why had she chosen Louisiana, when it would have been so much easier to stash everything in Texas? And what did she need with that stuff anyway, now that Alex was providing her with a counterfeit passport?

Melanie had some scheme brewing, and whatever it was, Alex planned to talk her out of it as soon as she pulled into the All Saints Motel. Because of the motel's location right near the airport, Alex suspected Melanie's scheme involved an international flight. But Alex was going to veto that the moment she saw her. The simplest way to slip into Mexico was by foot or by car, not by plane.

Alex's phone glowed again, and she glanced at the screen. Nathan. The phone went dark on the seat beside her as he left yet another message.

She wouldn't listen to it. She couldn't. He had a way of talking to her and—especially after last night—she knew she was much too vulnerable to him.

Nathan had Baton Rouge in the rearview mirror when his phone finally rang.

But the number wasn't Alex's.

"Devereaux."

"It's Troy Stockton."

Nathan bit back a curse. "Is Alex with you?"

"No, but I talked with her earlier, and I can tell you where to find her if you'll give her a message for me."

Nathan gritted his teeth. Why the hell was Stockton involved? "What's the message?"

"I just heard from the guy I hired to keep an eye on those vacant houses."

"What vacant houses?"

"The ones at Captain's Point," Stockton said. "Alex said she told you about them."

"She did. She just didn't mention they were vacant. I don't like the sound of that."

"Neither did I. My guy's been sitting on them for a week now, and one of them just got a big delivery."

"Of what?" Nathan asked.

"Lamps."

The dread that had been dogging Nathan for days now intensified. "He's setting up grow houses."

"Looks like."

"How many are we talking about?"

"Three," Stockton said. "But those are just the ones we know of."

Nathan gripped the steering wheel as the implications sank in. This operation was much bigger than he ever would have thought.

Cartels had been moving operations north ever since Homeland Security started tightening up the border. Suppliers had begun growing product deep inside state and national parks, and also in homes within urban areas. The mortgage crisis had been a boon to the cartels. Foreclosed homes were the perfect place to hide grows, and if you could get the product right onto the street, you cut out transportation costs and extra middlemen.

But the setup was complicated, which meant people and money. The more people and money involved in this thing, the more danger to Alex and Melanie for knowing about it.

"Here's something else you may want to know," Stockton said. "A friend of mine just called me from the Delphi Center. They identified the trace substance from an envelope Melanie Coghan gave Alex."

"Cocaine?"

"Meth. Along with some dolomite lime, which this guy tells me is commonly used on indoor marijuana grows. Not sure what it's for."

"Stabilizes the pH of the soil."

"Anyway, this sounds like a serious operation," Stockton said, stating the obvious. "Alex has underestimated what she's up against. Someone needs to warn her."

Nathan veered around an eighteen-wheeler. "So where is she?"

"On her way to meet with Melanie at the All Saints Motel out by the Louis Armstrong Airport. That's off I-10."

"I know where the goddamn airport is. Does she think she's going to be able to get Melanie out of the country? That's a bad plan. And it's not going to work."

"I don't know what she's doing, but whatever it is, I tried to talk her out of it. Maybe you'll have more luck."

Doubtful. Nathan's gaze dropped to the speedometer, and he pressed the gas.

"One last thing," Stockton said. "My contact says he's not the only one keeping an eye on those houses. There's some kind of police surveillance. Feds, I'm assuming."

That would be Nathan's guess. Probably the same guys who had been dragging the lake.

Craig Coghan was into some serious shit. This wasn't

just a love triangle—his money, his livelihood, his entire
life was wrapped up in this thing. And when he realized
it was unraveling, he'd probably react like a cornered
animal.

"When you find Alex," Stockton said now, "tell her
to back off this case. She's way out of her league here."

"You should have told her that earlier," Nathan said
bitterly. But of course, Stockton was probably too busy
working on his next book to give a damn. Murder, sex,
greed—this story had everything. "What's your big
interest in this case, anyway?"

"You mean besides Alex? I bet you can figure that
out."

Alex entered the Hyatt feeling tired, cranky, and in no
mood for bullshit. But given the way this trip had gone
so far, she felt certain she was in for some anyway.

She strode up to the reception counter. The clerk there
glanced up, and her perky smile faltered at the sight of
Alex's bruised face.

Alex gave the woman her name. "I'm meeting someone," she added. "She said she'd have a key waiting for
me at the front desk."

"Just a moment, Ms. Lovell." The woman's fingers
tapped over her keyboard. "And may I see some ID,
please?"

Alex dug her driver's license out of her purse and
showed it to the clerk. She typed more stuff into her
computer as Alex dropped her backpack on the floor
beside her feet and looked around.

Marble floors, bronze statues, a coffee kiosk. This
place had to be nicer than the All Saints Motel. And

why Melanie had decided to blow a chunk of her limited funds on a pair of rooms here remained a mystery. But she had insisted. She'd called Alex an hour ago and hit her with *another* change of plan: the All Saints Motel was booked, so she'd checked them into the Hyatt.

"You're all set, Ms. Lovell. Room 412." The clerk handed her a brochure containing a key card.

"Thank you." Alex shouldered her backpack and her purse and forced a smile. "Does my room have a mini-bar?"

"Of course. And twenty-four-hour room service."

Alex's mood lifted.

"Oh, and your friend called and left a message for you." The woman slid a white envelope across the counter. "She said it was important."

Her mood sank. "When?"

Another cheerful smile. "Just a few minutes ago."

Alex took the envelope and tugged the slip of paper out. The typed message was amazingly brief and infuriating: *Sidetracked with something. Will explain at breakfast. 8:00 A.M. hotel café.*

"*Un*-freaking-believable."

"I'm sorry?"

She glanced up at the concerned clerk.

"Nothing." Alex stuffed the note in her pocket and headed for the elevators. Once again, she was supposed to chase Melanie down just to do her a favor. Alex had had it. She was done. First La Grange. Then the airport motel. Now this. For months, Melanie had been silent as a tomb, and now this exasperating flurry of communications. Alex was sick of trying to keep up with all her—

She halted in her tracks.

That last e-mail.

It had come in hours ago, but Alex had been flying down the freeway at seventy-five miles an hour and she'd merely skimmed it: *Meet me tonight at the All Saints Motel, map attached.*

She jerked her phone from her pocket now. Her chest tightened with fear as she scrolled through this afternoon's mail. She found the message. She opened it up to check the header—

"Dammit!"

It had been sent from an AOL account, but not the one Melanie had been using recently. The more Alex stared at the address, the more she felt certain: this was the account Melanie had mentioned last fall, the one she'd suspected Craig knew about.

I'm not sure how he's doing it. Maybe he figured out my password or something, but I know he's been spying on me. Alex recalled the conversation, which had taken place at Lovell Solutions, just days before she'd helped Melanie disappear. *I guess I should change my password, huh?*

No, don't change it, Alex had advised her. *Then he'll know you're on to him. Better to keep using it, just for nothing important.*

Nothing important.

Like communicating her precise whereabouts to the man who wanted her dead.

CHAPTER NINETEEN

Nathan sped through the endless tupelo and cypress swamp and got an uneasy feeling in the pit of his stomach. It wasn't from the gloom of the bayou. It was Alex. She was just a few miles away, somewhere in the vibrant, pulsing city where he'd grown up. And his gut told him she was in danger.

Again.

He'd never met a woman so prone to hazardous situations. It was as if trouble came looking for Alex. Or maybe she went looking for it. Whatever the case, Nathan knew that getting close to her meant signing up for an infinite number of moments just like this, when he knew she was putting herself at risk, and no amount of logic and persuasion would make her change course.

So maybe he shouldn't get close to her. Made perfect sense. He should just wish her well and back the hell off.

But he couldn't do it. He liked her too much. At the heart of it, that was his problem. He couldn't leave her alone because he genuinely liked her, and although he didn't agree with whatever she was doing, he couldn't stand by and watch her get hurt.

His phone vibrated on the seat beside him, and he snatched it up.

"I've got a problem."

It was her. No hello. No preamble.

"Hey, thanks for getting back to me," he said. "Only took, what? Five hours? Are you at the All Saints Motel yet?"

"How'd you know about—"

"You need to get gone from there. Now. I'm pretty sure Coghan's on his way to Louisiana, and he's looking for you and Melanie."

"He is. That's the problem. I think Melanie lured him here so she could kill him."

Nathan clenched his teeth until his jaw hurt. He tried not to explode. "Is she there now?"

"*I'm* not there now. I'm on my way. I have to talk her out of—"

"Shit, are you crazy? Don't go anywhere near her! Call her on the phone and tell her to get her butt someplace else, someplace Craig won't come looking."

"Could you call the New Orleans police for me? I'm thinking, as a cop, you're a better one to explain. But don't tell them she's armed or anything. I don't want a big SWAT team rushing over there all locked and loaded—"

"Alex, *stop,* okay? Don't go over there. Let the police handle it. I'll call them right now, just—"

"Thanks," she said, and clicked off.

Melanie sat on the side of the bathtub and stroked her finger over the Smith & Wesson. It felt cool. Smooth. It wasn't as heavy as she'd expected, but the man who'd sold it to her said it packed a wallop. And she believed him because he'd had dozens of firearms beneath the glass counter, and his pawnshop seemed to specialize in them.

She rested the .38 on the Formica counter and stood up. Steam from the shower filled the room, and she wiped the condensation off the mirror with the sleeve of her sweatshirt.

A stranger looked back at her.

Short brown hair, where she'd always loved blond. Pale skin. She pulled up her sweatshirt and gazed at her doughy stomach that had once been so flat. As a teenager, she'd wanted a navel ring, a little silver hoop to draw attention to her perfectly toned abs. Now she was glad not to have one, not to have anything that would emphasize this new body she couldn't stand.

The worst were the scars. She brushed her fingers over the back of her neck. Even with makeup, they made her intensely self-conscious. The raised pink circles were a constant reminder of the most degrading moments of her life, and Craig's putrid, rotten soul, and the way he'd managed to control her every move.

And he wasn't done yet. Especially now, after what had happened with Joe, Melanie knew that no matter how far she ran, as long as Craig was alive, she'd always be looking over her shoulder. And one day, he'd be there.

She couldn't let that happen.

Melanie squared her shoulders and gazed at the mirror. The woman staring back at her had a steely glint in her eyes. She wasn't beautiful anymore, or even pretty. But none of that mattered, and she was beginning to realize it never had. The woman in the mirror looked determined. She looked like someone who could pull this off.

Thud.

Melanie whirled around. Beyond the door, over the sound of the shower, she'd thought she'd heard—

Thud, thud, thud.

—someone at the door.

Melanie picked up the gun. She clutched her hands around the grip. She stepped into the corner beside the bathroom door and waited.

CHAPTER TWENTY

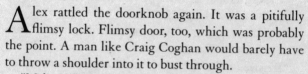

Alex rattled the doorknob again. It was a pitifully flimsy lock. Flimsy door, too, which was probably the point. A man like Craig Coghan would barely have to throw a shoulder into it to bust through.

"Melanie!" She knocked again, but stood off to the side while she did it, because she wasn't sure what exactly lay behind the door. "It's me, Alex. Open up."

She strained to listen. Nothing. Just the muffled *whoosh* of traffic on Airline Drive. Alex turned and looked at her Saturn behind her, which was conspicuously parked right in front of this door. Far from being "full," as Melanie had claimed, the All Saints Motel had plenty of vacancies, judging by the nearly empty lot.

Alex unzipped her purse and took out her SIG. She knocked again.

"Melanie, it's just me, Alex. Are you in there?" God, what if Coghan had already come?

"Melanie!" She pounded her fist. "Open this door!"

It swung back, and there stood Melanie, clutching a revolver. "What are you *doing*?"

Alex strode past her. "Just how stupid do you think I am?"

Melanie glanced at the SIG. "Why aren't you at the Hyatt?"

Alex slammed the door shut and threw the latch. She glanced around. The dim motel room smelled like must and mildew and the remnants of a thousand sleazy encounters. The shower was running. If Coghan had busted in here, he would have thought his unsuspecting wife was in there, totally defenseless.

"Clever setup," Alex snapped. "Did you even *stop* to think about how dangerous this is?"

"You can't be here." Melanie rushed forward. "You need to leave. Right now."

"*We* need to leave." Alex bent down and scooped up Melanie's backpack from the floor beside the nightstand.

"I can't leave. He'll be here any minute." She turned and cast a frantic look at the door Alex had just locked. "You've got to go now. I have a plan and—"

"Great plan." Alex zipped the backpack and held it out to her. "Use the two of us as bait? Get convicted of murder and spend the rest of your life in prison?"

"He'll be here any minute!" She clamped her free hand around Alex's arm and started pulling her toward the door. "You have to *go*."

"You're coming with me."

"No!"

"Yes." Alex shook off her grip and shouldered the backpack herself. She gazed into Melanie's face, trying to read her state of mind. She looked desperate, more desperate than Alex had ever seen her. Alex needed to steady her, talk her down from whatever ledge she was on, but she didn't have much time.

"Don't throw your life away," she said firmly. "He's not worth it, Mel. I can get you out of the country where you'll be safe."

"I can't do that."

"I *can* do that. I've got you all set up—"

"It's not just about me now."

Alex's gaze flicked over Melanie's shoulder. Something moved. . . . The door. To the adjoining suite.

Pop! Pop!

Alex's ears exploded as Melanie shoved her to the ground.

Pop! A lamp burst just above her head. She was on her back, a heavy weight on her chest.

Alex rolled Melanie off of her and took a shot at the doorway. Splinters flew, but the doorway was empty.

Her gazed dropped to Melanie, lying beneath her. Blood was everywhere—her face, her shirt.

"Oh God." Alex scrambled to her knees. She glanced at the doorway again. No one. A siren sounded faintly outside.

"Melanie!" Alex put down her gun and groped around, searching the source of all the blood. It was everywhere. She jerked up Melanie's sweatshirt and found the warm, sticky source of it at her side, near her rib cage.

"Melanie!"

The sirens grew louder as Alex yanked the spread off the bed and used the corner to try to staunch the bleeding. The sirens were loud now, right on top of them.

Brakes screeched. Car doors slammed. Fists pounded on the door.

"Police! Open up!"

Alex glanced frantically over her shoulder. "Bust it open! We need help in here!"

"Freeze!"

Alex whipped her head around. A uniformed cop filled the doorway where the shooter had just been. His gun was pointed straight at Alex's chest.

CHAPTER TWENTY-ONE

Alex was wounded.
Maybe critically.

Nathan squealed into the ambulance bay at Tulane Hospital and whipped into a space marked EMERGENCY VEHICLES ONLY. He hooked his APD hang tag on the mirror and jumped out of the car.

Both females were transported to Tulane. The words of the patrol officer Nathan had practically accosted in the motel parking lot kept running through his head.

One looked serious. Not sure she's going to make it.

Which one? Nathan had asked.

The brunette, I think. It was crazy here. I didn't really see her that good.

Nathan plowed through the double doors now and strode across crowded waiting room. He flashed a badge at the receptionist, who was talking on the phone. "I need to see a patient who just came in here."

She covered the phone with her hand and cast a glance over her shoulder, not paying a lick of attention to the badge that technically granted him zero access here.

"You're talking about the GSW, right?" She looked

up at him expectantly, and he forced himself to nod. "Through the double doors and to the left. Trauma 4. Although I don't think she's conscious—"

Nathan shoved through the doors and navigated the typical Friday night minefield. He cut a path through the gurneys and wheelchairs and harried ER workers until his gaze homed in on a placard beside one of the doors. TRAUMA 4. Medical personnel clustered around a table. Their movements were sharp and hurried, their expressions grim.

"Nathan."

He whipped his head around.

"Over here."

Just across the hall, sitting up on a table, was Alex.

Nathan's heart jumped into his throat. She was awake and alert . . . and covered with blood.

He stepped over to her.

"What are you doing here?" She frowned up at him as some kid in scrubs tended a cut on her arm.

"Are you okay?" He reached for her free hand, then jerked back when he saw that it was bloody, too. "What happened?"

Alex shook her head and gazed down at her lap. Her T-shirt and jeans were saturated.

"Alex, what the hell happened?"

She looked up at him, and the misery in her eyes made his chest squeeze. "He shot Melanie."

"What about you?"

"I'm fine." She glanced at her arm, and he could see her struggling not to lose it. "It's just a scratch. I hit the bed frame on the way down. Melanie fell into me."

The kid stitching up her wound looked calm and steady and about twelve years old.

"Have you seen her?" Alex gazed up at him pleadingly. "She wasn't conscious when they put her in the ambulance. No one's telling me anything."

"I'll find out."

"Alex Lovell?"

They both turned to see a uniformed police officer standing in the doorway.

"I've got some questions about the events earlier. Mind if I come in?"

"Not at all." Alex straightened her back. She looked fairly collected all of a sudden, aside from the blood. But Nathan saw the nerves beneath the surface. He glanced at the needle as it pierced her skin.

"You using enough anesthetic on that?" he asked the doctor.

The kid looked at Alex. "You tell me."

"It's fine." She turned to the cop. "Go ahead with your questions."

The officer gave Nathan a look he'd used a thousand times over the years: *Hey, buddy, mind stepping outside while I have a word with this witness?*

Instead of leaving, Nathan extended a hand. "Nathan Devereaux. Austin PD."

The cop glanced at the hand warily. He accepted the handshake, and seemed to accept the message, too.

Nathan eased closer to Alex's side and watched the doctor stitch her up as the officer rattled off questions. The questions were routine, and she answered each one in a clear, remarkably steady voice. She tucked her free hand under her thigh so no one would see that it was trembling.

"So you're saying you didn't see the shooter?" The officer looked up from his notepad.

"No." Alex bit her lower lip, and Nathan could tell that part was tearing her up. "But it *had* to have been her husband. She knew he was coming after her. He's tried to kill her before."

The cop met Nathan's gaze, and Nathan could see he wasn't convinced.

"Did you see anything?" The officer shifted his attention back to Alex. "Even a glimpse of his clothing? Maybe he had on a cap or something?"

"I didn't see him." She sighed, clearly frustrated. "I just saw the door move. And a shadow. Then Melanie was on top of me." She paused. Swallowed. Met the officer's gaze. "That's all I saw. But you have to find him. It was *him*." She glanced at Nathan, as if he'd jump in and back her up. He caught the flash of anger in her eyes when he didn't. "I know it was him! Who else would it be?"

The cop kept a neutral expression on his face while he jotted notes.

A commotion dragged everyone's attention into the hallway, where a team of people were wheeling a gurney out of Trauma 4.

"Where are they taking her?" Alex turned to the doctor working on her arm.

"I don't know."

"Will you find out?"

"I'll go," Nathan said, partly because he wanted the information, but also because he needed a word with whoever was running this investigation.

Plus he needed some space. From Alex. The last few hours had taken a few years off his life.

Alex wasn't dead.

She wasn't critically injured, even.

Nathan, on the other hand, felt like he'd just absorbed a bomb blast. He had to get some air. He slipped past the cop.

"Wait."

He turned and saw Alex looking at him, a combination of worry and confusion on her face.

"You never answered my question," she said. "What are you doing here?"

Nathan shook his head and walked away.

Alex rested her cheek against the passenger's-side window of Nathan's car and gazed out into the night. Office buildings and parking garages and alleys swept past. After a while, the mundane urban landscape gave way to something different. She saw brick walls and lampposts and ornate wrought-iron balconies. Neon signs reflected off pavement still damp from tonight's rain.

She turned to Nathan. "Is this the French Quarter?"

"Yeah."

Her sluggish brain tried to conjure up the map of New Orleans she'd looked at earlier today. Or was it yesterday? Whenever it was seemed like a lifetime ago.

The image wouldn't come, so finally she gave up and closed her eyes. "I'm booked at the Hyatt," she told Nathan. "That anywhere near here?"

"We're going someplace else."

Too tired to argue, she turned her attention out toward the street again. Wilted-looking party girls strolled the sidewalks, some in pairs, some alone. A man urinated in a doorway. She'd never been here, but it was quieter than she would have expected. Maybe it was really late. Or early.

Nathan rolled through an intersection and took a left without comment.

He was giving her the silent treatment. Or at least she felt like he was. He'd said almost nothing to her since they'd left the hospital with her arm in a bandage and a bottle of pain meds stuffed in her purse. Something was eating at him, and she felt pretty sure it had to do with her cross-country road trip.

But Alex was beyond caring. A deep chasm had opened inside her when she'd knelt beside Melanie and watched the life seep out of her. She was in a coma. The surgeon who'd treated her said she might never come out of it. And the man who'd put her in that coma was free. Still. All Alex wanted to do was curl up into a ball and cry.

There would be no crying in front of Nathan. That, she promised herself. She'd hold it together until he left tomorrow, and then she'd deal with all the emotions churning inside her. She didn't want an audience.

He took another turn, this time into a narrow cobblestone alley. The walls were so close, Alex could have reached out and touched them. She perked up a bit and looked around and realized the alley didn't lead to another street, but rather a tiny parking lot. Nathan pulled into a space beside an SUV.

"Is this it?"

"This is it."

He cut the engine, and they got out of the car. Nathan

came around and took her backpack from her, then led her through a narrow brick tunnel. On the other side was a spacious courtyard lit up with white twinkle lights. Alex blinked and looked up. Four levels of balconies festooned with lights and hanging plants shimmered down at her. Most of the windows between the tall black shutters were dark, but there was the occasional yellow glow.

Nathan led her past a gurgling fountain, then a cluster of cast-iron tables and chairs, all empty now. He pulled open a French door that led into a dim room.

A green banker's lamp shone from a desk in the small, carpeted lobby. The place smelled like cinnamon—the real kind, not the cloying air-freshener variety. Alex recalled the stench of the All Saints Motel and shuddered.

A slightly built man walked into the room and extended a hand to Nathan. He wore a black silk robe over black pajamas.

"Morning, Mr. Devereaux." Then he looked at Alex and smiled pleasantly. "We've got you in room 322."

Nathan took the key the man held out and nodded a thanks.

"The kitchen's closed at the moment, but we'll have coffee starting at six." He glanced at his watch. "Not too long now."

Nathan thanked him again and led Alex to an elevator. They stepped inside, and she looked at Nathan while it made its slow, grumbling ascent.

"You called ahead," she said.

He just looked at her.

She glanced away. Her gaze fell on the rolled cuffs of the windbreaker she wore. Nathan had brought it to her in the hospital to cover up her bloody clothes. It said APD in yellow block letters on the back, and it was lined with gray flannel. She'd already decided to keep it.

The door dinged open and Nathan led her down a hallway. She'd been led around a lot tonight, and she was too tired to care. He stopped in front of a door and opened it with the old-fashioned key. It had a chunky plaster fleur-de-lis on it, probably to keep guests from leaving town with it in their pockets.

Nathan pushed open the door and flipped on the light. Alex followed him inside and immediately noticed the duvet-covered king-size bed. Heaven.

After a shower.

She was already stumbling toward the bathroom when Nathan dropped her backpack onto a yellow wing chair.

"I've got to make a call." He opened the French door to the balcony, and she shut herself in the bathroom.

It was dark. She felt along the wall and tested three different light switches before finding one that illuminated the shower. It was a tub, actually. Claw-footed. Under different circumstances, she might find it charming. Under different circumstances, she might find Nathan charming and feel touched that he'd brought her to such a quaint little bed-and-breakfast in his hometown.

But right now she felt cold, right down to her core, and she knew even a scalding shower—or bath—wasn't going to make it go away.

She turned the water to hot and plugged the tub. She toed off her sneakers. Then she stripped her clothes off and left them in a pile beneath the pedestal sink. Avoiding even a glance at the mirror, she climbed into the tub and rested her bandaged arm on the side. At least it was her left arm. All she had to do was keep it clean for a few days, and she'd be fine.

Melanie was in a coma. She might never walk or talk or bathe herself again.

Alex used the hotel's shower gel and shampoo to clean up as well as she could. It smelled like lavender, but the scent did little to relax her because the bathwater had turned a pale pink from the dried blood on her body. Alex stood up, dried off, and wrapped the towel around herself.

She cracked the door and peeked out. The big bed was empty. She left the light on in the bathroom, but switched off the overhead one in the room. Using just the ray of light from the bathroom, she retrieved a clean T-shirt and panties from her backpack and slipped them on.

Then she climbed into the bed and let her head sink onto the cool feather pillow. She tucked the duvet around her shoulders and shivered at the chilly sheets. She couldn't get warm. She squeezed her eyes shut and thought of Melanie and felt colder still.

A hot tear slid down her cheek. Then another. She pressed her face against the pillow and tried to will them away.

The balcony door creaked open. Every muscle in her body tensed as she listened to the sounds of Nathan moving through the suite, taking off his shoes, using the sink. She listened to him toss his leather jacket over a chair, then empty his pockets onto the table. There was the soft thud of his holster and his gun, and she held her breath, waiting.

Finally the mattress sank down as he stretched out beside her. She tried to breathe evenly, tried to seem asleep. It was childish, yes, but she couldn't deal with sex right now. If he even touched her—

He hooked an arm around her waist and pulled her against him. He stroked her damp hair back from her face, and his fingers brushed over her wet cheek.

He pulled her closer against his warm, hard chest and she drew in a breath.

"It's okay," he whispered.

She squeezed her eyes shut tighter.

"Honey, it's okay." His fingers feathered over her cheek, and she choked on a sob.

And then the game was up, and she curled into a ball and didn't even try to hold back. She cried raggedly, noisily, like she hadn't cried since she was a kid. Nathan didn't say anything. He just held her close, and even through the duvet, she felt the solid heat of him.

When all the tears were gone, she put her hand on top of his and clutched it to her chest, and the warmth of it was the last thing she thought of as she finally fell asleep.

CHAPTER TWENTY-TWO

Alex came awake slowly. Her mind was foggy. Muddled. Her gaze fixed on a scarred leather jacket flung across a chair, and she remembered Nathan.

And Melanie.

She sat up in bed and immediately felt dizzy.

Then she remembered the pain pills. She glanced at the bandage on her left arm and pictured the baby-faced resident who'd stitched her up and brought her the little brown bottle. She glanced around and tried to orient herself. She faintly remembered waking up at dawn, and the room had been blanketed in bluish light, rain thrumming just outside the windows. A warm, strong arm had tightened around her and pulled her close.

The light was bright now, the sharp bright of morning. Or maybe afternoon.

She heard the low murmur of a male voice and glanced through the French door on the other side of the room. A pair of familiar boots was propped on a wrought-iron table there. He was on the phone.

Alex kicked off the covers and padded across the room. She dug her phone from her purse and touched the screen. One-*thirty*? She'd slept the day away! She jabbed the numbers for information and drummed her fingers on the table impatiently as the operator gave her the number and then patched her through to Tulane University Hospital. After a brief exchange with a hospital staffer, Alex hung up.

She rummaged through her backpack, but came up with nothing to wear, not even a pair of running shorts. For what she'd thought would be a brief overnight, she'd packed only a T-shirt, a travel kit, underwear, and a pair of flip-flops. The bloody clothes she'd left on the bathroom floor had disappeared.

Frustrated, she crossed the room and pulled open the door to the balcony. Nathan's gaze met hers as he listened on his phone.

She stepped outside and looked out, not caring that the flower boxes hanging off the railing didn't fully block the view of her standing there half naked. She surveyed the scene below. The sidewalks were crowded with tourists, the streets clogged with cars. Over the din of traffic, she heard the soulful moan of a saxophone being played somewhere close by.

"I got it covered," Nathan said into his phone. "Okay, then. Catch you later."

Alex turned around as he clicked off. He held her gaze for a moment and then his attention drifted lower.

"What happened to my jeans?" she asked.

"They bit the dust."

She arched her eyebrows.

"I've cleaned up plenty of jeans. Trust me, those were history."

She leaned back against the railing, and her gaze

landed on the white coffee cup sitting on the floor next to his chair. Behind him, on an ornate little table, she spotted a carafe and another white cup and saucer.

She stepped across the narrow balcony and poured herself some coffee. It was lukewarm, and she didn't bother with cream before taking a gulp. It tasted strong, like the coffee she'd had at Nathan's all those mornings ago when she'd shown up to take him jogging. The caffeine went straight into her veins.

"I don't have anything else to wear," she said, turning to face him.

"Yeah, you do."

"I didn't bring—"

"I got you a dress at the gift shop next door."

She blinked at him over the coffee cup. "A *dress?*"

"It wasn't exactly the Gap. They didn't have jeans there."

Alex bit back a comment. He'd bought her a dress. She didn't wear dresses. And she couldn't imagine what sort of selection they'd had in the gift shop next door. She pictured something black with feathers and maybe a Mardi Gras mask to go with it.

She'd deal with it later. She sank into the chair across from him, keeping her knees together to preserve some semblance of decorum. But his gaze settled on her legs anyway.

"I just called the hospital and—"

"No change," he finished for her. "I called, too. Twice."

"How long have you been up?"

"Since nine."

He'd barely had four hours of sleep, but he looked

showered and clean-shaven and completely alert. What had he been doing all this time? And how had she slept through it?

"It's the meds." He nodded at her bandaged arm. "You conked out."

Alex glanced down at her bandage. The sight of it brought back a flood of memories, and her stomach tightened. If only she'd gotten there sooner. Or gotten Melanie *out* sooner—

"You okay?"

She glanced up, and the intensity in his blue eyes startled her. He didn't usually look that way. He usually looked low key. Casual. As languid as his voice. She must have scared him yesterday. Not just the hospital part, but her meltdown afterward.

"I'm not going to cry all over you, if that's what you mean."

"I'm not talking about that," he said. "How do you feel?"

She shrugged. "Fine."

But he didn't seem convinced. She stood up. "I need to go the hospital. And I need to check myself and Melanie out of the Hyatt."

"You need to eat."

"Then I need to go get my cars. They're both at the motel still."

He stood up. "First, we eat. You can do all that after."

She looked up at him and knew she wasn't going to win any arguments right now. She'd save her chips for later. Something told her they'd have plenty to argue about in the coming hours, starting with the fact that he'd made no mention of any plans to leave. Nathan's presence here—in this cozy little suite—didn't factor into her plans right now.

He stared down at her, as if expecting her to challenge him. When she didn't, he stroked his hands up her shoulders and turned her around to face the door.

"You're a four, right?" He opened the door and steered her into the room.

"A what?" Her gaze landed on the rumpled bed, and she pushed away the memory of going to pieces in his arms last night.

"Size four," he said. "I'm usually pretty good at guessing."

She didn't reply. He was good at guessing because he'd been married, probably.

Alex was a six, but she let him have his fantasy.

She spotted the white shopping bag beside the door. She felt his gaze on her as she walked over and picked it up, then poked through the tissue paper.

It *was* black. But it wasn't bad, really. She held up the simple sleeveless dress made of some sort of rayon material. It buttoned up the front, and the skirt flared out a bit at the knee. Alex sighed.

"There's some other stuff in there, too."

She raised an eyebrow at him, but the look he gave her in return was completely unapologetic.

"Thank you. I'll pay you back," she said, and annoyance flickered over his face.

Rather than give him a striptease, she ducked into the bathroom to change. Besides the dress, which was just a bit snug, he'd bought her some black lace panties and a matching demi-bra, size 34C. More wishful thinking. Alex dropped the bra back into the bag and decided to go without. After getting dressed, she spent a few minutes brushing her teeth and scooping her hair into a ponytail.

The room smelled like shaving cream, and for a fleeting moment she felt nostalgic. When was the last time she'd shared a bathroom with a man? She hadn't had a serious boyfriend in . . . years, really. Troy didn't count. They'd known each other a long time, but the romance had been a brief flash.

What about Nathan? This whole arrangement felt intimate, and it made her uneasy. He'd come all the way here, most likely to rescue her from the perceived dangers of her job. But then what? Was he just going to walk away? He hadn't given her a lecture yet, but she felt like one was coming. Maybe the prospect of sex was keeping him here. She remembered his arms around her last night. They'd shared a bed for hours, and he'd simply held her. But that wasn't going to work again tonight. Part of her didn't want it to.

She finished up her face with some lip gloss, walked out of the bathroom, and slipped her feet into flip-flops. "Ready," she said, picking up her purse.

The elevator ride was quiet. They cut through the lobby, and she was surprised when he led her to the front door instead of the parking lot.

"We're walking?" she asked.

"Thought I'd show you around the Quarter."

She squinted at the bright sunlight as they stepped onto the cobblestone sidewalk.

"Which way?"

He caught her hand in his and started walking. The air was heavy with humidity, and she could almost feel the steam rising up from the sidewalk. Maybe a dress *was* better than jeans. It was certainly cooler in this muggy climate. Nathan pulled her through the throngs of tourists with their floppy hats and fanny packs. He led her past vividly colored doorways and ornate iron gates, and she caught glimpses of lushly planted court-yards as they passed by. Many doors were flung open, and music drifted out. Alex caught snippets of zydeco, rock, a Broadway tune pounded out on a piano. Most incongruous of all were the low, pulsing thumps coming from dark doorways where neon signs advertised GIRLS! GIRLS! GIRLS!

On the corner of Bourbon and Toulouse, they waited patiently as a horse-drawn carriage clomped by. Half a block farther and Nathan tugged her into an alley.

"Where . . . ?" But her voice trailed off as she realized it wasn't an alley, but an extremely narrow cobblestone street. He turned left, then right, then left again, seem-ingly oblivious to the sketchy-looking people who lurked in doorways and whose gazes followed them. Finally he reached an alley lined with potted ivies and flower boxes brimming with geraniums. A stream of people moved past them and they had to wait their turn to pass through the cast-iron gate.

A weathered wooden sign read MCLEAN'S.

Nathan pulled open a kelly green door and nodded for her to go ahead of him.

Inside was dim and cool, and Alex's mouth immedi-ately started watering. Fried shrimp. She'd recognize the smell anywhere.

Nathan didn't wait for a hostess, but ushered her through a narrow room with tables on one side and a long wooden bar on the other. He claimed a small table at the back, right next to a raised stage. The platform was empty now, except for a microphone.

Nathan pulled out a chair for her, and Alex was about to sit down when she heard a squeal.

The next moment, a red-haired woman was beside them, and Nathan lifted her off her feet in a big hug.

"It *is* you!" She slapped his arm as he finally put her down. "Mac said you were in town!"

She turned her flushed, smiling face to Alex.

"I'm Vera."

"Alex."

Her attention snapped back to Nathan, who was grinning at her. "How long you here for?"

Alex looked the woman over as she and Nathan exchanged chitchat. Besides saying vaguely that he was in town "on business," he didn't allude to what had brought him to New Orleans.

Despite the wine red hair, Vera had to be in her sixties. From the conversation, Alex gathered she was a friend of Nathan's family, probably his parents. Alex glanced around uneasily, suddenly wondering who else might turn up.

"What can I get you?

"Uh . . ." Alex glanced at Nathan.

"I'm having a beer," he supplied.

Alex remembered her pill-induced daze earlier and ordered an iced tea.

"You okay with spicy?" Nathan asked her.

"Yeah, sure."

"Two gumbos, then," he told Vera. "And a baguette."

They finally sat down at their table, and Alex looked

around. The bar was dark and noisy, and Alex couldn't believe she was sitting here in the middle of the afternoon. She checked her watch.

"Relax."

She sighed impatiently.

"We'll get to everything, I promise. But you need to eat first."

The drinks came, and Alex dumped sugar in her tea as Nathan and Vera exchanged more small talk.

"She's friendly," Alex said when she left.

"She and my folks go way back."

"They around, too?"

The corner of his mouth ticked up. "Why? Nervous?"

"Why should I be nervous?"

He leaned forward on his elbows. "You don't want to meet my family. Makes you antsy just thinking about it."

She frowned at him, and he smiled at her before taking a sip of his beer.

"My dad's in Baton Rouge," he said. "Has been since Hurricane Katrina. He lives with my only sister."

"And your mother?"

"She died eleven years ago."

Alex looked down into her tea. "I'm sorry." She felt like a jerk. She'd been dreading the prospect of meeting the woman. "How'd she die?" she asked, and immediately regretted the question.

"Breast cancer."

"I'm sorry." She blamed the drugs for her sudden lack of tact. When she glanced up again, Nathan was watching her closely.

"You're not tight with your family, are you?" he asked.

"Why do you say that?"

"You never talk about them. Seems like the whole subject makes you uncomfortable."

"Not really." She stirred her tea. "I just don't have much to say, I guess. They're pretty boring."

He waited for her to elaborate.

"They've lived in the same house for twenty-five years," she said. "Worked at the same jobs. They eat the same thing for dinner every Sunday night, right after *60 Minutes* comes on. There's nothing to say about it."

"That says a lot." Nathan turned his beer glass on top of the cardboard coaster. "Are they happy?"

Alex laughed at the straightforwardness of the question.

"Are they?"

She looked at him for a long moment. "No." She glanced away. "At least, my mom isn't. I don't know about my dad. He likes routine, so maybe he's fine with it."

"But your mom's stir crazy?"

Alex traced a finger through the condensation on her glass. How had they gotten onto this? "She's unfulfilled," she said carefully. "She's been teaching the same courses for twenty years. Grading the same mediocre term papers. Going on the same vacation every summer to Wisconsin."

Nathan's eyebrows tipped up.

"I think she's just, I don't know, bored. Settled."

"Too settled," Nathan said.

Alex shrugged again. Who was she to judge? But that was exactly what she thought. She'd go insane living that way. That was why she'd left rather than graduate college in her hometown with a degree from the school where both her parents had tenure.

He leaned forward on his elbows again. "That why you run away from relationships?"

"I don't run away from relationships."

"Uh-huh. But you've never been married, right?"

"So?"

"So you're beautiful. Smart. Successful. How come nobody's landed you yet?"

"What makes you think I'm sitting around waiting to get married?"

"I don't," he said. "Hey, don't get mad. I'm just curious. You seem timid about relationships, but you're not a timid person. It's an inconsistency. Inconsistencies get my attention."

"Don't psychoanalyze me. Jesus. I get enough of that from my mom."

His mouth curved into a slight smile. "So I'm not the only who's noticed it. That's good. I was wondering if it was something to do with me."

She cocked her head to the side. "You're really nosy, you know that? How'd you like me to sit here giving you the third degree?"

"Fire away."

"Okay. How come your wife divorced you?"

He lifted an eyebrow. "Who says it wasn't the other way around?"

"I do. You're old-fashioned. And your background's Catholic. I bet you would have stuck around to work things out if she'd wanted to."

He took a sip of beer.

"See? Isn't it fun being in the hot seat?"

He met her gaze. "Nicole and I wanted different things out of life. But we got married young, and we were too dumb to realize it."

"But you still see her."

"Occasionally."

Alex assumed that meant sex, but she didn't have the guts to ask. Instead, she scrounged up her courage and asked the question that had been plaguing her since yesterday morning. "Are you still in love with her?"

"No."

He watched her for a long moment. Then he reached across the table and took her hand. She wanted to pull away, but that would only prove his "timid" hypothesis.

"I don't know why we're talking about this," she said.

"We're getting to know each other. You're just not comfortable because you like to do all your snooping on the computer so you don't have to admit you give a damn." He squeezed her hand. "You've been pissed off at me since yesterday morning. I'm just clearing the air here."

"Gee, thanks." She tugged her hand away and picked up her tea. It bothered her to be read so well. She searched for a new topic.

"What about you?" she asked. "Why'd you leave New Orleans?"

He watched her for a beat. Then his gaze shifted around the room. "My dad spent his life here."

"Here, like, *here*?"

He nodded. "I practically grew up in this bar. But I was always more interested in what was happening outside."

Alex watched him, trying to picture a younger Nathan

Devereaux in this same setting. She glanced behind the polished wooden counter and imagined him chatting with customers and pulling on the taps. She could imagine it just fine, but she didn't blame him for wanting to go out on his own. Alex was in touch with that emotion.

"So," he said. "Now that we've covered pretty much everything else, are you going to talk to me?"

"About?"

"About what the hell's going on."

CHAPTER TWENTY-THREE

"What were you planning to do? Put her on a plane to Brazil?"

Alex stirred her tea. "I didn't want her on a plane anywhere. I was going to drive her to Mexico."

"With a fake passport."

"Yes."

She glanced up. He didn't look surprised by this news.

"Austin's a lot closer to the border," he observed.

"No kidding. But Melanie changed the plan. She wanted to meet in New Orleans. Said her safe spot was here."

"What's that?"

"A place she keeps important stuff," Alex said. "Though why she needed anything, I don't really know. I was lending her money."

Nathan shook his head, and Alex tensed. "What?"

"You and your lost causes. It's a wonder your business turns a profit."

The waitress appeared with a tray, cutting off Alex's retort. The lecture was starting, and she didn't want to hear it.

Nathan doused his soup with Tabasco sauce, and Alex ripped off a chunk of warm, crusty bread.

"You know, I didn't ask you to come here."

"I'm aware of that." He scooped up a bite.

"I didn't ask you for anything."

"I'm aware of that, too." He held her gaze for a long moment, and she looked away.

Alex dipped a chunk of bread in her gumbo and tried to collect her thoughts.

"Coghan's being sought for questioning."

Her gaze snapped up. "They haven't found him?"

"Not yet," Nathan said. "Supposedly, he was headed to his dad's place this weekend. That's down in Freeport. But you seem to think he came here."

"I know he did."

"But you didn't see him."

"It was him. He had access to Melanie's e-mail account. She lured him here—"

"But you didn't see him." He looked at her intently.

"No."

"You see the problem here, Alex? When he turns up, he's probably going to have an alibi."

"He always has an alibi." Alex picked at the bread, frustrated.

"He's a cop. What'd you expect?"

Alex shook her head and scooped a bite of soup. It was steamy and spicy, and she relished the way it burned a path down her throat.

"What did your electronic snitch tell you?" he asked drily.

She glanced up, and Nathan's expression told her he already knew what she was going to say. She'd checked the GPS tracking program from her phone in the emergency room.

"His truck was in Freeport last night," she admitted. "But that doesn't mean he was."

Nathan kept his opinion of this theory to himself. "You know what a grow house is?" he asked, changing the subject.

"No."

"Troy Stockton's got his eye on those vacant homes in Captain's Point. He thinks they're being outfitted as grow houses. Indoor marijuana farms."

Alex gaped at him. "Does anyone else know about this?"

"Evidently, a federal task force does. Hodges made some calls this morning. The feds have pulled the power records of at least a dozen homes in that neighborhood."

She rested her spoon on the table. "What do they want with—"

"Energy. The lamps, the ventilation systems eat up an incredible amount of power. It's one way to pinpoint the locations. Those three homes Coghan visited were just the tip of the iceberg, apparently."

"Why doesn't somebody arrest him, for God's sake? What's he doing on the job still?"

Nathan's brow furrowed. "I don't like it, either. My guess is, they're setting up some kind of sting op, hoping to get some people higher up the food chain. Coghan's involved in a complicated operation. The drug trade in Austin's tightly controlled by a few rival gangs with direct ties to Mexican cartels. It's very well organized. It's not possible those organizations would let him run his own gig independently. He's got to be connected. Which probably has the feds salivating."

Alex shook her head, unable to believe it. "Perfect. Our local drug czar's in bed with drug gangs. And yet he's still out on the street, trying to gun down his wife."

"I'm working on it."

"*You're* working on it?"

He nodded, and Alex watched him, confused now. Was he saying that to mollify her? Or was there really a case against Coghan?

He gazed at her for a long moment and seemed to decide something.

"I think he's good for three murders," he said. "If Melanie dies, that makes four."

"You think he killed *three* people?"

"I've got three open cases with the same MO. Three victims strangled with a length of baling wire. A sample of the wire's at the Delphi Center right now being analyzed by Mia."

Alex sat back, shocked. She saw the tension in his face, the spark of anger in his eyes.

"You *do* care about this," she said.

"Of course I care."

A burden lifted off her shoulders. She wasn't doing this alone anymore.

Nathan shook his head and gazed down into his beer. "Coghan's given every cop in the state a black eye. He's violated the public trust in every way that matters. He's responsible for at least three homicides, if not more. You bet your ass I care."

"I didn't realize . . . so are you going to go to the feds?"

He turned his glass of beer. "I haven't decided yet. I want him for murder one, not drug charges. He belongs on death row, not in some white-collar prison after he cuts a deal."

"Sounds like you've given this a lot of thought." Alex watched him carefully.

"Why's that surprise you?"

She shrugged. "I don't know, it's just . . . You've been pushing so hard for me to drop this case, I didn't think it mattered to you."

"Of course it matters. But you matter more."

He pinned her with a long, steady look, and her stomach fluttered. She didn't know what to do with that. How could she matter to him? He didn't even know her, really.

Alex's phone chimed, saving her from having to respond. She reached beneath the table and dug it out of her purse.

Nathan watched her take the call and wondered if he'd revealed too much. Hell, yes, he cared. About her. About this case. What had she thought? That he wouldn't give a damn that one of his colleagues, someone he'd once considered a *friend,* was responsible for a string of killings? For abusing his authority as a police officer?

He could see that he'd caught her off guard, and he found that ironic. She'd gone to bed with him. She'd shared her body with him. And yet, the whole time, she must have thought he was a callous son of a bitch not to care about this case.

Damn right he cared.

But he cared about her more, a fact that clearly didn't sit well with her.

She pulled the phone from her ear and frowned at the screen.

"Who did you say you are?" she asked the caller. A pause. "Sponsor of what?"

Nathan watched her brow furrow as she checked her watch.

"I don't think—" she stopped, obviously interrupted, and shot him a frustrated look. "Hold on a sec." She muted the phone. "You know where St. Louis Cathedral is?" she asked him.

"A stone's throw from here. Why?"

"This woman wants me to meet her there in ten minutes."

"Who is she?"

"She claims to be a friend of Melanie's. She says it's important."

"You told me Melanie didn't have any friends."

"I didn't think she did," Alex said. "But this woman's her former AA sponsor, apparently. Maybe she's the reason Melanie picked New Orleans for her safe spot."

"I don't like it," Nathan said, and that was putting it mildly. "She could be anybody. She could be with Coghan."

Alex pursed her lips. She got back on the phone. "I'll be there," she told her. "But I'm bringing my bodyguard, and he's armed. Heavily." She listened for a few more moments and clicked off.

"Your bodyguard?"

She dropped the phone into her purse and stood up.

"That's why you're here, right? To babysit me? Now's your chance." She pulled some bills out of her wallet and tried to leave them on the table, but he beat her to it. He took a last swig of beer and followed her toward the exit.

"How far is this church?" she asked over her shoulder.

"Not far. But you're not going near it until I check this out."

"Nathan—"

"No arguing. I'll call a friend with NOPD and see if they can get a patrol unit over there to sit on the location."

They stepped from the air-conditioned bar into the humidity, and Alex glanced up at the midafternoon sun. "This better be quick. I want to get to the hospital."

Nathan put his hand on the small of her back and steered her toward the street. "What was her name again?"

"Peggy."

"Peggy what?" He asked, heading toward Jackson Square.

"I didn't ask," Alex said. "She just said it was important. Maybe she has Melanie's valuables or something. All her important stuff was supposed to be stashed here in town."

Nathan fished his phone from his pocket and put in a call to a buddy. After a brief exchange, he clicked off.

"They've got units patrolling the Quarter," he told Alex. "He'll get someone to head over to the church, camp out there for a little while."

"Sounds good," Alex said, and quickened her pace.

But Nathan still wasn't happy. He glanced up and down the block, looking for anything suspicious.

Everything looked suspicious—it was the fucking French Quarter. He saw two drug deals go down and watched someone pick up a prostitute, all inside of five minutes. But by the time they neared their destination, the patrol car was parked on the corner just west of the church. Nathan caught the eye of the officer behind the wheel and they exchanged nods.

"There she is," Alex said.

"Where?"

"Red T-shirt, white visor."

"How do you know?"

"She told me what she'd be wearing."

The woman in the red T-shirt and white visor was seated on a bench across from the cathedral. Beside her was a young mom with a stroller and a toddler who was tossing bread at some pigeons. "Peggy" looked to be in her early sixties. And harmless. But Nathan still didn't like this. He kept his weapon hand ready.

Alex strode right up to the woman, but Nathan hung back, glancing around for potential threats.

"I'm Alex."

The woman gazed up from the bench, a worried look on her face. "Is Melanie with you?"

"She's in the hospital," Alex said. "The ICU, actually."

"What *happened*?"

"She was involved in a shooting last night."

"Oh, Lord." Peggy clasped her hands together in front of her face, like she was praying. "It was Craig, wasn't it?"

"The police are investigating."

"Oh, Lord," she repeated, shaking her head. "I was afraid of something like this. Is she going to be okay?"

"I don't know."

Nathan watched the woman's reaction closely. She seemed to be on the verge of tears now.

"You said you had something important for me?" Alex checked her watch. "Sorry to be short, but I'm on my way to the hospital."

Still shaking her head, the woman pulled her purse into her lap and started digging through it.

Nathan glanced around. The patrol officer was watching them with a bored expression. Tourists streamed back and forth along the sidewalk, stopping at hot-dog vendors and street artists. On the corner of Chartres and St. Peter, a silver-painted mime entertained a knot of kids.

Nathan checked all directions but didn't see any suspicious cars or pedestrians who didn't fit. Still, there were balconies and rooftops all around. He eased up close behind Alex and rested his left hand on her shoulder.

"Hurry this up," he whispered.

"You saw her yesterday?" Alex was asking.

"She'd been staying at my house off and on," Peggy said. "She came in on the bus, oh, about ten days ago, I guess it was." Peggy pulled an envelope from her purse and passed it to Alex.

Nathan's attention shifted from the patrol officer, to the mime, to the seemingly empty balcony above the nearest souvenir shop. The mom on the other end of the bench took her toddler's hand and led him toward an ice-cream stand.

Nathan's gaze homed in on the stroller. The hair on

the back of his neck stood up. Alex's shoulder tensed under his hand.

"She *what*?" Alex swayed backward, bumping into him.

He caught her around the waist. "What is it?"

She glanced up at him, wide-eyed.

"I thought you knew." Peggy cast a worried look at Nathan. "She didn't know?"

"Know what?" Nathan's gut tightened as Peggy's gaze moved to the stroller, the same stroller Alex was staring at now, mouth agape.

"About Grace," Peggy said.

A whimper came from the stroller, and Peggy stood up. Alex and Nathan stepped back and watched—speechless—as she clucked and murmured over the baby there. She picked up the bundle wrapped in pink blankets and settled it in the crook of her arm.

Alex stared, goggle-eyed, at the baby. She turned to Nathan.

"She has a baby." Alex held up the letter. "Did you know about this? She has a *baby*!"

"How would I know about this?"

Peggy stepped forward, and Alex recoiled as the woman tried to hand the infant over to her.

"*I* can't hold it!"

"She's fine." Peggy stepped closer and pushed the bundle into Alex's arms. Nathan heard her sharp intake of breath. The baby's cheeks reddened, and her face screwed up in a frown.

"She can't possibly think *I'd* take her." Alex whirled to Nathan. "She can't think that!"

"Calm down," he said, although he felt anything but calm. He looked at Peggy and tried to read her face. "This is *Melanie's* baby. You're sure about that?"

"Melanie and Joe's. Bless her little heart, she's not even three weeks old. And now Melanie's in the hospital." Peggy shook her head. "I knew she was in trouble. She wouldn't say what it was, but I knew. I knew something wasn't right from the second they showed up at my house. And her letting me babysit? Now, that was desperate, that's what that was. Mel knows better than anybody what a struggle I been having these last few months."

Alex held the baby out to Peggy. "I'm sorry. For the . . . inconvenience here. But there's really *no way* I can help you with this problem."

"Melanie said you'd say that." Peggy glanced down at the baby, who was whimpering and squirming now. "But she gave me your number and said to call you if she wasn't back by this afternoon. You're the only person she trusted in case of an emergency."

"But you're her *friend*—"

"So are you." Peggy picked up her purse and hitched it up on her shoulder. She stepped closer, and Nathan saw the tears glistening in her eyes as she looked at Alex. "I'd do this for her, if I could. God knows that husband of hers is evil incarnate. But I got my own demons to worry with."

"But—"

"I'll get by the hospital, soon as I can." She glanced down at the baby and bit her lip. "You tell her mama hi for me now, okay?"

Peggy turned and walked away.

Nathan watched her go, acutely aware of Alex's raspy breathing. She glanced up at him, and the look on her face was pure panic.

"She can't leave me with Melanie's baby!"

"Looks like she just did." Nathan pulled his phone from his pocket and dialed information.

"But . . . but I don't know anything about babies!"

The child's face crumpled, and she let out a wail. Alex gazed down at it, horrified.

"This is crazy! I don't know what to do with a baby!"

"I do." Nathan listened to his phone as the call connected. "New Orleans, please. Department of Social Services."

Alex stood beside the wrought-iron table and scanned the plaza for the thousandth time.

"You can sit down, you know."

"I don't want to sit down." She swayed side to side, which was the only thing she seemed to be able to do to keep Grace from crying. "How long has it been?"

"Almost an hour." Nathan sipped his coffee and picked up the last bite of a beignet.

"How can you eat right now?"

He licked the sugar off his fingers. "I'm hungry."

Alex rolled her eyes and turned her back on him. Just the thought of food made her stomach roil. She couldn't believe this. *How* had she not known? How had Melanie kept something so important from her for so many months?

Grace squirmed, and her little eyelids fluttered open. *Please, please,* please *don't start crying again.*

The sound of her crying made Alex crazy. She felt

helpless and stupid and incompetent, all at the same time. Grace had cried the entire distance across Jackson Square, howling in Alex's arms until her little face turned beet red. Finally, Nathan had secured them a corner table at this outdoor café, and Alex had discovered the side-to-side sway thing that seemed to help. She'd been doing it now for the past forty minutes, and her hip was sore, but anything was better than that wailing.

Grace squirmed again, and Alex swayed faster, praying she wouldn't start up once more. Maybe she should hum something. A lullaby. But for the life of her she couldn't think of a single one. The only song that would come to her was "Get the Party Started," which had been playing in some bar earlier when Nathan had led her through the Quarter.

She turned and looked at him.

"What are you *smiling* at?"

"You," he said. "You're funny."

"I'm glad you think this is funny. This child is a heartbeat away from being orphaned. What the hell's funny about that?"

"That's not what I meant, and you know it."

Grace's brow furrowed, and she wiggled some more.

She hadn't come with a bottle. Or a pacifier. Or a lactating nipple. Peggy had left behind a shopping bag crammed with baby clothes, diapers, and a half-empty carton of formula. The powdered kind.

Grace squirmed again. Alex shot a glance at the stroller, wondering if there might be some bottles stashed in the bottom part. But she didn't really want to check.

Even if she found one, she had no idea what to do with it. She'd never mixed baby formula before.

Exasperated, Alex turned around to look out over the square. Where *was* this woman?

"You told her it was an emergency, right?"

"You heard every word I said," Nathan reminded her. "She'll get here as soon as she can. Now sit down and have some coffee."

Grace whimpered.

"Shh . . ." Alex held her closer. "Shh . . ."

"You want me to hold her?"

Alex glared at him. "No."

"Maybe you should put her on your shoulder."

"Why?"

"Because when you hold her horizontal like that, she probably thinks it's time to eat."

Alex went still. She gazed down at the little mouth rooting around beside her chest. She glanced up at Nathan. Then she shifted the baby to her shoulder.

She quieted instantly.

Alex resumed the swaying and shot Nathan a suspicious look. "How'd you know that?"

He shrugged.

"No, really. You know about babies, I can tell. Where'd you get all these tidbits?"

He sighed. "I've got nieces and nephews. I pay attention."

Alex patted Grace's back through her terry cloth pajamas. She gazed across the square again.

"What did the letter say?" Nathan asked.

Alex glanced down at him. He'd probably wanted to

read it, but she'd stuffed it in her purse, right alongside the birth certificate that had been folded into the envelope with Melanie's note.

If you're reading this letter, Craig finally got what he wanted.

"It wasn't long," she told him. "It didn't say much."

Nathan watched her expectantly.

You have to keep her safe, Alex. Craig knows there's a baby, and he knows she's not his. You have to keep him from finding her.

Alex cleared her throat. "She thinks Craig would hurt Grace, if he knew where she was. She wants me to conceal her identity somehow."

If anyone can hide her from him, it's you.

"She says that in the letter?"

"More or less."

"You'd better hang on to that. It could be used in court someday, if we end up trying him for Melanie's murder."

Alex shuddered at the word and turned around again.

A tall, African American woman was making a beeline toward the café. Her gaze fastened on Alex.

"That's probably her," Nathan said, and Alex felt dizzy with relief.

She watched the social worker who had come to take charge of this mess. The woman had a thin, angular face and a determined stride. As she neared them, Alex saw that her brown eyes were warm and intelligent. Alex needed someone with eyes like that, someone who would listen and be willing to bend the rules for the sake of a little baby. Grace's real name couldn't end up on any of the paperwork that resulted from this.

The woman stopped in front of them. Alex stared at her across the low, wrought-iron fence that separated the café from the sidewalk. Nathan came to her side, and she felt the comforting weight of his hand on her waist.

The woman smiled at them. "This must be Grace."

CHAPTER TWENTY-FOUR

Nathan glanced at Alex in his passenger seat. Sitting there yesterday, she'd looked drained. Now she looked shell-shocked.

"You really didn't know?"

She glanced at him, startled, as if she'd forgotten he was chauffeuring her across town in his car.

"I had no idea," she said.

Nathan had done the math. Melanie had first gone to see Alex before her pregnancy would have started to show. But still, Nathan found it odd that Alex hadn't picked up any clues, especially when she'd seen Melanie just the other day.

"I know what you're thinking," Alex said. "You may as well say it."

"What am I thinking?"

"That I'm an idiot. I should have known."

"I don't think you're an idiot."

"Uh-huh."

"You do realize, though, that Melanie's probably involved?"

Alex frowned at him. "In what?"

"Coghan's operation. The grow houses. She gets out of that coma, she could end up facing charges."

"What makes you think she's involved?"

"My partner's been checking out her boyfriend, the one we pulled out of Lake Austin." He cut a glance at Alex to see if she knew what he was about to say.

She looked blank.

"Guy's name was Joe Turner," Nathan told her. "He was a real estate agent. His name's on the documents connected to each of those three vacant houses in Captain's Point."

"Does Coghan own them? He'd have to be making a hell of a lot of money—"

"We don't know who owns them. So far, it looks like a shell corporation. Hodges is looking into it, but there are a lot of legal smoke screens in place. Which just shows how elaborate this thing is. Coghan couldn't have set it up all by himself."

Alex looked away. "I don't think Melanie's involved."

"Her boyfriend was neck deep in this shit."

"Maybe so. But I don't think she was part of it. At least, not willingly. Coghan controlled her every move and treated her like garbage. I seriously doubt he'd give her any kind of important role in his business. And she definitely wasn't making any money off it. As long as I've known her, she's been practically broke."

"Didn't she have a job? I thought she was a clerk at some health clinic."

"Coghan controlled all their money. It took her years to pilfer enough to leave him."

Nathan gazed ahead at the road, understanding a little better now why Alex had agreed to take Melanie's case for next to nothing. The woman had been desperate. And Alex, being Alex, had felt compelled to help.

He glanced at her. She looked lost in thought again.

"You know she'll be fine, right?"

"Who?"

"Grace," he said. "I've seen situations like this after violent crimes. DSS has foster families on call. They'll probably have her placed in a matter of hours."

Alex crossed her arms and looked away, clearly unconvinced.

Nathan watched her uneasily. The idea of being left in charge of that baby had completely rattled her. But she seemed almost as upset by the idea of Melanie's child ending up with DSS. Nathan had seen Alex's hesitation when the social worker had reached out to take the baby.

Surely she wasn't thinking of stepping into this mess?

He turned onto Airline Drive, and the sign for the All Saints Motel came into view. It wasn't dusk yet, but still the neon red blazed, just above a blinking VACANCY sign. He pulled into the parking lot and spotted the Sunliner at the far end of the building, exactly where it had been yesterday night. The Saturn was parked right beside it.

Nathan looked at Alex. "You want me to come with you to the hospital?"

"No."

The speed of her answer irked him. He pulled into an empty space alongside the convertible.

"Don't you need to get back to Austin?" she asked.

He cut the engine and looked at her. It was a loaded question, and she knew it, too.

He smiled bitterly to himself. He'd driven seven

hours and ditched work to help a woman who, evidently, wanted him to take a hike.

"I figure you probably need to head back soon," she said, "for work and everything."

"I do." He met her gaze and didn't tell her how he wasn't really ready to leave yet, how he'd blow off another couple days of work—and probably get his ass suspended, if it wasn't already—if she'd just ask him to stay. But that wasn't going to happen.

"When are you going back?" he asked.

"I'm not sure." She glanced away. "Whenever I get this resolved."

"Resolved?"

She wouldn't look at him.

"Alex, it might not *get* resolved. Not like you want."

She didn't say anything.

He leaned closer. "She might never wake up, Alex. You need to get your mind around that."

"I have," she said, but the defensiveness in her voice told him she hadn't at all.

Nathan shook his head.

"She doesn't have anyone," Alex said. "I feel like I should stay a while until things have settled down."

"That could take weeks. Months. *Years,* even."

"I feel obligated."

"You're not," he said sharply. "She isn't your family."

"I know." She fidgeted with the strap of the purse in her lap.

"Where do you get this sense of obligation?"

"Why are you so opposed to me doing my job?"

"This isn't your job!" he snapped. "What is it with you and these women? You don't know when to quit.

You nearly took a bullet last night, and still you won't leave it alone."

He gripped the steering wheel and thought about the phone call he'd had with his partner this morning. "Were you planning to tell me about Thursday?"

"What about Thursday?" she asked, innocent as hell.

"How you got caught up in some *shooting* at the god-damn shopping mall?" He watched her reaction and knew she'd had no intention of ever telling him. "Alex, what are you trying to prove here?"

"I'm not trying to prove anything."

"Are you *trying* to get hurt?"

"Of course not."

"Then let the police handle this. Every time I turn around, you're deeper into trouble."

She glanced up at him, and he saw the storm brewing in her eyes. "You act like this whole thing is *my* fault! Have you forgotten that the person behind all this is a cop? Sorry, but my faith in law enforcement is a bit shaken right now."

Nathan took a deep breath and tried to rein in his temper. She was right. This whole thing *was* a cop's fault. And Nathan's faith was shaken, too. Much more than he cared to admit to her.

"Look, I'm trying to understand here," he said. "I know you want to help, but—"

"You really want to understand me?" She turned to face him, her cheeks flushed with emotion. "It's easy. My job is everything to me. It's all I have. Some people have their social life, their marriage, their Dewar's. I have my job. That's it."

"You really believe that?"

"I know that."

He watched her, battling the urge to argue the point. He'd had his feelings thrown back at him enough already today.

She peered around him, at her two cars. One would have to be picked up tomorrow.

Nathan started the engine. "Take the Sunliner," he said flatly, and glanced at her. She looked wary, unconvinced that he was done fighting. "It's a target, sitting here. You're lucky it didn't get boosted last night."

She nodded and pushed the door open. She turned to look at him. "Thanks. For the ride and everything."

"Yeah, no problem."

"Have a safe trip back."

It took two wrong turns and nearly an hour, but finally Alex managed to find the hospital. She located the ICU, where Melanie had been moved late last night after surgery. Then she got past the nurse's station, only to be held up at Melanie's door by a brawny U.S. Marshal.

"Sorry, ma'am." He stood up from his metal folding chair. "No visitors."

Alex let her face fall. "But she's my sister." She put a quiver in her voice and manufactured some tears. "I came all this way to see her."

He gazed down at her, stone-faced.

"Couldn't I peek in for just a few minutes?"

"Sorry, ma'am."

"But—"

"It's okay. She's with me."

Alex turned to see John Holt sauntering down the hallway. He was in full ranger attire, from the hat and boots to the star pinned to his lapel.

"Evenin', Alex." He nodded at the guard, then pulled a clipboard from a plastic holder affixed to the door. It was some sort of visitors' log, and he jotted both their names on it, alongside the date and time.

"We won't be long," Holt told the man, pushing the door open for her.

Alex stepped inside the room. The only light came from a fluorescent fixture above the sink and the greenish glow emanating from the machines lined up beside the bed. Alex let her gaze linger over the heart monitor and the IV before coming to rest on Melanie.

Her skin looked waxy. A patch of hair had been shaved, and a bandage wrapped around her skull where a bullet had grazed her. Alex knew more damage lay beneath the sheet, where a .22-caliber slug had nicked her kidney.

Her gaze moved back to Melanie's face. It was pale, almost gray. She looked like a corpse, and Alex had a sudden vision of the wailing, red-faced baby who'd squirmed in her arms just a short while ago.

"Doc was in not too long ago."

Alex turned. Holt lurked behind her, in the shadowy niche beside the bathroom.

"What'd he say?" she asked him.

"She has a cerebral contusion. They're monitoring the swelling."

"And the prognosis?"

"She got through the first day okay, which is something. But her chances fade as this drags out."

Alex pressed her lips together. It felt wrong to be talking like this in front of Melanie. Maybe she could hear them.

Alex went to her side and picked up her hand. It was cool and limp.

"How long has the guard been there?"

"Since they moved her up here." Holt stepped closer.

"How long will he stay?" She glanced over her shoulder, and she could see Holt knew what she was asking. Personnel was expensive, and this couldn't go on forever. Melanie's clock was ticking. Today, her life had value. Tomorrow, maybe not so much.

"Let's step outside," Holt suggested.

"I need a minute with her first." She waited a beat. "Please?"

He eased back into the shadows by the door but didn't leave the room.

Realizing it was the best she was going to get, Alex eased herself down on the bedside, taking care not to jostle anything. She stroked her thumb over Melanie's palm.

Did Holt know about Grace? If not, Alex wasn't going to be the one to tell him. The chances of a secret staying secret diminished with every person who knew about it.

Alex studied Melanie's eyes. The lids looked bluish in the fluorescent glow. She noted the artfully shaped brows that Courtney had worked on just yesterday morning. So much had happened, and so quickly.

Across the room, Holt cleared his throat.

She squeezed Melanie's hand and bent her head close. "I met Grace," she whispered. "She's going to be fine, don't worry." Alex tucked Melanie's hand beside her on the blanket and patted it gently. "You get better now, okay? I'll be back soon."

Outside the room, she gave the marshal a nod and followed Holt down the antiseptic-smelling corridor. At the end of the hallway was a visitors' area furnished with tacky purple sofas.

Holt gestured for her to sit, but she turned to face him instead.

"You guys find Coghan yet?"

He gazed down at her with those sharp gray eyes. "An officer interviewed him this afternoon at his father's house in Freeport. He has an alibi for yesterday night."

She folded her arms over her chest. "What is it?"

"Says he was down there fishing."

"And you find that credible?"

"It checks out." Holt rested his hands on his hips. "For now, at least."

Alex rolled her eyes.

"We think he's got an accomplice, Alex. You sure you didn't see anything yesterday? Not even a glimpse?"

"I told the police everything I saw. It's in the report."

"I read it," Holt said. "But he's not doing this alone. He has an accomplice, and we need to know who."

"Maybe it's that guy from the shopping mall. You ever identify him?"

"Sure did," Holt said. "When he showed up at the morgue."

A chill moved through her. "You think Coghan killed him?"

"Could be Coghan. Could be this mystery person."

"Maybe Melanie knows who it is."

"Maybe."

Alex gazed past him, down the long corridor. "How long for the marshal?"

"A week, max."

She glared at him.

"Budgets are tight," he said. "We can't pay to protect her indefinitely."

Not if she can't help us. Not if she's a vegetable. The words hung there, unsaid, in the space between them.

Alex shouldered her purse. "I'd appreciate a visitor's badge. Or some kind of clearance."

"Planning to be here a while?"

"Yes."

"I'll see what I can do."

"Thank you." She started to walk away.

"Alex?"

She turned around.

"Watch your step."

Alex felt sick as she exited the hospital. She was on her own now, but Nathan's departure hadn't brought the relief she'd expected. She needed someone to talk to tonight. Or even better, someone who wouldn't talk at all, but would take her to a place where she could forget everything.

Nathan could do that. He could make the rest of the world just float away until there was nothing but the two of them and their private cocoon.

But then reality would intrude, as it always did. Their one amazing night together would turn into two. Then three. Then four, with lots of daylight hours mixed in. And if she wasn't careful, she'd have a relationship on her hands.

And Nathan was right. She didn't like relationships.

He'd start expecting things. She'd start expecting things. He'd get disappointed. She'd get disappointed. She'd been through the cycle just enough times to know it wasn't for her. She had no interest in getting "landed," as he put it. She didn't know of a single happy marriage, and she'd looked around. Of course, a lot of that looking around involved tracking down cheating spouses and deadbeat dads, but still. Those were real-life examples.

Alex retrieved her car from the hospital parking garage and found her way back to the French Quarter. Her backpack was still at the bed-and-breakfast. And she still hadn't checked out of the Hyatt.

Maybe she'd stay there tonight. It was late to be moving around, but the idea of spending a night in that big bed all alone depressed her.

She pulled into the tiny lot beside the B and B and scanned the selection of cars. No black Mustang. A lump of disappointment lodged in her throat. She'd gotten rid of him, just like she'd wanted, and now she felt like a world-class bitch.

Alex trudged through the courtyard adorned with twinkle lights, past the tables crowded with people drinking and talking and laughing against the backdrop of jazz music. She opened the door to the lobby and was relieved to see the man she recognized from last night seated at the desk in front of a computer. Instead of silk pajamas, he wore a neatly tailored suit with a lavender pinstripe.

He stood up and smiled as she approached. "Miss Lovell. What can I do for you?"

She pulled out her wallet, even though instinct told

her Nathan would have taken care of the bill already. It was the sort of gentlemanly thing he'd do, even though he was ticked off at her.

"I need to check out," she said, tugging out her credit card.

His brow furrowed. "I'm sorry to hear that. Nothing wrong with your room, I hope?"

She heard a noise outside and glanced past him, at the sidewalk bustling with tourists.

Then she saw the car.

"Miss Lovell?"

"Sorry. Did Mr. Devereaux leave yet?" She held her breath, waiting for his answer and telling herself she was pathetic.

"To my knowledge, no." The clerk frowned. "I believe he's at dinner."

She let out the breath. She tucked the card back in her wallet. She walked to the French door and peered out, just to be certain.

"Is everything all right, Miss Lovell?"

She glanced at the clerk, who was watching her curiously.

"Everything's fine," she said. "Thanks."

She pulled open the door and stepped into the damp New Orleans night.

CHAPTER TWENTY-FIVE

A light drizzle started falling as she made her way through the crowded streets. By the time she crossed Toulouse, the drizzle had become a full-fledged rain. She spotted a familiar corner and turned left, then right again, trying to retrace the route they'd taken earlier.

The rain became a downpour. Tourists scattered, ducking into bars and restaurants, but none that looked familiar. Alex glanced around in despair. She'd been paying attention. What had she missed?

She spied the narrow alleyway. It was empty now, and shadowy, but the neon green sign in the window said MCLEAN's. She made a dash for it.

The bar was warm and noisy and crowded with water-logged tourists. Alex scanned the room. No Nathan. She elbowed her way to the back, to the raised platform where a sax player was warming up at the microphone. But the table they'd shared earlier was occupied now by a cluster of college kids.

Her shoulders sagged.

She glanced around, hopes fading. He'd grown up in the Quarter; he could have gone anywhere. What made her think she knew him well enough to predict his movements? Maybe that hadn't even been his car.

"He's upstairs."

Alex turned to see Vera standing nearby, a tray of drinks hoisted on her shoulder. She nodded across the room, and for the first time, Alex noticed the stairs.

Her heart lifted.

"Thanks," she told Vera.

"Sure thing." The waitress squeezed past with her load lifted high. "But fair warning, sugar. He's in a black mood."

Alex wove through the crowd. The stairs were steep, and she climbed them carefully because her sandals were slippery with rain. She must look awful. Suddenly nervous, she finger-combed her hair. At the top of the staircase, she heard a sharp *crack*.

Four big lights shone down on four green tables, all of them occupied with players. She spotted Nathan, and her pulse spiked. He was at the far end of the room, cue in hand, rounding the table as he scoped out a shot.

Alex moved toward him, heart hammering now. She watched his athletic movements as he leaned over the felt. Every detail was visible under the bright light, and she drank it all in—his strong profile; his jaw, shadowed with stubble; the way his muscles strained against his T-shirt as he lined up the shot. She knew the instant he sensed her, although his gaze never left the ball. The cue moved—a slight jab—and balls glided across the felt.

He stood up.

His gaze locked with hers, and the sheer meanness in it hit her like a punch. She froze. Her breath backed up in her lungs as he pinned her with all that hostility.

She forced her feet to move forward. His attention shifted back to the table. No longer sure of herself, she cast around for a distraction. She saw his jacket, draped across a bar stool, and decided that was as good a spot as any. A half-empty drink sat at his place. She dropped her purse on the floor and caught the bartender's attention.

"Rum and Coke, please."

She glimpsed her reflection in the mirror behind the bar. It was worse than she'd imagined. Her hair was dripping wet, and her thin rayon dress was plastered to her body—and not in a good way. She tucked her hair behind her ears and tugged the fabric away from her skin, but it was pretty hopeless. When the drink came, she took a big gulp.

She caught Nathan's gaze in the mirror, watching her, as he chalked his cue. She swiveled on the stool to face him. The intensity was there still, and she forced herself not to squirm. After a moment, she crossed her legs and tried to look nonchalant as she surveyed the pool table.

Nathan was stripes. He was winning, too, and Alex wondered about the black mood Vera had mentioned.

Did it have to do with her?

She watched his face as he took aim and called the pocket. He made the shot.

She turned around and stirred her drink. A minute ticked by. Two. She resisted the temptation to look in the mirror to see what he was doing. She'd made a mistake coming here.

An arm reached over her shoulder and picked up the abandoned glass.

She turned around and gazed up at him. "You win any money?"

He drained the drink. "Fifty bucks." He plunked the glass on the bar, boxing her in with his arm.

"Not bad."

His face was inches from hers, and she could feel his body heat surrounding her, seeping into her skin. Something dangerous smoldered in his eyes.

"I thought you'd be on the road by now," she said, somewhat hoarsely.

"Thought you'd be at the Hyatt by now."

She looked at her lap. He'd known she wouldn't be comfortable at the B and B alone, not after last night. What did that say about her?

She glanced up and cleared her throat. "I went by the hospital," she told him. "No change."

His gaze dropped to her mouth.

"They've got a guard there. A U.S. Marshal."

He eased closer and rested a hand on her thigh. The weight of his fingers burned through her dress and seemed to scald her skin. He bent his head down, and she thought he might kiss her, but he stopped just shy of her cheek.

"If you came here to talk," he said in a low voice, "I'm not interested."

He eased back and stared down at her. He smelled like sweat and bourbon, and the predatory look in his eyes made her throat go dry.

"I didn't come to talk."

His grip tightened on her thigh, and her breath caught. His thumb moved under the hem, and she nearly slid off the bar stool.

He took her wrist in his hand.

"Come on," he said.

And she did.

Her wrist ached as he pulled her behind him down the rain-slicked sidewalk. Half running to keep up with his long strides, she stumbled over the uneven cobblestones. He towed her across a street, dodging a taxi. She leaped over a puddle on the other side, and nearly landed on her butt, but he caught her and pulled her up.

"You okay?"

"Uh."

He didn't even look, just dragged her along beside him until they reached a familiar pair of French doors. He yanked one open and nudged her in front of him, into the chilly lobby.

The clerk jumped to his feet, no doubt startled by their soggy entrance. Nathan didn't even spare him a glance as he caught her hand in his and tugged her toward the elevator.

An elderly couple stood beside the call button, staring politely at the bronze doors as the elevator made its slow descent. He pulled her past them, past a planter and a bench, and pushed open the door to the stairwell.

"Watch your step," he said, tugging her up the stairs, and laughter bubbled up in her throat as she remembered Holt telling her the same thing, only he hadn't meant for her to "watch her step" as she sprinted up a stairwell to have hot, steamy sex with a man who looked like he wanted to strangle her.

They reached the third floor. Nathan pushed through the door. He snagged her purse off her shoulder as she tripped past him and immediately started rummaging for the room key.

"Side pocket," she said breathlessly.

They stopped in front of the room. He jerked open the pocket. Anger flashed across his face as he spotted her SIG. He glanced up.

Oops.

But, come on. Had he really thought she'd come here unarmed?

Shaking his head, he dug through everything else until he found the clunky fleur-de-lis. He jerked it free and shoved the purse at her, then muttered a curse as he fumbled with the old-fashioned lock. She watched him, tucking her hand in the back pocket of his jeans as she waited, heart pounding. At last, he jammed the key home and shoved open the door.

Finally.

He yanked her inside, and she barely had time to drop her purse on a chair before he had her flattened against the wall. His body was hard. His mouth and hands were everywhere. His hips pressed into her, and she felt the thick ridge of him through his jeans.

"Bed," she managed, tearing her mouth away.

But he wasn't listening. His hand was up, under her skirt, the other one crushed against her breast. He squeezed it through the wet fabric and seemed to realize she wasn't wearing anything underneath.

He pulled back and down looked at her, panting, and the desire in his eyes made her knees weak. He jerked and tore at the buttons until her dress gaped open, baring her to the waist. Then his mouth was on her again, licking and nipping and pulling. His hands slid to her

hips and suddenly she was up, off her feet, and pressed
against the wall. She wrapped her legs around him and
clutched at his head, his hair, whatever she could reach as
he went after her mouth again.

Then they were moving, and she held on tight as he
crossed the room. Adrenaline rushed through her as she
let herself be *carried* off to bed. It was amazing. Romantic. Amazingly romantic. And then he dumped her on
the mattress and gazed down at her, hands on his hips.
Her breath left her. The look on his face said nothing
about romance. It was raw and dangerous and made her
skin tingle.

"Don't like the bra I gave you?"

"Not really."

The mattress sank as he rested a knee beside her thigh
and slid his hand up her skirt.

"You like the rest of it."

She closed her eyes and tipped her head back as his
hand slipped under the lace.

"You like that?"

"Umm . . ."

His fingers stroked over her, and then his mouth was
on her again, kissing and licking its way down her body.
Somehow the buttons opened and the dress fell away and
all her skin was exposed and chilly, but then his mouth
glided over her, warming her, as his hands scorched
everything they touched.

"Oh my God," she murmured. Half-dazed, she fumbled for his waist, his jeans. Her fingers skimmed over
him, managed to find his belt somehow.

But he pulled back.

She grasped the belt and jerked him toward her, but he leaned back.

"Now," she said. *Right now.*

But he didn't stop what he was doing, and she couldn't make him stop. He didn't stop looking, either, gazing down at her with that fiery, triumphant gleam as she lay there, totally weak with need.

"Please?"

He lifted an eyebrow slightly. "You can't always have your way, Alex."

And then he slid his hands up her body, making her squirm and shudder, as he gently pulled her arms through the sleeves and removed the dress. He tossed it aside, and it landed with a *whoosh* on the chair. She shivered again, suddenly acutely aware of her damp skin, her wet hair, and the hot gaze that had zeroed in on the one scrap of covering she had left.

He slid it down her legs. Much too slowly. And she propped up on her elbows as she watched him. She reached for his belt again, and again, he backed away.

Impatient now, she got to her knees on the bed and tugged up his T-shirt as she hooked a finger inside his jeans. Finally he helped her, jerking the shirt over his head and tossing it away while she stroked her hands over that wonderful body she craved more than air. She started kissing him. She loved his smell, his feel, the salty taste of his skin.

But then he was nudging her back against the feather comforter and kissing his way down her body again. She squirmed and reached for him, and he caught her wrists in his hands and planted them up by her shoulders.

You can't always have your way. And he was proving it, right this moment, with every slow, languorous touch of his hands and mouth, while she quivered beneath him and he gazed down at her. He took her mouth, kissing her deeply, as she arched and pressed herself against him. He moved down her throat, lingered over her breasts, teasing her until she was ready to scream. And he knew it. He knew exactly what he was doing to her, and he was watching her, savoring every moment. He moved up to kiss her mouth again, and she hooked her leg around him, and the rasp of the denim against her bare skin frustrated her beyond belief. She moved under him and pleaded with her eyes. She was begging now, but the desire inside her was coiling tighter and tighter, and she knew she was going to explode if he didn't hurry.

She squeezed him closer, and he smiled down at her in the dimness.

He knew. He knew exactly where she was. He knew *her*—she could feel it in every cell of her body as he shifted over her and she heard the scrape of his zipper.

She closed her eyes and nearly wept with relief as he moved over her. She listened to the tear of foil, the thud of his wallet hitting the floor. She bit her lip and waited, afraid if she uttered a single syllable, she'd choke.

And then he caught her knee in his hand and pushed into her.

Every nerve cried out. She wrapped herself around him and pulled him as close as she could. Her hands were in his hair, pulling his mouth down to hers. She moved beneath him, but he refused to be rushed, and he tortured her for minute after minute until she thought she'd die.

He whispered her name.

She opened her eyes, and the look on his face as he gazed down at her made her heart skitter.

He was *making love* to her. With every slow, sweaty thrust of his body, he was proving her wrong, letting her know that they were connected, linked, that this wasn't just about sex, and they both knew it.

He must have seen the shock on her face, because he smiled slightly. He slid her hands from around his neck and planted them firmly above her head. She moved beneath him, lost in the pure pleasure of it, as she let go of all her resistance and gave him what he wanted.

He knew the instant she let go. She felt it in his body, his pace, as he pounded into her, fiercely and possessively, never letting her hands go, never giving her one single shred of control, as she gasped and reached and struggled to keep up. And just when she thought she was going to die from all of it, he freed her hands and said her name and she threw her arms around him and came undone.

In the morning, he was gone.

Alex squinted at the light shining through the windows. She reached back through the haze, trying to remember.

He'd left before dawn. The room had been dark. She'd been lying there, sapped and sated, after yet another storm of lovemaking. She'd heard the faint jingle of his keys as he'd slipped out the door.

She sat up now and rubbed the grit from her eyes. The bed was a wreck. So was the room. Her dress was on the chair, where he'd tossed it last night. Her purse was beside it, and her backpack, and the sleek, palm-size device that could tell her the time, the weather, and everything she needed to do today, if only she'd look.

She got out of bed and went to the French doors, dragging the comforter with her. She pulled it around her shoulders, then flipped the lock and stepped onto the balcony.

The sounds of zydeco and traffic greeted her. Another humid day. More rain probably, too, judging by the clouds. She looked out over the street, and her gaze went to the parking meter half a block away.

A black truck was there now.

She sank onto the chaise and gazed up at the sky. Her thoughts wandered back, retracing every moment from the instant she'd entered the bar. She realized what he'd done.

The old bait and switch, only in reverse. He'd given her exactly what she *hadn't* wanted, then everything she had. He was gone. She was alone. No commitment, no hassles, no headaches. It was just what she'd asked for.

She curled up on chair, tucked the blanket around her, and felt empty.

CHAPTER TWENTY-SIX

Mia stalked into her workroom and slapped the file onto the counter.

"Shit!" she hissed, snapping off her gloves and pitching them into the biohazard bin. She dropped her head into her hands and tried to will away the tears burning her eyes. These were the days she was grateful to work in a closet by herself. Sometimes it was all just too much—

"Rough morning?"

She gasped and whirled around.

Nathan Devereaux got up from the stool he'd been sitting on and stepped toward her. "They told me to wait in here."

"God, you scared me!" She clasped a hand to her chest and glanced around. No more surprise visitors lurking in the corners. Just this blue-eyed detective. "*Who* told you to wait in here?"

"Your friend next door. Think his name was Mark."

Mia glared at the door separating her little workroom from the larger DNA lab. Privacy was merely an illusion in this place. She needed to remember that.

The detective held out a paper bag from the coffee shop downstairs.

"They were out of chocolate, so I got cinnamon," he said.

She snatched it from him, both annoyed and embarrassed to be caught in a weak moment. She peeked inside, then placed the scones on the counter. "Thank you."

"You okay?" he asked, and the genuine concern on his face made the tears threaten again.

"I'm fine." She took a deep breath and tucked a lock of hair behind her ear. Time to act professional. "You're here about your baling wire."

"That's right."

She brushed past him and retrieved a file from her in-box. Delphi's ligature expert had printed up his report, and Mia had clipped it together with the DNA findings.

She skimmed through the pages to refresh her memory, then cleared her throat. "Your sample was identified as eleven-gauge baling wire," she said crisply. "According to our ligature tracer, it typically comes in fifty- or one-hundred-pound coils."

He whistled. "Lotta wire."

She glanced up from the file.

"Wonder what the chances are we might find some leftovers sitting around in his garage."

She could see what he was hoping for, so she went ahead and told him the rest. "According to our expert, this stuff's the farming equivalent of duct tape. It's ubiquitous. Also known as hay wire, it's commonly used to mend fences, bind haybales, or do any number of chores."

But the detective didn't seem put off by this.

"It might be possible to link it to a specific coil, if you had one," Mia said. "Do you have a search warrant?"

"Not yet." Devereaux propped a hand against the counter and nodded at the file in her hands. "What else you got there?"

"That's it for the wire itself. As for the DNA, the profiles you submitted—and I excluded yours from the sample taken from the handkerchief—were consistent."

His gaze sharpened. "You got a match?"

"Not quite. I recovered skin cells from the wire, but the sample was too degraded—probably due to improper storage—to get a full profile. I only got eleven loci."

At his questioning look, she backed up. "DNA is analyzed by comparing specific loci. The standard is thirteen. The eleven I was able to get are consistent with the sample from your handkerchief."

He folded his arms over his chest, and she wondered how he managed to make a blazer and slacks look so scruffy. Maybe it was the hair. It seemed longer than she remembered it a few weeks ago.

"Tell me straight," he said. "In your expert opinion, is it a match or not?"

"The odds of the samples belonging to the same donor are astronomically high," she said. "I think it's the same person."

He nodded. "Thank you."

"Anytime."

And suddenly the horror of this morning faded a bit as she realized she'd managed to help someone today, at least a little.

She sighed and put the file down, and he nodded at the other one sitting on the counter.

"Bad case?" he asked.

"Sexual homicide." He nodded. "Victim was eight." She didn't mention that the DNA sample she'd used to place the victim in the suspect's home had come from dried tears on a bedsheet.

"So," she said, changing the subject. "What do you hear from Alex Lovell?"

He glanced away. "Not a whole lot."

Mia tried to mask her surprise. The question made him uncomfortable, and yet last time she'd seen him with Alex, they'd seemed so close.

"I've left her several voice mails," she said, trying for a neutral tone, "but she hasn't returned my calls."

He didn't respond, and she decided to keep pushing. The Cyber Crimes Unit wanted Alex back, and they'd asked Mia to help make that happen.

"Her assistant, Sophie, tells me she's out of town on business," Mia continued. "You know if she's coming back soon?"

"No idea."

"She's been gone a couple weeks now. Sophie recommended I drop her an e-mail, said Alex was checking her messages every few days."

His eyebrows tipped up. "Every few *days*?"

"I thought it sounded weird, too." Mia tried to read his expression. Concerned? Defensive? She couldn't quite tell. "Is she okay, do you know? Because our cyber crimes people got the impression she really wanted to lend us a hand here. It seemed to be going somewhere, and then she just up and left."

He looked guarded now, and Mia knew her fishing expedition had come to an end. Once again, she'd come up with nothing. She'd talked to Troy, then Sophie, and now Devereaux, but no one seemed to know what was going on with Alex Lovell.

"Anyway, if you hear from her, please tell her to get in touch with us." Mia held out her report.

He took it and gave a stiff nod. "If I happen to see her, I'll pass it along."

Alex pulled into her parking lot and sailed down the row of cars. *Sailed.* It really was the only way to describe what it felt like to drive around in this boat. But it was growing on her. If it weren't for the lack of CD player, and air conditioning, and power locks, she might actually consider holding on to this thing.

She maneuvered into her parking space and glanced at the rearview mirror.

It couldn't be. She whipped her head around and looked over her shoulder.

And yet, it had to be. How many black Ferraris did she see in a year? She got out of the Sunliner and glanced around.

He sauntered toward her from the direction of the main office.

"Hi," she said.

"Hi yourself."

Troy stopped in front of her and peeled off his shades. His eyes were bloodshot, and it appeared as though he hadn't slept, showered, or shaved in at least a week.

He gazed up at the sign towering above the parking lot and sighed. "Extended Stay, Alex?"

"They have good rates."

He shook his head.

She looked him over, and she felt a wave of tenderness. She'd seen him like this before, but never this bad.

"Looks like you could use a cup of coffee," she said.

"I think I passed the coffee stage"—he glanced at his watch—"about ten days ago."

"Let's go." She led him across the parking lot to the greasy-spoon diner adjacent to the motel. He didn't talk, and she used the time to push aside all the emotions that he'd triggered just by showing up here.

They settled into a crescent-shaped booth, and she pretended to look at a menu, even though she'd memorized everything on it. Neither of them was good at just plunging right in. A waitress stopped by to take their orders, and finally they tucked their distractions away behind the ketchup bottle.

"How bad?" Alex asked, earning a glare from him. The mere allusion to writer's block pissed him off.

"Let's not talk about me yet." He leaned forward on his elbows. "What the fuck are you doing, Alex?"

She laughed. "What am *I* doing?"

"You're scared shitless, aren't you? That's why you're here."

"*I'm* scared?" She crossed her arms. "You're the one who drove eight hundred miles because you're afraid of shrinks."

"This isn't about me."

"Oh, right. My mistake. You came all the way here out of concern for my personal life. Who told you where I was?"

"Sophie."

Alex sighed. Sophie had flown to New Orleans to deliver Alex a laptop and some more clothes. She'd driven back in the Saturn, and Alex had paid her overtime for all her trouble.

"She shouldn't have told you where I was," Alex said now. "I need to have a talk with her."

"Ah, give her a break. She's a nice girl. Think she took pity on me after I hauled my ass all the way to Austin only to find out you were kickin' it in the Big Easy."

Alex noticed the look in his eyes. "Oh my God. You slept with her, didn't you?"

He raked his hands through his hair and leaned back.

"Troy!" She slapped her hand on the table. "*How* could you do that? She's my assistant! And she's underage!"

"She is not." He scowled at her. "She's twenty-three."

"How do you know that?"

"I checked. And I didn't sleep with her." He shot her a grumpy look. "She's hot, though. Don't think I didn't think about it."

Alex leaned back against the seat and watched him, a bit relieved. If he still had his sex drive, he couldn't be that far gone.

Their drinks came, and he gave her a few moments' peace before launching in again.

"You talked to Devereaux lately?" he asked.

"No."

"You planning to?"

"I don't know." She stirred her Coke with the straw and felt his gaze on her.

"How's Melanie?"

"Same." Alex glanced up warily. "How did you hear about that?"

"Friend of mine at the cop shop."

"APD?"

"Yeah. I spent half my drive on the phone. They've questioned Coghan, but word is, he has an alibi."

Their food arrived. Troy chomped into his hamburger. Alex peeled the undercooked bacon off her club sandwich and made a little pile on the side of her plate.

"Who do you know at APD?" she asked, in what she hoped was a casual tone.

"Plenty of people. Webb. Lopez. Hodges. Lopez told me something interesting."

"About what?"

"Coghan's alibi. The toll authority has a photograph of his truck going through a tollbooth near Freeport right around the time Melanie got shot. Coghan claims he spent the night at his dad's house, then got up and went fishing the next morning."

"Convenient," Alex said sourly. "I'm guessing this photo shows the truck, but not the driver."

"Points to an accomplice. *If,* that is, Coghan's the one who shot Melanie."

"He is." She picked up a french fry but couldn't muster an appetite. She glanced at her watch.

"Are you ready to talk about you yet?" she asked. "I've got to be somewhere in half an hour."

She could almost see his ears perk up. The newshound instinct, she guessed.

"Where you going?" he asked.

"To see someone."

"Melanie?"

"No."

"Then who?"

She sighed. "Melanie's baby. Her name's Grace."

Troy put his fork down and stared at her. "Have you gone completely off the deep end? Or is this just temporary?"

She forced herself to eat a fry. "Temporary. Until Melanie gets better. I'm trying to help out a little, spend some time with her baby."

"I didn't know she had one."

"Neither did I, until recently."

"I didn't know you liked babies."

"I don't." Except for Grace. She was special.

Troy lifted an eyebrow.

"The foster mom's really got her hands full," Alex said, and then wondered why she was defending herself. She didn't owe him an explanation.

"So when's this deadline?" she asked.

"Not so fast. We're not done with you yet. What's this I hear about you dumping the detective?"

"Where'd you hear that?"

"Think I'll protect my source on that. Is it true?"

"We weren't together, really. So no, it's not true."

Troy shook his head and polished off his burger. He had an appetite, at least. That had to be a good sign.

"You remember what you told me when we first hooked up?" he asked.

"No, but I have a feeling you do."

"You said you loved sex, but you hated relationships."

She frowned at him. "I don't remember saying that."

"You did."

"I must have been drunk."

He shrugged. "Maybe so. It was right before you told me I was the sexiest man you ever—"

"I was *definitely* drunk if I said that. Or you imagined it."

"Not the first part." He looked her in the eye. "You really said that, and I remember thinking, 'Hey, works for me. Finally a woman I can relate to.' But the thing is, you lied."

She sat back, annoyed. "You're saying I wanted a relationship with you? Even after you ditched me for that little tart at the party?"

"I knew you were still mad about that."

She rolled her eyes. "I'm not mad about it. And this conversation isn't going anywhere. You came all the way here for nothing."

"I don't think so. I think you *do* want a relationship, you're just scared of getting hurt. So as soon as you find someone who wants to be with you, you make a run for the door."

She gritted her teeth at his smug expression. He was enjoying this.

"I'm right," he said. "Admit it."

"You're wrong. I barely know Nathan Devereaux."

"Bullshit. You're in love with him."

Her mouth dropped open.

"What? You know you are. That's why you're acting like a coward, hiding in New Orleans while your business and your relationship go down the tubes."

"I'm not *hiding* in New Orleans." She pushed her plate away, angry now. "And who says my business is going down the tubes?"

"I do. Sophie's terrified. She thinks she's going to be out on the street in a week, looking for a new job. You don't man the fort, the work's going to dry up. All that effort you put in, gone. Plus, you've got the Delphi Center knocking on your door. Lots of people would kill for a chance to work there." He pointed a french fry at her. "And hey, here's a thought: What if Devereaux gets tired of waiting around for you to get your shit together and finds someone else?"

She felt a hot spurt of resentment. "I don't have to listen to this."

"Most guys I know won't sit around forever. First choice blows 'em off, they go for runner-up."

Alex clamped her mouth shut to keep from saying something particularly foul.

"Not a nice thought, eh?" The corner of his mouth curved up. "Told you. You're in love with him."

"You don't know me as well as you think you do. And you don't know Nathan at all."

"I know guys. And I *do* know you, like it or not. You're throwing away the best guy who ever happened to you, myself included."

She rolled her eyes and looked away. Where was the waitress? She needed to pay up and leave.

He popped the last fry in his mouth and pushed his plate away. He smiled at her. "I'm feeling better now."

"Now that you've trashed my life over sandwiches? Thanks a lot."

"I didn't trash anything," he said. "But I'm serious, Alex. Think about what you're doing here."

"I'm helping a friend."

"At the expense of the business you built? At the expense of a relationship that matters to you?"

She huffed out a breath. "You obviously think you're an expert on everything, but you're not. We don't have a *relationship*. And I'm not in love with him."

Troy shrugged. "Whatever you say."

"Why are you telling me all this?"

He met her gaze for a long moment. "I care about you. And Devereaux's a stand-up guy. I think he'd be good for you, if you haven't botched it already."

Alex started to feel queasy. She hated the food here. And yet she continued to eat it.

He nodded at the seat beside him. "He put that thing on your key chain, didn't he?"

"What thing?"

"That medallion."

Alex gazed down at the key chain sitting beside her purse. Nathan had attached something to it, just before he'd left her at the bed-and-breakfast. She remembered it being on *his* key chain, and her chest tightened every time she looked at it.

"It's a Saint Christopher medal," Troy said.

"What does it mean?"

He smiled slightly. "Why don't you ask him?"

She zipped the damn keys into her purse and folded her arms. "Okay, we're done with me. Now it's your turn. When's your deadline?"

The smug smile vanished from his face, replaced by that miserable look he'd shown up with. For a moment, she enjoyed it.

"Troy?"

"A week ago." He tipped his head back against the booth and closed his eyes.

"How much is left?"

He didn't open his eyes. "About half."

Ouch. "What are you going to do?"

He opened one eye and peered at her.

"Forget it."

He sighed. He'd told her before that sex sometimes helped. But that wasn't going to happen.

"Come on." She scooted out of the booth and left some bills on the table. "I think I know just what you need." She'd walk on his back for him. And maybe, *if* he was nice, she might give him a neck rub.

He eyed her suspiciously. "You're not going to hurt me, are you?"

"Probably."

"I knew it."

"If you didn't want my help, you shouldn't have come."

Nathan took a beautiful swing, but totally whiffed it.

"*Steeeee-rike.*"

He sent Hodges an evil look. "You mind?"

"Not at all." His partner leaned back against the chain-link fence and tapped his bat in the dirt.

Nathan focused his attention, refusing to be distracted by the cocky son of a bitch. Hodges had him on body mass and age, but Nathan had played college ball once upon a time and had the kid beat in the experience department.

The next one came fast. Nathan smashed it and smiled as it rocketed into the net.

"Alex back yet?" Hodges asked.

Another fast ball. He missed it completely. "No."

"You talked to her?"

"No. Why?"

"Just wondering if there's any change," Hodges said.

"Change?"

"With Melanie."

Right. What other kind of change would there be? He hadn't seen or heard from Alex since he'd left her in that hotel room. And with every day that ticked by, he was eaten up with dread. Maybe he should have stayed to fight it out with her. But he'd thought he could read her. And he'd thought if he gave her enough space, she'd decide she didn't want it.

The next pitch was a curve, and he blasted the shit out of it.

"Not bad."

He turned to see Nicole walking toward them. She'd dressed down for the occasion in jeans and cross trainers. As a setting for this officially unofficial meeting, Nathan had selected a Saturday morning and the batting cages on South Lamar.

"My turn," Hodges said, and traded places with him.

"You wanna hit?" Nathan asked Nicole as he held the gate open for her.

"No." She leaned back against the fence. "This is really clever, though. I couldn't even bring my briefcase. And you get my advice for free."

Nathan smiled because he'd planned it that way. He'd taken away all her favorite props so she'd be forced to let her guard down and give him her true opinion. Nicole had a sharp legal mind, and he hit her up for professional advice from time to time.

Hodges smacked one into orbit, and Nicole whistled. He sent her a look. She was in flirt mode, and he'd forgotten to tell her Hodges was married.

"I read your tracers' report," she said. "How'd you get Cernak to approve an expense like that?"

"Went over his head," Nathan said. "So what do you think?"

She twirled her Chanel sunglasses by the stem and looked at him. "I think you've got a case," she said. "And I think I could drive a truck through some of the holes in it."

"Let's have it," he said stoically.

"All right, let's start with the ligature," she began in her courtroom voice. "The DNA on it *could* be Coghan's, assuming your comparison sample's good—"

"It is."

"—but the results weren't totally conclusive." She hooked her glasses on the V-neck of her T-shirt. "Problem number one."

"The DNA's Coghan's," Nathan told her. "Trust me."

"*If* that's true, then it's your strongest piece of evidence. It links him to a cold case, provided he can't offer some other reason for his DNA to be on that murder weapon." She gave him a disapproving look. "And I should probably lecture you about the surreptitious collection of evidence—"

"Don't bother," he cut her off. "What else?"

"Okay," she said. "Then you've got a severed earbud. The blood on it comes back to a murder victim recovered from Lake Austin. He's been IDed as Joseph Turner. According to the tracers' ligature expert, whatever severed that earphone wire is 'consistent with' the baling wire from your cold case."

"The victim from behind the strip bar," Hodges said.

"Yes."

"So," Nathan said, visualizing it, "Joe Turner was at that fishing cabin, using Melanie's earphones, when someone—we'll say Coghan—walked up behind him and garroted him with baling wire. Then Coghan removed the body from the house, dumped it in the lake, and burned up the crime scene."

"That's a huge stretch," Nicole said.

"It's totally logical."

"I meant in terms of provability," she said. "And don't even get me started on that earbud as evidence. It was *allegedly* removed from a crime scene by a private investigator. A defense attorney would make mincemeat of it in court."

Nathan had known that from the beginning. But he was building a case here, brick by brick, and he needed every brick he could get.

"Fine," he said. "What else we got?"

"That's it," she said. "There's not much else."

Hodges groaned, but Nathan refused to be discouraged.

"What if we get a search warrant," he said, "and find some of that wire in Coghan's garage or some place?"

Nicole tipped her head to the side. "What's my probable cause?"

"Everything you just said. We can link Coghan to two killings, based the evidence you just listed—"

"Most of which a judge would balk at—"

"Not to mention the *new* victim that just turned up strangled behind a strip joint. That's three murders with the same MO."

"Even if we *got* a warrant," Nicole allowed, "you think Coghan would be stupid enough to leave that wire sitting around? He's a lot of things, but he's not stupid. Plus, as long as we're building a case here, what's his motive?"

"You mean besides offing the guy who was banging his wife? He wanted to eliminate threats," Nathan said. "Keep his operation going. Melanie, Joe Turner, the thug behind the bar, the CI who probably threatened to blow the whistle. All of those victims were in a position to expose him. He needed them dead."

"Makes a compelling story," Nicole said. "But where's the proof?"

Nathan tapped his bat in the dirt, thinking. "We need a search warrant," he muttered. "Who knows what he's got stashed in his house, in his car."

"Good luck with that," she said. "Oh, and FYI, now that he knows the feds are onto him, he's acting like a choir boy."

"How do you know?" Hodges asked.

"I've got a contact on the task force," she said. "They're all over him, but they can't get anything incriminating. He's not connected to the paperwork on those houses. Their evidence linking him to the operation at all is razor thin. They need witnesses who want to tell a story. That's why they wanted Melanie."

"We need the accomplice," Nathan said, thinking out loud. "Coghan likes to strangle people. It's quiet. No ballistics. But he's got an accomplice somewhere—someone with a twenty-two. Hell, maybe that person's in on the real estate deals, too. That whole setup involved money and legal expertise Coghan doesn't have."

"Maybe we're talking more than one accomplice," Hodges suggested.

"Who's the CI you mentioned?" Nicole asked. "I hadn't heard about him."

"It's a her," Nathan said. "One of Coghan's people. She was a hooker, killed with a twenty-two, two shots to the chest. Melanie was shot with a twenty-two."

"Hookers get killed every day," Nicole said. "And I don't have to tell you how common those weapons are. If you could get matching ballistics, that *might* be worth something, but—"

"Yeah, but those two women have something else in common," Hodges said. "They were both sleeping with Coghan. And they both have the scars."

"Scars?" she asked.

Hodges cleared his throat. "Turns out, Coghan likes to brand women with his cigarette while he's, you know—"

"Getting blown," Nathan finished for him.

"He *brands* them?" she asked. "Where did you hear that?"

"I interviewed some prostitutes who work for this guy Little J," Nathan said. "I thought it was their pimp's sick fetish, but turns out it's Coghan."

Of course, not one of those girls would ever go on the witness stand to talk about servicing a cop. And even if they did, a defense attorney would torpedo their credibility in no time.

Nicole unhooked her sunglasses from her T-shirt. "This is one hell of a case," she said.

"Tell me about it."

"I'm trying to." She looked at him, then at Hodges, and Nathan knew he was about to hear the closing argument.

"All your physical evidence? You can forget taking

it into court," she said. "You've got major admissibility problems. So unless you can get a warrant—which I doubt—and find something incriminating, you're going to have a bitch of a time building this murder case. Why don't you let the feds keep after him for drug charges?"

"I want him on murder," Nathan said stubbornly. Anything less was unacceptable.

"You asked me for my advice, Nathan. So here it is: drop this case," she said. "Politically and legally, it's a dog. And you guys have more than enough work as it is. Leave Coghan to the feds."

Nathan clenched his teeth.

"My guess is they'll have him on racketeering inside of three months."

"And then they'll cut a deal with him to get to the bigger fish," Hodges put in.

"Maybe, maybe not. But if you want him for murder, you've got only one hope left, and it isn't much."

"And what's that?" Nathan asked.

"You'd better hope Melanie wakes up." She put on her shades. "And that when she does, she's willing and able to talk."

Alex stepped through the hospital doors and gazed up at the sky. She felt light. Weightless. Like a child's balloon that had been let go, simply to drift up, up, and away into the cloudless sky.

She tipped her head back and smiled. Again. For hours, she hadn't been able to get rid of this silly grin, so finally she'd given up, and just let it stay. Now she stood on the sidewalk, enjoying the sun on her cheeks and the warm, fizzy euphoria coursing through her veins.

A siren pulled her back to earth. She opened her eyes. The area all around her buzzed with doctors and nurses and patients coming and going. She blinked up at the sky and realized what else was different. The rain had stopped. The slate gray sky she'd existed under for three weeks had transformed into a deep, rich blue.

Alex strolled toward the garage and decided to do something she hadn't done since San Francisco. It was the perfect day for it. Twenty minutes later, she was cruising down the highway with the top down. The engine hummed. The wind whipped her hair around her shoulders. She was going to arrive at the motel looking like Medusa, and she looked forward to seeing the expression on Troy's face.

If he was even awake.

He'd spent the past twenty-four hours immobilized on the sofa in her motel suite. She'd never seen anything like it. She'd come home last night and bustled around. She'd showered, and eaten, and watched TV, and pecked around on her computer, and he hadn't moved an eyelash. Only his deep, even breathing let her know he was among the living.

When she reached the motel, the Ferrari in her usual parking spot piqued her interest. He'd been out, which could be good or bad. Maybe he'd snapped out of his funk. Or maybe he'd gone on a bender. She'd been away for six hours, and that was more than enough time for him to find his way to the Quarter and get blitzed.

She paused in front of the room but didn't hear anything. She slid in her key card and opened the door.

The room was a cave.

"Troy?" She waved away a thick cloud of smoke as

she stepped inside. She turned around. He was seated at the desk in the living area. The computer screen in front of him cast his face in a ghoulish light.

"You're awake." She closed the door behind her and smothered a cough. "Jeez, how can you stand it in here?" She tripped over a fast-food bag and caught herself on the sofa arm. "God, this place is a mess!"

She picked her way through the flotsam covering the floor. He'd been to Wendy's *and* KFC, apparently. And now he was sucking down nicotine. The cup of herbal tea she'd made for him yesterday still sat on the coffee table, untouched.

"Hel*lo*! Troy? You alive in there?"

He frowned at the screen but still didn't look up. "Yo, Smoky. It reeks in here." She picked up the water glass he'd appropriated as an ashtray. Shaking her head, she walked over to the kitchenette and dumped the contents in the trash can. Then she watched, amazed, as he took a drag on his cigarette and ashed directly onto the desk.

"Oh, for heaven's sake!" She rushed over with the empty glass. "Troy!"

He glanced up. "Huh?"

"Unbelievable." She crossed her arms. "How long have you been up?"

He glanced down at the screen and frowned.

She took a closer look at him. He wore the same outfit he'd shown up in—a rumpled T-shirt and Levi's 501s—minus the cowboy boots. His hair was approaching the predreadlock stage, and his beard was filling in nicely.

And he was completely zoned out.

She stepped behind him and snapped open the blinds. He turned around and squinted at her. "Hey!"

"Finally! God. What is with you?"

He shifted the computer away from the glare and started typing something.

"Are you working? On *my* computer?"

He didn't answer.

She sighed. "Hey, don't you want to hear my good news?" She turned and gazed out the window at the cloudless sky, and felt the grin return. "It's been an *amazing* day! Magnificent! *Breath*taking!" She looked at the back of his head, and his hands continued to move over the keyboard.

"Melanie woke up. Can you believe it? Three weeks, and just *snap*." She gazed through the glass. Even the parking lot looked beautiful this afternoon. "I couldn't believe it. I walked in this morning, and there she was, sitting up in bed." She was talking to herself now, but she didn't care. "I mean, it was miraculous. She recognized me right away. You want to know the first thing she said? 'Where's Grace?' Isn't that great? I swear, I almost cried."

She peered out the window at her convertible, basking in the afternoon sunshine like a big red whale. It was a *beast* of a car, and she was starting to love it. The fins were actually kind of cool. And with the top down like that, it looked more proportional somehow. She imagined flying down the road in it with Nathan.

A lump rose in her throat. She stared at the car. Her gaze dropped to the key chain in her hand, to the medallion Nathan had put there before he left. Christopher, the patron saint of safe travels. Alex had looked it up.

Suddenly, she knew what she had to do now. It was clear as the sky.

"I'm leaving," she announced.

She strode across the room and jerked open a dresser drawer. She scooped up a pile of clothes.

"Troy? You hear what I said? It's time to go home."

She dragged her duffel out of the closet and dumped the clothes inside. Her sweatshirt was draped over the back of a chair, and she stuffed it in, too. Next was the bathroom. She picked up the items scattered across countertop and dropped them into her travel kit.

"Troy?"

"What?"

"I'm going back to Austin. Today. Wrap that up."

She zipped everything inside the duffel and glanced around. Why was her pulse racing? Why were her palms sweaty?

Nathan. She was nervous about seeing him. She hadn't called him in weeks. Maybe she should have. But he hadn't called her, either. She bit her lip and glanced around the room.

Running shoes under the coffee table. She snatched them up and shoved them in the bag. She parked her stuff by the door and grabbed a soft drink from the fridge. She looked around. That was it. Except for her computer bag.

"Troy, I need my computer."

She waited a beat. Nothing.

"Troy?"

"No," he said, without looking up.

"*No?*"

"I'm in the middle of something."

She walked over to him and fisted a hand on her hip. "Well, e-mail yourself a copy. It's time to go."

He tore his eyes away from the screen and gave her his full attention. "I'm not going anywhere."

"Well, *I* am. And my computer's coming with me."

He looked down at the screen again and resumed typing. "I need it," he muttered.

"So do I! It's got my files on it."

"I'll send them to you."

"Are you kidding? That's my system. You can't just keep it, just because you're in the middle of—"

"I'll give you a thousand dollars for it."

"I paid twenty-five hundred for it three months ago!"

"Ten thousand." His gaze never left the screen.

"Ten *thousand* dollars. For a laptop." She stared at him. He'd totally lost his marbles.

"Troy, that's absurd. I'm going back to Austin, and I need my computer. Don't bully me. Please. We need to check out and get on the road. I know you probably don't care, but I'm not crazy about driving cross-country late at night. We need to head out."

He kept typing.

"Troy?"

His hands stilled. He took a deep breath and looked up at her. "Alex. I love you. But if you don't stop talking, I'm going to have to hurt you."

Her mouth dropped open.

He started typing again.

"But . . . I'm leaving," she said.

"I know."

"What are *you* going to do?"

"Stay."

"Stay? At this crappy motel? With *my* computer?"

He stood up. He walked across the room and picked

up her bags from beside the door. She trailed behind him as he walked out of suite and dropped everything onto the passenger seat of the Sunliner.

"Have you completely lost your mind?" she demanded.

He stopped in front of her and patted her cheek. "Drive safe," he said.

Then he walked back into the motel room and slammed the door.

CHAPTER TWENTY-SEVEN

Nathan watched the crime scene techs load the gurney into the back of the van.

"You say you know this girl?" Hodges asked him.

"Deanna Perry, street name Britney. She'd been working this neighborhood a couple years now." *Since she was a kid.* "She and Tammy Dunn shared the same pimp."

"She another one of Coghan's informants?"

"Don't think so," Nathan said. "But who the hell knows? Maybe she knew something she shouldn't have, and he got rid of her, too."

Nathan glanced around. Not surprisingly, Coghan hadn't made the scene, even though this murder had occurred well within the narco squad's hot zone. Despite the late hour, the parking lot behind the convenience store was lit up like a stadium. Lights reflected off the rain-slicked asphalt. Several plainclothes detectives and a few uniforms were spread out in a line, conducting a grid search for shell casings or other physical evidence.

"I thought the feds were supposed to be keeping an eye on him," Hodges said. "You're thinking he ditched his tail somehow?"

"With this fucker, anything's possible."

Nathan lifted the crime scene tape and ducked under. Hodges followed. They headed back to the store, where the clerk was sequestered and awaiting an interview. The kid had called 911 after hearing a gunshot at about 8:55.

They rounded the side of the building, and Nathan saw the street corner where he'd picked up Britney for that last meeting. He remembered her fear, remembered her hands trembling as she'd shredded that tortilla and talked about her dead friend. The girl had been scared for her life—with good reason, obviously.

Her death was Coghan's doing; Nathan felt it in his bones.

Nathan stopped just outside the door to the store, then turned his back on the onlookers and reporters who'd already made the scene.

"We need to find Coghan, check out his alibi," Nathan said. "Why don't you make a few phone calls while I talk to this clerk?"

"I'm on it," Hodges said. And then he glanced over Nathan's shoulder, and his expression changed. "Heads up. Incoming."

Nathan turned around to see Alex elbowing her way through the crowd. The sharp punch of relief at seeing her nearly knocked him over.

She stopped in front of him and crossed her arms. "Hi," she said.

"Hi."

"I've been calling, but you didn't pick up."

"Scuse me," Hodges said, and made his escape.

"Been a little preoccupied."

"So I see."

She glanced around, and Nathan took a moment to look her over. Tousled hair, snug-fitting workout gear, Nikes. Even with all the chaos buzzing around them, she'd managed to attract the attention of some of the neighborhood lowlifes.

"How'd you find me?" Nathan took her by the elbow and guided her away from the leers and lights.

"My scanner. I couldn't reach you, so I tuned in and this is all over the police channel. Another strangling?"

"A shooting," he said, spotting an empty police unit. He led Alex to it and opened the passenger's-side door. "Sit down."

She glanced up at him with those whiskey brown eyes he hadn't seen in weeks. How long had she been back? What was she doing here? He didn't like her showing up at a crime scene—particularly this one—and he figured she had to have a good reason.

"Take a load off." He nodded at the seat. "You look beat."

"Thanks a lot," she said, but then she obediently parked her butt in the car and gazed up at him.

"When'd you get back?" he asked.

"Yesterday."

He noticed the damp hair clinging to her neck. Her cheeks were flushed, and something flickered in her eyes. Anger? Hurt?

"Melanie's awake," she said.

He watched her but didn't comment.

"She's being moved to a safe house. Holt tells me the feds are offering her a spot in the witness protection program if she'll testify against Coghan's associates."

"Who's Holt?"

"A Texas Ranger I know. He's part of the task force. Anyway, he's pretty much told me that they don't really have any dirt on her, but they're using her paranoia about Grace's safety to turn up the pressure."

"That's what's got you all hot and bothered?"

She blew out a sigh. "*No.* I spent the day staking out Coghan's health club."

Nathan gritted his teeth. She was working this case still. He should have known. "And what were you doing at Coghan's health club?"

"Following up on a lead,"

"What is it?"

"Coghan's mystery accomplice," she said, and her eyes got bright with excitement. "I thought about it the whole drive home, and I realized I might have him on tape."

Nathan frowned. "How's that?"

"Back in the fall," she said. "I spent two full days running surveillance on Coghan so I could learn his routine before I helped Melanie disappear. Last night I went back over the footage, and there it was. On two separate occasions, he's deep in conversation with people at the gym. Once in the weight room, once in the parking lot. In the parking lot footage, I even got a fuzzy license plate."

"So'd you get an ID?"

"No." She sighed. "But I e-mailed the clip to the Delphi Center. A guy I know there said he'd see if he can enhance the images."

Nathan gazed down at her but didn't say anything. Three weeks of nothing, and now here they were talking shop again. Noise surrounded them—emergency vehicles, onlookers, the squawk of a police radio—and for a long moment, they simply looked at each other.

Finally, she glanced away. "I went by your house last night."

"I was working."

"It was after two."

He bent his head down and stared at her until she lifted her gaze. "*That's* what's bothering you?"

She shrugged, and the knot of worry he'd been carrying around in his chest started to loosen. She gave a damn.

"I caught a case, Alex."

She nodded, looked away. Then took a deep breath. "I think we should talk soon. About . . . things."

She gazed up at him, and for the first time since he'd known her, her brown eyes looked vulnerable. She was going out on a limb here, taking a risk, and she seemed to be holding her breath, waiting for his response.

"We can talk," he said. "Your place or mine?"

She rolled her eyes. "That's not what I meant."

"I know what you meant." He reached out to touch her cheek, and she shivered when his thumb brushed over her skin.

Someone shouted his name across the parking lot. He turned around. Cernak.

"I have to go," he told Alex. "I'll come over later. We can talk then."

"Okay." She looked wary.

"It'll be late," he said. "Probably after midnight."

She stood up now, too, and she was so close, he could feel her body heat. He couldn't quite believe she was here. He'd been so sure that she had itchy feet again, that she was ready to pull up stakes and try her luck in New Orleans.

"I don't mind." Her voice was tentative, but her eyes were warm. And they told him she wanted to do much more than talk whenever he got done here.

He kissed her mouth. "Wait up for me," he told her.

"I will."

Alex was in bed with her clunky old laptop and a frothy Coke float when her phone finally rang. She glanced at caller ID. Then she glanced at the clock.

"This is *huge,*" she told Ben. "I can't tell you how grateful I am."

"Yeah, yeah. That's what they all say."

"Seriously, you didn't have to stay up so late just to help me."

He sighed on the other end of the phone. "In case you haven't figured it out yet, I have no life," he said. "And you won't, either, if you ever come to work here. Go check your in-box."

Alex clicked open her e-mail just as the message came in. "You use Photoshop on this?"

"I'm going to pretend I didn't hear that. You're clearly oblivious to the latest developments in photography software."

"I guess so." She slurped up ice cream as she waited for the first attachment to open. Her backup computer was agonizingly slow, and for the hundredth time tonight she cursed Troy Stockton. Finally, the picture came up, and her breath caught. "Whoa. This is incredible."

"Isn't it?"

"How'd you get such a high-res picture from a grainy video clip?"

"Trade secret," he said. "And I'll share it with you, if you'll get yourself back down here to work for us."

"I will." Alex scrambled off the bed and put the laptop on the desk, beside the dusty printer that hadn't been used in weeks.

"You mean it? You'll really come?" he asked.

The room was dark except for the glow of the computer, and it took her a second to find the cable beneath the desk.

"I'll really come." If she ever wrapped this case up.

"I'll hold you to that," Ben said, as she plugged in her machine and powered on the printer.

"So I assume you're trying to get an ID here?" Ben asked. "Does this help? Do you recognize these people?"

"I don't, but someone will." She gazed at the screen for a moment before clicking Print. The man next to Coghan in the parking could have been anybody—medium-height, paunchy, balding. But the woman talking to Coghan in the weight room was striking. Someone would know her.

"The third image is that vehicle tag," Ben said. "It's crystal clear now, so it should be a simple matter of looking it up. But if your program gives you any trouble, call me tomorrow, I'll see what I can do."

"You're a lifesaver," she said. "And I'll pay you back sometime."

"Promises, promises."

After they hung up, Alex collected the pages from the printer tray and stared down at the faces. "Who are you?" she muttered. Casual acquaintances? Alex thought not.

She'd been over and over the video clips, and the body language told her these encounters weren't casual.

She looked at the man again. There was something vaguely familiar about him, but maybe it was just because he resembled George Costanza from *Seinfeld*.

She'd go back to the gym tomorrow and shop these pictures around. She'd bet her right arm Steroid Boy could put a name to the blonde in about two seconds.

A thud sounded across the apartment. Alex whirled around.

Nathan?

It wasn't even eleven yet. She listened, but heard only the soft *pitter-pat* of rain on the roof above. Maybe she'd imagined—

Thunk.

The hair on the back of her neck stood up. Fear trickled down her spine. Alex spied her purse on the floor, beside her still-packed duffel bag. She crept over to it and pulled out her SIG. Slowly, cautiously, she tiptoed across the room. In bare feet, she moved quietly, the faint whisper of her satin pajama pants the only sound. Gripping the pistol, she peeked her head around the door frame and peered into the darkened hallway.

The apartment was still. Light from the porch seeped through the curtain on her door and cast a pale yellow glow on the living room carpet. Alex's gaze skimmed over the familiar silhouettes of her sofa, her armchair, her television. In the kitchen, the icemaker grumbled briefly, then stopped. She kept listening, kept looking, but detected nothing amiss.

Still, something tickled at her consciousness. Clutching the pistol in both hands now, she stepped into the hallway, crept past the bathroom, and poked her head around the corner.

Thunk. She jumped at the sound. *Thud, thud, thunk*.

The noise came from the front door. Then a plaintive *mew*.

Alex blew out a breath. Sugarpotomous. Probably wanting in out of the rain.

She crossed her living room and parted the curtains. Sure enough, a sopping wet cat gazed up pitifully from the welcome mat.

She reached for the door latch—

And froze.

The keypad on the wall was dark. No green light. No alarm.

Alex sucked in a breath. Her hand dropped away from the latch. She stepped back from the door.

She turned.

He lunged.

They crashed to the floor. Air *whoosh*ed out of her as he landed on her back with bone-crushing force. He gripped her wrist and smacked it against the floor. Her gun went flying. Pain ricocheted up her arm, and he stuffed something in her mouth. She couldn't breathe. Couldn't see. Something tasted sour, and her eyes burned with tears.

She kicked and twisted, tried to breathe, tried to scream, but all the air was gone and she was flattened by the *weight*. Her lungs tingled. Her arms wrenched back and she couldn't *breathe*. Something pinched her wrists. She tried to move her arms, her head, her legs, but everything started to go numb, and then the whole world turned gray.

* * *

She hadn't waited up.

Nathan closed his car door and gazed up at the dark apartment. He didn't blame her, really. It was late. She'd been tired. But she'd just have to get *un*tired. He almost hoped she'd answer the door ticked off at him so he could take her straight back to bed and make it up to her.

He hiked the stairs to her apartment and knocked on the windowpane.

Not a sound. He cupped his hand to the glass and peered through, then knocked again, louder.

A dog barked somewhere down the block.

His gaze landed on the door frame. Fresh gouges in the white paint.

Nathan yanked out his Glock and turned the knob.

"Alex!" he shouted, thrusting open the door. He swept the room with his gaze, his gun.

"Alex, you here?" He groped for a light switch, found one.

And his blood ran cold as he took in the scene.

"Alex!" He raced to the back of the apartment and checked the bedroom, the bathroom, the closet. Nothing. Back into the living room, where there had obviously been a struggle. Fear tightened his gut as the detective part of his brain calmly catalogued the signs: overturned chair, kitchen table askew, black scuff mark on the linoleum.

Bump.

He ran to the bedroom again, gun raised. Had he missed a closet? Maybe under the bed—

An opossum stood on the desk.

Scratch that. It was a giant, butt-ugly cat. With damp

gray fur and a wet, wiry tail. Nathan lowered his weapon and the animal scrambled off the desk, knocking something to the floor.

Alex's cell phone.

She wouldn't go anywhere without it.

A hard lump rose up in his throat as he carefully lifted the phone and placed it on the desk. He scrolled back through the call history, doing his best not to mar any prints. The Delphi Center, the Delphi Center. His number. His number. His number. Nothing else since the afternoon.

Something on the floor caught his eye. A slip of paper. Two. He picked them up.

And the world fell out from under him.

CHAPTER TWENTY-EIGHT

Alex's head pounded.

She opened her eyes, then winced in agony at the blinding light beaming down from above.

Where the hell . . . ?

Coghan.

Her apartment.

She shot up, then sagged back again as pain burst behind her eyeballs.

"Wake up, bitch."

Her skin turned to ice. She knew that voice. She forced her eyes to open and gazed up at the giant black shadow looming beside the spotlight. She lifted her hand to shield the glare.

It wouldn't lift. Metal clattered as she tried to pull her arm up. She glanced around. She was handcuffed to a pipe. She was naked. She jerked her knees to her chest and darted a frantic look around the room.

God, she was in a bathroom. A big fancy bathroom with giant glass shower and a Jacuzzi tub in the center. She was next to a bank of cabinets, and the doors were missing. Her hand was cuffed to the metal pipe beneath one of the sinks.

"Getting the picture here, Alexandra?" Her name rolled off his tongue, and her stomach heaved. She thought she might puke.

He stepped closer, eclipsing the spotlight with his huge body. She looked down. Her knees were bleeding. With her free arm, she pulled them closer to her chest.

He sneered. "I've seen it already. Not much to look at, but we'll have to make do, huh?"

Alex swallowed and discovered that her tongue felt thick, cottony. She tried to open her mouth, but it wouldn't move.

He reached down. She cringed. Then a loud *rip,* and her face caught fire.

She gasped for breath. He crumpled a ball of duct tape and tossed it aside.

"You can scream now, if you want. No one'll help you." With this news, he sank onto the side of the tub, rested his elbows on his knees, and leaned forward. He smelled like stale beer and sweat.

"We got some business to take care of, you and me."

The scent of cigarette smoke mixed in with the rest, and she felt a fresh jolt of fear.

As if reading her mind, he dug a pack of Marlboro Reds from the pocket of his olive green cargo pants. He slapped the pack a few times against his palm, then tapped out a cigarette.

"So," he said conversationally.

Alex darted her gaze around. Were they alone? Was there a guard?

Was he even armed?

She remembered her SIG skittering across the floor. She remembered the terrifying breathlessness, the weight, the bitter taste. Had he drugged her? Had he raped her?

He slid closer, and she spotted a Glock resting on the side of the tub. Looked just like Nathan's.

Nathan. Had he come over yet? Was he looking for her?

Coghan bent closer, and the stench intensified. The ice cream float she'd had for dinner was a cement ball in her stomach, and she leaned away from him, as far as she possibly could, while something hard and painful dug into her back.

"I got a question for you, Alexandra." His voice was low. Taunting. "We're gonna sit right here until you answer it." He dug a lighter from one of his pockets, flicked it open, and held the flame to his cigarette.

Her heart beat wildly.

He sucked in a drag. Exhaled through his nostrils. Leaned closer.

"Where. The fuck. Is my wife."

Sophie awoke to the thunder. She flipped onto her stomach, pulled the pillow over her head, and tried to reenter her dream.

More thunder. Getting louder.

She opened her eyes and sat up. She brushed the hair out of her face and looked around groggily.

The rain had stopped.

"Police!" *Pound, pound, pound.* "Open the door!"

Police? She scurried out of bed and glanced at the clock: 1:34.

The pounding continued as she snatched a robe off the chair and hurried across her apartment. She shoved her arms into sleeves, switched on a lamp in the foyer, and checked the peephole.

Nathan Devereaux. And an enormous, soaking wet man who could have been a lineman for the Dallas Cowboys. Sophie undid the latch and jerked open the door.

"What on earth—"

Nathan strode past her into the apartment.

"Sorry to disturb you," the big guy said from the doorway, "but—"

"Alex is missing."

Her gaze snapped to Nathan. "She's . . . *missing*?"

"Someone broke into her apartment, from the looks of it." This from the lineman.

Nathan thrust a cell phone at her, and Sophie recognized the lime green case. "I need you to get into that program she uses. That GPS thing. Can you do that?"

Sophie took Alex's phone and glanced up at him. Rain clung to his hair, his lashes. Little rivulets of water ran down his black leather jacket. He seemed oblivious to all of it, and his blue eyes pinned her like laser beams.

She looked at the phone again, her pulse racing now. "I can try. I—"

"I need you to *do it*. Now." Nathan flipped on the overhead light, and the living room brightened. Sophie gazed down at the phone again in dismay.

"The thing is, I don't really know how to work her phone." As the words left her mouth, Nathan cursed vividly. "But I can do it on my computer," she said.

"You can?"

"Sure, all I need is an Internet connection," she said,

and he was already across the room, jabbing at the computer sitting on the desk beside her futon. "Here, let me do that."

Sophie hurried over and settled into a chair. She was immediately conscious of the two large, intense males peering over her shoulders. She brought the system to life and took a moment to pull the lapels of her robe together. It was black and gauzy, and it actually revealed more than it covered, but these guys weren't paying attention.

Nathan leaned closer and rested a fist on the desk as Sophie keyed in the address for the GPS tracking service Alex used. An hourglass popped up as the site loaded.

Nathan's fist clenched tighter. He swore.

Sophie's heart was thudding now. "Are you sure she's really missing?"

"Coghan's involved," Nathan snapped. "We have to find his truck, ASAP."

The program opened up, and Sophie recognized the home page. A window requesting a password hovered in the center of the screen.

"Shit!" Nathan pounded his fist, and the desk rattled. "What's the password?"

Sophie stared at the screen. She bit her lip. If Alex was really missing, if she was really with Coghan, this might be their only chance of finding her. It could be too late already. Surely these guys knew that.

"The *password,* Sophie!"

She flinched. "Okay, okay. Let me think for a second."

"Shit, you don't *know*?" Nathan looked desperate now.

"Relax, Dev. She knows it." The big guy fixed her

with a look that was calm but no less intimidating than Nathan's. "You do know it, right?"

Sophie gulped. "Not exactly. But I have some ideas."

Alex tried to come up with a response. Her mouth moved, but it wouldn't form words. She ran her tongue over her burning lips.

"I don't know," she finally said.

"Wrong answer." He took another casual drag on the cigarette. Alex held her breath, watching.

His hand shot out and clamped around her arm. She tried to wrestle herself away from him, but his grip was like a vice. Metal clanged as she clutched the pipe with one hand and tried to wrench her other arm away. It was futile. A meaty hand squeezed her wrist and twisted her forearm, tender side up. He plucked the cigarette from his mouth and held it to her skin. Flesh sizzled.

And then the pain hit, and the only sound was her screams.

Fear burned in Nathan's gut as they raced down the highway in the Mustang. Ninety. Ninety-five. Ninety-eight. He would have traded his soul right now for his battered Taurus.

"This thing won't make triple digits," Hodges said from the passenger seat.

Nathan glared at him. "How much farther?"

He consulted Alex's phone. It had taken Sophie half a dozen tries to come up with the correct password from the many Alex used around the office. Since then, Hodges had managed to log onto the tracking site from

Alex's phone, and they were now using it to navigate. "Twenty miles, it looks like."

Nathan's knuckles whitened on the steering wheel.

"It's good, you know. That he took her to some house in bumfuck nowhere." Hodges—who wasn't normally a talker—continued the speech he'd been giving since they'd shot out of Sophie's parking lot. "If he just wanted to, you know, eliminate her, he could have done that back at the apartment."

It didn't take much imagination to come up with plenty of reasons he might have taken her to some isolated house on the shores of Lake Buchanan. Ditch evidence. Dispose of a body. A cold layer of sweat broke out all over Nathan's skin.

The yellow lines were a blur as they rocketed down the highway. Nathan flashed his brights and swerved around a pickup doing a sluggish seventy-five.

"You sure you don't want to call for backup?" Hodges asked.

Nathan shot him a glare.

"I'm just saying. Coghan's not operating alone. We got no idea who's with him, and—"

"I'll tell you right now who's with him! Probably half the badges in Travis County! Who we gonna call?"

Hodges didn't answer. The hum of the Mustang's V-8 was the only sound.

"You realize the implications, don't you?" Hodges asked. "Of those pictures at Alex's?"

Nathan gritted his teeth until his jaw ached. "Cernak's had a hand in every homicide case that's come in over the last five years," Hodges went on. "If the man's on the payroll of some drug cartel, and if the D.A.'s office is involved, too . . . Shit, we're talking mistrials. Overturned convictions. And who knows how many guilty people got off scot-free. It's a fucking mess."

Nathan pressed harder on the gas pedal. He focused his white-hot rage on the highway stretching out before him. It was nearly two. Traffic was light. That was about the only good news he could think of at the moment.

"And you really think it's Nicole?" Hodges asked.

"Yes."

"You're certain?"

"Yes."

"Because her face was turned away in that photo," Hodges said. "With that ball cap on, how can you really be sure?"

"Because I fucking lived with her for five years!" He pounded the steering wheel. "I know what she fucking looks like, all right? So just shut the fuck up and help me find Alex!"

The car fell silent as Hodges checked the digital map again. Nathan glanced at it and saw the green blip, which was them, slowly edging closer to the red blip, which was Coghan's truck.

Or so they hoped. Maybe he'd found the snitch and dumped it somewhere. Or put it on someone else's car. Maybe they'd find Coghan's truck, or even Coghan, but not Alex.

Nathan clenched his jaw. He floored the pedal. He said a silent prayer that Alex—wherever she was—was still alive.

Every cell screamed. Every nerve ending burned. How could something so small make her hurt everywhere?

He took another break, and leaned back, smiling. "Ready yet?"

She sucked in a breath. Blew it out. In. Out. In. Out. Her face was wet with sweat and tears, and she knew he was enjoying this.

She cradled her arm to her chest and gazed down at it, shocked. Six little circles. Melanie had had so many more on her neck. How could six little burns hurt so much?

Maybe because he'd lined them up neatly on top of her fresh pink scar, the remnants of her last encounter with him back in New Orleans.

"Hey, bitch."

She glanced up. With a shaking hand she wiped the snot from her nose.

"This is getting boring." He leaned closer. "I want information. Now." He reached onto the counter and pulled out the long, shiny thing he'd brought in earlier, when he'd gone to get that last beer. He set it on the side of the tub, and Alex got her first good look at it.

A wire.

It was thick. Silver. With patches of rust or . . . blood along it. The ends were twisted, and she tried to imagine—

"Where's Melanie?"

She glanced up at him.

"I *know* you know where they put her."

Alex didn't say anything. She'd already told him she didn't know where the safe house was. But this wasn't really about his getting information. He had to inflict pain. On her. The woman who'd helped his wife leave him.

She wished her brain would function better. She

felt dizzy. Disoriented. She was almost sure she'd been drugged. But she needed to shake it off. She needed a plan. Alex kept her eyes trained on his face, but she focused her mind on that Glock sitting beside him on the tub. If she could just get her hands on it—

He took his pack off the counter and lit another cigarette. One drag. Two. He leaned toward her, and she flinched.

He smiled.

Then he leaped up and grabbed her by the hair. He jerked her head back and jammed the burning ember against her neck.

Nathan blew past the private driveway, pulled off the road, and cut the engine.

"We got about half a mile to the house," Hodges reported.

"We'll hoof it from here," Nathan said. "We're probably outmanned and outgunned. Surprise is the only thing we got going for us."

"Roger that."

Nathan jumped out, popped open the trunk, and started grabbing up gear. "You any good with a shotgun?"

"Who isn't?" Hodges picked up a 12-gauge and tested it in his hands. "Sure you don't want it?"

"I want a hand free." *To help Alex.* "Anyway, I'm better with a pistol." Nathan shoved a few extra magazines in the pocket of his jacket. He grabbed the Kevlar vest lying beside the tire iron and held it out to Hodges.

"No way, man."

"Take it. Courtney's expecting."

Hodges stepped back, clearly surprised. "How did you—"

"People tell me shit." Nathan shoved the vest into his hands and slammed shut the trunk. "Now get rid of that white shirt and let's go."

Hodges leaned the shotgun against the bumper and quickly swapped the white Oxford that stood out like a beacon for the black Kevlar vest.

Seconds later, they set off at a brisk jog for the gate. It hung at an angle on one of its hinges, obviously broken. But if this place was some sort of command outpost or distribution center, there still might be guards or security cameras hidden around.

Once through the gate, they moved off the gravel driveway and cut through weeds and scrub brush in the direction of the house.

Snick.

Nathan's shoulders tensed, but he kept moving. Someone was behind them.

"What the fuck are you doing?" A voice. Not Coghan's.

At the sound of it, Coghan let go, and Alex slumped forward. Her neck burned. Her body quivered. She clutched her knees to her chest and tried to get her breath back.

"What the hell is this?" The voice was in the room now. Alex turned her head and saw a man. Light reflected off the top of his head. The parking lot guy.

Coghan picked up his beer and took a swig. "Just taking care of business."

Another figure stepped into the room. Tall. Suit. Female. The blonde from the weight room.

Alex shook her head and tried to clear it. She needed to *concentrate*. Sharpen her senses. Her situation was changing, and she had to find an advantage.

The woman's gaze swept to Alex, and her eyes bugged. "Have you lost your *mind*?" She turned to Coghan. "That's Nathan's *girlfriend*!"

Nathan. Her chest constricted.

"This is between me and her." Coghan pointed his beer bottle at the woman. "You two just pick up your money and get out of here."

"Like hell! We're accessories now!" She turned to the bald man. "I didn't agree to this. He's out of control. First New Orleans. Then the hooker. This is crazy—"

"Shut up." The bald guy scowled at the woman. "She's already here. We deal with it. Then we leave."

Alex inched closer to the drainpipe. She turned her attention to the handcuff. It was loose, but not loose enough to slip her wrist through. Maybe she could unscrew the pipe somehow.

"I'm leaving." The blonde turned on her heel, but Coghan stopped her with an arm across the door.

"You're not going anywhere."

Whoever was following them was about fifteen yards back. Nathan kept the pace up as he signaled Hodges. When they reached the next clump of brush, Nathan darted in front of a cedar and circled back.

A tall black shadow had stopped in the middle of the path.

Nathan charged him from behind. He landed with an *oof* on the ground, and in seconds Nathan had him on his stomach, a gun pointed at his head. "Police. Hands up."

Silence. Then the unmistakable slide-and-click of a shotgun shell being chambered as Hodges stepped out of the shadows.

The man lifted both hands off the ground. Nathan jerked a pistol out of one of them and tossed it into the grass, where Hodges promptly retrieved it.

Nathan leaned close, wanting to keep the noise to a minimum. "Who the fuck are you?"

"Relax, I'm a cop," he said.

"Yeah, well, that means shit to me right about now." Nathan did a rough pat-down and came up with a wallet, which he handed to Hodges.

"Name," Nathan demanded.

"John Holt. I'm a Texas Ranger."

Nathan glanced up at his partner, who was checking the wallet with a small tactical flashlight. Alex had mentioned a Holt. Hodges turned the light on the man, studied his face for a second, then gave a nod of confirmation.

Nathan stood up. The ranger got to his feet. Hodges returned the wallet, but kept the weapon tucked in his waistband.

John Holt's gaze shifted from Nathan to Hodges. "Who are you guys?"

"APD," Nathan snapped. "And we've got a possible hostage situation, so tell us something useful or get out of our way."

Holt's gaze narrowed on Nathan. "Who's the hostage?"

"Alex Lovell."

The man cursed. "Coghan has her?"

"Yes. And we don't have time to explain, so either—"

"Property's surrounded on three sides by a six-foot

fence. Gate's broken. Fourth side is lakefront. There's a second-floor deck with a boathouse under it, but no boat."

"How do you know?" Hodges asked.

"I got here fifteen minutes ago," Holt said. "Tailed a woman—"

"Who?"

Holt paused. "An assistant district attorney. She's been under investigation."

He was talking about Nicole.

"That's not all," Holt continued. "Looks like a crowd tonight. I saw four vehicles parked in back, three pickups and a BMW. I counted three guards milling around the kitchen, all armed with submachine guns. Everyone's busy. Looks like maybe a meth lab in there, and I'm guessing from the guards they've got some cash laying around, too. I took one look at those AK-47s, called for backup. ETA twenty-five minutes."

"You see Alex or Coghan?" Nathan asked.

"No."

Hodges pulled the ranger's weapon from his waistband and returned it.

"Stay or go, it's up to you," Nathan said. "But we're not waiting for backup."

"She's right." The bald guy fisted his hands on his hips, and Alex blinked at him. A *badge*. Clipped to his belt. That's where she'd seen him—he'd been at the crime scene earlier tonight with Nathan.

Oh God. Who *wasn't* involved in this? Was Hodges part of it, too? What about John Holt? Alex's stomach clenched, and she wanted to puke.

They were arguing back and forth now. Alex swallowed the bile in her throat and forced herself to listen.

"You let me worry about her." This from Coghan.

Baldy turned and glared at Alex.

"This is a business." The woman jabbed a finger at Coghan. "This isn't about *you*. This isn't about your slut wife, or your personal vendetta, and I will *not* be made an accessory—"

Smack! Coghan backhanded her, and she dropped to the floor. Blood trickled from her nose. She gaped up at him, shocked.

"Christ, Craig." Baldy now. "What'd you do that for?"

"Both of you, fucking stay out of this! This is *my* show. Take your money and get out."

"It's not that simple," Baldy said. "Melanie's talking, Craig. Don't you *get* that? Everything's compromised. And our prints are all over this place. We need to clear out, torch it, and hit the road. You stick around and draw this out, you put all of us at risk."

The woman wobbled to her feet and steadied herself against the shower. No one offered her a hand. Was she APD? A fed? Alex looked for a weapon, a telltale bulge under the suit jacket. Maybe if Alex could get the woman on her side—

Pop!

Shrieks filled the room. Alex ducked for cover under the sink.

Gunshot.

Nathan tore through the scrub brush, heart thundering, trying to throw together a plan. AK-47s in the kitchen. No one manning the front, which meant it was probably locked tight. Nathan plunged through the darkness, dodging trees and bushes, sprinting in the direction of the house as his heart jackhammered inside his chest.

The house came into view. Two-story. Limestone. A light glowing inside, illuminating a tall foyer and a curving staircase.

"Go around back and monitor the guards," he told Holt, who was bent over now, gasping for air. "Hodges and I'll take the front. We're way outmatched, so if anyone tries to escape, just let them go unless they've got Alex."

Holt took off jogging toward the back of the house while Nathan and Hodges sprinted for the front. Ducking low, they rushed up to the door. Locked.

Nathan heard a scream that chilled him to his bones. He threw his shoulder into the door. No use.

"Sounded like it came from upstairs," Hodges said, racing for the nearest window. He jabbed the shotgun butt against the pane. Glass cascaded to the ground.

"Cover me," Nathan ordered, and ducked inside.

The bald guy lay facedown on the tile, in an expanding pool of blood. The woman had backed herself into the corner, as far away from the corpse as it was possible to get without melting into the wall. She stared at Coghan, bug-eyed and terrified. She was hyperventilating.

Coghan pointed his gun at the woman. "Sit your ass down and shut up." Then he swung the gun toward Alex, and her stomach did a free fall.

The blonde bolted for the door. This time, Coghan ignored her.

Alex's mouth went dry as she stared into the gun barrel. She held her breath. She curled tighter. The *clink* of her handcuff echoed through the room. *Like shooting fish in a barrel.*

He stepped back until he was standing in the doorway. He smiled slightly. He lifted the gun.

"Good-bye, bitch."

Pop!

Alex's ears rang and she waited for the pain to come. It didn't. Footsteps stampeded outside the room. More shots. Shouting. A familiar voice—

"Oh, Jesus."

She opened her eyes and was stunned to see Nathan drop to his knees beside her.

"Are you all right? Are you okay?" He tried to pull her up, into a sitting position. Metal rattled, and his attention veered to her wrist, handcuffed beneath the sink. Then his gaze swept over her, and seemed actually to *see* her for the first time—the bloody knees, the bruised arms, the raw, red burns.

"Alex?" He brushed her hair out of her eyes and searched her face. "Alex, talk to me, honey. Are you okay?"

She nodded, still stupefied by the fact that he was *here* beside her, when moments ago she'd thought her life was over.

"Where'd he go?" Her voice sounded like a croak.

"I took a shot at him from the stairs, and he ran. Hodges went after him." He put his Glock on the floor now and started stripping off his jacket. "We have to get you out of here."

"Uh-huh."

He settled the jacket over her, and she used her free hand to clutch it to her chest. It was wet, but it was warm, too, from his body heat, and it smelled like him.

He bent his head down and peered up under the sink. "Shit, it's metal."

"I tried to detach the pipe." She'd spent five minutes frantically trying to unscrew the joint while Coghan had gone for a beer. "No luck."

Nathan flipped onto his back and reached up. All his muscles strained as he tried to twist the joint.

More shouts sounded downstairs. Doors slammed. In the distance, she heard a car start.

And then she caught a smell.

"It's stuck," Nathan said from under the sink. "I need a wrench. Or a handcuff key."

"Do you have one?"

"It's on my key chain, back at the car. I left the keys inside in case Hodges needed it before I did. God*damn* it!"

He sat up again, looking flushed and frustrated.

And Alex's stomach flip-flopped as she put a name to the smell.

"Nathan . . . I smell smoke."

He went still. "Shit, you're right." Then he rolled to his feet and crouched beside her.

"Don't leave," she said. She grabbed his arm with her free hand, but she already knew what he was going to say before he said it.

"I'll be right back," he told her, and her heart filled with terror. He picked up his Glock and folded her hand around the grip. "If anyone tries to hurt you, shoot 'em dead."

"But what about you? You need a gun."

"I'll be right back." He kissed her forehead. "I promise."

She wanted to grab a fistful of his damp T-shirt and beg him not to go. But instead, she bit her lip and watched him stand up. Her heart squeezed as he rushed for the door, and she realized it was now or maybe never.

"Nathan, wait!"

He turned around.

"I . . ." She blinked back the tears and forced a smile. "I love you."

His eyebrows shot up with surprise.

"You know, just for the record."

He looked serious now, more serious than she had ever seen him. "I promise you, Alex. I'll be right back."

And then he was gone.

The house was in chaos—doors slamming, people yelling in both English and Spanish, cars peeling down the driveway. A punk-assed kid armed with an AK-47 sat at the base of the stairs beside a can of gasoline. Shit, were they burning the place? Destroying the crime scene?

Nathan needed another exit. He darted down a dim hallway, following the same route Coghan had taken when he'd raced off.

Nathan had hit him. He was almost sure of it. At the very least, he'd nicked the son of a bitch with that potshot from the top of the staircase.

The potshot that probably had saved Alex's life.

A back stairwell. Bingo! Nathan raced down to the landing, turned the corner, and smacked into Hodges.

"Shit, you're hit!"

Hodges was pale as death and using the banister to pull himself up the stairs. Blood had soaked through the thigh of his slacks and was dripping from his pant leg.

"Get everybody out," he gasped. "They're torching the place." Sweat poured down his face as he tried to climb the next step.

"Alex is handcuffed up there. Quick, where's your key?"

Hodges reached for something, then started to slip as he lost his grip on the handrail. Nathan caught him.

"Right . . . pocket," Hodges said.

Nathan dug his hand in the pocket, hoping he wouldn't poke the bullet wound. He pulled out the key chain, and it was slick with blood.

"I'll get Alex," Nathan said, noticing the smoke now drifting up the stairwell. "You exit the back. You need help?"

"Hell no."

"Get as far away from the house as possible. If Holt's right about that meth lab, this place is gonna blow."

Alex pulled and twisted with all her might, but the pipe wouldn't budge. The smoke was thicker now. And she hoped it was her imagination, but the floor beneath her seemed to be getting warm.

"Come on, come on, come on," she muttered. Why hadn't she worked out more?

Something pulled on her ankle. She grabbed for the Glock.

"Whoa, there." Nathan dragged her out from the cabinet and ducked his head under. He had a key in his hand, and it was covered with something.

"Is that blood?"

"Hodges got shot."

"Oh my God. Is he okay?"

"We'll find out." Then a soft click, and the handcuffs clattered to the ground.

"Come on," Nathan took her hand and pulled her to her feet, not even bothering to unlock the other cuff. "Here."

Alex winced at the pain as he stuffed both her arms—along with the dangling handcuffs—into the sleeves of his jacket. He zipped the front, grabbed his Glock off the floor, and met her gaze.

"You okay to walk?"

"Yeah, I—"

"Good."

And then he was towing her out into the hallway that was quickly filling with smoke. Alex stumbled along behind him, trying to keep up. Her legs felt rubbery.

She bumped into Nathan as he halted in the hallway.

"Fuck!"

Alex gazed in shock at the scene below. The entire foyer was engulfed in flames, some already licking their way up the curved staircase.

Nathan pulled her in the other direction, down a hallway thick with smoke.

"Where are we going?" she asked, and her eyes started to sting.

"Back staircase."

She coughed and waved away the smoke. "Are you sure—"

Her feet flew out from under her as an explosion rocked the house. Alex blinked up at the ceiling, swirling with black. The impact had knocked the wind out of her, and she sat up and tried to get her breath.

"Shit, you okay?"

Nathan jerked her to her feet, and she could hardly see him for all the smoke surrounding them.

"I'm okay."

Nathan reversed directions and pulled her down another hallway. "We can't go through the kitchen," he yelled, over the crackle of flames. The floor seemed to sway. Something whined and creaked above them, and it seemed like the house was about to fall down.

"There! Look!" Alex pointed at what looked like a glass door at the end of the hallway.

They ran toward it. Nathan tried the knob. Then he raised his gun and shot out the glass. Shards rained onto the carpet and the decking outside.

Nathan glanced down at her bare feet and pushed the gun into her hands. "Hold this. Don't shoot me." Then he scooped her into his arms and ducked through the opening he'd just made.

Oxygen.

Alex tipped her head back against his arm and drank it in as they bounded along the wooden planking.

"Shit, no stairs!"

She glanced around and got her first good look at the house. It was huge. A palace. Only now it was an inferno, glowing orange against the night sky. Flames leaped from the downstairs windows. Black smoke billowed from the ones upstairs. Alex gaped at the structure, unable to believe they'd been inside mere moments ago.

Nathan set her on her feet and glanced around. "This way!" He grabbed her hand, and they ran down a narrow wooden walkway to a spacious deck over a boathouse.

Alex looked around frantically. "No stairs!"

Something screamed in the distance. A siren?

Another blast. Both of them hit the deck, face-first.

"Come on!" Nathan shouted, pulling her to her feet yet again.

"Where?"

As she said this, he reached the wooden railing and threw a leg over it. Alex peered down at the water below. It was littered with burning embers now, floating on the glimmering surface that reflected the blazing building like a giant mirror.

Alex hoisted herself onto the railing. The wail of sirens drew nearer. Nathan pitched his gun into a clump of reeds lining the shore. He grabbed her hand.

"Jump *out*!" he shouted.

And they did.

For the second time tonight, Nathan watched a gurney being wheeled away from a crime scene. This time, it carried one of his best friends.

"You think he'll be okay?"

He glanced down into Alex's concerned brown eyes. Her face was smudged with soot, her wet hair was plastered to her head, and she was the prettiest thing he'd ever seen.

"He's tough as they come," Nathan said. "He'll be all

right." At least, Nathan hoped so. *Tough* wasn't necessarily an antidote to a spray of bullets from an AK-47. Hodges had been awake and lucid when they'd rolled him up to that ambulance, but Nathan had listened closely to the paramedics barking back and forth, and it was clear the man needed surgery, fast.

"I called Courtney," Alex said now. "She's on her way to the hospital. I told her I'd meet her there as soon as I can make it."

Nathan surveyed the scene. Organized mayhem. Vehicles from federal, state, and local law enforcement agencies surrounded the burned-out carcass of the house. Several fire rigs and even a few boats had pulled up close to the action. Firefighters were busy tromping around the smoky ruins. A brief downpour had helped douse the flames, but mainly had added to the confusion.

"Like roaches."

Nathan turned to see John Holt walking up to them.

"What's that?" Alex asked.

"Goddamn gangbangers. Pardon my French. Scatter like roaches when the lights come on."

"Any sign of Coghan?" Nathan asked, without much hope.

"No." Holt's jaw tightened. "But we got a roadblock set up on every highway, byway, and wagon rut within twenty miles of here. Someone'll see him."

Nathan wasn't so optimistic. The son of a bitch's best asset was his ability to blend in with law enforcement. He'd slip through the cracks somehow.

"How you holdin' up?" Holt asked Alex, looking her over. He shot Nathan a disapproving look, probably due to the fact that Alex was still standing around in his dripping wet bomber jacket, which hit her about midthigh. She'd stubbornly refused the blankets the paramedics had tried to foist on her.

"I'm pissed," Alex said now. "The bastard got away. Hundred bucks says he's halfway to Mexico by now with a bagful of cash."

"If he is," Holt said, "we'll nab him at the border."

Yeah, sure.

The ranger's phone buzzed and he unclipped it from the holder at his belt. "Holt."

Nathan scanned the scene grimly. Three deaths—all bad guys, but still. An injured cop. An injured civilian. He glanced at the welts along Alex's neck and tried not to think about the rage that had been bubbling inside him since he'd pulled her out of the lake and gotten his first good look at her. She claimed she was fine—just a few dings and scratches—but Nathan knew better. He'd seen that look on her face when he'd first found her. She wasn't fine, not emotionally. And although she didn't know it yet, he planned to take her to the hospital tonight for a thorough exam.

"They got her."

Nathan glanced up. "Who?"

"The ADA."

Alex's gaze flashed to Nathan's. He'd told her about Nicole while they'd watched the firefighters battle the flames. She'd reacted with much less shock than he had.

"They're taking her downtown," Holt informed him.

"Good," Nathan said.

Nicole. Cernak. He could hardly get his head around it. He'd trusted both of them, and the bitterness he felt now—even with Cernak *dead*—it just kept growing.

Nathan's attention drifted over Holt's shoulder. The firefighter walking past that rig . . . He was big, tall, wore a helmet. Like every other firefighter out here tonight, except—

He pulled open the driver's-side door of a police unit. He glanced up.

"Gun!" Nathan yelled, whipping out his Glock. He saw the flash of the muzzle just as his finger squeezed the trigger.

Coghan slammed back against the car, then slid to the ground.

CHAPTER TWENTY-NINE

S hootings created paperwork.

That's what Alex told herself as she sat in the examining room alone, waiting to be poked and prodded by the ER doctor. She told herself the same thing again as she paced the hospital waiting room with Courtney, who was anxiously awaiting the results of her husband's surgery.

And hours later, when Alex stumbled into an empty apartment and collapsed, boneless, onto her bed, she reminded herself—yet again—that shootings created paperwork. Nathan had killed a man, and he couldn't have been with her right now, even if he'd wanted to.

She awoke with the sun beaming into her eyes and an enormous cat curled against her stomach. Her pillow smelled like smoke. She lifted her head and blinked at the clock. Two. Her senses kicked into gear as she glanced around the room. Her hair smelled like smoke. Her skin smelled like smoke. The scrubs they'd given her at the hospital smelled like smoke. She staggered into the bathroom and took a soapy shower, taking care to keep her burned arm out of the water. She put on a robe and went into the kitchen, then methodically filled the coffee carafe with water. Her gaze landed on the long black scuff mark on her kitchen floor.

Her stomach knotted. Her hands started to quiver. She abandoned the carafe on the counter, threw on some clothes, and went out.

When she returned several hours later, Nathan's car was in the driveway. She walked through the door Coghan had jimmied open less than a day ago and followed the trail: keys and wallet on the kitchen table beside the note she'd scribbled, boots outside the bathroom door. She collected the clothes off the floor and tossed them into the washing machine.

Then she stood in the doorway of her bedroom and watched him. He was passed out on his stomach, the covers tangled around his waist. A lump lodged in her throat. She thought of the groceries she'd just bought. She thought of feeding him. She thought of letting him rest.

Then she stripped off her clothes and slid under the covers.

For a few perfect minutes she watched his relaxed features. She traced them with her finger—his straight nose, his stubbled jaw, the faint lines at the corners of his eyes. She thought about what she'd said to him last night, and her chest tightened.

His hand found her thigh, but his eyes stayed closed. It stroked over her hip, her waist, then slid back to her thigh again. He opened his eyes.

"Hi," she whispered.

"Hi."

A full minute ticked by as he simply looked at her.

"Hodges is going to be okay," she said.

"I know. I talked to Courtney." He paused. "Did you get checked out?"

"Yeah, I'm fine."

His gaze drifted to the marks on her neck, and his eyes darkened, like they always did when he looked at her scars. She snuggled closer to distract him. He shifted position and resettled her head against his biceps. His hand stroked up and down her body, and it felt so good, she wanted purr.

"I'm sorry I wasn't here," he said quietly.

"It's okay."

"I would have been here sooner, but—"

"Shh." She kissed him to stop the words.

And then he wrapped her in those arms she'd missed, pinned her beneath him, and showed her he was sorry without any words at all.

Alex woke to the smell of bacon. She shuffled into her kitchen and found a half-naked man standing at the stove. This was a first. And she liked it.

He glanced over his shoulder at her and smiled. "Morning, sunshine."

She smoothed her hair self-consciously, and his smile widened.

"What?" she asked.

"You." He poured a cup of coffee and brought it to her. "Nice robe. Did I buy you that?"

She glanced down at the monogram over her breast. "I bought it in the hotel gift shop, after you left."

She opened the fridge and added cream to her coffee.

"Thanks for washing my jeans."

"No problem." She'd washed his shirt, too, but he hadn't managed to put it on, which was fine with her.

The newspaper sat on the table, and she read the headline splashed across the top: "Task Force Unveils Public Corruption Scandal." She sank into a chair.

He slid a plate of bacon and scrambled eggs in front of her. "I fixed that door."

"You did?" She glanced over at it. "Thank you."

"You got any Tabasco?"

"No."

"Picante?"

"Top shelf." She nibbled a piece of bacon and continued reading: "Following a house fire near Lake Buchanan, a joint state and federal task force unveiled a sweeping investigation into regional public officials. Arrest warrants were issued yesterday for more than a dozen central Texas cops and several public prosecutors."

"The D.A.?" she asked, incredulous.

"Nicole's boss." Nathan joined her at the table. "I always hated that guy."

"Isn't he involved in, like, hundreds of cases every year?"

"His office is, yeah."

Alex opened the paper, and the row of photographs caught her eye. She recognized Nathan's ex-wife. She recognized Nathan's boss. She stole a look at him over the top of the paper and saw the tension in his face.

"You've read all this, haven't you?"

"Yeah."

"What do you think?"

"It's a fucking mess."

She skimmed through the story. According to the

report, the task force had been formed more than a year ago to look into alleged ties between the Saledo drug cartel, out of Mexico, and various narcotics cops in key positions throughout the state. The probe had started with a few police officers, but had been expanded to include a huge array of public officials. The assistant district attorney had played a key role in Austin, according to a task force spokesperson. She'd used her legal expertise to paper fraudulent real estate deals that allowed the Saledos to buy foreclosed homes to use as grow houses. She and her boss also were accused of offering Saledo operatives who ran into legal trouble attractive plea bargains. Meanwhile, Saledo rivals were vigorously prosecuted.

It was the sort of corruption Alex expected to hear about happening *south* of the border, not in her own backyard. She shook her head as she finished the story. Who knew how many cases and trials and lives had been affected? Nathan was right. It was a fucking mess.

She looked at him. He'd just killed a fellow cop. One he used to consider a friend. And he'd just learned that the institution—the *people* he'd been working for his whole career—had betrayed him.

"Are you all right?" she asked.

"Fine."

And she knew he wasn't fine at all.

He stood up and took his plate to the counter. "Let's go for a drive," he said.

"A drive?"

"I need to talk to you about something."

Okay. Nerves fluttered in her stomach as she dressed and pulled her hair into a ponytail. They climbed into his car, and she watched him as he backed out of Thelma's driveway. This was bad news, and her mind ran through the possibilities. Maybe he'd been fired. Maybe he was facing criminal charges in Coghan's death. Maybe the task force had set its sights on him now.

He turned out of her neighborhood, and she took a deep breath. "Okay, hit me," she said.

He gave her a curious look.

"What?" she asked impatiently. "You've got something to say, say it."

"All right. I'm moving."

She stared at him across the car. He glanced at her.

"Moving," she stated.

"Yeah."

"When?"

"Soon. Probably this week."

He must have quit his job. He was fed up with everything, and he wanted to distance himself from it.

She looked out the window and tried to ignore the tears stinging the backs of her eyes. *Moving*. She hadn't expected it. *She'd* thought of moving. She thought of moving every few months or so. In her mind, she was always the mover, not the one left behind.

She turned to look at him. His profile was strong, and her attention was drawn to those arms bulging beneath the black T-shirt she'd washed for him. She loved those arms. She'd missed them. Missed him. And suddenly pride—which had always mattered to her—seemed like the most inconsequential thing in the universe.

"Stay," she said, before she could stop herself. "Please?"

He gave her a questioning look.

"I was thinking. About your, you know, job situation." Her nerves were jumping now, but she just plunged on.

"I've decided to hire some more help, now that I'm going to be splitting time between my office and the Delphi Center. Maybe you could come work at Lovell Solutions."

The side of his mouth curved up. "As a private investigator?"

"Why not? You're an investigator already. This would just be a change."

He smiled fully now.

"What's so funny?" she asked.

"You'd be my boss."

What was funny about that? But of course it would never work. "We could be partners," she said.

"Partners."

"Yeah, why not?"

And then she felt a shot of panic because, holy hell, was she really offering to give him fifty percent of the business she'd spent *years* building?

And she looked at him and knew that she was. That's exactly what she was offering. And she wanted more than anything for him just to say yes, so he could stay here in Austin and see this thing through.

Funny how coming inches away from death had made her realize all the things lacking in her life. She'd spent a lot of time lately thinking about Melanie. It was the weirdest thing. For all Melanie's screwed-up, terrible decisions, in some ways, she was better off than Alex. In less than a year, Melanie had managed to find, and lose, and then find again more love than Alex had known in a lifetime. As bizarre as it was, Alex actually envied her.

Nathan turned into a neighborhood off South Lamar.

"Where are we going?" she asked.

"I told you. For a drive."

She took a deep breath and gazed at her lap. Her idea would never work. He was an amazing investigator, yes. But the sort of work she did would make him crazy. The deadbeat dads, the insurance cheats—all of that would bore him to pieces. And the work she found meaningful—all those bleeding-heart cases he liked to chide her about—those cases belonged to her.

He hung a left at a stop sign and pulled over. He turned to look at her.

"I appreciate the offer." He leaned over and kissed her. "Come on."

"What?"

He got out, and she followed suit. They were parked in front of a white 1940s bungalow with turquoise awnings. Her heart started racing as he took her hand and tugged her up the sidewalk. He stopped in front of the turquoise front door and gazed down at her. "I said I was moving." He tucked a lock of hair behind her ear and rested his hand on her shoulder. "I didn't say I was leaving."

"So, your job . . . ?"

"I'm going back, soon as the review board clears me. It was a righteous shoot. Eight people witnessed it. The inquiry's just a formality."

He flipped through his key chain, then he unlocked the door and pushed it open. He gestured her inside.

Alex took a tentative step over the threshold. The room was empty. Her sandals sank into the pale pink carpet. She glanced at the walls, the ceiling.

"What do you think?" he asked.

She swallowed. "I think . . . it's very pink."

"Needs a coat of paint, I know. But look at this." He walked over to the corner of the room and knelt down. He peeled back a corner of carpet. "Wood floors."

"Wow, that's . . . wow."

She took a few more steps and peeked her head into the hallway. More pink carpet. "So . . . you bought this place?"

"Leased. With an option to buy in one year." He walked over and picked up her hand again. He led her past an empty bedroom, past a bathroom with a pedestal sink, to another empty room with sun streaming through the windows. Alex walked into the center of the room and looked around. The floor in here was a warm, honey-colored wood. And the walls were cream instead of pink.

"Do you like it?"

She glanced over at him. He stood just inside the doorway with a shoulder propped against the wall. His stance was relaxed, but she saw a trace of insecurity on his face.

"It's great," she said.

"When I first saw this room, I thought of you. I thought it would make a great home office for you."

She turned and stared at him. "When did you first see this room?"

"A few weeks ago. While you were in New Orleans."

"You . . . you decided to move *then*?"

He shrugged. "I knew I wanted to be with you. I knew we needed our own place. You've never unpacked a damn thing, and I knew you never would unless I gave you a reason. So I'm giving you a reason."

Her heart pounded so loudly she could hear it.

"You're asking me to live in this house with you?"

He walked over and picked up her hand. He kissed her knuckles, and the tenderness she saw in his eyes made her breath catch. "For starters, yeah."

"And then?"

"And then everything." He wrapped his arms around her and pulled her against him. "I love you, Alex. I want to be with you. Make a home with you."

She started laughing then, and she was crying, too. Happiness swelled in her chest as she searched his face. "Go back to the middle part."

He smiled. "The 'I love you' part?"

"Yeah."

"I love you. I want us to make a life together. Will you do that with me?" He kissed her. And it was tenderness, and heat, and this new thing, this joy she'd never felt with him before. And it went on and on and swirled around her until she forgot about words and the question he'd asked and the answer she'd wanted to say.

And when it was over, she looked up at him and smiled, and that was answer enough because for the first time in her life, she knew she was home.

Turn the page for a sneak peek
at the next spine-tingling Tracers novel
from Laura Griffin

EXPOSED

Available June 2013 from Pocket Books

Maddie Callahan's newest clients seemed to have everything—youth, looks, money—which was precisely why she doubted their marriage would work. But she kept her opinions to herself as she snapped what she hoped was the final shot of the day.

"That should do it for the church backdrop. So, we're all set?"

"What about the footbridge?" The bride-to-be smiled up at her fiancé. "I can post it on the blog with our engagement story."

"Whatever you want, babe."

Maddie stifled an eye roll and turned to check out the park. It wasn't overly crowded—just a few people walking dogs—but their light was fading.

"I know it's getting late." Hannah held her hands together as if in prayer and looked at Maddie. "But could we get something *real* quick?"

"We can if we hurry," Maddie said, collapsing her tripod and looping her camera strap around her neck. She waited for a break in traffic and led Hannah and Devon across Main Street to the park, where she deposited her equipment beside the lily pond. She glanced around, cataloging the details of the composition. The wooden footbridge formed a low arc over the water. Sunlight glistened off the pond's surface, creating a shimmery, storybook effect that Maddie had taken advantage of before. As one of the few natural backdrops in this congested college town, the park was a good place for wedding photos—or in this case, engagement shots. Normally, Maddie liked using it, but this appointment had run way over schedule, and she was anxious to get back to the lab. She opted to skip the tripod and keep this quick.

Maddie composed the shot as Hannah arranged her future husband behind her. In matching white oxfords, faded jeans, and cowboy boots, the couple's look today was what she thought of as Texas preppy. Hannah settled their clasped hands on the side of the bridge, putting her two-carat diamond prominently on display.

"How's this?" she asked.

"Perfect." Maddie snapped the picture. "I think I got it. Just a few more and . . . that's it. You're done."

Both pairs of shoulders relaxed. Devon looked at his watch, clearly relieved to be finished with what he probably thought was a marathon photo shoot. He had no idea what awaited him on his wedding day.

Hannah turned and smiled up at him. "Do I have lipstick on my teeth, sweets?"

He grinned down at her. "No. Do I?"

Maddie lifted her camera one last time as he reached down to brush a lock of hair from his fiancée's face.

Click.

And *that* was the money shot. Maddie knew it the instant she took it. The ring wasn't in the picture, but she hoped they'd order a print anyway. Maybe they'd put it in a frame on their mantel, where they could glance at it occasionally and be reminded of the genuine fondness they'd had for each other before the years set in.

And, really, what more could anyone expect from a wedding picture?

Her mission accomplished, Maddie collected her equipment.

"How soon can we see something?" Hannah asked as she joined her on the grass.

"Oh, I'm guessing—" Maddie checked the time. Damn, it was already 5:30. "I should have these posted to the site by tomorrow—plenty of time to pick one for Sunday's paper."

The bride-to-be looked crestfallen. "You mean not by tonight?"

Maddie took a deep breath. She mentally counted to three. Yes, her day job paid the bills, but freelance work was the icing on her cake. And that business relied heavily on referrals.

"I'll do my best," she said brightly, even though it meant turning her whole evening upside down. And that assumed she wouldn't get called out for some emergency. "I can probably get you something by midnight. If I do, I'll email you the password for the gallery."

"Thank you! I *really* appreciate it. Everyone's dying to see how these turn out."

Maddie wasn't sure who "everyone" was, but she managed to keep a cheerful expression on her face as they exchanged good-byes. Then she hitched her tripod onto her shoulder and trekked across the park.

Her stomach growled as she headed for the garage where she'd parked. She cast a longing look at the sandwich shop on the corner. Food would have to wait. She needed to get back to the lab and send out a half dozen files before she could possibly call it a day.

She ducked into the shade of the parking garage, avoiding the stairwell in favor of the ramp. The blustery February wind had died down, and the air was thick with car exhaust. Maddie hugged the concrete wall so she wouldn't get clipped by a driver rounding the corner. She reached the third level and spotted her little white Prius tucked beside a pickup. She dug the phone from her purse and checked for messages. Her boss, her sister, her boss, her boss.

Shoes scuffed behind her. The skin at the back of her neck prickled. Maddie paused and pretended to be reading something on her phone as she listened.

Silence.

Her pulse picked up. She resumed her pace.

More footsteps.

She whirled around. No one. She clutched the phone in her hand and darted her gaze up and down the rows of cars. She searched for anyone lurking, any ominous shadows—but she was alone.

Almost.

Anxiety gnawed at her as she surveyed her surroundings. It was light out. The streets below hummed with traffic. Still, she tightened her grip on the tripod. She tucked the phone in her purse and felt for her pepper spray.

In the corner of her eye, movement. She pivoted toward it and registered two things at once: *man* and *ski mask*. Fear shot through her. Maddie swung the tripod around like a baseball bat as the man barreled into her, slamming her against the pickup. The tripod jerked from her grip and clattered to the ground. Hands clamped around her neck. Maddie punched and bucked as fingers dug into her skin. She tried to scream. No air. Gray eyes glared at her through the holes in the mask.

She smashed the heel of her hand into his face and felt bone crunch. He staggered back. Maddie jerked sideways. He lunged for her, grabbing the collar of her jacket. She twisted out of it and bolted for the stair-well.

"Help!" she shrieked, yanking open the door. She leaped down the stairs, rounded the landing, then leaped down more stairs. Her butt hit concrete, but she groped for the railing and hauled herself up. Hinges squeaked above her. Her pulse skittered. Footsteps thundered over her head.

"Someone *help*!"

But they were alone in the soundproof shaft. Another landing, a door. She shoved it open and dashed through. She searched desperately for people, but saw only rows and rows of cars. Another door. Light-headed with terror, she pushed it open and stumbled into an alley. On her right, a passageway lined with Dumpsters. On her left, a gray car parked at the mouth of the alley. Someone was inside.

Maddie rushed for the car. It lurched forward. She halted, stunned, as it charged toward her like a rhino. Behind her a door banged open. Maddie sprinted away from the door and the car. The engine roared behind her as she raced down the alley. The noise was at her heels, almost on top of her. Panic zinged through her like electric current as her arms and legs pumped. The car bore down on her. At the last possible second, she dove side-ways behind a Dumpster and felt a great whoosh of air as the car shot past. The squeal of brakes echoed through the alley.

Maddie darted through the space between the back bumper and the Dumpster. She raced for the street. Despair clogged her throat as she realized the distance she'd covered. Where was the ski-mask guy? The people and traffic noise seemed impossibly far away. She raced toward the mouth of the alley as fast as her burning legs could carry her.

The man jumped from a doorway. They crashed to the ground in a heap of arms and legs and flying elbows. Her skin scraped against the pavement as she kicked free of him and scrambled to her feet. He grabbed the strap of her camera and her body jerked violently. She landed on her side as a fist pummeled her and pain exploded behind her eyes. She managed to roll to her knees as another blow hit her shoulder. She fell forward, but caught herself on her palms and kicked backward, desperate *not* to end up on the ground under him.

She struggled to her feet, but her vision blurred, and the strap was like a noose around her neck. The vinegary taste of fear filled her mouth. He heaved his weight into her, smashing her against the wall. The strap tightened again. Maddie gripped it with her hands. She tried to buck him off, but he was strong and wiry and determined to get her into a headlock. His arm clamped around her throat. She turned her head to the side and bit *hard* through the fabric of his T-shirt. The grip loosened for a moment, and she twisted free of the strap, the arms, the fingers clawing at her. Adrenaline burst through her veins as she realized this might be her only chance.

She rolled to her feet and rocketed down the alley, toward the noise and cars and people that meant safety. *Faster, faster, faster!* Every cell in her body throbbed with the knowledge that he was behind her. Her heart hammered. Her muscles strained. *Faster!* For the first time, she thought of a gun and imagined a bullet tearing through skin and bone. She surged forward, shrieking hoarsely and racing for the mouth of the alley.

Behind her a car door slammed. Tires squealed over the asphalt. She glanced back as the gray car shot down the alley, moving away from her. Taillights glowed. Another screech of tires as the car whipped around the corner.

Maddie stopped and slumped against the side of the building. Her breath came in ragged gasps. Her lungs burned, and it felt as if her heart were being squeezed like a lemon. Something warm trickled down her face. She touched a hand to her cheek and her fingers came away red.

Tears stung her eyes as she looked down at herself. Her purse was gone. Her camera was gone. Her phone was gone. *She* wasn't gone, at least. She was here—in one shaking, terrified, Jell-O-like piece. But her knees felt so weak she didn't know if they would hold her up. She closed her eyes and tried to think.

She couldn't stay in the alley. But she couldn't go back in that garage—maybe never again. She looked out at the street, at the steady flow of cars and people. Her gaze landed on the neon sign in the window of the sandwich shop. It glowed red in the gray of dusk, beckoning her to safety with its simple message: *Open*.

Maddie pushed away from the wall. On quivering legs, she stumbled toward the sign.

The two men were cops, she could tell at a glance. Maddie watched them from her place beside the patrol car, where she'd been sequestered for the past half hour answering questions from a rookie detective who'd probably been in diapers when she got her first speeding ticket. Maddie knew almost everyone in the San Marcos police department, but didn't it figure the first responder to her 911 call would be someone she'd never laid eyes on before—someone who didn't have the slightest interest in doing her a favor by moving things along. Added to the scraped chin, the swelling jaw, the lost purse, and the stolen Nikon, it was just another addition to the crapfest that had become her day.

And if her instincts proved right, the party wasn't over yet.

Maggie watched as the two mystery men walked up to the patrol cars parked in front of the sandwich shop. Definitely cops. But they were more than that, clearly. She pegged them for feds based on their dark suits, and that guess was confirmed when one of them flashed a badge and exchanged words with the patrol officers milling on the sidewalk. Stan Grimlich—a cop she *did* know—had just emerged from the shop with a steaming cup of coffee. He said something brief and gave a nod in Maddie's direction, sending them her way.

Damn. Maddie checked her watch. Whatever these two wanted, it wouldn't likely be quick. She looked them over. The one leading the charge appeared to be in his midthirties, like she was. His shaved head, coupled with his solid, stocky build, would have made him look like a bouncer—had it not been for his suit and the determined scowl on his face that said *cop*.

Maddie shifted her gaze to his friend. Taller, probably six-one. Broad-shouldered, muscular, lean at the waist. He had sandy-brown hair that was cropped short on the sides and longer on top. The word *military* popped into her head. It wasn't just the haircut and the build, but the supremely confident way he carried himself. He was watching her, too, but in contrast to his partner's expression, this guy looked utterly relaxed.

"Are you *sure* you don't want to get this looked at?"

She turned her attention to the EMT handing her an ice pack. Maddie pressed the pack to the side of her face, where a bruise was forming.

"I'm good."

"Because it's entirely possible you could have a concussion."

"Thanks, but I'm fine." And a trip to the emergency room was the last thing she needed tonight. She had an aversion to hospitals.

"Well." The woman shrugged and flipped shut the lid to her first aid kit. "Suit yourself. I can't *make* you take commonsense precautions."

"Madeline Callahan?"

She turned, startled. She'd known he was coming, but she hadn't expected such a deep voice from someone so young. He stared down at her, hands resting at his hips, suit jacket pushed back to reveal a semiautomatic pistol and—as she'd suspected—an FBI shield. She returned her gaze to his smooth, clean-shaven face. If she was right about the military thing, he must have graduated from the Academy about a week ago.

"I'm Special Agent Brian Beckman with the FBI. This is Special Agent Sam Dulles." He nodded at the bald guy. "We'd like to ask you a few questions, ma'am."

Dulles leaned back against the patrol car parked perpendicular to the one where Maddie stood. Clearly, he intended to hang back and observe. Maybe this was a training exercise.

"Ma'am?"

She looked back at the young one. Beckman. He was watching her intently with those hazel eyes.

"Could you take us through what transpired here, please?"

Transpired. Typical copspeak. Maddie folded her arms over her chest and leaned against the side of the car. "It was a mugging."

His eyebrows tipped up. "Could you be more specific?"

"Someone attacked me in the parking garage. Stole my purse, along with my brand-new camera."

"Your camera?"

"I'm a photographer. I was doing a photo shoot down at the park—a couple getting married."

Both men were regarding her with frank interest now, and she had the feeling she was missing something.

Beckman eased closer, as if to hear better. "We'd like you to walk us through the entire incident, ma'am. Step-by-step."

Irritated by the ma'am-ing, she shot a look at Dulles. "Since when does the FBI have jurisdiction over a mugging?"

No answer.

"Maddie?"

She turned to see Stan walking toward her, hand outstretched. Her brown leather purse dangled from his fingers.

"Oh my God! Where was it?" She beamed a smile at him and snatched up the bag.

"Nicholson found it under a truck near your car. Phone's in there, too. You just had a call come in."

"Thank you! You have no idea how much trouble

this saves me." Maddie already had the phone out, and her heart lurched when she saw the text from her boss. It was just as she'd feared. She was needed at a crime scene, ASAP. He'd sent her a message coded 911, followed by a street address.

Maddie stashed the ice pack into her purse and shoved the phone into the pocket of her jeans. Now she *really* needed to leave.

"Ms. Callahan?"

She glanced up. The young agent was watching her expectantly. So was his partner.

"Listen, you see Officer Scanlon over there? The one with the notepad? I guarantee he'll be turning in a full report before he clocks out tonight. You can get the details from him."

"We need them from you," Dulles said, speaking up for the first time. He was still leaning against the side of the car, with a disapproving look.

"Is there a specific reason the FBI is involved here? I told you, it was a mugging."

"Looks to me like an assault, too," Beckman said evenly.

"Okay, fine. But I really need to be somewhere, like, an hour ago, so unless you can explain how this is relevant—"

"We're investigating a federal case."

"A federal case involving . . . ?" She waited as they exchanged looks.

"There was a theft across the street from here at about five thirty." Dulles nodded toward the park. "Given the timing, we think it could be connected to your incident."

Maddie glanced across the street, where a bank faced out onto the park. A bank robbery certainly would explain the feds, but why weren't there any police cars?

"Take us through what happened," Beckman said, all trace of politeness gone.

And so Maddie did.

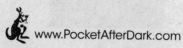

Want a thrill?

Pick up a bestselling romantic suspense novel
from Pocket Books!

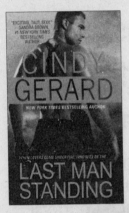

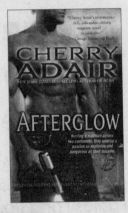